THE SHADE

Enjoy the book

Matthew Tarr

MATTHEW TALLMAN

Note: This is a work of fiction. All characters, organizations, and events portrayed in this book are either products of the author's imagination or used fictitiously.

THE SHADE
Copyright © 2014 by Matthew J. Tallman

All rights reserved. This book or any portion thereof
may not be reproduced or used in any manner whatsoever
without the express written permission of the publisher
except for the use of brief quotations in a book review.
Printed in the United States of America
First Printing, 2014
ISBN 978-0-9916192-0-7 (Paperback)
Cover Illustration and Design by Lisa J Wilson of Pixel Pixie Design

Formatting and Interior Design by: E.M. Tippetts Book Designs

*For Ashley,
For always believing in me,
even when I did not*

PART I:
ARRIVAL

Through me, you pass into the city of woe:
Through me, you pass into eternal pain:
Through me among the people lost for aye.

Justice the founder of my fabric mov'd:
To rear me was the task of power divine,
Supremest wisdom, and primeval love.

Before me things create were none,
Save things eternal and eternal I endure.
All hope abandon ye who enter here.

-Dante Alighieri

I

An intense wave of pain shot its way up my spine, telling me I needed to get up. The hard hospital tiles had broken my fall with the gentle care you would expect. Slowly I opened my eyes, getting my first look at the ceiling of the room I had been thrown into. My bloody fist clinched a hand full of tile fragments and crushed them into powder.

That didn't go as expected.

My hands shook as they slowly lifted my body back to an upright position.

Once on my feet, I scanned the empty room quietly. There was nothing significant about it; the room looked just like the hundreds of others in the abandoned hospital. The paint on the walls was cracked and peeling from years of neglect, along with a floor covered in a thick layer of grime. However, I wasn't scanning the room to look at the scenery; my eyes were looking for something far more—sinister. My legs quivered as they tried to keep me from doubling back over.

Then I felt a presence in the room with me.

It wasn't something tangible that I could see with my naked eye, but I knew that something was there. My breath remained slow and steady.

2 MATTHEW TALLMAN

The fall must have been harder than I thought.

My hand rubbed the back of my head as I tried to get my bearings. Then it happened, coming out from the wall in front of me, the specter emerged.

It looked like a man in shape only. Truly, it was more like a cadaver that had been charred in an unholy fire. I gazed in horror at the creature, black as pitch. As I stared into the blackness that comprised it, the darkness seemed to swallow me up, almost like falling through space with nothing to grasp onto. Flesh from the specter's body was peeling away, matching the paint on the walls. Its eyes, if you could call them that, were as black and deep as the ocean depths. It moved closer to me, with a twisted look on its face that seemed to say. *"You, you're screwed, and there's nothing you can do about it."*

With my fists balled tightly, readying myself for an attack. I could feel the color draining from my clenched fists as the creature leapt at me, its arms opened wide, ready to take me to the ground. I instinctively ducked, letting my body slam against the hard tile floor, causing my assailant to vault over me. I rolled forward—creating more distance between the creature and myself—and then sprang back to my feet.

The specter landed softly, only a few feet behind me.

I spun around to face the creature.

It turned to face me, but before it had time to attack; my fist was already rocketing towards its face. The power encapsulated in my closed hand crushed itself against the creature's face and as the two forces made contact, a thunderous boom erupted in the room.

Take that you piece of—

The specter recovered quickly, and before I knew what was happening it had latched its arms around my waist and we were tumbling towards the ground. We slammed against the floor, rolling a few feet. When we stopped, my legs heaved upwards with all their strength, breaking the specter's grip on me, hurling it across the room.

The creature hit the floor as I quickly found my way upright.

THE SHADE

Using the confusion to my advantage, I ran for the door. I made my way through the door and immediately turned right, heading down the long hospital hallway. My breath was stuck in my chest, as if my lungs refused to work. My heart thumped quickly inside me as I ran. I felt the side of my body begin to burn as the pain the specter had inflicted became apparent. Halfway down the hallway, I found a room and ducked into it to avoid the specter. My hand met my mouth to stop myself from breathing too heavily. My heart pounded so loudly in my chest I thought that it would give me away.

From down the hallway, I could hear the specter moving closer towards me. My eyes shut tight as the sound of footsteps came closer towards me. Closer and closer the footsteps of the creature passed by the room. It breathed heavily as it searched the hallway for me.

My muscles tightened.

I could feel the creature as it passed by the room.

One, two, three.

I counted in my head and then took off down towards the opposite end of the hallway. I ran back down the hallway, leaving the specter behind me. I had only fooled the creature for a moment, because almost immediately after I emerged from the room the sound of heavy footsteps running towards me echoed down the hall. I would have looked back, but I knew what chased after me, I knew the unending horror of what a monster like the specter could do to a man. I tried with all my might, to will my legs to move faster, but with no success. The noise from the creature behind me grew closer, and closer. Each step that I took down the hallway the creature gained another few feet on me, I knew that within a few seconds it would be on top of me again.

So in a split-second decision, I stopped to make a stand.

My foot pivoted and my whole body turned to face the specter. My eyes grew large seeing that the creature was only a few steps away from me. I balled my hands into fists and readied them to defend myself. Just then, the creature lunged off the ground, leaping through the air towards me.

In that moment, as my eyes watched the creature fly like a missile towards me. Time seemed to slow down, and for one second, it almost seemed to stop. However, as soon as the creature struck me, time sped back up again. We fell towards the floor together, slamming each other against the hard tile, making it crumble like autumn leaves. We wrestled with one another, grappling for the best position to finish each other off. Together the specter and I rolled across the tile, as we did the specter grabbed my shirt, pulling me towards it, only to slam my head back down into the ground.

My head felt woozy from the blow; while I was recovering, the specter positioned itself on top of me. Its arms reared up and its fist plunged down towards my face. The first blow landed. It felt like being hit by a car. A quick second later, another fist slammed into my jaw; then another in my eye, then another.

I can't take much more of this.

With all the strength I could muster, my hand shot up, catching the specter's punch that had been meant for my face. I summoned all muscles to tighten and crush the creature's hand. My body called every muscle in my body to throw the specter off me, and for once in my life, my muscles came though. With one quick jolt from my arm, I shoved the creature away from me. It stumbled backwards towards the wall, unable to stop itself from making contact. I continued to watch it from the floor waiting for the inevitable moment when the creature crashed through the old sheetrock; but the moment never came. My eyes fixated on the specter as it disappeared into smoke.

My breath was heavy, as my lungs finally allowed me to breathe. I moved my hand towards my face, letting my fingers touch it, but as they did, I winced as a wave of pain shot through me. I could tell that my face was a jumbled mess of broken bones and blackened bruises. My arms pushed me to my knees and from my knees; I rose to my feet. My body felt dizzy, like when you stand up too fast and all the blood rushes to your head.

I knew that the specter was still near, my eyes glanced around, looking for the creature.

He's playing with me. He knows that he had me dead to rights, so why did he let me go?

I tried to focus my eyes on the grime covered walls but it was hard to focus; my vision became a blur every time my head moved in the slightest. Then my whole body stiffened as the presence of the creature filled the hallway. The presence made it feel as if someone else was in the room with me and yet I was completely alone. I searched the dusty corridor with my eyes, taking note of everything. The amount of lights hanging haphazardly from the ceiling, the discarded beds and gurneys left in the halls, all of the dust moats that seemed to dance in the air in front of me, I took inventory of everything.

I looked downward to find my hand trembling in fear.

In fact, my entire body shook with anticipation of what was coming next.

The specter leapt out from the wall towards me. My body ducked, causing the creature to miss me. The specter was headed for the floor but before it made contact, it disappeared once again. My eyes began to scan again, waiting for the next attack. Then from my left, the creature burst from the wall. This time my body was prepared. As the creature flew by me, I grabbed hold of it. While holding the specter, I gave it one solid toss, managing to send it crashing into the closest wall. The action was so fast by the time the specter hit the wall it had only just realized what had happened. The wall caved in where the creature struck it, creating a thick cloud of white dust before me. Frantically my eyes searched the dust for any signs of movement.

Where are you?

I continued to search as the dust began to settle.

Where are you? Where are you?

My eyes turned up nothing. Then from behind me,

something slammed into my back, which sent me stumbling forward towards a wall. I hit the wall, cracking the sheetrock in places.

I found him.

I turned my body around to face the specter. Its hands grabbed my shirt and threw me to the ground. I hit the floor in a seated position, that was, until the creature kicked me in the face. The blow snapped my body completely backwards, causing my head to smack the tile.

"Is that all you've got." My voice choked out through layers of blood and saliva.

Taunt the specter, that's a great idea.

The specter looked at me as if it were annoyed. As if any emotion could be distinguished from a face so evil. I watched as the specter stood above me, then in one swift motion its leg went back, and then came forward towards my gut. My hands moved to intercept the foot but they did nothing to soften the blow. The kick sent me sliding across the floor towards the wall, only stopping when my back made contact with the wall.

I opened my eyes. The world around me was out of focus and a dark figure approached me. Time itself seemed to slow as the specter walked, each stride taking longer than the last. I fluttered my eyes to regain focus but by then the creature stood over me. Slowly my eyes looked up at the creature. Blood dripped from my face, and my body ached, but I knew there would be no mercy, no repose. Then I watched the creature raise its leg in the air, and then propelled its leg down towards me.

Two point five seconds until his foot slams me into the ground and I'm nothing but a stain on the tile.

Two point five seconds was enough time for my mind to think of everyone that I was about to leave behind. My family, my friends—Angela. Then my mind moved from those I'd leave behind to the things that I'd never get to do. All the things that I would miss out on, all of the things that I regretted not doing, everything, all at once passed in front of my eyes.

THE SHADE

Let me back up for a moment. To truly understand how precious those last seconds were you'd have to understand everything else that led up to that moment. I'll have to take you back six months. Back when I was a regular high school student just trying to make it through my senior year. But that was before, before the accident, before I met Virgil, before The Speakers.

My name is James Langley, and this is a chronicling of events that would change humanity's future, forever.

The warm sunlight filtered in from behind the half closed blinds. The light flickered and lapped my cheek with its soft warm glow. A shallow breath left my lungs as I wished that the morning would never end, but then I remembered what day it was.

"Monday" I softly said to myself as I rolled over onto my back.

I gazed quietly at the ceiling, while it quietly gazed back at me. I squinted, trying to count the small off colored speckles that adorned the dust covered ceiling. As I continued to count the dots, they seemed to jump out and mock me, screaming at me to get up.

I've got to get up.

The proposition of continuing to count the dots became less and less appealing as my eyes began to blur the dots I'd already counted, and those left to be. I let out a slow even breath as my eyes glanced over at my alarm clock, the large octagonal numerals told me it was time to get up— 6:30 A.M.

The first day of school was never something I'd dreaded, but this year was different. As I lay in my bed, it didn't feel like I was beginning a new school year but more like I was a prisoner waiting for the hangman. Just like someone waiting for their executioner, I'd hoped that the day would never come, but time marches on.

My mind was a mess of jumbled thoughts and constant worry. It didn't help that it had become impossible for me to sleep through the entire night, I'd even started to think of myself as something of an insomniac. My sleep deprivation was due to constant nightmares, which came both when I was asleep and awake. No matter what I did, my mind could never shake them away for very long. I closed my eyes for a quick second as I thought of the nightmare. It was always the same, every night the dream fell upon me. I was alone, in a cold, dark, hole. When I looked upwards to see the top of the hole, it seemed as if the pit stretched up into the heavens. Then I began to climb, I climbed faster and harder than I'd ever pushed my body before, but no matter how fast my hands tried to pull me to the surface, the bottomless pit only rose up further and faster around me, faster than I could climb.

That was about when I would wake, most of the time in a cold sweat.

I'd thought about telling my parents about the dream, however I knew that they'd only say it was anxiety or that it was some sort of jitters about finishing high school. When I awoke, it always left my stomach feeling sick, it was the same feeling that you get when you know someone's lying to you.

As I continued to think about it, the sickening feeling washed over me again.

That's my cue.

My mind told me that I needed to get out of bed. I slowly rolled my body off the bed, twisting my torso that I could plant my feet on the ground. I stood up, cracking my knees as they straightened out. My eyes blinked a few times to adjust from the harsh whiteness of the ceiling to the soft blue painted walls of my room. I finished stretching so I scratched my face, and then moved towards the door. As I walked out of my room, I grabbed only the watch off my desk, careful not to disturb any of the overturned picture frames and other items that adorned my workspace.

I made my way out of my room and down the narrow hallway towards the bathroom. After a few steps down the hallway, my body gave a quick pivot to the right and walked into the bathroom. My feet touched the cold tile of the bathroom and my whole body flinched at the sudden change in temperature from the carpet. I shuttered from the cold but didn't let it phase me as I closed the door behind me. The bathroom was small, containing a tiny sink to the left as you walked in, with a mirror above it, a toilet that sat next to the sink, immediately followed by a standing shower. I turned towards the mirror and peered at the figure that stared back at me. My mind wasn't entirely sure if the person that I was looking at was still me, my fingers ran themselves through my greasy brown hair just to make sure that it was me that was still in command of my body. The person mirrored my movements and as it did I let out a heavy sigh of relief. My body leaned over the sink and my face drew close to the mirror, I touched the large dark circles that swelled under my eyes; they had taken up residence there ever since I'd started having my nightmare and they showed no signs of leaving.

I'd never considered myself more than an just average high school student. My friends came from every click there could possibly be in a high school, even if I didn't conform to any particular one. I was smart, but in no way was I the smartest student. I stood at a height of six-one with an average muscle build, so I wasn't the strongest nor the best looking, and as I stared at my form in the mirror those traits became apparent. I matted my hair down with my hand, disrobed and then got into the shower.

My shower was cold as usual.

The pilot light must have gone out again.

I thought as the cold water cascaded over me. My eyes shut as I let the feeling of the cool water cover my body. The water didn't bother me that much, I'd become used to that sort of thing happening. It had felt as if my body had been reliving the same morning for the past month, and like a machine that repeated the same action time and time again, it had become habitual.

I'd wake up. Lay in bed until my mind finally allowed me to get up. I'd take a cold shower then get some food; the rest of the day was spent around the house, it eventually became so ingrained it was like my own morning ritual.

However, this day would be different.

That was because this was the first day of my senior year of high school. The first day of school had always been a day that kids sought to avoid, but for me, I had my own reasons altogether. It was the same reason I had constant nightmares, why I had spiraled into a sort of sleep walking oblivion; this reason of course, was because of a girl.

Her name is Angela, she and I had been together for almost three years, but that was until last month. Until Angela started becoming more and more hostile towards me, almost as if she wanted *me* to break up with her. Then she told me we couldn't see each other any longer, there was no more explanation than that.

I called and texted her, but each time I was met with the same set of empty responses. She seemed to be avoiding me, and as the last month of summer rolled to a close, I began to avoid her as well. But the first day of school was different; during the summer I could stay inside for the most part, avoiding any chance of actually seeing her, intentionally or by accident. Still, with the beginning of the school year, it would be near impossible not to see her at one point or another.

I tried to clear my head of thoughts of her as I dried myself off and put on a pair of sweatpants. My hands tied the cords together and with that, my feet slowly stumbled down the hall towards the kitchen. As I approached, I heard my mother making her early morning cup of coffee. I slowly stepped into the kitchen where I found my mom sitting at the table drinking her coffee. "Good morning James." she said to me in a happy tone as she sipped her drink.

"Morning." I mumbled under my breath, attempting to pour myself some orange juice.

"How are you feeling?" My mother asked. "You know about the whole Angela thing?"

My mother was always straight to the point; it was something that we had in common, but not something that I particularly cared for. "Mom we broke up a month ago." I said quietly as the juice reached the top of my glass. "I'm about as good as I can be I suppose." My face feigned a smile to satisfy her.

"I just want to make sure you're okay." She said.

"Yeah." I told her not looking up from my glass and then there was a momentary break in our conversation.

"You'll be alright, there—," she started to say.

"I know, there's plenty more fish in the sea." My voice was quiet as my hand made a motion that was supposed to look like a fish. It was easy to tell that she wasn't finished with the subject and instead of fight it I decided to sit down.

My hand pulled a chair out and I sat to meet her gaze.

"Well, you hadn't mentioned anything about her for the last few weeks," she remarked. "You don't want to talk about it?" My mother knew full well why I hadn't talked to her about it, it was the same reason that I'd shut myself in for the past month, I was avoiding it.

"I know mom, I know." I tried to tell her to get her off the subject. "I'm working some stuff out right now."

Working out some stuff, which would have meant that there was still some sort of hope for Angela and me.

"Well, I just think—," she began again.

"Mom I don't feel like talking about this right now, besides I can't even begin to explain what happened." I interrupted and then sipped from my drink. The orange juice travel down my throat and into my stomach, it felt more acidic than normal and burned as it went down; it was a welcome change to the numbness that normally accompanied my early mornings.

My mother was quiet so I saw that as an opportunity to get out of the conversation.

I forced myself to finish off the oddly acidic orange juice as quickly as possible to avoid any more unnecessary banter with my mother. With what little breakfast I could stomach out of the way, I started to get up from the table. My eyes looked at my mother and it was clear that she could have talked for days about Angela, but she knew not to push it. That's what I liked about my mom; she was a lot like me, she knew when people couldn't be pushed to talk and didn't bother them if she knew they wouldn't offer any more information. She kept her thoughts in check and mostly to herself.

My lips feigned another smile to assure her that everything was all right, we both knew that that was a lie. I appreciated that she was trying to be supportive, which was more than I could have said about my friends. I turned from the table and walked back into my room.

"One more thing James—," she broke the silence as I was just about to leave the kitchen.

She couldn't hold her tongue.

I turned back to face her.

"—your father needs to speak with you before you leave today." She requested.

"I'll talk to him after I get dressed." I assured her and then turned away from her to leave the kitchen. I moved out of the kitchen and once again walked slowly down the long hallway towards my bedroom. When I entered the room, my eyes noticed the clothes that hung from the closet doorknob.

I don't remember setting these out.

My eyes tightened on the clothes as my hand reached for them.

I stared at them for a moment and then shook my head. Lately I'd started doing things that I couldn't remember doing, I didn't think too much of it, it had become such a common occurrence for me. It was rare for me to keep my mind on any one thing for more than a few minutes. I'd read somewhere that was a sign of attention deficit disorder. Of course, it would have been a relief if I could attribute my absentmindedness to something medical rather than the real reason. Even so, I knew what really caused my mind to wander aimlessly in thought, why I spent my waking hours lost in a zombie like stupor. The real reason of course was that I was still very much in love with Angela.

Thinking about her moved my thoughts into dangerous territory, like a man walking through a minefield I had to tread lightly. I had found that prolonged thoughts about her made me feel sort of sick, so when my mother had changed the subject, telling me my father needed to see me, served to help me get my mind off what was really bothering me. I looked down at the clothes that I didn't remember setting out the night before—a grey hooded sweatshirt and my worn out black jeans. My hands touched the fabric and as my fingers worked over the different textures, my mind told me to finish getting dressed. The last thing that I threw on was an old blue jacket that I hadn't worn in about a year; then headed down the half lit hallway to my parent's bedroom.

My father sat on his bed, getting ready for work; he was a park ranger at the local nature preserves. My relationship with both of my parents was just like any other teenager; we had our disagreements but nothing out of the ordinary. My father was my main opposition in the household, he was a bit hardheaded, and I supposed that was where I got it from. He had a very strong work ethic, which combined with a very firm set of morals made him come across as overly strict at times. Our normal exchanges seemed more like lectures than conversations with his usual three main points, school is important, take care of your truck, and get a job.

If I was lucky, sometimes I would get a combination of all three, I knew he meant well but it always seemed like an uphill battle when speaking with him. He had just finished putting on his large black work boots when I strolled into the room.

"Hey son." He said as he finished lacing his boots.

"Good morning." I said in a low monotone voice as I entered the room. He didn't have to say anything to me; I knew what he was going to say because it was the same thing that he'd harped on the entire month before.

"James, I noticed that your tires are still leaking air, you need to get the valve stems replaced so you can make it through the winter." He told me.

"Yeah, I had been meaning to get to that." I said trying to shrug off the remark.

"Just make sure you take care of it James, it's—,"

"It's very dangerous, I know, I know." I interrupted him.

"I'm just concerned about your safety." He said sympathetically. My eyes didn't want to meet his because in my head I knew that he was truly just looking out for my well-being.

"I know dad, I've just really distracted lately." I told him.

"Your mother and I were talking about Angela—," he told me as he finished putting on his jacket as if it were the punctuation at the end of his sentence. He looked me over as if he had something left to say, an awkward pause hung in the air until I broke the silence.

"Did you need me for anything else?" I asked.

He let out a sigh at my blatant attempt to end our conversation.

"No, just make sure you get those tires fixed this week, okay?"

"Okay, will do." I told him and then turned myself around to leave the room. I walked slowly back to my room and as I entered my eyes looked down at my desk, noticing the copy of Dante Alighieri's The Inferno that sat on it. The book had been a gift from Angela, she had given it to me the last day of junior year; it quickly became one of my favorite books. Unfortunately the book sat open on my desk, it had flipped itself back to the spot where the spine was most creased; the middle of the book. This wouldn't have normally been a problem for me except that in the middle of the book Angela had written a personalized note for me. As my eyes glared down at the pink ink that adorned the page a sickening feeling started to work its way into the pit of my stomach. I glanced away and then without looking reached out and closed the book.

That was one of the little pieces of Angela that I couldn't bear to look at, she was everywhere I looked, in my books, my wallet and she was the reason that the picture frames on my desk were overturned. There was even a small odd shaped blue box at the corner of my desk that I couldn't bring myself to open.

The reason for my anxiety was that she had never given me a solid reason why we broke up, I'd suspected another guy but that thought was only fleeting; Angela was too respectable to do anything like that. We hadn't spoken with one another in over a month and the only interruption in our cell phone silence was when we agreed that we would return whatever possessions that belonged to the other person after the first day of school. It made me upset to even think about, I wasn't sure how Angela felt about me, but I still cared about her. Even thought I wanted nothing more than to hate her with every part of myself, I couldn't bring myself to do it. I let the thoughts of her clear from my head, allowing my sadness and anger to go along with it for the moment. I drew in a breath and let out a heavy sigh, grabbed my backpack and threw it over my shoulder. My hands checked my pockets for the keys to my truck before leaving my room.

I called to my parents as I walked to the door. The door to their room was closed so they didn't answer me back. I rolled my eyes and let out a tiny scoff at them as my hand turned the knob and opened our large wooden front door. I stepped outside the house and looked up into the sky, the clouds were large, fluffy for the time being; but I knew that later, they would turn cold and grey as they always did.

Good thing I brought my jacket, it always seems to rain.

THE SHADE

Eugene, Oregon was where I lived, and in Eugene, rain was especially common in September—quite frankly it was common for most times of the year. Eugene seemed to be one of the wettest places in the United States. I looked away from the clouds overhead and made my way towards my truck. I fumbled with the keys as my hand tried to dig them out of my pocket, clanking the keys together the way that a bunch of loose change does. After a few seconds of this, I pulled the keys from my pocket and found the one that belonged to my truck.

I stood in front of my truck, a 1999 Chevy S-10.

The faded blue paint had chipped in places, the tires had become extraordinarily difficult to keep inflated, but other than a small oil leak, the engine worked a majority of the time. I grabbed the handle and opened the door, pulling myself up into the cab I ducked down to make sure that my head didn't hit the doorframe as I got in. Once inside I closed the door and put the key into the ignition. My hand gently turned the key making the engine turn over, and eventually it roared to life. I listened to the hum of the engine as the truck idled in the driveway, basking in the fact that it had started on the first try. I struggled as my eyes attempted to focus through the dirty windshield; it was just something else my reclusive summer months had let slip.

I shook my focus away from the unclean windshield and resituated it on the dysfunctional look of my parent's home. The house was one story with a basement, with a large archway adorning the front doorstep. It had strange oblong shaped windows, and with its tan paint it looked dull and mute against the early morning sky.

I pulled out of the driveway and began the long trip to Sheldon High School; the drive always took me through downtown Eugene. The city isn't that large, it's quiet and for the most part, kept off the radar. The University of Oregon was about the biggest attraction we had. Really one of the biggest things to happen to Eugene was a string of unsolved arsons almost fifty years ago. I was, for the most part a quiet person, but when among friends I was much more outgoing. I enjoyed the quiet things; I figured that was why I had always enjoyed living in Eugene.

Eugene had been good to me. I had lived there all my life but after high school, I planned to leave it. If there was one thing that I had going for me, it was the fact that at an early age I'd excelled in school. I'd written an essay and gotten noticed by Dartmouth College when I was junior. It seemed that I would be able to pinch a spot in their early acceptance program and needless to say, I didn't have any reason to remain in Eugene. As I got to the edge of the city the small one lane road changed into a double lane, which let me know that I'd entered the city proper. There was always something interesting to me about the dynamic in Eugene. For the most part the city was just like any other its size, but on the outskirts, houses were spaced fairly far apart, and most of the land still belonged to the wilds.

But what the road change really signified was that I was one step closer to school.

As I moved further into the city my heart began to race, it knew that soon, I would have to face the one thing that I had been dreading. Today was the first day in a month that Angela and I would see each other. I looked to the north as rain clouds had already started to invade the skies over the city.

Twenty minutes later, I made it to school. The line to park wasn't any longer than it usually was at the start of a new school year. I parked my truck and tried to concentrate on what I needed to get done, trying not to forget anything that I needed to take with me. My lungs drew in a deep breath and looked down at my watch, 7:52 A.M. I still had plenty of time before class started.

I could always play hooky.

I tried desperately to find some reason not to enter the school. Slowly I worked my fingers into the shape of a gun and put them against my head in an exaggerated manner. I sat there in the truck for a moment and then pretended to pull the trigger. My mouth made a noise that sounded like a gunshot and then I let my head slump over and hit the ice-cold window. "That would be too easy." I said to myself making my window fog up with my hot breath.

The thought of death never really crossed my mind, at least the thought of killing myself never did. My mind wasn't imbalanced in any way, I just wanted more time. Time to heal and get over her, but time was something that I seemed to lack. The time I had was supposed to help me get over the aching feeling that I felt every time I remembered anything about her.

My mind wanted me to believe that everything would get better on its own, that *it* would be able to deal with my problems without any help from me. My mind had been my only friend during my month of seclusion and it knew everything about me. It shared in my pain, it knew my frustration, and in a way— it had become my best friend.

I still maintained some contact with my real friends but none of them really understood what I was going through. My eyes gazed at the front of the school and noticed that the influx of people going into the building had all but stopped; I looked at my watch, it told me that the time had come to stop procrastinating. Slowly I moved out of my truck and onto the asphalt that was damp from the morning dew. My eyes watch the building that sat before me, and with a heavy sigh, I slammed the door to the truck. As I approached the school, my mind searched for any sort of reason not to set foot inside the building. But as I reached the door to the school, I realized that I couldn't find one.

My hand began to shake as my arm reached out to open the door. I grasped the cold handle and then tugged it open. The air inside hit me like a baseball bat to the chest and as I crossed over the threshold into the school, I knew that this was the end.

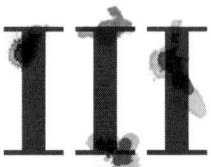

III

I walked into the building and a cold chill worked its way down my spine. The lights in the school seemed extraordinarily bright, my eyes watered as the sudden change in brightness almost blinded me. It took some time for my eyes to adjust to the light but as I strolled down the long hallway towards my locker, the same one I'd had for the past three years, they recovered.

My fingers fumbled with the worn out combination lock. Finally, after about three attempts, the dull green locker door swung open revealing that it was entirely empty, just the way I'd left it at the end of last school year. I tossed my backpack inside, knowing that it was no longer needed. I'd never really used my books in class and never saw the reason to carry an empty backpack around all day. Since there was nothing for me to get, I just stood in silence as my eyes glared at the back of my locker.

This is the 'homestretch'

It was September, which meant there were only a few more months that separated me from the end of my high school "career". My eyes still glared at the back of the locker waiting for it to open up and swallow me whole. I'd have wished for anything to end my day so that I'd not have to endure it. As I stared blankly at the locker, my ears heard something faint, that grew louder and louder as the sound approached me. "James." A voice called.

I gave no response.

"James Langley?" It said again questioning me.

"Hey man." The voice said louder than before. My eyes snapped out from the back of the locker and they looked towards the noise. I looked up from the locker and my eyes focused on the voice that had been calling my name. I slowly adjust from the darkness of the locker to the light of the hall as the figure approached me.

The voice belonged to my friend Rich, his cheery demeanor and scruffy blonde hair greeted me as I looked over to him with half closed eyes. Rich was a bit shorter and stockier than I was, but what he lacked in height he made up for by being the captain of our schools' wrestling team. He was an all around good person, just a little too eager to please, a people pleaser by nature who wanted to make everyone happy and never leave people out of anything.

Unfortunately for Rich, I wasn't in the mood for his usual repertoire.

"James, good to see you." Rich said lively. "How was the summer?" He asked still apparently very excited to see me.

"Didn't get up to much actually—," I told him, letting my voice trail off in the hopes that our conversation might putter to a stop. I felt bad for doing it, but I wasn't in the mood. The thing was, Rich's lively attitude was something that on any normal day would have helped to put me in a better mood. However, because of what day it was, my bitterness wouldn't allow me to enjoy the company of someone like Rich. "Look James, I heard about you and Angela and just wanted to know if you wanted—,"

"Rich it was good seeing you, I've really got to get to class."

I interrupted him trying to end the conversation quickly

"Okay well if you change your—," Rich started to say something, but I turned away from him and slowly started to walk away. The rest of his sentence was buried in the white noise of the busy hallway. My body lumbered down the hall slowly and without a sense of direction, making unnecessary twists and turns on the way to class. I soon found myself in the cafeteria where the handmade posters for the annual back to school dance were everywhere.

The student government started early this year.

My eyes rolled at all of the ridiculous things that were printed on the posters.

Already pairing us off for the school year, what a crock.

But after I'd passed them I realized my accusation wasn't fair. I just felt jaded and that didn't put me in any kind of mood to think about things like the back to school dance.

My schedule informed me that my first class of the day was English, one I was not looking forward to. It was my one class with Angela, and there wasn't anything that could get me out of what was coming. It just meant that she and I were one-step closer to the end with each other, and I hated that. I hated the idea because it meant that everything was final, and that wasn't something that I wanted, I didn't want finality, I wanted *her*.

Then, as I often did, I began to think about what Angela looked like, what I would see in the classroom when I came in. As I thought of her, my heart began to beat faster and faster in my chest. My legs quaked as I approached room 142. I took in a deep breath and held it in my lungs as I stepped across the threshold and entered the room. As soon as entered the room my eyes darted quickly around the class.

No Angela yet.

Then I let myself exhale. My heart rate began to lower, knowing that even though Angela wasn't there yet, it would only be a matter of time before she was. I knew I might have only bought myself a few extra minutes, but they were minutes

I could relish. Deep down however, subconsciously I knew that no matter what, I'd eventually have to see her and that didn't comfort me. I found some of my friends and sat down at the desk behind a dark haired boy named Eric. "Hey James, how's it going?" Eric said pushing up his glasses as I sat down.

"Hey," I started to say hesitantly. "I'm doing okay, a little tired but can't complain otherwise." I told him as my hand dug into my pocket for a pen.

Eric turned back to the front of the class for a moment and then used his pencil eraser to scratch the stubble underneath his chin. Then he turned back to me, staring with his dark green eyes. "That's good man. Where's Angela?"

I looked over towards the door to see if Angela was going to be joining us for class. My eyes glared at the doorframe as my heart began to jump; each second that passed made me feel more and more sick to my stomach. The door sat there as I wished for no one else to cross its threshold. Eric's question filled my mind but I didn't answer him, I couldn't. My eyes sat so intently on the open door that it almost seemed as if it would suddenly disappear and I wouldn't have to see it any longer. The simple truth of the matter was that I wasn't going to be able to shed the bonds of my grief quite so easily.

"I don't know, and frankly I don't care." I told him shrewdly.

"Okay James, don't worry about it, I was just asking." He said as he turned away from me to talk to someone else. I looked forward and class began after the bell rang. My heart began to slow down as my mind realized that Angela wasn't going to be in class, I wasn't sure if she changed her schedule or if she was just late, but it seemed for the time being, I was safe. I didn't know if I would be so lucky tomorrow. My luck usually dried up after twenty-four hours.

I imagined having to relive the day again and it made me feel even more anxious. My eyes turned towards the front of the class, our teacher introduced himself as Mr. Murphy. I had had him for Composition the year before so he and I were already acquainted. He started the class by passing out a syllabus and then after taking attendance he proceeded to go over it with the class. It took all of my strength not to fall asleep; English was a class that always made me tired, something about learning a language that I was already fluent.

After the bell rang, I left the classroom and meandered down the hallway, knowing that chemistry class would allow me to get my mind off Angela, even if it was only for an hour.

As I walked to the classroom, I noticed a large gathering of girls near one of the lockers. I examined their faces, I knew some of them; some of them were friends with Angela. I stopped dead in my tracks, my palms started to sweat as I contemplated what to do. I knew I could walk straight past them—that would only serve to make me feel uncomfortable—or I could take the long way around the entire building to try to circumvent seeing them.

I decided to take the latter.

I couldn't bear to walk past them and be poked or prodded in any way.

It took me an extra two minutes, but I finally made it to class. Mr. Johnson who I'd had for biology my sophomore year, stood in his white lab coat waiting by the door to greet the students as we came in. I greeted Mr. Johnson and then entered the room. I looked around for any of my friends, after a moment of searching I found them. Zach and Gabriel were sitting at the back of the room; Zach gave me a wave with his long lanky arm, letting me know they had saved me a seat. I nodded to show him I had seen him.

As I walked towards the empty seat, my eyes glanced down and I met eyes with Shaun.

Shaun was, to put it lightly, the weird kid in class. That was partially because he never looked like he was fully aware of what was going on. Shaun stared at me, his eyes deadlocked on mine, something that—if it had been anyone else—wouldn't have bothered me much, but Shaun's eyes had always tended to freak me out. With one being blue and the other green, even when he wasn't looking at you, it always seemed like he was staring off into space at something. Shaun looked up at me through his long bangs; his black hair seemed to be more kempt than usual. As I walked to my seat at the back of the classroom his eyes never left me, I could feel him staring at my back as I walked past, he peered through me, his eyes like razors cutting into my back as I walked away from him.

Finally I found my chair and sat down. My eyes quickly glanced over to Shaun, discovering he was no longer staring at me. I breathed a sigh of relief and then turned towards Gabe. "Hey James what's happening?" Gabriel asked in his slight Dominican accent. Gabriel was one of the only Hispanic kids in the school. He was slightly heavier but still fit, his buzzed hair made his head look more round than I remembered. My eyes moved over his face noticing the small soul patch that he must have grown over the summer and chuckled to myself.

"Not much man, just trying to make it through today." I said feeling a little more open than earlier. "The first day of school always sucks."

Zach leaned over across the aisle. "Agreed," he added and then flashed us a smile. Zach was, to put it nicely the pretty boy in our school. There was no girl that didn't swoon when Zach flashed his baby blue eyes at them. He was also the quarterback on the football team, which meant he was always in perfect shape; he was definitely a contender for the Mr. Irish pageant the school hosted every year for charity.

"How was your summer?" Gabe asked. "Better yet how are you and Angela—,"

I put my hand up to silence him.

"Please don't mention her, I got enough of that from Rich already." I told him. My frustration didn't stem from the fact that he brought up Angela but more the fact that he already knew how Angela and I were.

"Hey we just don't want to see you so gloomy." Zach said. "It's senior year man cheer the hell up."

"I'm not gloomy Zack, I just need—," my voice paused to think about what to say. "—time."

"Have you seen her yet today?" Gabe asked.

Have I seen her? No thank God.

"Nope I haven't seen her today." I told them trying to play it cool.

They both looked at each other and then looked back at me, as if they could tell that I was secretly stressed, they didn't say anything. There was a break in conversation during which I took the opportunity to get out my pen. I felt the pen in my pocket but as I sat there, my eyes staring blankly at the front of the classroom I began to get lost in thought. Then I felt a nudge on my arm, my eyes looked up, it was Gabe, trying to get my attention about something.

"Hey James." Gabe said quietly.

"Yeah, what is it?" I told him still trying to get my hand to respond to my commands.

"Check out the freak, he's staring at you again." He pointed up to Shaun.

My eyes moved across the room towards Shaun. To my astonishment, he was staring at me with his eyes wide open.

Had I done something to offend him?

He looked at me with a white-hot intensity that seemed to burn holes straight through my body. Shaun had a habit of freaking the class out; he even had seizures sometimes, fits of rage almost. Last year he had one of his episodes and it took three of us to hold him down before the nurse showed up. He kept screaming gibberish about shadows or something of that nature. Needless to say, Shaun had always made me feel uneasy, it didn't help that he was Angela's cousin either.

Why is he staring at me? Is he angry with me because of Angela?

Angela and he hadn't been the closest, but when it came to family, Angela had always protected Shaun, especially from the bullies at school. I snapped out of my staring contest with him and looked back over to Gabe. "Yeah, wonder what he's looking at?" My voice fluctuated as I said trying to move away from the subject quickly. My eyes gleaned Shaun turning around to face forward, and as he did a sigh of relief left my lips and my mind finally allowed me to pull a pen from my pocket.

"Does he know about you and Angela?" Gabe asked, his voice rose as he said the words.

"I don't know; keep your voice down okay." I told him with a begrudging look. "I'm not sure why he's being abnormally creepy today."

"He's starting off strong this year." Gabe said with a laugh. Zack joined in too as I watched Shaun. "Whatever man. As long as he doesn't have another major freak out during class I'll be happy."

"I think I've got three classes with him this year." I told the two of them.

"Oh man you hit the crazy jackpot didn't you?" Gabe said with a laugh. My mouth formed into a tiny smirk back at him.

"Hey Gabe you got a pen?" Zack asked with his hand already out to receive the utensil. Gabe turned to look at Zack.

"Are you telling me that you came to school, on the first day of classes, unprepared to write? Why doesn't that surprise me?" Gabe asked in a playfully annoyed tone. Zack moved his mouth to the left and right as if he was chewing on something.

"I suppose if you're going to be like that I don't even want a pen from—," Zack began.

"Good, because I don't have one." Gabe said back to him with a laugh.

"Oh what?" Zack said. I reached into my pocket while this was going on and grabbed an extra pen that I'd brought with me. My arm extended and handed it to Zack. "Hey thanks, I don't care what Gabe says, you're not a bad guy." He said, laughing while he spoke.

"James if you just give him what he wants he's never going to learn to be responsible for himself." Gabe joked back at me. The whole ordeal made me chuckle as well, which startled me at first. It was the first time I'd laughed in weeks. The class began and I started to think that the day wouldn't be as bad as I had originally thought. I had never considered myself an optimist by any means, but something about being able to speak to another human being made me feel better about everything. When class ended I grabbed the papers we'd been given and the three of us walked out of the.

"Catch you later James." They said as they walked the opposite way down the hall towards their next class. My next class however was only a few doors down from the one I'd just left. I turned around to start towards my class. Then my eyes looked to the end of the hallway and what they saw hit me like a punch in the chest.

She had just turned the corner into the same hallway as me. It was the one person that could take my mood and spin it completely on end. She was the one person that could turn my entire world upside down. The hall was crowded, so it seemed like she hadn't seen me. I knew that any sort of interaction with her would be too much for me; So, in a split second decision I turned my whole body and proceeded to immediately walk in the opposite direction. My feet moved as quickly as they could to try to get out of Angela's eyeshot.

Not until I finally went around a corner and felt there was sufficient space between us did I begin to feel more at ease. With my heart still pounding in my chest I rushed into the nearest bathroom. My hands fumbled with the facets as they turned on the water and let it heat up. My hands made a cup shape and held the water, splashing it on my face intermittently. The steam from the hot water rose up and covered the mirror in front of me while my hands continued to splash water on my face, trying to get the image of Angela out of my head. After a minute or so, I grabbed a paper towel, wiped my face off, and then tossed the crumbled tissue into the trashcan. With that, I left the bathroom. I wasn't sure how much more school I could take.

How many more times can I see Angela's face before I go completely insane?

I walked back down the hallway to my next class. I decided

to take the long way around to avoid Angela at all cost.

The rest of the day felt like a blur of useless information, one class after the next passed without any narrow escapes or interruptions. I fell asleep twice during the school day, due to my sleepless nights. As I drifted in and out of sleep I couldn't keep Angela from invading my thoughts, as the day dragged on it became harder and harder not to let myself slip into thinking about her. The problem was, the more it happened, the more my head began to pound. My first reaction was to fight the feeling, but eventually I decided to just succumb to the thoughts, thinking maybe the end of the day would allow my mind to be at ease.

The end of the school day didn't come soon enough, it never did. I stumbled like a drunken man out of my last class and slowly made my way out towards the parking lot.

I knew it would only be a short walk to my truck and then I would be home free, for the day at least. But as I walked to the parking lot, the thought of having to repeat what I'd gone through again tomorrow filled me with so much dread it made my legs wobble. "I just have to make it beyond the double doors that led out of the school." I told myself as I walked alone down the hall.

Once my feet hit the pavement I quickly walked towards my truck. My eyes glanced at the ominous clouds that had gathered over the course of the day. They looked like large grey ships that had parked themselves in a harbor right over Eugene. The wind blew strong across the parking lot and sent a cold shiver down my back.

The simple walk to my truck seemed to stretch out for an eternity, a sea of students passed around me, hindering my progress as I walked. While my feet moved forward, my eyes darted around the crowd in search of one person and that's when I heard it.

"James!" I heard from across the lot.

The voice belonged to Angela and although I hadn't seen her, I didn't have to, because with that one word I knew exactly whose voice had called out my name—because I'd heard my name said by that voice a thousand times before. I pretended not hear the shout as my feet hurried me towards my truck. In my moment of hurry, I imagined her dark brown eyes and dirty blonde hair, all of those things haunted my mind as it listed each one of her features that I missed one-by-one. Her face came out so clearly in my mind; it was the same face that haunted my dreams, every time I closed my eyes. Angela wasn't a tall person. She was of average height. She was slim and had a peppy attitude that could always bring me out of a bad mood. However, her peppy voice meant something very different that day.

It meant that after everything that I'd been through to avoid her through the day, was for nothing. This was the moment that I'd run from for over a month; Angela had sent me to the edge, now she was there to finish what she had started and push me over. My eyes closed and I breathed heavily, all I wanted to do was to ignore her and walk to my truck. Something in my body told me not to stop. I pretended that I couldn't hear her, that my problems would just disappear if I didn't stop.

"James!" I heard again, only louder than before. It wasn't until I felt the hand on my shoulder that I knew that I couldn't run any longer, that I would have to face the thing I had been avoiding.

"James—," I heard, this time quieter and more sympathetic.

I don't need this right now.

I had never needed anything like what was coming. After feeling like a prisoner on the run, it felt like the police had finally caught up with me and now I was going back to my cell. It didn't matter what I thought, nor did it matter how hard I fought it. I had tried to run, but without any real hope of escaping what was coming, and as if I had no control over my body, I turned and faced Angela.

IV

My body turned to look at the predator that had stalked me through the parking lot. My eyes met hers and her brown eyes held unnervingly still as they looked up into mine, I gasped a tiny breath in and with a final huff, I released it into the air. My mind had prepared me for that moment; it had prepared me for everything that was going to come after it. But when the moment finally came, I didn't want it to. "How are you doing?" She asked quietly. My eyes continued to watch her, my throat felt dry as the muscles in it tried to speak.

How am I doing?

The question filtered slowly through my mind. I stood completely still, trying to process a response. It felt like time had stopped, my eyes glanced down into Angela's. In my mind she was no longer waiting for my answer, she was frozen in time because the question she'd asked couldn't be answered. It would have taken a lifetime to answer the question and another just to explain I still cared for her. But as my eyes blinked slowly down at her I began to process thought once again, the imaginary gears in my brain began moving and the only thing it could come up with was a measly.

"I'm alright." The words finally left my lips. I even faked a smile as well.

Her eyes squinted into a worried look. She peered into my eyes and it was easy to see she didn't buy my response, or the smile that went along with it. She seemed like she wanted to say something but then quickly moved on to something else.

"Are you really alright?" She asked again, as if she needed some sort of extra clarification.

"I told you I'm fine." My voice was as still as I could make it, which wasn't very much. "Really, I'm okay." I reinforced.

Her eyes were trained on mine for a moment then her mouth made a slight shift to the left as if she was debating on calling me out. "You're a bad liar, you always have been Langley." She told me with a slight smile on her face. I knew what she was trying to do, I knew she wanted to lighten the mood, but for some reason my mind didn't want to give ground. My heart felt like it was slowing down inside of my chest. My eyes fell and stared for a moment at the black asphalt. Angela placed her hand on my shoulder, which made me look back up at her.

Her eyes looked more concerned than they had in a long time.

She almost seems— I paused in thought. *Sad.*

I finally found the correct word.

In my belligerence, I shrugged her hand off my shoulder, as I tried to suppress the memories that had started to flood into my head. My mouth took in a deep breath and then spoke I spoke. "What happened today? I asked. "Don't tell me you weren't in class because you were avoiding me."

She looked shocked at my sudden outburst and she retracted from me.

"No, I wasn't avoiding you." She told me, her tone was less concerned than before. "I was on a college visit, but you wouldn't care about that, would you?"

"You know what?" My voice paused. "You're right, I don't care." I lashed at her. My face cringed at my own remark. I wanted to take it back as soon as the words left my mouth.

They were words that I would regret saying, but in the heat of the moment, it was all could come up with.

I'd never considered myself a mean spirited person, but there was no other vent for all of my frustration. My emotions had become so twisted and entangled with each other it was hard for me to distinguish sadness from anger and vice versa. The boiling point in my heart had been reached, for the past few days it seemed like the contents of my heart were about to spill over.

After the month that she'd used as a buffer time to think about our relationship, it felt like there was nothing left to talk about, but there was so much more I wanted to tell her. Things like how she drove me crazy even when she wasn't around, that she was always on my mind. I wasn't sure if she truly knew how much I cared, that sometimes it seemed that without her I felt lost.

"Anyways James—," she seemed hesitant to get to the point. "Do you think you could come by today to drop off my things? I've got some things of yours that you may want back." She said breaking my train of thought. Over the three years, that Angela and I were together there had been a huge exchange of various boyfriend/girlfriend paraphernalia. The problem with that being, we now had to collect all of our memories, all of the things that made us, us.

After all of the different trinkets and gifts had been collected it was as if someone had boxed up the past three years of my life and they were about to be taken away. It was going to be as if those three years never happened and that was the thought that terrified me the most. The box that I used to collect Angela's things sat by my bedroom door, and if I leaned my head in just the right way, it was visible from my bed. There had been many nights when I couldn't take my eyes off it. My eyes would stare at the box wishing for it to just disappear while my mind tried to recount all of the items the box contained. It was there every time I went to sleep and every time I awoke.

Maybe if I were finally rid of the objects that connected us, I would finally be rid of the pain.

Even though the thought sounded promising, I knew in my heart that it wasn't true. It would take more than getting rid of some *stuff* for me to get over Angela. "Yeah, I'll bring your stuff by today." I told her as my eyes found the ground and focused there.

"Are you sure?" She asked curiously. "I don't want you to have to make a special trip." Her tone made it seem as if she was trying to console me, but it wasn't enough to squelch the frustration I felt.

"Any trip's going to be a special trip now, I suppose." I told her as my eyes came back up to hers. "I told you I would bring it by today, I'll come over after I get home." My voice was thick with frustration.

Angela paused for a moment before she spoke. "Alright, just call me when you're coming over." She told me with a smile. My eyes tightened as I examined her uneasy grin.

What could she possibly be smiling at?

And as the thought floated across my mind, she turned around and started walking back to her group of friends. The smile that she had flashed me was the same one that she had always greeted me with at the end of the school day. It was the smile that I saw in my dreams, and the one that caused me so much grief.

My eyes followed her until she disappeared into the crowd of people and then vanish from sight. As I approached my truck, I knew it would have time to think on the drive home, which was never a good thing. When my mind had time to itself, it was always a bad. I'd always had a natural talent for reading people and a talent for overanalyzing things. It didn't matter where I was, at school, in the city or completely alone, I was always an observer, it was one of the things that I did best. However, when I would overanalyze situations, I'd tend to twist them into some sort of perversion of what they really were, creating farfetched scenarios that caused me to worry.

THE SHADE

My hand popped the handle on my truck and I climbed in, placed my key into the ignition, and turned it until the sound of the engine echoed in my ears. My hand reached down and flipped on the radio. I pulled my seatbelt down over my shoulder and heard it click firmly into place. Then I pulled out into the row of cars that were waiting to leave the parking lot. My breath was heavy as my forehead came down and met the steering wheel; there was nothing that I wanted more than to scream as loud as my lungs would let me.

My mouth opened to let out the scream but the only thing that came out was my hot breath and silence.

"Damn." I said into my steering wheel. Then my eyes closed and lost myself in thought.

Then suddenly a loud *honk* came from behind me.

My head immediately lifted from the steering wheel and looked through my rearview. In a state of panic, I searched for the person who had honked. The person directly behind me was waving their hand in the air, which told me they wanted me to move forward or get out of the way. My foot pressed down on the accelerator and I began my drive home. My fingers fumbled as they cranked up the volume on my radio.

I'd decided it would be better if I let someone else's thoughts and ideas fill my head, instead of turning over control of my thoughts to my mind. Music had always had the ability to calm me down. It was a chance to relax and take my mind off the things that had gotten me worked up. As the music blared in my truck, my foot tapped the accelerator harder and I began to speed down the old curved road towards my house. On most days, I'd have waited to hammer on the gas until I was out of the city, but I was in a hurry to get Angela's things. Not because I wanted to see Angela necessarily, but because it meant I wouldn't have to stare at the box any longer. The thought that I would no longer have to look at the box as I fell asleep filled me with a grim hope, a hope that without all the things to remind me of Angela, that maybe the nightmares would stop.

After about twenty minutes, I made it back to my house.

As I looked upon it from a distance, its shape and size sent a strange tingle through my body. After a month of not going outside or noticing much of anything, the odd shape of houses roof and the way it stood like an obelisk on the outskirts of the woods, seemed to stand out so clearly.

The clouds had come in heavy, which made the building look like some kind of haunted house from a B-rated horror flick. I made it up the curved driveway and then parked the truck, my hand twisted the key, and the engine died. I leaned back in my chair and sighed as my eyes glued themselves to the trucks headliner.

There has to be a better way.

However, I knew all the things that had happened the month before had led me to that point. Slowly I opened the door to the truck and got out; after I shut my door, my feet began moving me towards the house. My hands fumbled with my oversized key ring trying to find the correct one.

Finally, after a few seconds I located my house key.

I opened the door, went inside the house, and let the door closed behind me. The living room was dark, cold and the smell of burnt coffee grounds that my mother most likely forgot to take out of the coffee maker filled the air. I found the coffee maker, the strong aroma filtered through my nostrils as I lifted the filter cover to clean the machine. My hands worked hard to try to remove what was left of the coffee filter from the machine that held it.

Mom, how did you forget to turn this off?

Then I pulled the plug out of the wall with one swift yank. It seemed like I wasn't the only one in my family with other things on their mind. I was sure that that was where my forgetfulness came from. After I left the kitchen, I strolled into the dining room. My eyes noticed a note that had been left for me. I was sure it was from my mother and I could only imagine what it said.

"Wash the dishes, do the laundry, clean your room, blah blah blah." I said out loud imagining what the note said. The thought made me chuckle as I said it.

The sound of my laugh startled me.
Twice in one day, I'm on a roll.

My feet carried me heavily down the dark hall, then into my poorly lit room. The box of Angela's things sat quietly by my door and as my body crossed the threshold my foot gave it a slight kick. I took my jacket off and threw it on my bed as I examined my desk. I grabbed two of the overturned picture frames and stared at them for a moment. The sting I felt wasn't new, the sensation was the same I'd known for the past month. I decided then that the faster I accomplished my job the better off I would be. So, without much thought I tossed the two frames into the box. My hand moved across my desk gathering books and other trinkets that had not yet made it into the box. I moved with haste, not wanting to see the items being removed; that was, until my hand touched a small odd shaped blue box that sat by itself on my desk.

I stared at the box.

Slowly they measured and traced the lines on the box. With a heavy sigh, I returned the container to my desk. It was the only thing of Angela's I wanted to hang on to. My shoulder shrugged my backpack off. I let it hit the ground with a loud thud, bouncing a little bit as the content inside shuffled about.

My homework would have to wait. I've got bigger things to worry about.

I walked down to my bathroom and looked into the mirror. My eyes lost in the eyes of the person staring back at me.

"What should I do?" I asked myself aloud as I stared at my reflection.

"There's nothing left to do." The reflection said back to me. "The decisions have been made. Now you've just got to live with them."

I went back to my room and grabbed the large box by the door. It was much heavier than I'd thought it would have been, and then I surmounted that three years' worth of stuff could have been heavier.

"Ready to go?" I asked myself.

There wasn't an answer, I wasn't expecting one. So with that I walked out into the living room, at that moment I heard my phone ringing, the faint ring tone was coming from my room. I'd forgotten my phone in the bedroom, so I quickly darted back to my room, with the box still in my hands to grab my phone. I arrived too late, missing the call. The bright LCD display told me the caller had been my father. I didn't feel like calling him back because all I wanted to do, with every fiber of my being, was to get my current task over with.

I'll talk to him when he gets home from work today.

Then I stuffed the phone into my pocket, made my way out the front door with the box in hand. The sky looked even more ominous than before, the dark clouds whipped up a cold, and bitter wind once again, sent a bitter chill down my body. In my hurry, I'd forgotten to grab a jacket and it was clearly about to rain. In Eugene, it was easy to tell when it was going to rain because there was a very distinct smell into the air. It was like smelling a freshly cut pine tree or the way freshly washed clothes smell so clean. It was a bitter smell, but it was also refreshing. I tossed the box into the truck and started to pull out; I nearly hit the mailbox in my haste just narrowly avoiding it at the end of my driveway.

I made my way out onto the main road back into Eugene. Angela's house was on the other side of the city, which was only about a ten-minute drive. I decided to make a stop at the local wildlife preserve. There was something about the outdoors that allowed me to clear my head, for me, clarity had been in short supply for a long time. I couldn't face Angela without having some sort of peace of mind.

I arrived at the reserve just outside of the downtown area. From one of the ridges you could see a clear view of Eugene, but by the time I got there, it was almost entirely overshadowed by the clouds. The coming storm had created a thick blanket of puffy gray clouds descending upon the city. I shifted the truck into park, silenced the engine, and left the vehicle. My feet stepped out onto the grass and moved quickly into the reserve. The rustle of the leaves were the only audible sound as I walked to the mouth of the forest, the leaves had started falling off the trees and the magnificent browns and reds now covering the forest floor seemed to resemble flames shooting up from the earth.

The smell of rain and the sweet smell of fur trees filled me with a sense of bliss. My feet carried me into the forest almost without me thinking about it. I seemed to move deeper and deeper until I finally turned to look at my truck and all I could make out was a tiny blue dot in the distance. "Hello?" I yelled to the forest.

My voice echoed off the trees, each syllable reverberating off the trunks and rocks. The forest was silent for a moment, the wind had stopped, but the leaves held their sway. It was as if my voice had seemed to halt the earth's rotation and stopped time, at that moment, I finally felt at peace. Everything around me evaporated, it was as if all my problems had fizzled out inside me and I was truly happy. My head shook and I quickly snapped out of my trance, the crackle of the twigs and leaves underneath me broke the silence and brought me back to reality.

I turned to make the long walk back to my truck all while I tried to take in as much of the forest as possible. After some time my eyes caught the glint of my truck, finally able to see it again. Then from my periphery, I noticed a strange rustling sound in the leaves. My head turned slowly but saw nothing.

It was just the wind.

Then as if the forest had heard my thought, a faint moan left the interior of the trees and at the same time, the wind began to whip up almost as if the moan had commanded it to. My pace quickened to a fast walk as I tried to get back to the truck.

If there's one thing I don't need, to be mauled by a wild wolverine.

My father had always told me about the carnivorous

animals around Eugene. He was a park ranger, so anytime there was an animal attack I always heard about it, sometimes for days.

Thunder boomed in the sky as I quickly climbed into the truck.

The rain began to pelt my truck. My fingers locked the door and then started the engine. I backed the truck up and headed for Angela's house. My truck lurched slowly out from the park and I didn't look back. I'd forgotten to call Angela so I pulled out my cell phone and dialed her number. Each keystroke of the numbers seemed to make me more and more nervous until I finally finished dialing. The phone began to ring and I waited.

"Hello James." Angela said.

"Hey Angela, I—," I stopped mid sentence. Out of the periphery, I saw something that seemed to be moving in the back seat of my cab. My eyes stared at the rear view mirror as they tried to see what had occupied the space in the corner of my eye, but they found nothing.

"Hello?" Angela called back to me, her voice sounded like she was worried.

"Nothing Ang, I just thought I saw—," my eyes glanced away again to check the cab of my truck, as Angela's voice became like white noise in my ears.

Then my eyes saw it.

It looked like a blur, I only saw it for a second, and then it was gone.

My eyes searched the cab for a moment until they noticed a small black shape sitting in the back of my truck. As soon as my eyes fixed upon its position it vanished like magic, as if it wasn't even there. My hand came up and rubbed my eyes. After a moment, Angela's voice began to come through clearly, she was yelling at me to answer her. The rain came down now harder than ever, it was hard to hear Angela over the noise.

"James, are you there?!" She said over the phone.

"Yeah I'm here, I just—," I tried to explain the situation.

"Look I know you want to—come over—but right now," Angela's voice weaved in and out as I lost reception.

"What? Ang I'm losing you!" I exclaimed as the connection dropped.

My fingers scrambled to redial the number, but as they started to dial, I glanced into the back of the cab. The dark figure sat in the back and then disappeared again. My foot slammed down on the brakes, my whole body twisted to glance into the cab. My heart beat quickened as I realized there was nothing there.

Am I hallucinating? Am I really that desperate not to see Angela that I would make up something to keep me away?

I looked one last time into my mirror then took off again toward Angela's place.

I felt a chill move its way down my back. The chill wasn't the kind of chill that a cold wind gives you but a different type of chill entirely. The sensation sent a pulse through my entire body and the feeling made my heart skip. What I felt was almost indescribable, it was as if I wasn't whole, like I wasn't truly all there. Like someone had taken a piece of me away, and without it I was just an empty husk. Slowly my eyes moved to the passenger seat of the truck, my eyes widened as I saw the figure cloaked in darkness beside me.

Our eyes met for a second and I slammed on the brakes once more.

Franticly looked around my truck, but just as before the only occupant of the truck was me. My heart began to beat furiously in my chest, my hands tightened around the steering wheel until my knuckles turned white. The rain outside drummed against the top of my truck and with one last look I glanced in my rearview and slammed the accelerator.

The truck roared down the road.

"I'm only a few minutes from Angela's and at this speed I'll be there soon." I thought to myself, my heart still pounding hard against my ribcage. I glanced back; the figure was still there, but I didn't stop.

I didn't dare to look back again.

Just kept going, faster and faster.

The turn to Angela's street was within my sight. I was home free. I approached the turn and my hand spun the wheel to take the turn quickly.

My truck ran the stop sign and half way through the turn, something happened.

All of a sudden, there was a loud screech and then the truck lowered for a brief instant as if I had hit a pothole. The next thing I remember was the truck flipping, the sound of broken glass and crunching metal filled my ears as everything began to spin.

My body was like a rag doll as I flipped inside of the truck, until finally I came to rest upside down. My eyes opened out of focus and they blinked, trying to see. The only thing I could hear was the ringing in my ears and the drum beat of the rain on my now overturned truck. The drumming was interrupted when my phone began to ring. I closed my eyes and listened, there was only the faint sound of the ringing phone, and then, nothing.

V

My eyes were closed, my breath still. The first impulse that crept over me was the pain; almost instantaneously my body felt as if it was on fire. But at the same time, even though the pain was coursing through me, I felt more free than I had in my entire life.

So my first natural thought was.

Am I dead?

Then a strange sensation washed over my entire body, and the world around me was as black as coal. My nostrils flared as the smell of the outdoors entered my lungs. It smelled sweet, like that of nothing I had ever smelt before. My eyelids slowly rolled back, they blinked furiously trying to adjust to the light of the sun that hung in the sky overhead, filtering through the thick layer of clouds. I looked up into the air and tried to count the number of clouds that went by. My eyes were fixated on the sky when I noticed a sharp pain coming from the back of my head.

My hand reached clumsily to the burning sensation coming from my skull. My fingers slowly moved towards the source of the pain, and I touched a wet goop that had matted my hair.

My hand moved in front of my face and my eyes focused on the dark red liquid that clang to it. I blinked as if the blood on my hands would just disappear, but no matter how many times I tried, the blood remained. My body sat upright and a sting of pain shot over me. My hand held my chest as my eyes winced and then tried to focus on the shapes around me.

I looked around for a moment, and then noticed that I had been sitting in the middle of the road. My head turned to look behind me, my truck sat overturned.

What the hell?

I tried to fixate my gaze on it but for some reason I couldn't focus on it. The sun above me was still out, although I couldn't find it in the sky. I'd assumed it was obscured by the clouds.

Did I black out or something?

My mind tried to remember, but every time I thought about what had happened, I came up with nothing. My eyes glanced down at my shirt; the fabric was adorned with rips and tears.

What happened to my shirt?

I tried to stand up, but my first attempt ended in failure and with me back on my ass. I breathed heavily and tried once more. The second time I made it to my feet, only to find that my knees shook, betraying me as I rose and straightened myself out. My back cracked as it straightened back into alignment, and once upright, dizziness set in on me as it tried to adjust to the strange saturation of color around me. It felt like my eyes couldn't exactly focus on everything at once, like things were constantly being blurred.

"I have to take this slowly." My voice croaked out.

I walked slowly towards my truck to make sure that I wouldn't accidently take another spill. As I approached the overturned truck, I began to notice things about it that seemed, out of place. The metal on the truck had almost completely rusted; the paint was almost gone, leaving it a dull brown that seemed to make it mute against the fog. The next thing I noticed was that the tire on the passenger's side was shredded. The rim was bent and the sides of the truck were crushed inward.

I've got to find help.

I looked around and slowly walked down the road to try to get a sense of where I was. As I walked, I began to notice the buildings seemed to be much older and rusted out in than I remembered. I continued to walk down the long road and as I did, the fog started to clear out.

That's when my foot struck something in the road.

CLANK!

The object sounded off with a metallic ringing. The reverberation from the ring sent a hum that floated into my ears. I bent down to pick up the object; it was an old address sign. I flipped the sign over, noticing there was more than just the street sign, but a mound of metal waste lay in the middle of the road.

What was this doing here?

My hand wiped the dirt off the sign and my heart began to race as I read the numbers off the plaque: **2215 Birchwood**

That was Angela's address.

My heart started to crush against my chest as it beat rapidly back and forth.

"Where the hell am I?" I said as I threw the sign back down.

I looked back up at the house that should have belonged to Angela; its broken and decayed facade looked as if it had been vacant for years. The paint on the outside was peeling just like all the other houses on the street.

Why do all these houses look like this? Where is everybody?

I walked quickly to the front door and pushed it open. The door opened slowly squeaking as it slammed against the doorstop. I stepped into the house to take a look around and then my eyes noticed something perplexing. The outside did not do the inside justice. The inside was well kept and seemed to be semi furnished; it seemed like someone had maintained the house on the inside but left the outside in disrepair.

What's going on here?

I glanced up the stairs and began to climb. I'd made the walk from the front door to Angela's bedroom many times, but this time it was different.

What happened to my truck? Where was the box I was supposed to deliver and how would Angela respond when I told her I couldn't find either of those things?

Thoughts flooded my head as I ascended the staircase towards Angela's room.

The door to the room was already open, so I walked inside to find it empty. The bed had been slept in, the drawers had been picked through, and most of her clothes were strewn about the floor. It almost seemed as if they had been robbed. I moved through the room and sat on the bed; my body laid back and looked at the ceiling. My eyes stared at the odd colored ceiling and thought about Angela staring up at it, as I was staring at mine.

Then I remembered, I was bleeding.

"Shit, the blood." I said as my hand reached up and touched the back of my head. But as my fingers grouped through my hair looking for the moist spot that had once been there, they found nothing. "That's odd, could have sworn—," my words trailed off.

My confusion over how I'd started bleeding was quickly overshadowed by the fact that a few minutes later I wasn't.

I've got to call for help.

My hand dug in my pocket and drew out my phone. I turned it on but as it came to the home screen, everything on it blurred out and went black. I gave the worthless piece of technology a few good taps and then gave up on it. "Damn, I've got to find a phone." I said to myself as I headed back downstairs. Angela's parents had done away with their landline years ago, so I knew I'd have to find another somewhere else. I left the house and made my way back out to the street. I glanced back at what should have been Angela's home for a second; the entire scene was a mystery to me. My eyes looked around trying to make sense of the area around the house, I didn't know how long I'd been lying in the street or if my parents had started looking for me yet.

Am I dreaming?

All I knew was that I needed to get home before my parents began to worry. Alone and empty the street resembled the way I'd been feeling lately. I scoffed at the symbolism and then strolled carefully down the road towards Angela's neighbors' to see if I could find a phone to use.

I knocked on the door, but there was no answer.

I knew the house belonged to the Mitchell's a nice old couple that had lived there for as long as I could remember. My fist knocked again and again but there was no answer.

"Well, maybe I'll just go in." I told myself and then twisted the doorknob and let myself into the house. The home seemed to be the same as Angela's had been, decayed on the outside, and picked through on the inside.

Did someone rob and pillage all the homes on this street?

It was a highly unlikely thought, but nothing else seemed to explain what was going on. I searched the house to see if anyone was home; but after a few minutes of searching, it was clear the house was truly empty, empty of the life and light that should have adorned it.

Finally, I found their phone. It was a classic rotary style, like the ones you'd see in a movie from the fifties. I picked it up and put my ear to the receiver. However, instead of hearing a dial tone, it had been replaced by a static that screamed in my ear. My hand dropped the phone at the sound of the static, the receiver bobbed up and down as the cord acted like a bungee. Unsure if It was just the phone I decided to look for another. My body turned and I walked into what looked like the dining room, and then I saw it. It looked as if the back half of the house had been ripped out, torn completely from the rest of the home, it had just been destroyed.

I peered out from the gaping hole in the wall and then jumped out of it, onto the soft earth below. I ended up in the backyard, that's when my eyes turned their attention to the other houses on the street. I looked down the line of homes, from inside it was hard to see, but outside it was unmistakable. The blemish that scarred the Mitchell's house was not random. It looked like almost every house down the line had some sort of twisted deportation that marred their surfaces. Many of the homes had walls and windows broken and some had scorch marks that looked like fire had charred them, the area seemed more like a war zone than a friendly neighborhood. I walked through the backyards of the decimated buildings and as I moved further and further, a dangerous thought worked its way into my mind.

How long was I out for? Had something happened and no one found me?

And the thought that stuck out so prevalent in my head was.

Where is everyone?

I decided to walk on, trying to look for help elsewhere.

I had wandered for about a mile, the streets and homes were empty as far as I could tell. There didn't seem to be anyone around for miles. "I've got to be dreaming." I said as my hands smacked against my face. "Wake up, wake up, wake up." I told myself.

I knew that if I was dreaming it was only a matter of time before I woke up and was rid of my nightmare. My hands rubbed my eyes and then pinched the bridge of my nose while I tried to focus on where I needed to go next. Home was the only thing on my mind, so it seemed like the next logical step. Knowing it would take me more than an hour to make it home on foot, I decided to search the street for a vehicle. This posed a problem because all of the cars looked as worn and abused as the houses. When I gave up looking for some sort of transportation my eyes fell to the ground glaring at my shadow, knowing that if I couldn't find anyone else my shadow may be the only person I would be able to talk to.

The edges of my mouth formed into a smile as the idea

filtered into my brain and fizzled out. I looked up from the road and suddenly caught eyes with someone, it had only been for an instant and I wasn't sure who it was but it was someone, it was another person.

My heart began to jump in my chest.

Knowing there was someone still around filled my chest with hope. However, before the words *hello* could even leave my mouth the figure was gone, the figure moved so quickly it was as if they had disappeared. I looked for the person as my eyes tried their hardest to follow their movements. I could barely keep up with the figures speed, so I began to run after the figure.

"Hey! Come back!" I yelled as my body pushed my legs to their limit.

The figure turned a corner and I followed shortly behind. I'd never been a runner of any kind, but I was in good enough shape to keep up a healthy pace. I rounded the corner of the nearby house and saw the figure had gained at least twenty paces on me. I tried to keep up the best I could, but my lungs began to burn inside my chest and my heart felt like it was going to give out, I knew sustaining my run for much longer would cause me to collapse.

"Hello!" I shouted, trying to get the figure to stop. The chase continued out of the neighborhood and into a large grassy field, when the figure arrived at the middle of the field it stopped and then turned around to face me. I finally made it into the clearing, slowly coming to a stop myself. Even though the figure and I were at least forty feet away from one another, I could feel its eyes tearing holes into mine.

I glared intently back at the figure trying to make out who or what it was, and then it broke its stare, looked up at the sky and looked back up at me. My heart began to beat the same way it did when I had seen Angela in the parking lot, my breath hastened which only intensified the dryness I felt in my throat. The figure looked up and we caught each other's eyes, finally I was able to distinguish that this was indeed a person, a man.

How is he running so quickly?

My hot breath filled the air around me.

"Hello? Hey can you help me?" My raspy voice said trying to catch my breath. The man stood still, almost like a statue. My eyes adjusted, trying to see if I knew the man. "Hey, can you help me!?" I yelled once more and then stepped forward to confront the man.

I stepped my left foot forward and like a mirror the man took one-step backward.

What kind of game is he playing? My head is bloodied and my shirt is torn, it's obvious that I need help, right?

I moved closer again and again and he stepped away from me. The man reached out his arm and pointed at me. The one finger sent a feeling of dread that worked its way over my entire body; then the man dropped his arm and continued to run away from me. He didn't run as quickly as before, almost like he was running in tune with my pace which allowed me to keep up much easier. I quickly followed the man to wherever he was going.

We entered back into a residential district and just like all the houses I'd seen before, the ones there sat decayed and destroyed. The man entered a small house that at one time had been blue, the worn out and faded paint was now an off colored white. Slowly I entered the house and looked around. Upstairs I heard footsteps; my eyes followed the noise up the stairs trying to hear what was going on. I knew he was up there, and I knew that I wasn't going to get anywhere by standing where I was.

My foot stepped onto the staircase as I made the internal decision to go upstairs. Slowly I ascended the staircase to the second story, my heart was calm, but my mind had an unnerving feeling it couldn't shake.

What if this was a trap, what if this person wants to do me harm?

I couldn't think about that, I'd just have to be cautious and use good judgment. I looked at the room the noise had been coming from. The door had been left slightly ajar which I assumed was on purpose. My hand pushed the old wooden door open making it creak as it slid slowly forward. I peeked around the threshold, and then hesitantly stepped into the room. As I entered, I noticed a young man who sat quietly on the bed in the middle of the room.

The man looked as if he was in his mid-twenties; he wore a worn out pea coat, black jeans, and a white shirt. His face matched his clothes, worn and tired. His short-cropped black hair was a mess on his head. His eyes were a shade of pale yellow that gave me an uneasy feeling and as he watched me, I continued to make my way across the room. I turned towards the man and stared back at him. "So, you are real." He said with a slight smile as his hand wiped something invisible away from his eye.

Real? Of course I am.

I swallowed the dryness in my throat and out of discomfort I gave the stranger before me an awkward look. "Where the hell am I?" I asked ignoring his odd introduction. The man then began to chuckle to himself as if something I'd said had been funny. "My name is James Langley; can you tell me where I am?" I pleaded with him.

"Well James." The man's yellow eyes looked up at me. "You may call me Virgil and I'll be your guide through hell today." He said with a grin.

VI

The man who called himself Virgil pushed his body off the bed and stood in the middle of the room. He looked at me motionless, his eyes searching their way up and down my body. I watched as the man's pale yellow eyes examining me, after a few moments of this he looked into my eyes and without speaking a word, he seemed to be screaming at me. I could tell that my face was a blank sheet, as my mind began to comprehend what the stranger was telling me.

There was a long pause and then.

"I'm just kidding." Virgil said laughing. "You're not in hell, but not far off." His voice felt more lax than before. He laughed as he pulled his duffel bag off the bed and began to fill it with clothes from the closet.

"What are you doing?" I asked as my voice's pitch moved up and down.

But the man named Virgil didn't stop; He just continued to pack the bag full of clothes, sometimes stopping to hold them up to his body for measurement, but never to acknowledge me.

"Hey, excuse me, I asked you a question." I tried to get his attention.

THE SHADE

He continued to look around the room at seemingly random objects; he even got on top of the bed and took the light bulbs out of the ceiling fan. Looking at me, he smiled and said, "You never know when you're going to need these." He passed me on the way out of the room shaking the light bulb by his ear. Quickly, I followed him out of the room as he made his way to the next bedroom. We entered what looked like the master bedroom; Virgil walked over to the closet and started to pilfer clothes from it almost instantly.

Just like before, he threw the ones he didn't want on the ground and the rest made their way into his bag. He did this with such violent haste that it almost scared me. I sighed trying to understand what exactly he was doing.

Why steal clothes? There are a lot more valuable things around the house I'm sure. Why does he only seem interested in the clothes and light bulbs?

I walked over to Virgil who had his back to me and my finger tapped against his shoulder. "Hello. Um—Virgil." My voice was hesitant and then he glared up at me. "I don't know if you can help me out but—,"

I tried to tell him, but before I could finish he put his finger up to silence me, his body rose up from where he had be squatting and said. "I know—," he seemed annoyed. "—I heard you the first time, I thought you might shut up about it if I ignored you, but apparently I gave you too much credit." His tone was half-jocular and half-cruel tone of voice.

"Look, I just want to know where I am." I said so that I might get some sort of real answer from him. Virgil sighed, looked at the floor, and shook his head as he turned his back to me and began to sift through the closet once again.

"Can you hand me that bag?" He asked pointing to the bag already stuffed with clothes.

"What?"

He remained silent.

"Hey!" I shouted at him.

Virgil turned and met my eyes, and in a slow calm voice said. "Hand me the bag."

"You're unbelievable—," I started to say.

"Look—," his voice was raised. "—you seem like a nice enough kid, so please hand me that bag because you're either helping me out or you're leaving, it's your choice." He told me threateningly.

My hand gripped the bag and I threw it at him as hard as I could.

"Thanks." He said with a smile, catching the bag with ease.

"Yeah, no problem." I said as a long sigh left my lips.

Virgil threw the bag's strap around his neck and looked at me with a grin. He walked out of the room and as he did, made a hand motion for me to follow him. I followed him down the stairs, my mind racing through thousands of questions nagging and chewing at my brain.

Once at the bottom of the stairs Virgil looked out the small window beside the front door, I could see the little ray of sunlight beam its way into the house. Virgil turned from the window towards me. "First off, I'm going to ask you to do some things, what you're going to do is answer with a nod of your head, is that clear?" He asked calmly.

"If I do, will you answer my questions?" I asked, breaking his rule before we'd even begun. Virgil grabbed my shirt and pulled me closer to his face. "I am going to ask you to do some things to help me—," he spoke slower and more clear. "—please nod if you understand me."

I nodded my head to indicate that I understood his request.

"Good—," he smiled then released me. "—look, we got off on the wrong foot before, but I'm sort of on a schedule here. So for your safety please pay close attention; in a few moments we're going to go outside, do you understand that?"

I nodded to him.

"When we leave the house, you follow as closely behind me as possible, do you understand?" The calm in his voice told me that I could trust him. Virgil then peeked out the window a second time and then looked back to me.

My head nodded yet again.

THE SHADE

I wanted so much to ask what had gotten him so uptight. Every word that rolled from his mouth seemed to drip with a sense of urgency that I couldn't understand.

"James, are you ready?" He asked as he placed his hand on the doorknob.

"I suppose." Answering, not knowing what I was supposed to be ready for.

Virgil turned the doorknob and turned back at me with a smile. "If we don't die, I'll explain everything to you."

DIE?!

Then he opened the door and left the house. I stepped outside with him; the sun was extraordinarily bright against the muted grey background. The white glint of the sun blinded me and without thinking, my hand moved to shield my eyes. With my makeshift visor, I could see the northern part of the city; the jagged towers in the distance looked like spears trying to pierce through the clouds.

This isn't right.

Before my mind could dwell on the thought, Virgil grabbed my shirt and pulled me down off the steps towards a large tree in the front yard. "I told you to follow me." He said looking around. "Don't look at the sun; keep your eyes on me." He said. Then pushed off the tree and started running towards one of the houses across the street, I followed suit and we hit the shaded wall of the house at the same time. I leaned out from the side of the house and Virgil pushed me back against it.

He looked at the ground and then followed what seemed to be an imaginary line up the side of the house with his eyes. I tried to see what Virgil stopped to stare at, but couldn't see it. My body leaned out from the wall and again Virgil turned to me and slammed me back against the brick. I tapped Virgil's shoulder. "Hey, what are we waiting for?" I asked him to get some information.

"We're waiting for the clouds to move." He said pointing up into the sky. Slowly I peered into the air trying to figure out why he was waiting for the clouds to move. The sun flared and shot its intense rays at the earth below. Then suddenly, just as Virgil had said, clouds rolled in and draped the sky in overcast.

Virgil turned to me.

I could infer what he wanted; that was the moment he had been waiting for, his arm that was still holding me against the wall released me. "Run quickly, move fast, if I tell you to freeze, you freeze, got it?" He shouted.

"Yeah, I understand." I replied and then we began to run across the street, he ran much quicker than I did, at times he even slowed down so I didn't get left behind. We ran from the house across a small field into another neighborhood. Quickly we went down the street until it ended with a T-shaped intersection. Before us was a large white house with pillars that accented the outside doorstep. The white door seemed to look abnormal amongst the rest of the decay of the house. We each ducked behind one of the large pillars as the sun began to shine down through the clouds once again.

"Don't move!" Virgil told me as we clung to the pillars. My back stiffened against it as I tried to make myself as thin as possible, holding my breath to keep from moving even in the slightest.

"Virgil what are we waiting for?" I asked to understand what was going on.

"When I tell you to run, follow me closely, I doubt we'll have much time to move." He told me, his voice was panicky. Then once again the sun dropped behind a group of large clouds and as it did, Virgil signaled me to follow him quickly. "Let's go!" He yelled.

We ran out from the pillars and across the open street towards another house, running the length of the house until we made it to the backyard. I sprinted through the large backyard that seemed like it would never end. We ran across several more yards until we finally found a small house on the edge of the neighborhood. It looked as if the home had sustained serious damage in some sort of explosion. The wall closest to us had scorch marks around a large hole that had been rudimentarily patched and some of the larger holes had been covered by tarps of sown together clothing. Virgil entered through a makeshift entrance at the rear of the house and I followed him inside. My hand pushed the blue tarp that covered the entrance out of the way as I walked in.

The house was dark, ill lit, and empty; there wasn't much furniture to speak of.

My feet stepped slowly across the floor to Vigil who had sat down on the only armchair in the room. Slowly I made my way to the center of the room and stopped to catch my breath. My hands immediately met my knees, doubled over in exhaustion my lungs demanded the air that they had been deprived. I gasped for air for a few seconds and then looked up at Virgil. That's when I noticed that he was very calm, even though he had run the same amount I had, he didn't seem to be out of breath. "Remind me not to do that again." Virgil said with a sense of humor that rang in his voice. "It was fun though right?" He smiled.

"You aren't tired?" I said as I tried to catch my breath.

Virgil didn't answer my question. Instead, he opened his bag and started to search through it. He sifted through the bag until he found a light bulb, held it up, and jiggled it beside his ear making sure it was still good. Virgil got up out of his chair and stuck the light into the vacant ceiling fan fixture. The room lit up instantly, sending a shock of light through my eyes, finally letting me get a good look at the room. That's when I noticed there was a small black chair located behind me. My hand reached for the chair and pulled it up to where Virgil was.

I'd trusted him to make good on our deal and answer my questions. However, Virgil didn't pay any attention to me as I pulled the chair up to where was. Even when I sat down and stared at him, he still did not look at me. I had moved uncomfortably close to him when he finally looked up. "I can't help but notice you there." He said as I continued to look at him. "Can I get a moment here, I know you have no idea what kind of danger we were just in, but for those of us who can appreciate it, let me finish doing a victory lap in my mind." He told me.

"I need your help, can you tell me anything." My voice pleaded.

Virgil's eyes winced a moment and then he drew in a long deep breath. "Fine, I suppose that's enough celebrating." He told me. "I'll tell you what you need to know."

A ton of questions flooded through my head, the most prevalent one being my location.

Virgil read my expression like a book. "First off James you're not dead."

"What do you mean not dead? I didn't realize being dead was an option!" My voice had risen sharply as I spoke. Suddenly my palms were wet with anticipation of his answer.

"James—," a tiny sigh left his mouth and then his worried eyes set in on me. "—you obviously don't understand the gravity of the situation you're in. This is more serious than you know." He told me with concern in his voice.

"What's going on?" My brow furrowed in anticipation of his answer.

"What's the last thing you remember before ending up here? I do assume you woke up somewhere you didn't recognize." He asked me the questions as he leaned forward, his hands balled together.

"The last thing I remember." I said thinking back. I searched my head trying to find out what had happened but everything seemed fuzzy and hollow in my head. However, no matter how hard I tried my mind couldn't recall the events which made me feel uneasy. "All I remember is that I was on my way to Angela's house—," my voice trailed off as I said Angela's name. Virgil snapped his fingers a few times bringing me back to what I was saying. "—then the sound of metal crunching—," I searched my mind until my head began to pound but I couldn't remember anything else. "—that's all I remember." I told him.

"Sounds like a crash." He said back to me.

"Crash? I was on my way to see Angela." My mind snapped to the thoughts of my overturned truck. "Wait is that why my truck was flipped?"

"Yep, sounds like a crash." Virgil said.

"If I only wrecked my truck, then how do you explain what happened to Angela's house—to everyone's house?" I questioned, raising my voice as I asked. "And if I was in a crash how come I'm not in a hospital?"

"Angela?" He said looking at me intrigued. "You mentioned her three times, that's interesting." He seemed to let the words roll off his tongue as he said them. The softness of his voice matched the amount of care in which chose each of his words. "James you're in danger, I am going to need you to listen to me very carefully." His tone had drastically changed from a second before.

"I don't understand." I told him, confused about the situation.

"I know you don't, but the best advice I can give you right now is to not panic—," Virgil stated, but when someone tells you not to panic it's normally the first thing you do. "—the thing is James, you've been in an accident. This is going to be hard to believe, but you need to accept what I'm going to tell you—," my heart had all but stopped in my chest. "—you're in a hospital, only—you're in a coma." He spoke his words softly.

"Wait, I'm what?" My voice said in disbelief.

"You're in a coma, your body sustained heavy trauma in what seems to be a car crash. You're body is alive, but you're mind is stuck—," he swallowed hard as he struggled to get the last words out. "—here."

"What!?" I exclaimed to him.

"James, I know it's hard to believe but you have to understand—," he began to say.

"Understand? What you're trying to tell me is insane!"

"You don't have to believe me but I am here to help you." He said calmly. My heartbeat had accelerated so fast it felt like it was going to burst from my chest. Denial filled my head, what Virgil had said was impossible and everything in my body knew he was wrong.

"What you're saying is crazy, these kinds of things don't happen." I told him as I got up from my chair.

"Look you don't have to—,"

"CLEAR!" A voice rang out in my head obscuring Virgil's voice.

"—because this is just something you'll have to take my word on." Virgil tried to explain.

My head tilted to the side because I'd not heard clearly what Virgil had just said to me.

"Did you hear that?" I asked as my finger tried to dig out the sharp ringing that had entered my ear.

"Hear what—,"

"CLEAR!—CLEAR!"

Virgil's mouth was moving but it felt like someone else was screaming straight into my ears obscuring his voice. My head suddenly felt light and then the room began to get fuzzy as it spun in front of my eyes. I could feel my body becoming lighter as my legs gave way under my weight. My body dropped to the floor and as it did, my eyes caught Virgil, who had jumped from his chair and tried to catch me. He was too late however; my body and head hit the floor with a loud thud that reverberated off the empty walls.

I felt my eyes close but instead of a darkness coming over me I saw nothing but a tiny single ball of light. Then the small light was replaced by an extremely brilliant one that filled my eyes and seemed to warm my body. My ears could still hear Virgil, who was trying to tell me something that was indecipherable. As my eyelids became heavy the only thing I could hear was the sound of my own heartbeat, it beat slower and slower, until it came to a stop, and then I felt my body drift into the whiteness.

VII

The whiteness turned back into darkness, and suddenly I could feel the shallow beating of my heart. My eyes were closed, not by choice, but for some reason I couldn't will them open. Then I felt air fill my lungs and my chest came back to life. From the pressure on my back I could tell that I was laying down, face up. That was when my nerves sprang to life. Electrical currents from my brain sent signals out to my limbs then back to my brain.

The electrical signals ran up and down my skin, which felt, normal and completely new all at the same time. My eyes remained shut, no matter how hard I tried to get them open. My heart sank as the sudden sense of paralysis crept its way slowly into my mind. I tried to move my body but found my efforts were wasted. No matter how much I struggled, my body didn't respond to my commands. The beating in my chest picked up quickly as my muscles laid there motionless.

The nerves in my arm twitched, but even as I struggled to move it with all of my strength, I couldn't make it move an inch. The paralysis was not limited to just my arm, but all of my appendages. I knew that I needed to get up; everything in my body told me that I needed to leave where I was. My mind thrashed and yelled; but my body stayed completely still.

Where am I?!

That's when I heard a ringing sound and as it continued it became sharper, more focused somehow, morphing into the sound of squeaky wheels resonating down what seemed to be a very long hallway.

Good it looks like not all my senses are gone.

My body felt the sensation of motion. Someone was moving me on a cart down a hallway. My ears could hear footsteps and sense the slightest of movement, even though I couldn't move myself. It seemed that with some of my senses dulled my remaining ones had gotten much stronger. Finally the squeaking stopped and with it so did the cart. The sound of footsteps stopped as well, replaced by the low rhythmic sound of machinery. My ears listened to the humming of the machines as they played a sort of orchestra of sound in the room. Finally, the music fell silent when a man's voice broke through the empty air.

"Erica, are the parents on their way?" The voice asked to his someone named Erica.

Erica? Who's Erica and where am I?

"Yes Doctor Burke, they should be here shortly." The voice belonged to a woman that I assumed was Erica.

Doctor? I'm in a hospital!

Then a voice came from the left side of the room. It was a voice that I knew, and a voice that I had heard earlier that morning. "Oh my goodness, James!" My mother cried out. My body felt the pressure of her body against mine as she sobbed over top of me. I wanted nothing more than to reach out and tell her that I was okay. I could hear my father in the background, his low breath was easily distinguishable as he leaned over me, and even though my eyes were closed tightly, I could almost feel his eyes bearing down on me.

"Doctor, it's a nice to meet you." My father said to the doctor.

"I wish it were under different circumstances." The doctor replied. I imagined my father and the doctor with arms extended to shake hands. The thought made me want to roll my eyes. While my father was making friends with the doctor, my mother didn't say anything, she just continued to sob over me in a state of despair.

"So doctor—," my father began.

"—Burke, Edwin Burke." The doctor quickly responded with his name.

"Doctor Burke, what happened?" My mother asked with a sense of helplessness in her voice.

"Well, the police report that we have says that he suffered blunt force trauma to the head. As far as they could tell his vehicle rolled several times then came to a stop upside down." The doctor tried to explain the situation without a whole lot of technical jargon. "He was wearing his seatbelt which didn't help him much, he was almost crushed inside the truck, and if it hadn't been for the paramedic's quick reaction, it could have been a lot worse." He continued.

"So what's wrong with him now?" My father asked with a clear lump in his throat.

"Well, James seems to be stable for now; we had a hard time resuscitating him though." Burke stopped for a moment and then continued. "Did you know he has an acute blood disorder?"

"We had no idea." I heard my father say.

"It's called Megaloblastic anemia, it's a genetic abnormality that causes some issues when receiving transfusions." He said. "I'm sure it's nothing to worry, about we just have to make sure he gets plenty of Vitamin B and he'll be fine." I could sense a sigh of relief wash over my parents as they heard the news.

I have a blood disorder, great. What other fun facts will I learn about myself today?

"Now that he's stable our only issue is that he doesn't seem to be reacting to any sort of stimuli. As of right now, he's in a coma and there doesn't seem to be anything we can do." He explained to my parents.

Coma? Virgil was telling the truth.

"How long will he be like this?" My mother asked.

"Well, Mrs. Langley. He could come out of the coma in a few days, or a few weeks. I've been doing this for a long time, in fact Michael, the gentleman in the bed next to James has been in a coma for the last sixty years. Don't worry, his is a very rare case, and I'd not expect anything so severe in James'. These types of issues are treated on a case-by-case basis. Most of the time, it's up to the patient."

Up to me? I's not like I can will my way out of this bed.

My thoughts insulted the doctor's clearly naive comment.

"Mr. and Mrs. Langley I have a lot of patients, if you would excuse me. If you need any help the button over there will call a nurse." Burke said to my parents and left the room.

The room then fell silent. The only thing that I heard was the quiet sniffle of my mother and the heavy breath of my father. I could hear the EKG machine in the background, my pulse determining the green line as it rose up and fell back down. The room remained silent for a few minutes until a shriek from the hallway caught my attention. I heard the light footsteps of someone as they walked frantically before entering the room and stopping beside me.

"Oh James."

As soon as the words floated into my ears, I knew whose voice it was.

Angela!

"Mrs. Langley, Mr. Langley, I'm so sorry." Angela said worried.

"Angela we're so glad you came." My mother told her as I felt her walk to the bed.

"I'm sorry, this is my fault, if James wouldn't have come over he wouldn't have been in the truck when—," her words trailed off and she began to cry. The muffled sound of her sobs told me that my parents must have embraced her to calm her down. If there was one thing I didn't need, it was her crying over me. I felt bad enough as it was, I didn't want her to see me in my current state. I felt Angela move in closer to me, sitting on my left, she buried her face into my arm. I felt her tears roll down off my arm and wet the sheets below. There was nothing that I wanted more than to tell her that everything was okay, that she didn't have to worry about me. My brain screamed as it tried to open my mouth and when nothing came out, I was left frustrated.

"How long will he be like this?" Angela asked.

"The doctor said that there is nothing else that they can do, it's up to him." My father told her. Out of the corner of my ear, I heard my mother start to cry again. "Angela, I'm going to take Mrs. Langley to get something warm to drink." He told her.

"Alright—," she answered back sniffling as she spoke. "—I think I'm going to stay here with James for a few more minutes." My parents left the room. I heard their footsteps continue down the hallway and once I could no longer hear them, I felt Angela lean over me.

"What did you do James?" Angela asked me. She began to cry again, it was easy to imagine her tears slowly rolling off her flushed cheeks and landing on my arm. I felt her lean down onto me and lightly kiss my forehead. She remained there for a while, time seemed to blur into the abstract. It wasn't until she spoke again that I realized any time had passed at all. "James, I'm sorry this happened. I don't know what to say. I'm going to check on your mother I'll be back I swear." She told me. I felt her lean down and kiss my cheek. She moved her lips to my ear, her hot breath breathing on my neck. "I love you James, I always will." She whispered.

Love!

My mind screamed as my body tried to move even in the slightest.

It's no use!

Angela got up and left the bedside, I heard her footsteps as she left the room. As soon as Angela's footsteps faded out of earshot another heavier pair took its place, I felt the individual walk into the room and lean over my bed.

The only thing that I could hear was the sound of someone pressing a button repeatedly, as the person did I felt my head become heavy. My mind felt sluggish, like it had been working too long on a complicated math problem, my heartbeat became even shallower, and my breath fell flat. My mind seemed to fade out slowly and it became difficult to concentrate. The intensely bright light of the hospital changed to a deep darkness that seemed to consume my body, mind, and soul. Like Virgil had said, my body was alive but my mind was lost.

I fell back into the darkness and blacked out once again.

The room was dark, cold, and damp; it felt more like a cave than a room. My back felt like I'd been lying on the same bed for years as a sharp pain shot through me. Quickly my eyes fluttered open and suddenly it hit me as my mind allowed me to remember exactly where I was. The hospital room looked dirty and old, filled with newspapers, and discarded books; it looked as if no one had set foot in the room in years.

How did I get here?

My head tilted down, to my surprise I was no longer in my regular clothes; instead I somehow had ended up in a hospital gown. I looked at the gown for a long moment, examining it, questioning it with my eyes. That was until; a ripple of pain coursed its way through my head. Instinctively I reached up and touched the source of the pain, what I found there shocked me even more than the gown. A tight cotton cloth sat stretched around my head, wrapped many times; it started at the bottom of my forehead and covered my head the rest of the way up.

I pulled myself upwards so that I was sitting upright on the bed. As I looked around the room, a cold shiver worked its way down my back.

I've got to get out of here.

Slowly I worked myself off the bed and as my feet hit the ground, I stretched out my arms and legs. Then a sound came from the hallway.

I swallowed hard as I heard the sound ripple down the long dormant hall. Then my hands fumbled around the ground for anything that I could use as a weapon. After searching, I found a rusted pole that I held up like a baseball bat. Slowly I crept out into the hall, stopping in the middle with my weapon ready to strike. My head turned to the right to see the empty decrepit corridor before me. Then I looked left. The hallway was dark, but through the ill-lit passage, I made out a shape, not a human shape, but that of an animal the size of a bear. Its black body moved haphazardly through the hospital, and as it rounded a corner, I lost sight of it. I let out a slow sigh of relief and let the hand that was holding the pole fall.

"James, are you in there?" A familiar voice called out from behind me.

My hands tensed up and quickly readying my weapon. I turned to see who had spoken my name; I was ready for anything, anything except what actually happened.

I lowered my weapon as Virgil walked up to me, pushing me back into the room I'd come from. He had a duffel bag slung around his shoulder and as he herded me into the room, he looked at me with a sort of relieved smirk. I wasn't sure what he was smirking about but I was glad that I was no longer alone. "Great, I found you. Took me three hours and two hospitals but I found you."

"There was something out there—," I told him. "—some sort of animal."

Virgil looked back into the hallway then looked back at me. "I think he's on his last leg, you don't need to worry about him." He told me.

There was a brief moment of silence between us.

"Why are you here?" I asked. "More to the point why am I here?"

Virgil looked at me for a moment and then said. "I told you before, you're in a coma."

I looked at him in disbelief.

He returned the look and threw the duffel bag at me. "Here, these are for you—," he said as I caught the bag. I unzipped it and to my surprise, there were clothes inside. "—thought that they would be better than the hospital gown." Virgil smiled.

I let out a deep breath as my mind raced with thousands of questions. The entire situation was overwhelming, I didn't even know how or where to start. A dizzying feeling set in as my head filled with so many thoughts I wanted to scream. "Are you alright?" Virgil's voice broke through my stupor. My eyes looked up at him, hoping this was just a dream and in a few moments, I would wake up and be back in my bed. My eyes blinked, but Virgil and the grim hospital remained.

This is not a dream, this is real.

"Where am I, and why am I in this gown?" I asked him.

Virgil turned his back to me and walked towards the door. He poked his head out into the hallway for the briefest of moments, then with his back turned said. "Get dressed, it will be night soon, and that's when we move. If you have some questions, I'll do my best to answer them." My hands hesitated for a moment as I stared at the man in the doorway, unsure if I could trust him. Then after a few seconds, I began to disrobe.

"So what is this place?"

"To be honest James, I don't know what this place is." He said, his voice sounded sorry that his answer couldn't be any better. "It's had many names given by a lot of different people. Some call it Limbo but most of the people here like to call it "The Shade." He told me.

"The Shade—," my tongue mauled over the word. "—so where are we?"

"It's a mirror of the real world, with a few differences. Put simply, it's a place between."

"A place between what and what?" I asked for clarification.

"Not any two physical places, but between life and death,

heaven and hell, who knows? Your body is alive and it's stuck in what we—,"

"—We? You keep saying we, are there more people here?" I interrupted.

"Yes, there are more people here, but that doesn't matter right now." He told me and then continued his original thought. "Your body is stuck in what we call, 'the real world', but your mind—your soul, as it were, has been trapped here. When your body fell into a coma, it separated from your mind; if and when your body recovers your mind will leave here." He explained as I finished putting the white thermal shirt that he had provided over my head.

"So why was I in the hospital gown?"

Virgil let out a bit of a chuckle then said. "It's enduring self image, or something like that, I'm a bit fuzzy on all the science. When your mind or soul returns to your body, it acquires an image of yourself. When your mind separates from your body it uses that image to determine what you look like, for example what clothes you're wearing. When you returned to your body you were in a hospital gown and when you woke up here, you were in that same gown because your mind thinks that's what you look like." He finished as I pushed my legs into the dark blue jeans that Virgil had given me, they were a bit snug, but they would fit.

"So how did I get from the house we were at to the hospital?" I asked him as I pulled out the large brown combat boots from the bag.

"The Shade works like a door, wherever your mind comes in from the real world is where you end up." He answered. "You must have slipped back into your coma in the hospital, thus you woke up here, which was good for you because I knew to look for you here."

I tied the boots laces up and as I did, Virgil turned around and looked at me again. He examined me for a moment. I wasn't sure if he was looking at me or seeing how well the clothes fit but in either case his cold yellow eyes made me uneasy. "So if I'm in a coma can't I just wake up?" I had hoped for some easy way out.

"It's not that simple, you can't just wake up. There are ways to get you back to your body, but there's nothing I can do." He told me.

"I don't believe this, so I'm a ghost?" I asked.

"You're not a ghost; ghosts are minds without body's to go back to." He reassured me as he looked at his watch. "It's about time—," he seemed to say to himself. "—let's get going."

He left the room and I followed behind. As we entered the hallway, my eyes began to search the long dark corridor for the way out, but the hospital proved a labyrinth of overturned stretchers and broken down equipment. I'd been to the hospital a few times and I knew that they had colored lines on the floor that lead to different places. However it didn't matter, Virgil walked on as if he knew exactly where he was going. The hallways were barely lit from the ambient light outside, which was almost worse then it being completely dark. There were cracks in the walls and as we passed each crack a bit of sunlight filtered in. We found ourselves at a staircase, which we proceeded to take downstairs. Once downstairs we were almost to the lobby. Virgil approached the large glass automatic doors and looked outside.

I walked to the window and did the same. The sky was gloomy, and the sun was up; clouds had moved in and settled themselves in a way that blocked most of the light outside. That's when I remembered what Virgil had said.

"I thought you said that it was going to be night soon?" I asked.

He looked over at me tilting his head down from the sky.

"God you ask a lot of questions, the sun never sets here." He explained. "When the sun is masked by clouds we call that night, when the sun is out we call that day. Try not to rack your brain to much about it."

My eyes looked again at the clouds covering the giant white colored sun.

THE SHADE

So it's night now because the clouds are covering the sun. Why does that matter?

Without a word, Virgil quickly walked out of the hospital and into the street. Seeing this broke my train of thought and I hurried after him. We headed out onto the street and my eyes got their first glimpse of downtown Eugene. It was hard to process everything that my eyes took in; the buildings that normally made up the skyline of Eugene were torn and broken. The streets remained eerily empty, lined with rusted cars and as my eyes looked over the wreckage of the city, a strange tingle of fear scratched at my mind.

I turned back to look at Virgil who was looking up into the air.

"We're going to need to get inside soon." He told me.

"Why, what's going on?" I asked as Virgil signaled me to follow him into an abandoned warehouse.

"We're too far from my house and the sun will be back out soon." He told me.

"Why does that matter?" I asked him repeating my previously internal question.

Virgil turned around and looked at me, his eyes sharp like daggers. Then he paced over to me so quickly I thought he was going to push me over; but he didn't, he stopped a few inches short of me and said. "James there are things in this world unlike the one you left. People think that predators and murderers are what they should be afraid of but the truth is—," he hesitated. "—the real things that go bump in the night live here, and that animal you saw in there is one of those things, so if you'd kindly come with me."

I was reluctant to move as Virgil backed away from me.

"The sunlight draws them to us." He almost shouted as his voice became more urgent.

My feet remained planted on the ground, unsure of what I should do.

"Let's go! What don't you understand, bug—," Virgil pointed at me. "—zapper." He pointed at the sun. "I'll explain, just get inside." Virgil said as he hustled me indoors. We arrived inside the building; it seemed to be an old warehouse of some kind. I found a seat on a large spool of rope. Virgil stood up, half paying attention to me half intermittently looking outside.

"James before we go any further I need you to realize something." He told me firmly.

"What's that?" I told him ready for what he had to say.

"There are things that inhabit this world, things you could have only imagined in your darkest nightmares. You're going to need my help to survive here, so you need to listen to what I say, understand?" He asked as he looked into my eyes.

I felt a sense of despair creep up on me as what Virgil had said started to sink in. This world was something very different from the one I'd been born into. My mind thought of these 'things' and what they actually were. I shook the thoughts out from my brain and then looked back at Virgil. "So you're human?" I asked.

Virgil let out a long sigh then smirked at me. "Yes I'm human; I'm not some monster out to get you." Then he returned to looking out the window.

"I get you. So what about my family?" I asked him quietly.

"Your family." He paused as he thought about his words.

"Yeah, I heard them talking while I was unconscious, they were talking to the doctor, it was difficult to make out what they were saying." I told Virgil.

"Wait!" Before Virgil's attention seemed split between our conversation, and what was happening outside, but now his attention was fully on me.

"What is it?" I asked worried at his newfound interest.

"The doctor! Who was the doctor?" He asked as he put both of his hands on top of his head.

"Uh, Brooke, or—," it was hard to remember.

"Burke?" Virgil stated in a low voice.

"Yeah that's it, Burke." I confirmed his correction.

Virgil's eyes seemed to grow twice their size and his voice became serious and nervous at the same time. "Damn, this is worse than I thought. If Burke is involved you are in danger."

"What do you mean in danger?" I asked him as my body stood up to join him.

"James, you shouldn't be here, the fact that you're here is not an accident. Someone did this to you." He said as he looked into his duffle bag.

"Who?" My voice filled with worry.

"Burke." He stated.

"Why would the doctor do this? He's the one who's keeping me alive!" I tried to plead his case.

"James, he wants you here for a reason, you're different, and the way your brain works compared to the way that most people's brains work is different. Since Burke is involved we have to tread carefully—," he paused for a moment to choose his words. "—and because Burke is involved with this, don't get your hopes up about waking up."

VIII

We sat in the cold warehouse as we waited for the sun to recede behind the clouds allowing us to escape. Virgil sat on an old unlabeled wooden crate staring out the murky, dust covered glass; his eyes pointed upwards towards the sky for what seemed like twenty minutes. I couldn't be entirely sure. Virgil sat alone on his side of the warehouse while I did the same on mine. My body ached with unseen pains, I felt exhausted, as if I'd used up every ounce of energy in my body. Slowly my heavy eyelids sank down over my eyes and I felt myself nodding off.

My eyes suddenly opened and a sense of vertigo shot its way through me. The sensation snapped my mind back to the present.

You cannot sleep. I told myself. *If you sleep, you can't defend yourself.*

I knew that if I was asleep I couldn't move when Virgil said it was time.

If these "monsters" don't kill me the sleep deprivation will.

So many things flashed through my mind, I tried as hard as I could to concentrate and sort through them, but if I tried to concentrate on any one thing, I instantly felt lightheaded. The images of my friends, my family, and Angela all flashed across my mind and I knew that I'd better distance myself from those thoughts before they started going wild in my head.

I got off the wooden spool that I'd been on ever since we'd gotten to the warehouse and started to walk to one of the dust covered windows near Virgil. I glanced at Virgil as I made my way to the window; he looked at me briefly and then went back to watching the sky. My hand moved up and wiped the dust away to create a small porthole which allowed me to get a better look at what was going on outside. My eyes peered out, looking at what the world had become. The cold and hard shell of what Eugene was in another world.

I looked over at Virgil. "What exactly was that thing?" I asked to break our long silence.

"The thing from the hospital?" He asked for clarification. I nodded.

His jaw moved left to right as he mauled the question over. "We call them wolves, or wolf singular. They're incredibly strong pack hunters, as large as a bear and more ferocious than anything I've ever seen. They can stand on their hind legs and walk upright as well." He told me.

"Like a werewolf?" I felt embarrassed the word werewolf had just come out of my mouth.

Virgil nodded. "Sure if it helps you keep it straight, they bare a resemblance to a werewolf." Virgil's words circled around my head and as I took in what he had said, my mind began to work overtime. Thousands of thoughts filled my head and then fizzled out of existence.

"Is there, anything else I should be worried about?" I asked.

"The specters." He said in a short, loathing tone. "They look more human, but I'm only using the word human to compare them to the wolves. They are terror incarnate. They're drawn by the light of the sun so if you ever have the misfortune of seeing one, run." Virgil's grim tone made me shiver, and then his eyes shifted back to the window.

I looked at Virgil and thought of what he had told me about Burke.

What's Virgil's part in all this? How did he get here?

That thought seemed to lead into another.

Can he be trusted? He seemed to be in a hurry when we left the hospital, and when I mentioned the doctor, Burke, his attitude changed almost immediately.

He seemed distracted by something ever since we had gotten to the warehouse, and that set my mind ill at ease. I knew he wasn't giving me the whole story, and it was clear that he knew more than he was letting on. That wouldn't have worried me but the fact was, I didn't really know Virgil and he wasn't exactly a fountain of information. He answered my questions with haste and only gave me information he felt was relevant. I felt as if I'd be more inclined to trust someone that would at least give me a solid answer when I asked them a question.

Just as I began to get lost in thought a loud noise came from the right, I turned away from the window to where the sound came from. Virgil had tapped the window with his finger making a loud clacking noise; his eyes looked over at me. "You ready to go?"

"Yeah, as ready as I'll ever be." I answered quickly.

We both walked to the door and out onto the street, the sun was no longer out, which, according to Virgil, meant we could move freely outside. The road ahead of us was long. The buildings that once stood as proud monuments to the city crumbled in rot and ruin before us.

"We go north." Virgil said as he started walking up the street. "We need to get out of the city as quickly as possible."

"Why's that?" I asked.

"I only have one rule; it's one that's kept me alive for a long time. Never go into the city. The city belongs to the monsters, it's a deathtrap." He told me, a harsh seriousness in his voice.

I nodded to him to let him know that I understood.

We continued up the street. The asphalt lay torn apart;

cars littered the streets with their rusted remains. The scene looked more like a battlefield than a city, something you see on the news. The street was eerily quiet; the only sound was the rhythmic pattern of our footsteps on the cracked asphalt. Virgil footsteps were so light I could barely hear them at all. We walked down the road quietly without a word to one another. There was so much that I wanted to ask but I didn't know how to go about asking; and then Virgil broke the silence.

"Who's Angela?" Virgil asked abruptly. My thoughts instantly snapped to Angela's face. It was warm and inviting and in that moment, no questions I had mattered. Virgil snapped his fingers at me. "Hello?" He said. I shook myself from the thoughts and looked up at him.

"She's my girlfri—," I stopped midsentence. "My ex-girlfriend."

"Ex-girlfriend huh?" Virgil said. "So why was she the first thing you remembered when you realized you'd been in an accident?" My mind pondered the question and as the gears in my head turned over, I slowly formulated a response.

"I was on my way to see her." I told him.

"She must be someone important to you."

"She is." I confirmed. My eyes glanced to Virgil; he seemed to have a calm air about him. When Virgil and I first met, he seemed only concerned about himself. However, since we had left the hospital and ever since I had mentioned the doctor named Burke, he seemed to look at me with more sensitivity. I was unsure of the reason why his attitude had changed but his curiosity about Angela helped me relax a bit. Our footsteps changed from the hard patter of asphalt to the soft crunch of grass as we made our way out of the city proper.

"Virgil, tell me more about this place." I said inquisitively. It seemed that he had been in The Shade for a while and any information he had was going to be of great use to me. He turned to me with eyes that told me to proceed. "What's Burke's connection to this place?" I asked him, trying to make as much sense of the impossible situation I found myself.

Virgil stiffened for a moment and then spoke. "My history's a little fuzzy, but around fifty years ago there was a string of arsons around Eugene—,"

"—sure yeah, everyone knows about that." I confirmed that I knew the stories.

"Well at that time Burke was a young doctor, one that was just starting out his medical career, he'd even make house calls. He would take patients in, ones that were in comas, trying what he could to save them. Even people who came to the hospital with the flu ended up in intensive care, he'd put them under, and they'd never wake up." He said.

"Wouldn't someone catch on to what he was doing?" I asked.

"He's sly, he spread the deaths apart that way the statistics couldn't point to any sort of wrongdoing on the hospitals part." He said through his teeth.

"Why would he need to do that anyway?" I asked trying to investigate further.

"Science, like my history, is a bit fuzzy, but to the best of my knowledge when you're asleep or while in a coma, your body produces a natural endorphin called Dimethyltryptamine, or DMT for short. It's also produced when having a near-death experience, combine that with adrenaline and your body can do things most people could never even imagine. Burke's plan was to harvest this from his patients—," he stated slowly.

"—and then he destroyed the evidence." I filled in the rest of Virgil's sentence, knowing where he was going with it.

"The patients weren't the only ones, anyone he considered a loose end would meet the same fate as the individuals that were "sick"." We continued to walk, at that point, we were a sufficient ways away from the city, and the grass was thick and as tall as my knees.

"Why does Burke need the endorphin?" I asked as my hand ran along the top of the grass.

"Burke needs it to stay alive, his real body is almost eighty years old and—,"

"Wait, eighty? He didn't seem much older than his early thirties; of course I'm estimating that based on his voice." I told him.

"The Burke you've seen—or heard rather, isn't the real Burke. That was his mind, his projection of himself, like you are right now, a projection of yourself. Burke's real body is old and frail but his projected self has become strong enough to be corporeal." He said as we continued to walk. "He's also strong enough to enter The Shade at will." He added.

"So where do you fit into all of this?" The question that had truly been on my mind since Virgil had told me about Burke finally came out. Virgil stopped in the middle of the field and looked at me. His yellow eyes peered into mine and with a look of concern turned away from me.

"You're special James. Simple as that." He said cryptically and then continued to walk. We had made it out of downtown Eugene and were close to the house, I felt as if the questions I'd asked only served to fill my mind with even more questions. I contemplated asking more but held my tongue as we continued to walk.

We made our way across a field and back into the neighborhood, slowly closing in on the house. The grassy field gave way to the suburban landscape before us. That was when I felt an overwhelming sensation that I was never going to get out, I'd be stuck in The Shade for the rest of my life. My head boiled over with these thoughts and I couldn't help myself, I couldn't hold my tongue any longer.

"Virgil, is there a way out of here?" I asked as I tried to calm my mind.

"Yeah we should be back at the house soon." He answered misinterpreting my question.

"No I mean out of this place." I tried to clarify what I had meant.

"Like I told you before, you can snap out of a coma at anytime, but there may be some people who can help us. The thing is, Burke is blocking the way out. He's guarding the one exit, he's the gatekeeper, and he holds all the keys." He told me with a grim half smile on his face.

"What does that mean?" I was taken aback by his sudden burst of happiness.

"That means for us to get out, Burke will have to die." His smile told me there was more going on between Virgil and Burke, and it went deeper than what Virgil had let on.

"When you say he has to die?"

"That means we have to kill him." My eyes must have widened because Virgil's expression turned from curiosity to anger. He knew I was judging him and he hated it.

"Why?" My voice squeaked out.

"Which reason do you need, the fact that he's a murderer or the fact he's been getting away with it for years?" He answered back. I ran my hands through my hair as I felt the tension in the air from the conversation. It was clear that Virgil's personal feelings towards Burke were strong.

"I agree that if he's done what you say he needs to be stopped but—,"

"*If*?" Virgil questioned. "What do you mean *if*? He's done things, unspeakable things and you and I are his prisoners here." He exclaimed.

I put my hands up in a gesture of surrender. Virgil wasn't particularly wrong about anything that he'd said. I knew if Burke was as dangerous as Virgil claimed, then he needed to be stopped. "Wait—," I drew in a deep breath. "—you said you and I are both his prisoners. What do you mean by that?"

Virgil looked at the ground, as if he'd misspoke or something.

"It's nothing, this isn't about me." He said, discounting what he'd previously said.

I stared at him for a long moment, and then suddenly, like a puzzle coming together I remembered what Burke had said to my parents in the hospital. "I'm sharing a room with another man—in the hospital. A man named Michael, according to Burke he's been there for almost sixty years." As the words left my mouth, Virgil's body flinched. "Your name's not really Virgil is it?"

Virgil stopped moving and looked intently at the ground. Then unexpectedly his head snapped up and he paced quickly towards me. "Now you listen to me, this has nothing to do with me James! This is about everyone, including you!" He shouted at me. The Virgil that had asked about Angela was gone; the person in front of me was someone completely different. His nostrils flared in anger as he looked at me.

"I'm not going to kill someone unless you tell me what's really happening here." I scolded him. "Something else is going on and you're either going to tell me what it is or I'm not going to help you."

"You little bastard." His voice was snide as he shrugged off my comment. "I've helped you, kept you alive! You owe me more than you know. If you feel like you can do better on your own feel free to leave." He motioned, by pointing in the opposite direction.

"Fine, I'll go." I felt like a child when the words left my mouth; but it was too late. My body turned and I began to walk the opposite way of Virgil. As soon as my foot took the first step, I immediately regretted the decision to leave. However, there was no time to think about the choice I'd made. As I walked away from Virgil and I looked back I saw him walk towards the house, he shook his head as he ascended the front stairs to the house.

Who am I to judge who's right and who's wrong?

I made my way into an ally between two of the abandoned houses and decided to take a seat to collect my thoughts. My eyes glanced upwards towards the sky. The air was hot and heavy which made it harder to breathe. I didn't know what to make of Virgil. He was right, Burke needed stopping; but it seemed like something more for him, almost like a vendetta. I didn't have all the facts and that's why I was hesitant. I didn't know what to do about Burke and frankly I didn't have any time to think about it, I needed to find someplace to go. The world of The Shade was foreign to me, there were so many new rules, and many things I yet to discover, but as I thought of my own survival, my mind ran back to the same questions.

Who was right and who was wrong? Had Virgil's morality been warped by his time here?

A rustle came from my left, my neck snapped to the side to examine the noise. My eyes scanned the alleyway looking for the slightest bit of movement. The figure that emerged from the side of the house was Virgil.

"James." He said as he walked over to me and sat down next to me.

"I didn't think you were going to come back for me." I told him.

"Yeah, well I decided someone needed to help you, you're useless on your own." He smiled at me as he slowly walked over to where I was sitting.

"So you came here to insult me? Or did you have something to say?" I asked him again.

Virgil made it to where I was sitting, and then he got down on the ground and sat with me. We sat there together looking at the sky as the cold of the ally washed over me. Once again, I felt I would never see my family, friends, or anyone ever again. The words that Angela had whispered to me in the hospital still haunted me, mostly because I couldn't tell her how I felt. My emotions seemed to twist my focus away from Angel and redirect them towards Virgil. I wondered why I couldn't bring myself to trust him. The reason I had so much apprehension seemed to stem from the way he casually talked about taking another human being's life. It was obvious that Virgil had been in The Shade for a long time, he might have had to do things to survive that some people would consider immoral.

There was a long silence and then he finally spoke.

"I know you don't have any reason to believe me James, but I am not here to hurt you, I want to help. Burke is the enemy here and if someone doesn't stop him then he can wreak havoc on anyone he wants."

THE SHADE

"Yeah I understand, but you do realize that it's a little tough to swallow, unless you give me all the facts I can't help anyone, not even myself. If I go with you, will you give me the answers I need?" I asked to him as he got up.

"I'm not going to compromise with you. The less you know the safer you'll be, if that means you won't trust me, so be it; but if you want to get out of here, you're going to need help, it's up to you." Virgil told me.

"You seemed happy at the thought of killing Burke, why is that?" Virgil's eyes grew distant and the anger and frustration written on his face faded to a sort of dull pain, like a wound he had lived with for years, had suddenly been ripped open.

"He took something from me." His voice a river of sadness. "That's all you need to know right now." He told me to end our conversation. My eyes searched his face. He looked like the same man that had asked me about Angela, the man that seemed to have a heart. At that moment, I knew whatever had warped Virgil had not fully taken hold of him. In that moment I thought that if I could remind him of his humanity, I might be able to trust him.

"Alright." I said. "Let's go then."

"I'm going to help you and if you can, you'll help me." Virgil said as he offered out his hand to me. My hand met his and he helped me to my feet. My hands brushed myself off as I stood upright. I looked at Virgil and knew he was being as sincere as he could.

We started to walk out of the ally when I turned to him.

"Virgil can I ask you a question?"

"What is it?" He said in a snappy tone.

"Why did you end up coming back for me?" I asked.

For a long moment, Virgil said nothing but then as if an idea sparked to life inside his mind he spoke. "Honestly, I don't think we can do what's ahead without you." He said as we continued to walk out from the alley.

IX

My eyes slowly adjusted to the darkness in the living room of Virgil's repossessed home. My back cracked as I rolled off the old lumpy sofa. My feet hit the floor with a loud thud, and I reached for the jacket I had been using as a blanket. I put the jacket on slowly, while my eyes tried to adjust to how dark the room was. Virgil's home was almost too dark for comfort, what little light there was, fluttered in through the small holes in the makeshift tarps that covered the house.

I stood up and walked over to the four full bookcases that occupied the corner of Virgil's living room. My eyes scanned the books, medical journals; catalogs on science, there were even a few about Greek and Roman mythology. I took a book from the shelf entitled, "Human Disease & Medical Treatment". My hand flipped the book open, inside I was surprised to see the pages covered with notes, in fact, entire paragraphs had been highlighted, and the margins had been scribbled on so harshly that the main text was almost indiscernible.

It had been a few days since our conversation in the alley. Even though I knew everything that was going on was real, it all still felt like some sort of dream. Virgil had been sitting on the front porch, waiting until it was clear to leave the house. He had planned to get some extra supplies from some nearby houses and with enough persuasion on my part, I was able to convince him to take me along. My eyes peered down at my clothes, the ones Virgil had given me in the hospital must have been hand-me-downs. They were riddled with holes, torn at the edges and fraying at the seams. My fingers pinched the fabric and my nose smelt the yellowed shirt. "Stinks to say the least." I said to myself.

Light crept into the house from one of the window and touched the skin on my hand. My fingers dropped the fabric and my hand twisted until the light was sitting in my palm. I stared at the light, waiting for it to jump out and grab me. Virgil seemed so scared of the light and the sun, he told me it drew the creatures out.

I still hadn't seen anything abnormal since the day in the hospital.

Then again, if the creatures were half as bad as Virgil made them seem, I wanted no part of them. Dust particles filled the air as I walked back to the couch. Each step brought more and more dust moats into the air and as I inhaled, I could feel the tingle of each one in my nose. I sat back down on the couch and waited, it was the only thing I'd become adept at since I'd arrived in The Shade.

I felt tired again. That was because over the past couple days I'd gotten a total of eight hours of sleep. My head fell back onto the armrest and with my eyes half shut; I sighed and looked over to Virgil's armchair. There in his chair sat a small leather bound book that I hadn't noticed until just then. I squinted as my eyes focused on the book. It had a faded red cover and the binding was frayed in places, clearly something Virgil had had for quite some time. My instincts told me not to mess with the book, but there was something calling about the tome. However, as I looked at the book, my better judgment had taken a back seat to curiosity.

My head lifted off the armrest as I sat back up. I got off the couch and walked over to the armchair. The chair was covered in dust, just like everything else in the house; its red leather seemed muted by the darkness in the room. My hand slowly started for the book. I could see it more clearly now, it had a red wax seal that had a shield and eagle symbol burned into it. My hand stretched out for the book but as it did, the front door flew open. Before Virgil could enter, I jumped back onto the couch, pretending to be asleep. His footsteps were loud as he walked into the living room. "Hey, you ready?" He asked.

"Yeah, I'm good to go." I told him as I pretended to get off the couch for the first time.

"Here, you're going to need this." Virgil said as he threw an extra duffle bag at me. I caught the bag and looked at him.

"Thanks." My voice filled with an inquisitive excitement.

"Some clouds just rolled in, they should give us enough time to get where we need to go and back. Just follow me and do exactly what I tell you." Virgil instructed.

"I know the drill." I answered him sarcastically as he began to walk towards the door. Before leaving the room, he looked back at me. That was my cue to follow him. I left the couch's side and walked to join Virgil by the doorway. My heart sank as we approached the door and I felt the same way I did when I knew something was going to go wrong.

You wanted this. Just don't panic.

We made our way out of the door; it had been the first time I had been outside in days. Even though there was no sun, the light still scorched my eyes. As my eyes adjusted, I looked out at the new world as if I was seeing it for the first time. The broken down houses, the rusted cars, and the bluish tint that seemed to mask the seemingly war torn streets all flooded my eyes.

I followed Virgil off the doorstep and as soon as his feet hit the grass, he took off in a dead sprint. I panicked as my eyes tried to follow his movements. Before I knew what had happened he was already a good fifty yards away from me. I took off after him, but my legs felt heavy, like trying to run

THE SHADE

with bricks tied to my feet. As we made our way into the open field directly across from Virgil's house, he continued to pull away from me. I glanced at the sky above and when I looked back down, I'd lost sight of Virgil, as if he had disappeared.

My eyes glanced around, looking for any trace of Virgil. *Where did he go?*

I began to panic, trying to figure out where he had gone.

He hadn't told me where we were going and I knew if I couldn't find Virgil before the sun came out I would learn firsthand why he was so afraid of it. I felt my heart begin to beat faster, my head felt compressed.

Pressure built up in my chest and slowly climbed into my head.

My heart began to pound against my chest and my breathing began to slow. I looked down at my hands as my vision became fuzzy, my hands blurred out of focus when suddenly. The area around me burst into full focus, like a switch being flipped inside my head. Everything around me, the knee-high grass, the clouds in the sky, the rust colored dirt beneath my feet, all of it seemed to stand out with a new brilliance that I had never noticed before.

Everything had become clear as my legs began to pick up speed. I started to run fast, faster than I had ever run in my entire life. Everything around me seemed to be a blur as my body darted through the rest of the field. My speed wasn't the only thing that had changed. My eyes began to see the tracks Virgil had made when he ran through the field, the tracks seemed to glint in the pale blue light of The Shade, almost guiding me to my destination.

I focused on the tracks and continued to follow them into a residential area with some newly built houses in it. My eyes darted, following the tracks towards a brown one-story house that had no cars outside of it. As I approached the house, all the small nuances about it seemed to pop out at me. Everything about the house seemed to be calling out to me, and something told me I was at the correct house. I approached the house and as my body got closer to the door, I could feel my heart start to slow and the pressure that used to occupy my head seemed to dissipate, returning to normal. The door to the house was slightly ajar, telling me that someone had been there.

I walked inside; the lights in the small foyer were off.

In the foyer, there was a small table and upon it was a scarlet red lamp. Without a second thought, my hand tilted the lampshade downward; looking inside I noticed the light bulb had been removed.

Virgil's been here, no doubt about it.

A loud thud came from the back of the house, my head quickly snapped up. I looked down the hallway that led to what I believed, were the bedrooms. I walked slowly down the hall and entered the room where the sound had originated from, only to find Virgil packing his duffle bag full of clothes. "Hey, glad you could make it." Virgil said to me as he looked up from his duffle bag.

"Glad you could make it! What the hell happened?" I said as the anger from him leaving me surfaced. Virgil zipped up his duffel bag and looked at me as I quickly approached him.

"I was testing something, seems to me you made it here okay." He said casually as he got up off the floor and walked past me.

"Testing something?" I watched while he exited the bedroom. "What exactly were you testing?" I said to him as I followed behind him. Virgil passed into another bedroom as I hurried quickly behind him. When I entered the room, it was abundantly clear it was the master bedroom. A large king sized bed sat in the middle of the room with a nightstand on either side. By the time I made it to the room Virgil was already looking through the closet for clothes.

"I need to know why you're so important to Burke, seems he knows how to pick'em." Virgil stopped collecting clothes and placed his duffle bag on the bed behind him.

"Are you talking about what happened to me in the field, the feeling that I got, the speed, the clarity?" My mind searched my body for the same clarity that I'd felt when I was in the field but couldn't find it.

"You felt something?" Virgil stared at me. "That feeling was your mind using adrenaline and DMT together." He told me as he moved past me and into the hallway. Virgil was quiet as he moved down towards the next room. He seemed like he was lost in his thoughts unable to decide what to say to me.

"So is running fast the extent of what I can do?" I questioned him, curious about my newfound ability.

Virgil paused in the hall right at the threshold of the next room. "No, you have to keep in mind that this place isn't like the real world. The same rules don't apply here, things like sleep, fatigue, hunger, you may get urges like those here, but there is no need to act on them." He explained to me.

"So that's why I never see you sleep." I said, letting him know I understood.

"Right, and don't worry about the other stuff, I'm sure it will come later." He reassured me as he continued to walk into the next room. The room seemed to be a study, filled with old books and leather furniture. "So what we're looking for anything we can use, light bulbs, clothes, medical books, medicine, things like that." He explained.

"Alright and what about these other books?" I asked him as my hand traced the spine of an old leather book on the shelf.

"Those are books on law, so unless you intend on taking someone to court, leave them." He said sarcastically. We began to search the room for the items that Virgil had mentioned. My head was filled up with so many questions I almost blurted them out in normal conversation. I found a medical book that looked like it could be of use, so I stashed it in my bag.

"Why do we need light bulbs? I mean where does the electricity even come from?" I asked.

Virgil turned from whatever he was doing and looked at me, his eyes in a half squint as if his face was telling me he was thinking. "I'm not sure where it comes from, it just does." He finally said.

"And that doesn't seem worth investigating to you?" I said with a chuckle.

"I don't look a gift horse in the mouth, if electricity is one of the simple comforts we have here, then I'll take what's given to me. I'm not going to question it." He almost seemed annoyed with the question, but I knew that he was probably more annoyed with the fact that he'd not ever considered it before then.

"So what about water and other utilities?" I asked.

"As far as I can tell everything works just like in the real world, now can we stop talking and concentrate on the task at hand please?" He said more as a command and less like a question.

Virgil returned to his work and me to mine.

"I'll go check somewhere else." I said to him as I left the study and moved to the bedroom across the hall.

"Hey, make sure you hurry up we don't have long." He said as I left the room. I shook my head as I made my way cross the hallway towards the last room in the house. The walls were a mat blue color with a full sized bed in the corner of the room. The bed sheets looked as if they had been tossed from the bed haphazardly, as if someone had jumped out from it. As I broke the threshold of the room, I found a small dresser with a television sitting on top. If I had to guess, I'd say that the room belonged to a boy.

Maybe I could find some clothes that actually fit me.

I started to search when my ears detected a sound coming from outside the house. I swiftly walked out of the room and back down the hallway, passing the room that Virgil was in.

That's when I heard the noise again.

"Hello?!" I heard it call, desperate.

Another person!

My mind shouted to me.

I made it to the front door in the foyer of the house and peered out the window looking for the source of the noise. "What's going on?" Virgil asked me as he glided gently down the stairs.

THE SHADE

"There's someone out there, I heard them." I said as I headed for the door. Virgil peaked out of the window, pushing the white curtains aside with his fingers and looked into the air. The figure was walking down the middle of the street—alone.

"Hello! Is anyone out there?" The man yelled in extreme anxiety.

My eyes gazed out the window and observed the man, my hand reached for the doorknob, but before I could touch it, Virgil's hand caught mine. "No James." He said to me.

"I was just going to let him in." I said, ripping my hand free.

"We can't do that."

"What are you talking about? He needs our help!" My voice began to rise.

"There is nothing we can do for him now." He said with a straight face.

"How can you say that? We can help him." I tried to push my way to the door again but Virgil's hand was too quick. Before I had even touched the knob, he grabbed me once more. With one hand holding onto me Virgil used the other to rip down the white curtains covering the window, revealing that the sun had started to emerge from the clouds.

"Look at the sky James."

"I can't just leave him out there. Stay if you want, I'm going." I told him for the last time.

"Apparently I didn't make myself clear. You're not leaving this house." He said through his teeth. My hand started for the doorknob a third time, but as my fingers touched the cold brass knob Virgil grabbed my shirt, as he did, my feet left the floor and my body flew across the room. My back hit the wall and I slid down towards the floor. The impact caused me to hear a sharp ringing in my ears. I shook my head to get the sound out, but with no success.

"What was that for?" My voice screamed at him.

"It's for your own good." He said as he walked over to me.

He offered his hand to help me. I pushed it out of my way as I got up on my own and then made my way back to the window.

"He's already dead James; he just doesn't know it yet." Virgil told me.

I watched the man outside who was still shouting. Virgil pointed at the sun and then back down at the man. "Watch him." He directed me. The man was still in the middle of the street, the sun was now fully out and was beating down on him.

That's when I saw it.

I couldn't be entirely sure, but for a moment the ground seemed to shift slightly below the man's feet. "I don't understand." I asked Virgil. "What am I watching?"

"Just keep watching." He instructed. Then it happened, something that resembled a hand appeared out of the man's shadow. The appendage was horrifyingly hideous, so much so that I didn't want to see the creature it was attached to. An arm followed the hand, the arm looked burnt and bloodied, and then another arm shot out from the shadow. The arms placed themselves firmly on the concrete and drudged up a figure so hideous I had to turn away for a moment. The figure stood at least six feet tall and seemed as though it was the embodiment of death itself. Its skin peeled off in places exposing the moist red flesh underneath. The majority of the creature was covered in black scorch marks.

"That's a specter." Virgil said quietly.

The burned and blackened specter grabbed hold of the man's leg and began to pull him down, not onto the ground, but into the shadow itself. The man screamed for help as the specter tore at his torso trying to make him sink into the once solid pavement. The man's arms caught himself while he was waist deep in the ground. The man let out a terrifying scream as he lost his grip on the asphalt. Almost instantly, the man's head was totally submerged and as he finally went down he shouted for help one last time, and then silence filled the street. "What the hell was that?" I asked as my heart pounded against my chest.

"That's why we don't go into the sunlight." He told me.

"It was his shadow—his shadow turned into the specter and then took him—," my voice trailed off, my eyes still glaring at the street as my mind tried to process what I'd just seen. Virgil patted me on the shoulder. "—how did they even do that?" I added.

Virgil looked around the entryway until he found what he needed. He picked up two sheets of paper on the small table beside him. He took the two sheets and began to fold them in an accordion like fashion, so that when he was done the paper had points and valleys. "Okay, when you think about The Shade think of it like an onion, in the sense that it has layers. If we want to put the real world as the first layer that's fine, with The Shade right beneath that. Now the layers that come after that are unknown, at least to me."

He then placed the papers on top of one another, letting the peaks of the bottom paper touch the valleys of the top piece of paper. "Where the two layers touch are where breaches happen, like spillovers into the different layers. It happens in the real world all the time, things like Bigfoot and the Lochness Monster, can all be traced back to a breach. The specters and wolves use the shadows of living people as portals to this level of The Shade, but that means they have to be in the right place at the right time on their end." He explained.

My head began to ache as he continued. Virgil dropped the papers to the floor, apparently done with them. "Let's say I go outside right now, and a specter were to attack me, they would use my shadow like a door. If that specter entered our level of The Shade and the sun becomes obscured, making my shadow disappear, then their door back to their level is closed."

"So that's why that wolf was in the hospital." I said, beginning to understand.

"Exactly." Virgil said. "Most of the time a trapped creature will head for the city, it's where they have the easiest time hunting. Another thing—," he said remembering something else. "—it's the shadows that are cast by the sun that attract them, don't worry about light bulbs or fire."

Everything that Virgil had told me made me feel better about my situation, setting my mind at ease. My heart rate lowered and my mind began to focus again. Given what I'd witnessed, the ability to calm myself took a feat of unimaginable strength. "So now what are we going to do?" I asked him.

"Now we have to stay here until the sun goes down, so start getting stuff together and I'll tell you when we're leaving." He told me as he walked down the hallway. Still unsure of what had just happened, my mind was reeling from the horror I had witnessed. Nevertheless, I did as Virgil told me and I made my way into the bedroom to see if that could calm my nerves.

***

Our figurative night didn't come quick enough. Virgil had been silent the entire time until he finally said it was okay to head out from the house. "James let's go." He said as he passed by me on the couch.

Finally.

I rolled my body off the couch and followed him out of the house. We began our way across the street, but halfway across I stopped at the spot where the man had been pulled through by the specter. My foot stepped on the solid pavement, checking it repeatedly. "So what exactly are the specters?" I asked.

Virgil looked at me hammering away with my foot and said. "Sometimes when people die, their souls or spirits get stuck here, they don't move on for whatever reason. The fact is, you and I are not supposed to be here. The specters are simply trying to balance the equation by getting rid of us." He explained.

"This isn't some sort of math problem. Someone's dead and you're acting like nothing even happened." My voice had grown louder as the words spilled from my mouth.

"People die every day, people dying here isn't uncommon, it's just a part of life." He said. His attitude about the situation put me in a bad mood and I remained silent for the remainder of our walk back to the house.

We continued to walk through the grass when suddenly Virgil stopped, and threw his arm out to stop me as well. "Something's wrong." He said.

Virgil began to run quickly, headed straight towards his house.

I couldn't muster the clarity that I'd felt earlier, but I ran as fast as I could with him. A bright light filled the sky as I approached the house and a wave of heat hit me. Flames covered the home, seeming to touch the sky as the fire roared out of control. Virgil was nowhere in sight but the door had been opened, telling me he was inside the burning house. Frantically my eyes searched for him, waiting for him to come out of the home. Finally, Virgil burst through the front door, smoke trailing him as he ran towards me.

He walked up to me, wiping the soot from his face as he approached.

"Where do we go from here?" I asked.

"There is a place, a refuge, that's where we're headed. This is Burke's doing, we need to go." Virgil said.

X

The fire bellowed from the house, covering the sky with a thick coating of smoke and ash. All of the light seemed to vanish from the sky as the black plumb coming from the house spread itself like a blanket across the horizon. Virgil and I glanced at one another then back to the fire. The house was lost. Virgil and I both knew it.

Virgil turned away from me and began to walk. The direction seemed random but his legs carried him as if he had a purpose. My eyes glanced one last time at the house and then I turned and followed Virgil. We walked in silence, his eyes intent on what was ahead of him not bothering to look at me. His yellow eyes peered forward, intent on his goal, whatever that was. We walked back across the field and from time to time, I looked over at him, just to make sure he was okay, but we never made eye contact. We wandered around for at least an hour before I finally worked up enough courage to say something to Virgil.

"Virgil, are you doing okay?" I asked as I tried to understand what he was thinking.

"I'm fine, why?" He said. I could tell he was trying to brush me off.

THE SHADE

"Well, your house just burnt down, all of your stuff's gone and you haven't said anything since you mentioned Burke, so, just a hunch." I said sarcastically.

He grunted at the comment continuing to walk towards his unseen destination. His face looked worried, the lines on his forehead seemed to standout because his brow was furrowed. It took a few minutes but finally Virgil said. "It wasn't my house, and I'm trying to think, which works a lot better when you're not speaking." He glared at me as he said it.

"How do you know Burke did that?" I asked. "I mean, why would he just burn down your house?"

Virgil stopped and thought for a long moment and then turned to me. "He knows I'm with you James, he knows we're trying to get you out and he destroyed the one place that was safe for us." Virgil said his tone that of someone who was concerned and angry at the same time. "Trust me James, the less you know the better off you'll be." His voice trailed off as he began to walk again.

Silence fell over me.

Better off not knowing? Why is he so afraid of Burke?

The thought bounced around in my head, only serving to frighten me. Over the few days that I'd been with Virgil he seemed to always shrug off danger. Virgil had to be the calmest person I'd ever met, especially in the face of danger and death. That thought made me worry, I worried because if something could scare Virgil so badly that he'd seek help from someone else, then it was probably something I should be scared of too. Especially since it felt like Virgil was the type of person that hated asking for help. I didn't know Virgil well, but it was easy to tell what kind of man he was, and he'd never ask for help or do something that wasn't on his own terms unless he absolutely had to. That was what scared me the most.

"Why can't we just move to a different house?" The silence shattered around us and Virgil's eyes peeked in his peripheral vision at me.

"It's too late for that." He told me. "Burke knows I'm with

you and I can't protect you myself, so we're going to need help." He told me. It felt good that Virgil had finally started to let me into his world, but it would be meaningless if he couldn't keep me alive. The clouds hung still in the sky above us as we walked slowly through the still grass; the long reeds hit my open palms as my hand glided across the grass like a skate across fresh ice. Virgil gazed over at me and my eyes met his. He still made me feel uncomfortable when he looked at me.

His yellow eyes took some getting used to.

"Where are we going exactly?" I asked him.

"The refuge, it's a church located on the other side of town." He told me, reluctant to offer up any more information. I knew that I'd have to push to get anything else out of him.

"Why do you seem so hesitant to go?" The question sprang from my lips and as Virgil heard the words, it was as if he smelled something putrid in the air. He met my question with utter silence. That was my first indication that Virgil didn't want to go to the refuge unless he absolutely had to, and if he did, he wasn't going to be happy with it.

But why? I asked myself. *Why seek help from people he didn't like?*

My thoughts of Virgil seemed to run around in a circle, so I put the thoughts to bed and looked at him. "Why are we going to the refuge—," before Virgil could interrupt I put up a finger. "—it's obvious you don't want to go. My question is, if you don't want to go somewhere that badly, why get help from them?"

Virgil was stunned. His face went from his usual angry demeanor to a softer confused one. He looked at me as though I'd figured some great question out. "It's complicated." He told me, his voice calmer, smoother than before. "I've got my reasons for doing everything that I've done. All I can say is I'd rather see you protected than not." He told me with concern and then looked ahead. His sentiment was something new. It was the first time that I believed without any doubt what Virgil was telling me. Virgil was usually always about business, always about trying to survive. It was the first time since I'd met him that I felt I could relate to him.

"Thank you" I told him quietly. I wasn't sure if it was because he hadn't heard me or he didn't care, but he remained silent. "What's at the refuge?" I asked.

Virgil looked at me, then back ahead. "People—well not people exactly, but people with very different skills and abilities." He told me. "Every myth, every legend that has ever been told has had some kernel of truth to it."

"So who are these—refugees?" My voice stammered out.

Virgil chuckled a bit.

"They call themselves 'The Family'" He informed me. "They're people, real people. Some of them are just like you and me, only with power unlike any human. They live at the refuge because there's nowhere else for them to go."

"So this family—," my voice said questioning. "—how do you know they can help us?"

"Burke is a threat to all of us, but he's not the only enemy we face. He's a problem, but nothing compared to the real enemy that the members of the refuge have been struggling against—," his words trailed into a silence.

"Against what?" My voice cried out in the silence to get him back on track.

"—we—they don't know. We're not sure about their motives, they take people and as quickly as they appear, they vanished. You see, over time evolution branches out and creates certain sub-species. Some of the family members belong to those genetic offshoots. The family's adversary takes those people who they believe are special, different from everyone else. The people of the refuge try to stop them, think of them as the police for this world; we're going to need their help." He told me.

"So why is that not a good thing?" I said inquiring about his tone.

"The family and I had a falling out. It's complicated, hard to explain." Virgil sighed.

"*You* had a falling out with someone? That doesn't seem hard to believe." I said sarcastically.

"Sarcasm noted. I've been here a long time James. Some of my choices have been questionable at best, but all that aside, we need to hurry, the sun will be out soon." Virgil hastened. We made our way over a large hill as we left the field, entering into a small residential area, I could see a church start to form just over the horizon. Its large spires scraped the sky and if that was indeed where we were going, it didn't bother me. Light blazed from the windows making the church light up like a beacon in the dark lonely world of The Shade. We walked through the outskirts of Eugene, the location unknown to me because of my seldom visits to that side of the city. Once we were within a hundred feet of the church, I could see the magnificent stained-glass windows; they shined beautiful colors out into the ever-present darkness that seemed to encapsulate the church.

A beacon of light.

The thought of light pierced through all the things that clouded my mind, leaving only the thoughts of Angela. I wondered how she was getting on without me, and if she'd spent every day worrying about me.

She's probably sitting with me in the hospital.

Someone had probably told her to leave and she'd more than likely thrown one of her fits, making a scene just to stay. The thought of her brought a smile to my face.

"Are you alright?" Virgil said to me.

I stared at him inquisitively. "Of course I'm fine why?"

"Then why are you crying?" He asked.

My hand reached up and plucked a single tear off my cheek, I held it in my hand as I slowly watched it soak into my skin. My mind pushed my emotion down so that I could focus at the task before us. We approached the front of the church, at which point, we were close enough for me to notice the exterior had been reconstructed. There wasn't a single scratch on it, the paint was new and it seemed to be maintained. In my opinion, the refuge was beautiful. Finally, we arrived at the stoop and then slowly ascended the steps to the door. A sign hung on the large wooden double doors. The sign had been spray painted in blue paint, a circle with a star in the middle of it. When we got to the final step of the stoop Virgil turned to me.

"James. You may not understand everything that's going on in here, but for your safety, please don't make eye contact with anyone, is that understood?" Virgil instructed me.

"I understand." I confirmed.

We opened the door and the light from the inside of the church hit us in the face. It flooded over me, making me feel unimaginably warm, it coursed through my body and for an instant, I felt whole. Then the warmth of the light left me, as the large wooden doors slammed shut behind us. Suddenly all eyes were on us, and as I looked out on what appeared to be at least one hundred pairs of eyes, a cold draft swept from one end of the church to another. We stepped further inside, and as we did, all of the onlookers returned to what they had originally been doing. The floor was a sheen white marble with a long red carpet stretching all the way down from the door to the altar.

There were twelve pillars that lined the church walls. Grouped together in sets of four, they made a square shape. Those squares extended upwards towards the ceiling eventually coming together into a point. The ceiling itself had been painted with beautiful mosaics of a forest changing throughout the seasons. At the entrance, the trees were budding, further along they were a lush green, even further the trees had begun to lose their leaves but the ones that remained were brilliant shades of red and yellow, unlike anything I'd seen before. At the end, above the altar the mosaic depicted the trees barren, without leaves, and although I knew that the picture signified death, the last piece of the mosaic seemed to speak to me the most.

As my eyes looked down from the mural on the ceiling, I decided to stare ever so intently at my shoes. As Virgil and I walked, I heard a group of women whisper amongst themselves, and as they did, another group started to approach us. "Virgil, nice of you to come." A woman's voice said. My eyes teetered upwards to catch a glimpse of the person who had stopped us. The woman had flaming red hair, her face was full, and the way she stood with two larger men behind her, it was clear that she was the leader.

"Yes, well you know why I'm here, please let me through." He asked, more polite than usual, he kept moving but the two men stepped from behind the woman and blocked our path.

"What I can't understand is why someone who's claiming to be neutral would come *here*?" One of the men pressed him.

"Then I suppose you will be lost in your ignorance." Virgil said as he turned away from the trio and motioned for me to follow. Virgil pushed the two men aside and I did as Virgil had silently asked.

"What was that?" I asked.

"They're called naturals. They're called that because they can enter The Shade in their real world bodies." He explained.

"So those are real people?" I questioned him.

"Yes. You and I are representations of our minds, if we went back to our bodies in the real world we wouldn't have any of the advantages that we do in The Shade. Even if we did make it back to our bodies we could never amass enough power to reenter The Shade, although it's not impossible, just unlikely." Virgil explained. "Naturals however can tap into the DMT inside them, giving them the same power in the real world that they have in The Shade. Everyone here could pass you on the street and you'd never know about the secret life they live."

"And why did they call you neutral?" I asked him.

"I'm not on either side. I'm not a part of their fight." He told me as we continued down the long aisle. The pews that would have normally been in the church had been removed for one reason or another. It seemed they used the space in the church as a common area. As we moved I felt a hundred little sets eyes staring at me, each set of eyes burning holes straight through me as if they wanted to see into my soul.

"Virgil, you've come back to us." A woman said to Virgil in a slight English accent.

"James, get behind me." Virgil whispered to me.

A young woman that couldn't have been more than twenty approached us. The girl was pale, with black hair running down to her shoulders, she couldn't have been more than 5' 4" but still exuded a sense of fear when I looked at her. "Is that your new pet, love?" The woman said.

"He's with me Kate; you know not everyone is something you can eat."

She cocked her head and smiled at Virgil. "You know I've been clean for longer than you've been alive, so why has our favorite ghost come to visit us?" She smirked knowing that Virgil would take offense to the word ghost.

"Well it has nothing to do with our resident blood sucker, now does it?" He threw it back in her face. Kate's eyes glowed red, she blinked, and they were green again. "Did you need something from me?" Virgil asked.

"Virgil we all see the storm that's coming, why can't you?" She questioned him.

"I'm not here to defend myself, tell me where he is!" He demanded from her.

"Continue running Virgil, we all know that's what you're best at." She taunted.

Virgil looked annoyed, more than that, I could tell he was biting his tongue; the way people are cordial with one another even if they hate each other. "I don't have time for this." He said, pushing his way past Kate who stood there with a dumbfounded look on her face.

I waited until I was absolutely sure that Kate was out of earshot before I spoke to Virgil again. "What was that?" I asked.

"Remember when I told you about those things that weren't *exactly* people?" I nodded to affirm what he'd said. "She's one of them. Humans call them vampires, but they hate that name, they think it's sort of racist. They're really just creatures that find sustenance from human blood, but she's the last one in the world." He informed me.

"Should I worry about her?" I asked him with a hand on my neck.

"About Kate? No, she's been off human blood for like a hundred years, she made a vow never to create another one like her, something about a war between humans and her kind." The information felt like something out of an old black and white horror film. Then my mind snapped back to the reason Virgil had taken me to the refuge in the first place.

"Virgil, you never told me who we're here to see."

"I know, why would that be relevant?" He chuckled as he asked. "It's not like you'll know the guy anyway." We walked further down the aisle. Virgil started to point out the different groups as we made our way to the front of the church. "Those are the leeches, one touch from their hands and they'll know everything you know." He told me. The group he had pointed at was a group of nine or ten seemingly normal looking "people" and as Virgil had said, they all wore gloves to cover their hands. "The folks over there in black, dressed like Goths are called wraiths. They're hot headed, very powerful in a fight. Their anger is the source of their power." He said.

"What about Bur—,"

I almost said, but before the words left my mouth Virgil covered it with his hand. "Don't say his name, not here." He told me as he removed his hand from my mouth, my brow furrowed, unsure as to why Virgil stopped me so quickly. Slowly I looked around to make sure that no one heard me, I quietly looked down to the floor and made my way with Virgil to the altar. We stood at the altar, Virgil looked worried as we waited for our mysterious host to appear, and then out from behind the large throne like chair that sat in the middle of the altar, a figure walked out.

The man took position in the middle of the altar.

Slowly I looked up from the carpet and met his eyes.

Shock flooded over my body, as I realized that Virgil had been incorrect in his assumption that I wouldn't know the person we had come to meet. As I stared at the man in front of me, his set of blue and green mismatched eyes stared back.

PART II: ENEMIES

"Audentes Fortuna iuuat"
Fortune Favors the Bold
- Virgil

XI

The eyes that met mine were familiar and different at the same time. The thought of the eyes sent a word to my mouth and the only thing that could spill over my lips was. "Shaun." He moved to the large chair at the middle of the alter and sat down. He crossed his legs and looked down at Virgil and I.

What's Shaun doing here?

My heart raced as I pondered the question. Suddenly the silence that had filled the church around us was broken by the voice of the boy who had been my classmate only a few weeks before. "Virgil, Virgil, Virgil." He said in an almost disappointed tone. "What are you doing here?" Shaun questioned.

"You already knew I was on my way, didn't you? It must be nice to be able to see what's coming your way, makes it easier to hide." Virgil scolded him.

Virgil leaned over and whispered in my ear.

"He's a seer, he can see the future." He said in a whisper to fill me in.

"You should know all about running and hiding right Virgil." Shaun shot back. "Why are you here?" The room was silent, the tension palpable. My muscles tightened in my arms and chest. My lungs held on to each breath, unsure if they could grasp another. "We're here for your help. This is James—," Virgil began to say.

"I know who he is, we go to school together." Shaun informed him. Virgil didn't look surprised as Shaun's eyes moved to me. "How are you adjusting James? I heard about the accident, you've generated quite a lot of commotion around Eugene." Shaun told me.

I ignored him.

"How's Angela?" I asked, needing to know anything about the real world.

Shaun sighed and then with what looked like reluctance told me. "She's fine I assume. She's not been at school for a few days; my aunt told me that she's been taking it pretty hard." Turning back to Virgil, he said. "And you Virgil, why in the world would I help you?" A smirk spread across Shaun's face.

"Because this isn't for me, James needs protection and I don't need the burden." Virgil said in a shrill voice.

"He needs protection from whom? You?" Shaun questioned, his eyes locked on Virgil. I looked at Virgil trying to understand what was going on between him and Shaun, they might as well have been speaking nonsense, and it would have been just as clear to me. Slowly I looked to my left, then the right. It seemed that everyone who had previously been in their separate groups had made their way to us and created a half circle shape around Virgil and I.

No way to get out now, not even if we wanted to.

"Shaun, it doesn't matter what you say he's safer here than with me." Virgil said, seeming as if he wanted to dump at the refuge. They stared at one another for a moment and then Virgil added. "Please." In a voice that almost seemed pleading.

My focus shifted from Shaun to Virgil.

Why is he so desperate to get rid of me?

I peered up at Shaun. His black stringy hair hung down near to his shoulders. Shaun put his hand on his pointed chin as if he were pondering something of great importance, after a minute of the showy gesture he said. "You have to be kidding Virgil. You walk in here demanding favors. After what you did? My answer is no, he's your problem." Shaun told Virgil bluntly, pointing in my direction.

"What are you—?" My voice tried to call out before being interrupted.

"—quiet James, the grownups are having a conversation." Shaun said to me. I was taken aback by what Shaun had said. Not in a million years had I ever thought that Shaun was capable of speaking to anyone with such pompous arrogance. I'd misread him the entire time I'd known him, which had been since grade school, I wondered how I could have been so wrong about someone for so long.

"Shaun we need to get him back to his body." Virgil pleaded.

Shaun's look changed from frustration to a sort of confusion.

"Even if I could help him, and I'm not saying I can." Shaun paused for a moment. "Why would I put the rest of my family—," he spread his arms out towards the half circle of people around us. "—in danger?" His voice filled with harsh conjecture.

Virgil began to walk forward.

"Look Shaun you don't have a choice, he's here and you can't hide it. You're already involved, there's no going back at this point." Virgil said.

Shaun walked down to meet Virgil and stopped a few feet from his face. "No!" His voice boomed. "You listen to me, you're no longer welcome here, turn around and leave. You take James and help him yourself." Shaun said angrily.

"We can't do this alone. I—we need your help!" Virgil yelled.

"And I told you, I don't care." Shaun said back.

With lightning speed, Virgil grabbed Shaun's shirt and pulled him closer. "Virgil, what are you going to do? You don't have a chance." Shaun said as he smiled. A sound of shuffled feet came from behind me. My head turned and looked at the crowd of people behind us, they had gone from a position of ease to a stance that looked like they would pounce on us with a single word.

"Virgil, we've got a problem here." I put my hand on Virgil's shoulder, trying to get him to notice the crowd that was about to crash down on us like waves on a beach.

"James I know what I'm doing." He tried to quiet me. I turned back, meeting the gaze of a hundred sets of eyes. It was clear we were outmatched, but it was something that Virgil refused accept. I swallowed hard and turned back to face Shaun.

"Listen to James, Virgil. I know you're strong, but you don't stand a chance. Let me go and leave now." Shaun told Virgil as he tried to talk him down.

"We need to make a deal, we won't stay here, but we need to talk." Virgil's hands released Shaun. "Please, in private." I watched as Shaun brushed himself off. Confusion filled me as the man that I had considered almost statuesque was pleading for someone's help. Virgil's words were filled with desperation, as if he was out of options, but even more distinct than that they were filled with worry. Virgil cared if Burke found us, he cared if we couldn't make it back to my body. I tried to process it all and the man that I thought I knew stood out more than ever before.

There was a long pause and then Shaun finally let out a long exaggerated sigh.

"Fine, let's talk." Shaun said he motioned for Virgil to follow him.

"James, stay there, be good." Virgil told me as if I was his pet, and then they vanished into a small room behind the altar. The crowd behind me loosened up, returning to what they had been doing. As I watched the crowd disperse, I found it hard to make sense of everything that had happened.

What did Shaun mean when he asked if I needed protection from Virgil?

I knew that Virgil's story went deeper, but as the thoughts sunk into my head, I felt as if it was deeper than I'd ever imagined. I knew he hadn't taken me to the refuge because he wanted to get rid of me, that much I was sure of. It was something else; in the back of my mind, I knew the person who had set Virgil's house ablaze was responsible. Something had scared Virgil and now Shaun was scared too.

It became hard to concentrate. My hands covered my face as I lay back on the marble steps of the altar. The old chapel ceiling stared down on me, but the beauty of the paintings made it look wonderful. I closed my eyes to relax. The thoughts that ran like a river through my mind had begun to spill over the levees. A throbbing pain crept its way into my head. I breathed in deep and then a sigh left my mouth. As soon as it left my lips, my eyes shot open.

A slender woman stood over me, but the light blinded me and I couldn't make out her face.

"Angela?" I said to the woman.

"No love, my name is Kate, who's Angela?" She said to me. Her voice sounded sultry, like the same feeling you get when you touch a soft piece of fabric. I rose up and looked at her; to my surprise, it was the woman Virgil had called a vampire. Closer to her than I had been before the features on her face became even clearer. Her almond shaped eyes looked at me with worry. I stared at her for a long time, probably to long because she interjected. "Did you forget?" She asked in regards to her previous question.

"Uh no—She's a girl." I told her my voice with a tinge of disappointment in it.

"Well she's very lucky to have you to think about her. How are you doing?" She asked.

The question caught me off guard.

Why does she care?

"I'm doing okay, a bit confused, but other than that I'm fine." I answered the question.

"Don't be put off by Shaun; he's just trying to do what he believes is best for us." She said as she sat down beside me. Her hands clasped one another around her knees making her body tight like a ball.

"Yeah he's different from the Shaun that I know—or knew."

I told her as I stood up.

"You're in a coma correct? The things in this world must seem so different from the one that you left." She continued to say.

"Do you think he can help get me back to my body?" I asked.

"He's able to step between the two worlds. If anyone can help you, Shaun would be the one to do it." She said to me with a smile. "Please be patient with him, he's cautious because he wants to protect us."

"You sound like you've known him for a long time." I pointed out.

"I have been here for him since he was born." She said with a smile. I raised my eyebrow to question what she'd said. "Shaun is very special; very few can do what he did. Shaun was born premature, almost four months early. Normally being so underdeveloped would have killed him, but it seemed that he was not meant to die. Somehow, he was able to travel here. Once he arrived, The Shade took care of the rest, healing his body, making him healthy. Doctors called it a miracle, but the truth was that he was meant to lead us." She smiled at me. "You see James, The Shade is his refuge, from the real world." She explained.

"That explains a lot, everyone at school thinks he's a bit off." I thought of all the times that Shaun had an episode at school, all the times he was picked on for being different. He was different, but nothing could have prepared me for the truth. "Virgil said he has visions."

"He can see the future." She said to me. "It's a side effect of the way he was born."

A heavy breath left my nose and then I looked back at Kate. "Why doesn't Virgil have any friends here?" The question was blunt, haphazardly flowing out of my mouth. Kate chuckled to herself quietly for a few seconds and then looked over at me. I gave her a blank stare, confused as to why she was so being smug.

"He hasn't told you?" Kate looked at me.

"Told me what?" I asked.

"Virgil was cast out of here because of his obsession with Edwin Burke. He has a vendetta against the man." Kate told me. "I'm surprised he took you to us at all."

"Why's that?" I asked.

"You're not his first companion. Let's just say, he's had a long history of losing those closest to him." She immediately looked down at her knees. She seemed vexed, as if she realized that she had told me too much.

Others had died in Virgil's care. Could that be the reason for his apprehension?

"But Burke is undeniably a bad person, he needs to be stopped." I said.

"We don't support one man's vendetta, regardless of how justified it may be."

I looked down at Kate. She sat there, as still as a stone; her pale skin shining like marble against the lights. I peered down at her trying to detect the slightest movement from her but came up with nothing. My eyes glanced up, darting around the room I saw most of the people who had been in the church before were gone.

"Where did everyone go?" I questioned her.

"You don't expect everyone to stay here do you? Most of them are human, just like you. They have families and lives outside of The Shade. The only difference between them and everyone else is they can walk between both worlds." She explained to me. I noticed a few people make their way down to the basement of the church. Without everyone in the church, the expanse between the altar and the door seemed even greater. Suddenly a chill worked its way through me, the hair on the back of my neck stood on end and my breath was visible in the air as I sighed. My lungs inhaled back in the ice-cold air and it pierced my lungs like sharp daggers. I walked towards the large wooden doors that stood like sentries at the entrance to the church.

I reached out and touched the doors.

They're beautiful. I must have missed them when we arrived.

My hand moved away from the doors and I turned and faced back to the altar. Kate sat on the step as I walked back to her slowly; then I sat down beside her. My thoughts were restless; everything seemed to run through my head so quickly.

How long had Virgil and Shaun been talking?

I peered over to Kate and she looked at me.

"When are they going to be finished?" I asked in anticipation.

"You are to restless child, please be still and relax." She tried to comfort me.

"Not all of us are supposed to be here." I snapped at her.

I felt bad after I said it.

I knew she was only trying to comfort me. "The time will come when you will receive the answers to your questions, but you must be patient." She calmly told me, as I fixed my eyes on the door that Virgil and Shaun had left through a short while before. Keeping time in The Shade was, to put it mildly, almost impossible to do. It was irrelevant anyway. So instead of dwelling on time, I tried to remember what Kate had suggested about being patient.

That didn't help.

Being patient was something I couldn't afford at that moment. I began to tap my foot incessantly, it was a nervous habit; something that I did to keep my mind from running away with my thoughts. My eyes glanced over at one of the old stained glass windows, noticing the light that reflected through the colored glass and unique dance it did across the floor.

The tapping of my foot stopped.

I looked at this little bead of light and I felt the first sense of real beauty since my accident. The mosaics had been beautiful but there was something so much more natural and organic about the light, the blues and greens that melted together with the reds and purples. I lifted my hand up into the light and touched it as it filtered through the window.

And for a moment, I was lost.

A loud thud came from behind me, and two sets of feet started towards me. My head didn't lift from the light and the euphoric feeling it had given me—until a voice broke the silence.

"James! Stop playing with the light." Virgil said, almost mocking. My eyes twitched and my head snapped around to see Virgil and Shaun standing together behind me.

"You kept me waiting long enough." I told him in rebuttal.

"We're leaving, let's go." He told me sharply.

Virgil and I began to walk to the door.

We didn't look at Shaun as we left. We walked past him and he just stared with his empty eyes as we passed. The lack of emotion led me to assume that negotiations did not go well. We left the church and as the large wooden doors closed behind us, the words that flooded from my mind and spilled out of my mouth. "So it didn't go well I take it?" I asked him.

"We need to talk." His tone serious. "This is going to be important."

"Then talk, I'm not going anywhere."

"We've made a deal." He said looking at the ground.

"What kind of deal?"

"Well the good news is, we're going to get you back to your body." He said as he started to walk down the church steps.

"And the bad news?" I called as he reached the bottom.

"You're going to have to kill Burke." He stated as he headed out into the street.

XII

I quickly followed Virgil down the church steps. My mind raced with thoughts about what Virgil and Shaun had discussed. I caught up to Virgil. He was walking more quickly than normal, more determined, as if he finally had a purpose.

"Hey!" I called out to him.

There was no response.

"Hey! What did you mean when you said we're going to get my body back?" I asked, but Virgil continued to walk at the same pace in a seemingly random direction.

I matched his speed to keep up.

"We'll talk, but first we have to find a new place to stay." He told me. "Keeping you safe is my number one priority." He said as his long finger pointed at me. I wasn't sure what had changed when Virgil and Shaun had talked, but Virgil's attitude had done a complete 180.

It concerned me, as it would have anyone else.

Slowly the refuge of the church faded into the gray-blue fog of The Shade. My eyes squinted to try to find the building, but they came up with nothing. It had faded from sight and for a moment, it seemed as if the old church had been just a figment of my imagination.

Had it ever existed at all?

My head shook away the thought as we entered a residential area. I turned to Virgil—his pale yellow eyes had gone wild, up and down, up and down—scanning the houses laid out before us. We continued to walk, slowly. This went on for another thirty minutes. Up until that point, Virgil had been doing his methodical checks on each house without a sound from me. That was until I couldn't bare silence any longer. "If you tell me what you're looking for I can help you." I offered.

Virgil turned and gave me a good once over. "I've got it. Just let me figure this out." He began to walk away from another house. I wasn't sure what was wrong with it, but like the twenty before it, they all looked the same.

"I'm just trying to help. I don't know what was wrong with the last twenty—,"

Virgil held up his finger at me.

"—you're right. You don't know, so please let me do this. I've done it a few more times than you; I know what to look for." He told me. His tone wasn't angry, he just seemed burdened.

"What about Burke." I asked. "What if he finds us again?"

Virgil eyeballed another house from across the street and began to walk towards it. "If he finds us you run like hell back to the refuge." He said with his back to me. "But that's what I'm trying to prevent. You see methodical, I call it thorough." He chuckled a bit when he said it. I wasn't sure why but he found the conversation amusing. We continued for another few minutes before Virgil had his eureka moment. His eyes widened like a child looking at presents on Christmas morning. "I think we have a winner." He looked back at me with a smile.

The house sat on a corner. The bright white door seemed a substantial difference against the red brick that made up the outer skin of the house. There were hardly any windows on the face of the home, which made it seem more like a business than a house. I didn't care about the color of the house or the amount of windows it had; I was just thankful he'd finally made a decision and we could take a rest.

So many questions circled around in my head like buzzards circling an animal carcass. We walked towards the house. Virgil jiggled the knob on the front door, which appeared to be locked. Virgil gave the door a hard thrust of his shoulder. The locking mechanism broke, allowing him to push the door open and walk inside, with me close in tow. The home had been all but abandoned, dust was settled thick on the floor, and as my feet stepped through each one of the rooms, my shoes left small indentations that told the world that I'd been there. We were greeted by absolute darkness. We searched the house, the entryway led into a large expansive living room with an open ceiling. To the left of the front door was a long narrow hallway leading down to the three small bedrooms. The interior was painted white with hardly any furniture to speak of.

Someone must have picked this house clean years ago.

The halls were the brightest part of the house but those were still barely lit. I stepped into the living room and noticed Virgil had found the only armchair and had taken his place in it immediately. There was a small couch against the wall at the back of the room, as far as I had seen these were the only two pieces of furniture in the house. I sat down on the old dusty couch, sending dust everywhere. "Why is this place so special?" I questioned.

"Low amounts of sunlight, best view of the street, and plenty of doors to escape from on the back side of the house." He told me as he crossed his leg over the other. The logic made sense. I knew then, I wouldn't have put in that much effort into picking a place.

At least he knows what he's doing. That or he's the greatest scam artist ever.

Virgil sat forward in his chair. It was easy to see that he was uncomfortable. He let out one final huff filled breath and then looked at me. His eyes caught mine, which told me that it was time to listen. "I suppose you want to know what Shaun and I talked about." He said.

That was a stupid question; of course I wanted to know what they'd talked about. It only determined the rest of my life.

"So—," the words crawled sluggishly off my tongue. "—what did you two discuss?" Virgil remained silent for a long moment.

"We talked about you."

"What about me?" I asked.

Virgil hesitated. I wasn't sure why, he seemed like he needed to say something but didn't know how to. "I—," he paused. "—we decided to help you get your body back." My heart fluttered to life when he said the words. A smile began to tug at the corners of my mouth. "Don't get excited." He told me. "We've got a lot of work to do and not a lot of time to do it in."

"How long before this happens?" I could barely contain myself.

Virgil paused for a long moment and then spoke. "About five months, maybe less." My heart sank back a little at the news. It was as if all of my hopes had come true and Virgil smashed them before me.

"Five months. Why so long?" I exclaimed. Virgil's brow furrowed at the tone of my voice.

"That's the time it's going to take for Shaun to get everything ready on his end." He said. "That's barely enough time for me to train you to be worth something in a fight."

"Fight?" My words stammered as they came out. "I didn't say I was going to fight." My arms motioned 'no' in the air. The tension in the air started to grow as Virgil looked at me as though I'd said something crazy.

"Did you think you were going to talk Burke to death? How else are you going to kill him?"

"That's another thing. Why do *I* have to kill Burke?" I questioned.

Virgil's hand came up in an answer to that question.

"Stop." He told me. "Just stop." His hand lowered back down as I fell silent. "Do you want to hear the plan or not?" He asked.

I nodded at him.

"The plan is simple but it's going to be difficult to execute." His tone got more serious. "Shaun's web of informants and spies runs deeper than I thought. The day before we get you out, one of Shaun's people will turn off the drip that's keeping you in your coma."

"Seems simple enough."

"That's the easy part." Virgil said. "The next part's going to be a bit tricky. He's then going to hide a handgun in your room to use against Burke. Do you have any experience with a gun?"

I nodded my head. "My father's a park ranger he's taught me how to shoot."

"Good. That will work." Virgil said as his hand stroked his chin. "So you get the gun. Find Burke in the hospital, kill him and then you're free to go." He told me as a tiny smile spread across his face. His head bobbed up and down as if he was trying to convince himself that the plan was palatable.

"What about me?" I asked.

"What's that?" Virgil said with so much haste he snapped out of his premature bliss.

"I mean if I kill a doctor in cold blood wont I go to jail?" I said pointing out a flaw in an otherwise well constructed plan.

"We've got you covered there too. You see Burke's body is just his mental image of himself, sort of the way you're an image of yourself right now. The only difference being, he can interact with things in the real world. Once you kill the projection it should just disappear." Virgil said with a sense of satisfaction.

"Should?" I asked.

"More than likely." He reaffirmed.

Virgil's confidence in the plan made me feel a bit better about my chances. In the few weeks that I'd been in The Shade it was the first time I felt like there was some sort of hope. Shaun and Virgil's plan was sound, I was capable of doing my part, or so I assumed.

Can I take someone's life, no matter how insignificant?

The thought entered my head but I quickly shook it away. There was a piece of me that knew Burke was pure evil, but there was another part, a much larger part, knew any type of killing was unacceptable. The thoughts slowly filtered their way out of my head and then I was brought back to reality. "If Burke is as powerful as you say he is, won't he see me coming?"

Virgil pondered my question for a brief moment and then said. "He's powerful yes. But he shouldn't be onto us, especially because it's you who's going to be coming after him."

"What do I do if he figures it out?" I asked. "What's my back up plan?"

Virgil's hand met his face and he shook his head slowly. "He won't figure it out. If he does then we can kiss your asses' goodbye because there's not much we're going to be able to do." Virgil's words stunned me, leaving me with a feeling of emptiness.

"So in other words—,"

"—he'll kill us." He finished my sentence.

I'm screwed.

The thought crept over me. It found a place in my mind and nested there. It was like seeing insects on T.V. and then feeling an itching sensation all over your body. My body squirmed as the realization—not only was I going to be killing someone, but also there was a good chance I could be killed in the process—crept over me. Virgil must have seen the dismay on my face because he quickly spoke up. "But I'm going to show you how to defend yourself." He tried to calm me down. "There's a chance that you—,"

"—what can you teach me? What can you show me that will make any difference?" My voice suddenly became pessimistic. My eyes moved from Virgil to the floor. I breathed a quick sigh of frustration and then I looked back at Virgil who was then standing up. My eyes looked in shock at Virgil's sudden change in position.

"Burke may be strong, but he's overconfident." He told me, his voice steady and still. "He's like a ruler run unopposed for too long, he's become soft. There's more than a chance you could hold your own in a fight."

"How can you know that?" I asked.

"You're special James." He walked towards me. "That's the whole reason you're here, you have untapped power that scare men like Burke." He crouched down so that he was at my eye level. "James. I'm not going to let you get yourself killed. I promise you." The promise would have meant more if I would have known Virgil for longer than a few weeks. However, for what it was worth, I appreciated the gesture. I nodded slightly so that he understood that I was alright, which was a lie. Virgil got up and went back towards his chair. He sat down with a grunt and then looked at me. He feigned a smile and I shot him one back.

"So how strong is Burke?"

"Do you want to know? I don't want to make you more uneasy." He said.

"It doesn't make a difference now." Virgil nodded in agreement as if by having the conversation it had sealed my fate. Virgil twisted his neck and it popped as he turned it from side-to-side. After he was finished, he leaned forward in his chair and said.

"Burke draws his strength from anger. That's the thing about DMT, if you let it take you over it can consume you. The drug unlocks things inside our minds but it's a double edged sword. It grants us power, making us stronger, but too much of it can—," Virgil's voice trailed off for a moment before coming back to reality. "—let's just say that it can change a man into a beast and a beast into a nightmare. You see after a while, you begin to crave power; you need it. That's when you begin to change and that's when all hope is truly lost for you."

His words rang in my ears. I swallowed something heavy in my throat and felt it as it slid slowly down into the pit of my stomach. Virgil's eyes focused on me, intently, never looking away.

"Come on." He told me. "We've got a lot of work to do."

XIII

My eyes were closed tight because I didn't want to wake. The aroma of something sweet entered my nostrils, I opened my mouth to taste the aroma. Then warmth filled my body, it touched my skin and danced over me. It warmed my mind, thawing its frozen state. My head twitched to the side, and a sound reverberated off the walls and bounced into my ears.

"James—," the voice called out to me. I held my eyes shut so that I'd not lose the warmth. I welcomed the sensation as I let it move over my fingertips and up my neck. I felt the light run down to my legs and back up to my chest, when I heard it again.

"James!" The voice cried out. The voice made my eyes snap open, it had won, and the warmth disappeared. When my eyes opened a bright light hit me and for a moment all there was in the world was whiteness. I forced my eyes closed to stop the pain, and as soon as I did, the euphoria that I felt returned and washed over my body.

"James, what are you doing?!" Virgil's voice cried out again. I opened my eyes once more and again the white light blinded me. Then from behind, something grabbed my shirt and with a violent tug, I felt myself flying through the air. I landed on the floor and slid to a stop several feet behind Virgil who had been the one who threw me. My eyes finally adjusted, Virgil stood by the front door, which was wide opened. The light from the outside poured into the house, Virgil grabbed the door and slammed it shut. The sunlight from outside had been beaming in on me, that was the warmth I felt.

"What the hell do you think you're doing?" Virgil scolded me.

"I— I don't know." I told him, not sure what exactly had happened.

"Are you insane? Do you know what could have happened?" He asked.

"I didn't mean to do anything, the last thing I remember was going to sleep, and when I woke up standing in front of the door." I tried to explain but Virgil looked at me as if I was speaking another language. "Oh don't look at me like that." I told him. "I felt warm, it must have been the light that I felt, and I couldn't help but move towards it."

Virgil stared at me for a moment shaking his head in disapproval.

"Do you know what else feels warm and moves towards light?" He asked the question obviously rhetorical. "Bugs, right before they get zapped." His finger flicked my shoulder.

"Enough with the bug zapper stuff I get it. I didn't mean to do anything, I couldn't help it."

"Are you alright?" He asked.

"Yeah thanks." He gave me a slight nod.

Virgil's tongue moved in his mouth. "Then I guess we can overlook what happened." He said as he offered me a hand. I grabbed it and a second later, I was back on my feet. My hands brushed the dust from my clothes and then I looked at Virgil who was sizing me up. Our eyes met for a brief moment, silently asking what we were going to do.

Then he spoke.

"Do you need to change before we go?" He asked quietly.

"Before we go where?" I asked looking down at myself, to the thermal shirt that I'd been wearing for the past week. Originally, the shirt had been just plain white, but due to the fact that Virgil rationed clothes so conservatively, it was becoming more of an off-white color. I was lucky that dirt was all that was on my shirt. Virgil had told me that in The Shade you don't sweat. Which at first I found odd but as time went on I found useful, seeing as it kept you cleaner. That was the thing about The Shade. Most bodily functions didn't work or didn't need to happen for a person to survive. There was no need for food or water because those were needs of the body, and my body was resting comfortably in a Eugene hospital bed.

My eyes glanced down at my shirt, pulling it towards my nose I sniffed it. It was, in relative terms, *clean;* so there wasn't a need to change. "No I think I'll be fine in this." I told him.

Virgil stared out the windows towards the sky. "Good because some clouds just rolled in and I'd like to get this lesson done as soon as possible." Virgil said as he looked back in my direction. His hand twisted the knob of the door he'd just slammed closed, and opened it back up.

"Another one—," I moaned. "—please tell me it isn't sparing again?"

It had been a week since we had visited the refuge. Since then Virgil had wanted to show me a few moves of basic combat. He had used the opportunity to use me like a human punching bag for almost two hours. He thought it was hilarious, me not so much. "I told you that I had to teach you things that way you'd be useful in a fight." He said casually as he walked out of the house and down the three steps off the porch.

I knew from experience that was my cue to follow him. As I got outside my head began to ache. My hand held my forehead while the dull pain worked its way through me. The headaches weren't a new phenomenon; they had slowly started happening every day for the past month. Each time it happened a bit of my memory of the crash would return. I shook off the feeling and joined Virgil on the lawn.

I looked upwards at the grey clouds.

No surprises today.

My thoughts were echoed as Virgil spoke. "There should be no surprises today." He said as he looked at the sky and then started down the street.

It took us well over an hour to get a meager five miles. The sun had decided to come out twice in that time, which meant we had to hide, wait for it to recede again and then continue. When I questioned Virgil about why we didn't just use our speed to run everywhere he chuckled at me. He told me that it was because using our speed wasted energy, energy that we might need for a fight if we got into trouble. So, as Virgil had instructed, we walked. We headed together towards a small commercial area of town that I recognized. I remarked at the stores as we passed them, up until that point Virgil and I had stayed strictly in residential areas.

"Where are we going today boss?" I joked.

"Into town." He told me shortly.

I snapped and said. "Why are you even helping me if you're not going to be open with me?" Virgil had made a habit out of being short with me, it wouldn't have gotten on my nerves as much as it did but my body was tired, and so was my mind. A heavy sigh left his lips and he continued to walk. Disappointment and frustration filled me as a huff of air exited my lungs, as I continued to walk as well.

A short while after, the frustration left me.

No use in getting angry over something I can't change.

I let my mind drift. I thought about where Virgil was taking me, and what he had in store for me when we got there. So with those thoughts in my head, we walked down the road in complete silence, and although I trusted Virgil, any sort of idol banter would have been appreciated. Virgil rarely opened up to me. Ever since visiting the refuge he almost insisted that we didn't talk about his past, so I didn't push it.

As time passed, the trip began to feel more like a death

march. The weather had gotten colder, which was a direct result of the seasons in the real world changing, or so I Virgil told me. The ground was noticeably more wet than usual, as if it had just rained.

After some time, we reached a large grocery store. The store stood like a monument in the middle of an oversized parking lot. The building was large, made from old brick that looked as if it had held the place up for at least the past twenty years. It had a large friendly welcome sign above the two broken sliding doors.

We're going grocery shopping?

The thought made me chuckle. Virgil's eyes looked at me with a sharp glance and my smile fell flat. I continued to walk with him, but to my surprise, we didn't go into the building. Instead, we went down a long alleyway on the side of the building that sat vacant, littered with garbage. The alley was most likely used for deliveries but I wasn't sure. Finally, Virgil stopped with his back against the old outdated brick of the grocery store. I stopped along with him as my eyes began to trace the spaces between the small red bricks, supplementing for the lack of conversation.

Virgil turned towards the wall, so close in fact that I thought he was going to tell it a secret. His hand touched the walls surface, and then nodded for me to come over and do the same. Not entirely understanding what the point of the exercise was I let my hand stroke the wall. The brick was cool to the touch, its rough surface felt like sandpaper that could have taken the skin clean off my hand. "I don't get it." I stated, breaking the silence in the alley.

Why am I petting this brick wall?

"I just wanted you to know that this wall was solid." He told me cryptically. Virgil stepped away from the store and bobbed his head to signal me to follow him. We backed a good ten feet away from the brick wall. Virgil stood there next to me with a smile on his face, which meant he had something up his sleeve. "Tell me what you see?" Virgil asked.

The question was ridiculous. I looked at him with a smirk on my face as the words left his mouth. His pale eyes looked at me and quickly I pulled myself together saying. "It's a wall." The obvious answer seemed like the safest.

"Right but look past the wall what is it?"

Uh. It's a wall, can't be much clearer than that.

"I mean it's a wall—," my voice hesitated trying to understand. "—okay, um—it's used to divide things, something that keeps the outside out and the inside in."

"You're being general." He told me.

I shrugged my shoulders at him with a perplexed look on my face.

He let out a heavy sigh and said. "This building is a grocery store. If you were inside, there would be shelves, and on those shelves there would be food like breakfast cereals, cans of soup things like that?" He told me.

My hand rubbed my mouth and I finally said. "I still don't understand."

The purpose of this lesson escapes me.

Virgil smirked at me as he shook his head. "Okay, let me explain. Solid objects in the real world are just that, solid. However here, things you would consider solid or whole aren't always that way. Even though you see the wall in front of you, your mind knows that inside this building there are shelves and on those shelves there's food, drinks—," he waved his hand in a rolling motion at me. "—and so on. The point being, that just because we can't see the things inside, doesn't mean they're gone, those things are still there. So the wall is, in and of itself, meaningless. Having the wall there doesn't negate the fact that there is an inside, and yet even though you can't see the objects inside you know they still exist and just because you *can* see the wall outside, doesn't mean the wall does." Virgil said as he stepped toward the wall.

Virgil's explanation sent my head into a tailspin. I wasn't sure where to begin with all the information he'd given me. However, before I had time to ask a question, Virgil approached the wall and as he did he placed his hand upon it. Not thinking much of the action because I'd seen someone touch a wall a million times before and nothing was going to be no different.

However, it was different.

As Virgil's hand pressed against the wall, a tiny light outlined his fingers. He then pushed harder against the wall and suddenly his hand passed through the place where it should have met the brick. My eyes widened, dumbstruck at the sight of the impossible.

After his hand was gone his arm followed, then his shoulder, his torso and then finally he stepped into the wall and disappeared. A few seconds later, he stepped back through the wall and looked at me. I stood there, astounded. Words escaped me.

"Your turn." Virgil said to me with a smile.

"What? I can't, I mean that's—impossible." I stammered.

"Why is it impossible? You just watched me do it."

"No it's impossible because that's a solid wall and I am a solid person and that's not the way those things work." I told him.

"You watched me do it, you know it's possible."

"No—," I pointed a finger at him. "—you know it's possible, I—"

"—stop making excuses and get up here, this is self defense 101, you need to do this." He told me. My eyes shut tight, feeling the overwhelming urge to stand completely still. I hoped that somehow Virgil would forget I was there and he would just leave me alone. My eye peeked open to find Virgil's face twisted in frustration. I opened my eyes and slowly moved towards the wall.

"Touch it." He instructed me as I got to where he was standing.

My hand reached out and touched the wall. The brick was solid, that much I knew for sure. As my hand touched the wall I began to panic, this was because even though I could see that the wall was completely solid, Virgil still wanted me to pass through it. "Now, this isn't all that difficult, all you need to do is breath deep, close your eyes, and step through." He said. "You can do this, I know you can." He said with an unusual amount of encouragement.

I closed my eyes and waited for something to happen. My breath slowed and I tried to make myself as calm as possible. I let my mind wander, until I held an image of a quiet stream running down a mountain. It was quiet, everything around me fell out of focus, and the loudest thing in my ears was my own heartbeat. As I finally fell into a deep state of calm, a sharp pain entered the right side of my face.

The pain was familiar although strangely new.

My eyes sprang open to see Virgil's open palm coming in for another strike.

I stumbled back from him and said. "What the hell was that for?"

"Sometimes it helps if you feel like you're in danger." He suggested with a grin across his face. I glared at him as my body stood upright once more. "What? I'm only trying to help."

"You just wanted to hit me didn't you?" I said.

Virgil looked in the air for an exaggerated second then put his hands on his head. "No, if I wanted to hit you I'd just ask to spar with you again." He said with a chuckle. It was funny, but I had to hide my smile because I was still mad at him for breaking my concentration.

"Look I don't need your help, I'm fine." I finally said. Once again, I closed my eyes and tried to envision the peaceful river, knowing that the sound of slowly running water would calm me down. However, the more I tried to concentrate on the river the less focused I became. My mind had to find something else to center me. Then a spark flashed in my mind and it knew exactly what I needed. A picture of Angela made its way into my head and seeing her instantly set me at ease.

I raised my hand up and proceeded to move it closer and closer towards the wall.

The hand reached out and grabbed—nothing.

My finger never met the wall.

I peeked open my eyes and saw the tip of my ring finger inside of the brick wall, just in time to snap out of my tranquil state. Like falling from a great height, my mind brought me hurtling back to the alley of the grocery store, back to The Shade, back to where I really was.

The relief of going through the wall left me immediately and like someone who hears a pile of books drop in a quiet library, my heart leapt from my chest in a panic. The fear was almost instantly replaced by the sensation of pain shooting into my ring finger. Franticly my eyes look down at my finger. The wall had encapsulated the tip of my ring finger, everything before the first knuckle. My eyes tightened as I struggled to try to pull myself free.

"Damn it!" I yelled.

"You're fine, try not to move. The wall just has your finger." Virgil said casually to me.

"So how do I take it back?" I asked him with a panicked tone. The pain was excruciating.

"We just—," he began as he pulled out a small knife and smiled a tiny smile. "—have to take it back."

"You're enjoying this aren't you?" I remarked. "Oh God this is going to suck."

"Hold still, this is going to hurt." He warned.

Virgil brought the knife to the knuckle on my ring finger, the one furthest from my hand. He glanced up to me. I knew he was watching me, but I couldn't help but wince at the thought of the knife cutting my finger off. "This is sharp enough." He tapped the blade against the brick. "It should make it through on the first cut."

"It should—," the words left my mouth just as the blade sank into my finger. My eyes immediately filled with tears and just as Virgil had promised, one cut was all it took. The pain in my finger amplified as I stumbled back from the wall. The blood traveled down my hand and curved around the contours of my knuckles. Virgil tore a piece of fabric off his shirt and wrapped it around the finger. "See you'll be fine." He told me as he finished the bandage. "It could have been worse."

"What do you mean fine, I'm missing the tip of my finger!" I exclaimed, mostly out of pain with just a hint of anger.

"What?" He said. "You'll be okay."

"What happened?" I asked.

"What do you mean? You came out of focus and when you lost focus you lost sight of what you were doing—causing you to lose your finger in the process." He wore the same grin he had been wearing for the past few minutes.

"I'm glad you find this funny."

"Look, the moment you phase through objects you technically no longer exist, you're somewhere between here and the real world. You came out of your phase inside of the wall, and the wall, as we say, took you into it. Just try not to do that with something important or you'll be killed." He explained.

"Well I'm never trying that again."

"You know how to do it, that's all I needed to teach you. If you want to practice on your own, that's on you." He said.

"So what was this supposed to show me, how to lose a finger?"

He looked at me and then sat down on the wooden bench that sat against the building opposite the grocery store. The bench was rickety, most likely used for smoke breaks. I followed him and sat down. The bloody cloth became redder by the second as my finger spewed warm red liquid into it. "The point of this was to show you two things." He held up two of his fingers. "One was to show you how to phase through objects, but it was also to teach you something about life and death." he told me.

"What about life and death?"

"It doesn't matter if you lose a finger in here. You're just a projection of yourself created by your mind. Your real body will still have all of its fingers when you get back. Remember this." He told me. "The mind can live without the body, but the body cannot survive without the mind. That means if you die here, you're dead." He stated.

I breathed a heavy sigh.

There was an awkward pause, letting the moment pass I looked up at Virgil and finally said. "Does it get easier?"

"Does what get easier?"

"Being like this, being different?" I clarified.

Virgil's head sank for a long moment. So long in fact that I'd almost thought he'd fallen asleep. After the long pause, Virgil finally chuckled and said. "You remind me of myself." My eyes flexed as I tried to figure out what he was talking about, I opened my mouth intending to speak but just before I did Virgil added. "You're curious, I was like that once, but now—," his voice trailed off for a moment. "—but now I just do what I have to do to survive. It's not pretty, but if you want to stay alive, you've got to think that way."

I stared at Virgil and as my eyes searched his face, I could tell he was upset. I wasn't sure why my question had triggered that response from him but it seemed as if he didn't really believe what he was telling me. "Do you really believe that?" I asked after a few minutes.

He groaned and ran his hand through his hair. "I don't know anymore." He said as he got up off the bench. "How's the finger, you ready to move?" Virgil asked looking down at me.

I nodded my head to him as I got off the bench. I didn't say a word to him as we left the grocery store, my mind was too busy trying to process what he had told me. It was true that in the real world, people made decisions every day that determined whether people lived or died. Firefighters, military, police officers, they all had to make split second decisions that affected whether people lived or died. I didn't know how anyone could make those kinds of decisions, and I prayed that I never had to.

XIV

My eyes watched the knife twirl in my hand as I turned it over, inspecting it. Virgil had given me the knife to use in case of an emergency. Its five-inch fixed blade was slender, serrated on one side making it useful for cutting clothes into bandages. As I watched the knife spin in my hand, my eyes slowly drifted to my finger, or lack thereof. I stared at it for a hard moment then a hand met my shoulder. "You still hung up over that finger?" Virgil said.

"It's just a bit odd to get used to." I told him as I put the knife back in my holster.

"It has been two weeks. You'll get it back as soon as we get you out of here."

I let out a grunt at his comment, making my finger flex as I clenched my fist. It didn't matter what Virgil said about the finger, there was no getting around how strange it felt to be missing part of an appendage you've had all your life. "Look don't be like that," he said trying to sympathize. "There are some extra clothes upstairs, go see if any of them fit you."

I nodded to him and without a word; I began to walk up the stairs to the second level of the large home. Since the day behind the grocery store, Virgil had slowly taken me under his wing, bringing me along with him when he went to look for supplies. He had even shown me a few things that would keep me alive in a fight against Burke. Over the weeks that Virgil and I spent together, our relationship began to morph. It was subtle at first, but as time went on it became easier to talk to him. However, even with all of the improvements one thing still rattled my brain about Virgil. He'd not once told me about his family, or how he came to be in The Shade that still made me apprehensive about him.

Other than that, we were two peas in a pod.

I reached the top of the staircase and then entered the first room on the left. The closet door swung open, my eyes scanned the clothes trying to find a new shirt to replace the torn one that sat draped over my body. I looked for a minute at the selection of clothes; I reached out and took a thin grey hoodie, along with an olive green jacket to wear over it. I took my torn shirt off and replaced it with the new clothes. The mirror in the door of the closet reflected back how the new garments fit; they were a bit large but they would have to do. I began to inspect myself, seeing if any of my other clothes needed replaced. Looking down I saw my frayed pants, but couldn't decide if I needed a new pair. That's when a loud noise echoed its way through the house.

THOWMP

With my eyes closed, I listened to where the sound was coming from.

THOWMP

Again, the sound echoed through the house. I ran straight out of the room and into the stairwell. I looked down the stairs and Virgil's eyes met mine, seeming to ask what the noise was. We'd both heard the mysterious sound, and we both knew exactly where it had come from. Virgil ran up the stairs quickly and joined me as we walked into the room across the landing from the one I had gotten the clothes from. We entered the room looking for the cause of the noise. Quickly my eyes were drawn to a shattered lamp on the floor. Virgil put his finger over his mouth then pointed at the closet door.

Slowly we crept closer to the closet door, as we did my heartbeat began to rise.

What's in the closet?

Virgil gripped the doorknob of the closet and slowly twisted it. As he did, I readied myself for anything, his hand held up three fingers, two, then one. He balled his fist to signify zero, put his fist down and swung the door open. What we found inside we both did not expect.

There in the closet, sat a young woman curled in the fetal position. She didn't look very old, maybe the same age as Virgil, maybe a bit older. She sat in the dark closet, her arms held herself as she shivered, cold and alone. "What the hell is this?" Virgil said.

"It's a girl—," I moved closer to her. "—she's scared and alone." I got down on my knees and looked her in the eyes. Her light green eyes met mine and I smiled, after a moment she looked up, smiling back. "Hello, I'm James, who are you? Are you okay?" I asked her.

The girl looked tired. The black bags under her eyes matched the sunken look of her face. "Ye—yes, I'm okay. My—my name is Christina." She told me, her voice hoarse. She spoke with a sense of exhaustion in her voice, but as she sat in the closet, quiet and still, I could tell that she was barely breathing.

"I don't care what your name is, get out!" Virgil said over my shoulder.

Quickly I turned to face Virgil. "What are you talking about Virgil?" I got up in his face. Virgil pushed me back an inch with two of his fingers and then grabbed my arm. He pulled me across the empty room away from where Christina was starting to rock herself back and forth on the floor.

"What are you doing?" He asked me, his voice sounded nervous, almost reluctant.

My eyes squinted at him. "What do you mean what am *I*

doing, what are you doing?" My voice shouted in a whisper. "That's a girl, she's helpless. So let's help her." I told him as I turned to walk back to the closet, but Virgil caught my shoulder. He spun me back around so I was looking at him and said. "Look James this could be a trick, we have to do whatever it takes to survive—,"

"—so it's okay to let people die?" I shrugged his hand off my shoulder and stared at him. "I'm not like you Virgil I can't leave this woman to die." I added then turned back to Christina, trying to put what Virgil had said out of my mind. It was no use; Virgil's words stung deep like a hive of bees had been shook up in my brain. I turned around and walked back towards him. "If we have to lose who we are to survive then what's the point of surviving?"

Virgil stared at me. His teeth clinched and I could tell that he was angry. He wanted to say more, but fell silent as I walked back over to where Christina sat.

"Do you know where you are?" I asked her.

It was a stupid question.

I knew she had no idea where she was but it seemed like the right thing to say.

"No, I remember being at home. I was sick, but that's it. I went to sleep and ended up here." She explained, bringing her hand up as she let out a violent cough. She moved her other hand to her mouth and continued to cough. When she finally stopped, her hands trembled as they moved away from her bloodied mouth. I looked back at Virgil who stood with his arms crossed at the back of the room.

"James seriously, can I talk to you?" He asked and then Virgil left the room and went out into the hallway, I followed him out and we left Christina alone, still in the closet.

"What is it?" I asked him, in no mood to have another conversation on survival.

"You can't save her, she's terminal."

"What do you mean terminal?" I asked.

"With or without our help, she's going to die James. She

must have a brain tumor or something because she can hardly sit upright." Virgil noticed the look on my face. "Look she's coughing up blood, she's got memory loss, and her voice is hoarse." He tried to explain to me.

"Those are all symptoms of strep throat Virgil." I told him, grasping at straws.

"When was the last time you had memory loss and slipped into a coma because of strep throat?" His voice rose slightly. "We can't save her and to be honest I'm not fully convinced that she's not an agent for Burke." He said shrewdly.

"Why are you so paranoid?"

"Because I—,"

"—save it." I held up my hand to him and then walked back to the room to check on Christina. Virgil followed close behind me as I walked back into the room. In a faint whispering voice, he spoke over my shoulder. "We have to make her go." He said.

"So we're going to toss her out on the street?"

"She's going to die either way—," Virgil began.

"—and that makes it alright to leave her. What about me, would you have left me to die?" My anger was finally starting to come through. Virgil seemed caught off guard by my tone, so much so that he had to think for a moment to come up with a response. I faced him, waiting for an answer.

"You—you were different James, you have a chance." He tried to reason.

"That doesn't matter, chance or not, she's coming with us."

"Wrong. She's not coming with us, either we lose her, or you lose me." He told me.

My brow furrowed as the words left his mouth. Virgil had snapped and given me an ultimatum, one that went against everything I stood for. My eyes glanced at Virgil and then to Christina. I studied Christina's face carefully, memorizing every line, every shape, and every hue of color in her eyes. I stared at her and the only thing I saw—was myself.

Could this girl have been me? Would Virgil have left me to die if I slowed him down?

Then a thought crept into my head. One that I hadn't wanted to think about but at that moment it seemed to be the only thing that I could think about.

How much had this world twisted Virgil's mind, how much of him had he been warped to allow himself to reason the way that he did?

My eyes looked back over to Virgil. "No, I'm not going to leave her to die."

"Fine." He said with some finality. "If you can do better on your own, be my guest." He told me, and then stormed out of the room. The heavy stomp of his feet hit each of the stairs as he went down, finally the slam of the front door marked his exit, echoing through the house as he left. I walked to the closet where Christina had sat since this whole ordeal started. She was cold; it was easy to see because of the way her body shook all over. I knelt down beside her and looked back into her eyes. "I'm sorry about your friend." She said to me.

"It's okay." I reassured her. "I'm not going to leave you here alone."

"Why, what is this place?" She questioned. I decided to ignore the question; I didn't want to start out our conversation with the fact that she might have been dying.

"Can you stand?" I asked as I got to my feet.

"I think so." She told me as she took my hand to stand up. Her hand felt weak, cold and clammy.

She was sick. Virgil was right, but that still didn't give him the right to leave her.

It took me ten minutes to help Christina down the stairs and to the living room. She hobbled through the house as if her legs had become too weak to hold up her frame. As we got into the living room, I sat her down on the couch and placed a pillow underneath her head.

"Are you okay?" I asked once again.

"I'm fine James, how are you?" She asked.

"Why are you concerned with me?" I asked. "Tell me about yourself." I sat beside her on the couch trying to comfort her with small talk.

"I'm a graduate student, I was studying architecture." She told me.

"That's great, what happened?"

She smiled at me but her eyes told me she was reluctant to say what she really wanted to. Her lips pursed together, they were white and chalky as if she was dehydrated. "Your friend was right," She said abruptly. "I have a tumor—," she paused. "— in my head." Her shaky finger moved and pointed at the side of her head as if she knew the exact spot the black growth was located.

"I'm sorry I—," I began but couldn't get the words out.

"Don't be sorry James. It's not your sympathy I need." She said with a smile.

"And what is it you do need?" I tried to figure out.

"Talk to me for a while." She told me. "Do you have a girlfriend?" She asked.

My mind wandered away from the conversation briefly, as the thought of Angela trickled through me. I wondered if Angela even still considered herself my girlfriend. Then my mind snapped back into place. "Uh no—not at the moment." I stammered.

"What's her name?" She asked without hesitation.

"Angela—how did you know?" I asked.

"When I asked about your girlfriend your eyes lit up. She must be special." She stated.

"Yeah, she is—was special to me." I told her.

"How old are you James?"

"I'm 18, 19 in a few months. Why?"

"You just seem to be very mature for your age." She smiled at me and let out a loud cough.

She looked tired, like her essence had been spread too thin. Her body hunched over in the chair and slowly lurched forward out of the seat. She fell towards the floor, almost colliding with it, but I got to her before she hit. She looked up at me as I held her in my arms and whispered to me. "James, can we keep talking?" She asked softly. Her breathing had increased dramatically and with it so did my heartbeat.

"Of course we can." I assured her, my heart racing in my chest.

"Is everything going to be okay?" She questioned.

"Of course it is, I've got you, and everything is going to be alright."

Virgil was right.

The thought ran through my head at least a hundred times that second. Christina was going to die in my arms and there wasn't anything I could do about it. As she stared up at me with her green eyes, I would have given anything not to look down at her, but I knew I couldn't deny her that, not when she needed someone the most. "When did you graduate from high school?" I asked her.

"Almost nine years ago now." Her voice answered soft and wispy. "I thought I would be able to make it back for my reunion—," she began to cough.

"Don't say that of course you will be able to make it." I made my best attempt to reassure her again.

"Don't lie to me James, I know what's happening." She called my bluff. I wasn't sure how I was supposed to comfort someone before they died. Christina began to cough violently again and twitch in my arms. "Thank you James." She said with a half smile.

"You're welcome, it's okay I'm here." I said. My arms held Christina as my eyes peered down. She was still, like a tree without the wind, she no longer moved. Even her soft breath had stopped. Her chest lay still, no longer moving up and down. Slowly my body rocked her back and forth, as she slipped away. "You're welcome, it's okay I'm here." I said. "It's okay I'm here." My voice repeated. I didn't know what else to do. I slowly lowered her body to the floor and backed away from it. I sat on the hard, wooden floor beside her. The house sat empty and cold, with the smell of death creeping up around me. A woman was dead. A woman a lot like me, someone scared and confused in a dangerous new world. However, for her it was over. I sat in the dark house, with someone I hardly knew, and for the first time I truly felt, alone.

XV

A strange kind of darkness washed over body and mind, like everything I knew about the world had been turn upside-down. I put my hand on my head as a white-hot pain hit me. It felt like a high-speed train had derailed inside my head. Suddenly a flash of memory came back to me, more memories to fill the empty places before my accident. I didn't care though, I was filled with so many thoughts and questions and each one eventually led to the same dark place in my head. I shook my head, trying to clear it, but to no avail. My thoughts ran hazardous and destructive through me until they turned to one simple truth.

How am I going to get home?

I knew that without help, there wasn't much of a chance for survival in The Shade. My heart slowly hit against my chest as my hand tried to clear the dirt from my eyes.

It didn't help.

I moved my hand away from my face, allowing my eyes focus on it. My hands were dirty, just like my face. I'd finished burying Christina's body a few hours earlier or at least it seemed to be a few hours. Time in the endless void seemed very trivial; hard to count, everything seemed to blur together. I laid flat against the cold hard ground, eyes peering directly at the ceiling so hard they could have ripped it apart.

Maybe that would be a good thing.

I began to ponder how if I let the sunlight into the room I might be free of the worry that tormented me. My heartbeat began to speed up as my mind posed the question to itself; slowly at first then it grew louder and louder in my chest. I told my body to move and yet I remained. My heart wanted to stay in the spot forever, but my mind knew there were still things that needed to be done.

My legs slowly moved toward my back and bent upwards, my arms twitched as I instructed them to pick my worthless body up off the ground. I planted my palms firmly on the floor and pushed with all my strength. My body rose off the ground and then I looked around the vacant room. The darkness in the corners seemed to shout out at me as my eyes moved slowly passed them. My mind had drawn a blank as to what to do next. I'd decided that going for help was out of the question, there was no way I could find Virgil and definitely no way I could make it back to the refuge.

Even if I could, would Shaun take me in?

My eyes blinked out the last of the dust left in my eyes as my mind blinked out the thought of going for help. I turned to walk towards the door. My footsteps fell heavy in the hallway, not even attempting to be quiet. When I finally arrived at the door, my hand reached up and touched the knob. The metal shocked me as I touched it, which sent a shiver through my body. I shook the tingling sensation out of my hand and then slowly turned the knob, letting the door open and with it, the rays from the sun began to flood into the house.

Suddenly my mind snapped back to reality.

I slammed the door shut in an attempt keep the light away. Then a loud crash came from the back of the house. The sound was ear shattering. An explosion of broken boards and shattered glass filled the house. In a natural reaction to the noise, my body had gone prone with my hands covering my head. My eyes opened slowly and then turned upwards as they searched the hallway.

Everything was silent.

With caution, I picked myself up off the floor and walked towards where the explosion had emanated. I moved through the hallway, past the living room and then I rounded the corner into the kitchen.

That's when I saw it.

The loud explosion had come from where the back of the house once was. I only say *was* because the entire back half of the house had been torn apart.

What happened here?

I stood in the middle of the kitchen, glass and splinters from broken boards were everywhere. Although my heartbeat was abnormally fast, my entire body felt a sense of warmth all around it. I closed my eyes to drink in the new sense of euphoria. Yet, the more I basked in the new sense, the faster my heartbeat grew. I placed my hand over my heart in an attempt to calm it.

Then like a ping, a single tiny signal pulsed into my brain.

My eyes flashed open, frantically looking all around me. In my wandering state, I had walked directly into the sunlight, which was flowing gracefully in through the huge hole in the kitchen. My heart had tried to tell me I was in danger but my mind wouldn't listen. I glanced quickly to the floor, looking for my shadow.

Then it moved.

The shadow moved from where it should have been behind me, towards a point in the middle of what I assumed was the dining room. My mind raced as I tried to determine what to do, the shadow—that should have been beneath me—was still flat on the floor. Then the floor rippled, like when a rock hits a body of water, making the hardwood floor look like liquid. I started to walk towards the shadow, even though everything in my body told me to turn around and run. I was curious about the specters.

I knelt down beside the shadow and stared into it, the shape had morphed from an outline of my body into a large circle. My hand moved towards the ash colored circle hovering in place over it. I trembled as my hand hung over the shadow. The fear I felt in that moment was greater than any I'd ever experienced, but as scared as I was in that moment, I couldn't bring myself to move away. I tried with all my might to pull away but I couldn't. My hand sat idle over the circle for a good minute until my mind finally decided that it was satisfied, and it relinquished control of my arm back to me.

As my hand drew away from the shadow, something happened.

A hand shot out from the blackness and grabbed my wrist.

Its cold icy fingers sent shivers up my arm as it began to tug me down into the darkness. The specter's mutilated hand gripped my wrist with no intention of letting me go. The black shadowy arm pulled me closer and closer towards the darkness, so close in fact, my fingers touched the black spot on the floor. My original observation had been correct; the solid floor not only looked like a liquid but felt like it too. My eyes closed ready for the end. I knew that if I let the creature take me, all of my worries and my suffering would be over; I could finally be at peace.

Then my eyes snapped open.

No, this is the easy way out. Not like this!

As if I'd been kicked out of a stupor, I began to fight the specter that was dragging me under. I felt the adrenaline surge through my body. My hand twisted and grabbed the wrist of the creature; with all my strength I ripped the hand and everything that was attached to it from the dark hole.

I flew backwards and landed a few feet from where I had been standing, landing in the living room, which had also been bathed in sunlight. The specter had come out of the hole entirely. Its charred black form stood menacingly before me. The figure looked like it had once been a person, but in that moment it only looked like a shell of what used to be a human being. The specter breathed a lumbered heavy breath as it slowly trudged towards me. My eyes widened as I tried to back away as quickly as possible. My feet scrambled to get under me and as I tried to get off the floor the creature moved ever closer. It twitched its head around as it moved in close; as the specter reached me my mind snapped to something that Virgil said.

"Don't fight those things. If you see one, you run and hide."

Virgil's words rang out and my hands tightened into fists. Suddenly my vision sharpened and everything around me became clear just as it had in the field. I felt the cocktail of chemicals flowing through my veins, heightening my reflexes, making me faster, making me stronger.

The specter bellowed out a terrifying scream, the howl echoed through the house and when it finished, it dashed towards me. It grabbed hold of my shirt and in one quick motion, my fist swung up and made contact with the side of its head. It flinched slightly but continued pulling me towards the floor. My fist slammed against its skull repeatedly, hitting the creature in jaw and cheekbones, but nothing seemed to deter it. The specter stared at me and for the first time I had gotten close enough to see that it didn't have eyes; all that remained were the hallowed out sockets where its eyes should have been. With one final push the creature's overpowering strength pulled me down.

My legs gave out and my body dropped to the floor.

The specter positioned itself on top of me, pinning my arms to the floor with its knees. It then centered its head just above mine, opening its mouth twice the normal width of a human. It let out a wail that caused my body to stiffen with paralysis. The specter moved its mouth just above mine and as it did, I could feel myself getting weaker and weaker. My legs thrashed to break free of the grip that held me to the floor. As each bit of strength left me, I felt myself slipping further away from life. My eyes became heavy, struggling to stay open as the specter continued its assault.

The thought of Angela pierced my mind. Her smile radiated out and touched me.

I love that smile, but if this thing takes me, I'm never going to see that smile again.

My body was growing cold, my heartbeat became more faint. I knew I had to fight it, so with every bit of energy I had left, my arm shifted to the side, slipping free of the creatures knee. The specter immediately stopped, which gave enough time for my fist to strike it in the face. The specter drew back, freeing my other arm and allowing me to shove it back across the room. My body felt its strength returning slowly as I tried to stand up. My eyes came back into focus as my legs finally allowed me to stand upright. The dust from where the specter had landed started to clear, allowing me to anticipate its next moves. My fingers twitched as they readied for the next attack. Knowing I couldn't let it take me to the floor again.

The specter screamed, shaking the house around me. It locked eyes with me and started to move towards me once again. My feet stepped backwards but I ran into the dining room table. My head twisted left to right looking for an escape. I knew that staying in the house would only serve to get me killed.

I need to get outside, the more distance I can put between this thing and me the better.

I stared at the specter—still a few feet from me. I readied myself, then dashed towards the creature. As I approached the specter, I ducked under its attempt to grab me and ran towards the ruined remains of the kitchen.

I made it to the kitchen within seconds and from behind me, a low growl erupted from the specter. My head twisted around to see how much time I had before the specter was on me again. When my head turned, my eyes were looking directly into hollowed out sockets of the Specter that was only inches away. With both hands, the creature slammed hard against my chest.

Time seemed to flow in slow motion as my body flew through the air.

I felt my back hit the something hard as I flew through the gaping hole in the kitchen wall. As my body soared out of the window, and subsequently out of the house, I knew that impact would was only moments away. I looked up towards the sky, the clouds that swelled and circled as if a storm was coming. It wasn't until I was only a few feet from the ground that everything seemed to speed back up.

The impact with the ground knocked the wind out of my lungs. The loud thump it produced along with the sound of my back crackling was like some sort of sick symphony of pain. My body crashed into the dirt and I was unable to move. My eyes flickered up towards the hole in the house as they tried to regain focus. The specter peered out the hole at me, and then suddenly it disappeared from the house, reappearing seconds later a few feet from me.

With my eyes still adjusting, I slowly staggered to my feet and readied myself for the next attack. Starting inside my chest a strange sensation began to wash over my entire body. The adrenaline started to fill me, so instead of running, I began walking toward the specter.

As I approached it, I threw a punch.

But I only hit air.

The specter had disappeared. My eyes darted around trying to find where it was hiding. Then out of nowhere, it suddenly appeared beside me, it tried to grab me but I ducked under its attempt and hit it in the abdomen. It was stunned for a moment.

That's when I saw my opportunity.

My fists began to punch wildly into the specter. Unfortunately, swing after swing I hit nothing but air. The specter was quicker than anything I'd ever seen before. Then, mid-assault it disappeared again. I scrambled, trying to figure out where it would appear next. Somehow, even though I couldn't see the creature I could still sense that it was there. It was like when you're being stared at from across the room, a gut feeling that tells you to look up. I could feel the specter around me, as if I were blind.

Then a sharp pain hit my back.

The creature's fist rammed itself into my spine. I fell to my knees from the intensity of the pain. The creature reappeared again beside me, hitting me again, this time in the face. The pain of which echoed down through my legs.

I glanced in the direction the attack had come from.

Nothing.

Then I looked forward to find the charred mass standing in front of me. The specter kicked me in the chest. The blinding pain of the kick fought for dominance over the other sensations that were coursing through my body. I flew through the air and upon impact, my body slid across the ground then rolled to a stop.

I breathed out a solemn breath, kicking up a dust cloud in front of my face. My muscles trembled as I picked myself up out of the dirt, pushing myself up onto all fours I tried to find the strength to get back to my feet. I spit some blood at the ground in frustration.

I need to get out of here!

The specter moved in closer.

Still on all fours, I began to crawl backwards. The specter's hollowed eyes glared down at me as it moved in, only a few feet away from me. My legs continued to move me back until my back finally hit a wall.

There was nowhere left to go.

The specter closed in, only two feet away, and then it did something I didn't expect.

It stopped.

It began to look around as if it couldn't see me. My eyes looked down at the ground. I was standing in the shade of the building that my back was against, when I realized.

They must be having trouble finding me when I'm not in the sunlight.

The specter sniffed the air in front of my face. It could tell I was still around but it didn't seem to understand where I had gone. Then it all made sense. It was the reason why Virgil had kept us in the shadows when we ran from house to house, why he was afraid of the sun.

My eyes moved back to the specter. It looked around for a moment and then found a shadow and sank back down into the ground. My eyes glanced around trying to determine if it was safe to come out of my shaded sanctuary. The sun above still beat down strong and heavy. I decided to stay in the shade as long as possible to avoid another incident. The houses next to me had a small alley between them, which were completely shaded. My hand clutched my ribs as I stumbled towards the alley.

While I walked, it became apparent the specter had inflicted more damage on me than I had thought; the adrenaline in my body was starting to wear off and for the first time my wounds were beginning to hurt. My back met the brick wall with a thump and my body sank down the wall to the soft green grass below.

I sat in the shade staring into the sky.

I can't survive another encounter like that.

Closing my eyes, I tried to rest; but right as my lids made contact a rustling sound came from the entrance of the alley. The figure that appeared was just a silhouette, completely obscured by the sunlight. It walked slowly toward me causing my knuckles to tighten, ready for one last, futile attack.

Then my eyes adjusted and I noticed the familiar shape.

It was Virgil.

He sat down next to me against the wall. "What are you doing here?" I asked him, sighing in relief that the specter hadn't come back to finish what it had started.

"What do you mean?" He said back.

"You said I was on my own, so why did you come back?" I cleared up the question.

"The explosion." He said pointing at the house. "The gas line must have gone up and must have torn the house apart. I saw the fight too, you did well." His demeanor was smug, almost happy. Anger built in my chest as I realized that he'd let me fight the specter alone. There had been a million things I'd wanted to say to Virgil after he left me with Christina, but at that moment there was only one thing that came to mind.

"You're a bastard!" I told him, allowing my anger to swell inside me.

"You were never in any real danger, if something was going to go wrong I would have stepped in. I wanted to see how you'd do on your own." He told me with a smirk.

"Why are you smirking?!"

I glared at him with intense eyes; I was in no mood to be joking. He'd sat on the sidelines while I was almost killed by a creature made entirely of darkness. He must have taken the hint from my furrowed brow because before he spoke again he huffed out a long breath. "I'm here because I promised you that I'd help you get your body back, I was smirking because I thought it was funny." He admitted to me in a surprisingly sincere tone.

I looked downwards at my feet and said. "Why the change of heart?" My voice was cold, unwavering as I continued to stare at my shoes.

"Personal reasons." His answer was short and sweet, typical Virgil fashion.

"Virgil we can't keep doing this." My tone was a mixture of frustration and exhaustion. "This back and forth is not going to work. You can't hide things from me, especially if you need my help."

"It's for your protection—," he began.

"—I know. I've heard that song from you before." I interrupted. "You can tell me all you want it's for me, that you're just trying to protect me, but the truth is you're running from the things that you've done—," I stood up and faced him. "—I get it Virgil, you've done things you're not proud of, but you're scared of opening up—," Virgil looked away from me so I stopped.

He stared down the alley and then his eyes looked back at mine. Virgil's eyes screamed a sort of sadness that you only see in someone that's truly broken inside. Then I realized something, up until that point I had only been worried about myself, it never occurred to me that Virgil was also trapped in The Shade. Suddenly I felt as if something had been taken from deep within my chest, it was the first I felt as if Virgil was a real person, not someone who was made up, but an actual human being. "Virgil, how did you get here?" My voice asked quietly. "Are you the man in the hospital with me, are you Michael?"

Virgil hesitated for a long moment and then finally said. "Yes."

There was another long pause.

"Burke is the reason I'm here." He told me. I could hear the anguish in his throat as he spoke the words. "I had a family once James. A wife, a little girl named Sarah. We were happy together, but it didn't last. One day Sarah came down with a fever, something simple, non-life threatening. Burke was her doctor—," Virgil looked away from me. His eyes sank slowly down to the floor as if he were lost in thought. After he had a few seconds to compose himself, he looked back at me. "—he murdered my daughter. He murdered her, kidnapped my wife and all of it was to get to me."

Virgil paused as I took in the story he was weaving for me.

"That's how I ended up here. Burke killed my daughter, kidnapped my wife, and destroyed my family just to get to me. You and I are the same James. We have the same genetic abnormality that makes us so useful to Burke. For most people, the supply of Dimethyltryptamine is finite. You and I on the other hand can produce an endless amount, that's why we're so useful." He confessed.

"I'm sorry—," I tried to say.

Virgil's eyes looked worse than I'd ever seen them, his pain shown through them as if they were beacons. "I don't want your pity. I want my revenge, I want to set things right." He told me.

We sat in silence as my mind raced with the new information that Virgil had given me. That was when Virgil finally seemed human to me. He was no longer the indestructible force that I'd once seen him as. Everything inside of me wanted to scream at him for not opening up to me sooner, there was no excuse for someone to suffer at the hands of someone else like Virgil had. My hand reached down to cradle my ribs, when I noticed. The pain was gone, no aches or bruises. I looked at Virgil; his head hung low staring at the ground.

"Virgil." I called his attention to me. He looked up at me and as he did, I offered him my hand. He took it and I pulled him up towards me. "I'll help you." I muttered.

"With what?" He asked.

"I'm going to help you kill Burke." I said to him.

XVI

We stood silently in the alleyway. Virgil looked stunned by what I had said to him, I didn't expect anything less. He knew that killing Burke wasn't something I'd been alright with since he had first mentioned it. The truth of the matter was that Virgil's story made me see something I'd not seen before. He made me *feel,* and for the first time in a long time, I felt like I knew what was right and what was wrong.

"Why." Virgil paused for a moment. "Why are you so sure now?"

"Your story. You were right, Burke's a murderer and he needs to be stopped." I explained.

"How do you know I wasn't lying to get you to do it?" He questioned me.

"You weren't lying. The look in your eyes was one of loss, I know that look, I've given it enough to know what it really looks like." I told him. His pale yellow eyes searched me; it was almost as if he was looking for what had changed as if it were physically noticeable.

"So you're with me then?"

As Virgil asked me, he reached out his hand towards me, waiting for mine.

"I'm with you." I told him as I put my hand in his. We shook hands, but it was more than that, it was a bond, an agreement only my death could undo. It was my promise to him and his to me, for the first time since I had arrived in The Shade I finally felt like an equal to Virgil, rather than a burden.

Virgil looked towards the sky. "Let's get going while the sun is gone." He suggested.

"We're going to have to find another place to stay." I told him. "This house is destroyed."

"Right." Virgil's voice trailed off. We left the alley and went out to the street. I wasn't sure where we would go, nevertheless Virgil always seemed to know where he was going so it didn't concern me. Virgil stopped at the edge of the street and looked in both directions as if he was trying to decide which way to take us.

After a few seconds of deliberation, he stepped out in the street and began walking towards the center of the city; I stepped on the street to follow behind him. We walked up the street in total silence for about five minutes. I wasn't sure if Virgil was angry with himself because he had let me see into his world, or if he was embarrassed because he'd never thought he'd tell anyone the things he'd told me. Whatever the reason, the way I saw him had fundamentally changed. From the streets, we passed into a large field. The field was sloped upwards, making it impossible to see what was over the hill. After some time walking, Virgil and I crest the hill and could see a small residential area on the horizon. To our left there was a lust forest, with trees growing uninhibited by man and on our right laid a road, broken and cracked. It struck me as a cruel duality that without humans the manmade structures seemed to wilt, while nature seemed to prosper. "Virgil are you alright?" I asked, breaking the silence as we walked down the hill.

Virgil looked over at me, his face a mixed bag of emotions. "I'll be alright." He told me, then he looked up into the sky, twisting his head from right to left, then refocusing on the tiny speckles in the distance. I glanced up towards the sky. The grey clouds above swirled in miraculous formations, every so often letting a tiny ray of light through, then quickly closing back up again. My eyes glanced back to Virgil who was walking into some tall grass. "Why did you tell me all of that—back there I mean?" My voice broke the still air.

Virgil looked back at me and said. "Honestly—I'm not sure. It just felt that you needed to know."

There was a long pause.

"We're going to get him." I said. Virgil's eyes turned back to the horizon. "Burke, I mean. We'll make him answer for what he did." I tried to reassure him, but Virgil didn't say anything, he was lost in thought once more. We walked through the field with the specks growing in the distance. Periodically I glanced upwards, noticing something peculiar in the sky. I'm not sure what compelled me to look at the clouds again, but as my eyes searched the clouds I noticed they no longer swirled. They remained still, like grey statues in the sky. I blinked, trying to see if the clouds would move again.

Nothing happened.

"Virgil—," I said in an almost whimper. He didn't answer me. The clouds began to separate letting light through, like rips in a sheet of paper the light tore through and began to fill the air. "Virgil." I said a bit louder. Then in an unimaginable burst of power, the sun tore through the clouds like a fist through paper. In an instant, the warmth of the suns light replaced the grey shadows that had filled the air. "Virgil!" I yelled. That was when he finally took notice; Virgil looked over at me and instantly knew what was going on. His eyes widened as he watched the sun's rays filter down to the ground.

"James run!" He yelled.

I did as Virgil commanded. My eyes set to the horizon, the shapes looking more like houses, but the closest one was still four hundred yards out. My heart cracked hard against my chest as my mind struggled to make my legs run faster.

Three hundred yards out.

My head twisted back to see the rays of the sun, they were pushing down from the sky and coming straight for us. "Don't stop running!" Virgil yelled. My eyes snapped forward focused on the house in the distance. The sound of loud footsteps filled the soft air in the field as we ran.

Two hundred yards out.

I felt warmth on my back. I knew what it was but didn't dare look back for confirmation. Then from behind us the stampeding sound of two—no four, more sets of feet. Growls erupted as the new sets of feet moved forwards after us.

One hundred yards out.

The sun's rays had past us. There was never any chance we could out run the light. The growls from behind us had become louder and louder. Closer and closer, the creatures that chased us drew in for the kill. I could see the house we were running to, only fifty feet away from us. My legs burned as they pushed my feet against the ground and made me move faster.

Forty feet to go, my legs pushed harder.

"James, we have to split up." Virgil yelled at me as we approached the house.

Almost instinctually, my body shifted course to run to the right of the house. My head twisted back to see if the creatures following us had separated, what I saw was nothing short of pure horror. I saw what pursued us, two massive wolves. Just like the one I had seen in the hospital, the two beasts that followed us were enormous, almost the size of a bear. They didn't really look like wolves, but they ran on all fours. Their black skin shown through the wispy hair that stuck out from their bodies. I turned away from the nightmare that chased us just in time to see Virgil phase through the wall of the building I'd chosen to round.

An instant later, the wolf following Virgil dove through the wall after him. However, the wolf didn't phase through the house as Virgil had, instead it smashed its body against the wall. The sound of the animal ripping through the wall was like a clap of thunder. I continued to run just as Virgil had instructed me. To my left another explosion ripped out through the air. As I ran down the line of houses every so often, I could see Virgil phasing in and out of homes, as the wolf that chased him smashed haphazardly through walls. My head twisted back to see my assailant, but to my surprise, there was nothing there. My body slowed to a stop and for a moment, I was in the street alone.

When suddenly from behind me I heard. "James run!"

My head snapped quickly to the sound of Virgil's voice. I looked at him as he ran towards me, a second later the wolf chasing him burst through the side of the house he had exited. It used its powerful hind legs like a spring to launch itself towards Virgil. Virgil who was only a few feet from me didn't see the beast flying towards him.

There was no time to warn him.

The wolf landed, instantly tackling Virgil. Without thinking and without any regard for my own life, I took the knife from my belt and ran at the beast. It took me only a few steps to get within striking distance. Once I was in range, my arm raised the knife up and with one swift motion, it plunged into the wolf's eye. The wolf reared up onto its hind legs, making it stand upright and knocking me backwards. Instantly I thought of what I had originally called the beasts—werewolf—if there ever could be such a thing. Virgil saw that as his opportunity, his leg kicked the enormous animal in the chest making it return to all fours. What came next was so lightning fast that my eyes nearly missed it. With my knife stuck in the wolf's eye, Virgil grabbed hold of the knife, pulled it out, and brought it down into the beast's skull.

The wolf whimpered for a moment, then fell over, and didn't move again.

Virgil breathed heavily as he picked up my knife and handed it back to me. It was covered in a black viscous liquid that I assumed was the animal's blood. "Thanks for the help—,"

Virgil didn't complete the sentence. From out of nowhere,

the second wolf slammed its body against Virgil, throwing him across the street and into a fire hydrant. All I could do was watch as Virgil's body rag dolled across the road and slam into the yellow hydrant.

He was still, lifeless.

The wolf then turned to me rearing up on its hind legs as if it were human. It stepped towards me letting its front legs drop like arms beside it; the wolf once again resembled a werewolf as it suddenly swung its massive paw at me.

I sidestepped the swipe, which put me in position for attack. With the knife still in my hand, I stabbed the wolf in its hind leg, cutting flesh and muscle. As soon as the knife entered, the wolf howled in pain. I withdrew the knife and stabbed again, then again and again.

After the fourth time I thrust the knife into the wolf's leg, its massive body rammed into me, throwing me away from it. I stumbled backwards a few feet, seeing my chance to escape. I looked at Virgil who was still unconscious and quickly ran towards him. Once I reached him I grabbed his arm and threw him onto my back. Virgil wasn't heavy, but he wasn't light either. Luckily, the stab wounds in the wolf's leg seemed to slow down its reaction time.

Quickly I ran down the street, unsure if the wolf was closing in on me.

In that moment, I was unsure of many things. I had no idea if the sun was still out or not, or if Virgil was still alive. I felt like my life was hanging in the air, like a coin tossed just waiting to land. Given everything I didn't know, all I could do was run. The sounds of the wolf behind me propelled me forward, pressing me to fight through the pain of making my legs work overtime. I poured every ounce of energy I still had left into my legs in the hopes that they would give me just a little bit more speed.

I ran.

I ran and I didn't look back to see the jaws creeping up after me. I didn't look forward to see where I was going, I focused my eyes on my feet and willed them to keep moving.

Just keep putting one foot in front of the other James.

The thoughts echoed in my head as the muscles in my legs began to tighten, I could feel my muscles scream out at me as they cramped. I pushed through the pain. I gave my body one last burst of energy before the pain overwhelmed me; and suddenly I fell to one knee with Virgil still on my back. It was over.

I waited for the end to approach me from behind.

I closed my eyes and waited for the wolf to come and snuff out the light of my existence. But as I waited for the end to come with my eyes closed, I couldn't hear the growls behind me any longer, in fact I hadn't heard them for quite some time. My eyes came open slowly, and my head rose up from the tired black asphalt. As my eyes rose up, the sight before me was one of complete dread. Sprawled out before me was the blacked and destroyed skyline of Eugene. I had made it all the way to the interior of the city.

The one place Virgil had told me never to go.

XVII

The air was still all around me.

My eyes traced the outlines of the tall grey monolithic buildings on all sides. I swallowed hard to choke back the fear that had begun to rise in my chest. I sat on the street, Virgil's limp body at my feet and no energy to get us both out of the city. My eyes searched the nearby buildings for shelter then looked up at the sky. The sun had retreated behind clouds, which meant for only a few moments, I was safe.

Somehow, I mustered enough strength to pick myself back up; once fully upright I bent down, wrapping my arms underneath Virgil's armpits. Slowly I dragged Virgil's body towards an old office building. Paper and glass covered the street as I pulled Virgil's lifeless body towards a temporary safety. The building looked like it was made of black garnet; its once smooth face had been riddled with holes and abrasions.

With my back towards the front door of the building, I used my body to prop the door open as we entered. Virgil's body slid across the floor with relative ease, once inside the building I dropped him to look around. The lobby of the building was laid out fairly simply; the room was large, about fifty feet across with a large security desk in the center. A large metal sign stood in front of the desk, which I could only assume, was the building directory. Directly across the room from me sat a set of stairs, adjacent to the steps were the elevators. After a long moment looking around the room I picked Virgil's body back up and started to drag him towards the elevators, knowing that the more distance that I put between us and the wolves the better.

A minute later, we were there. My finger pressed the faded yellow button expecting it to light up; it did not. I pressed the button again; still, nothing happened. Virgil had told me that in The Shade electricity, along with other utilities were spotty. I let a heavy sigh pass over my lips and then grabbed Virgil's body once more dragging him towards the stairs. We were at the foot of the staircase in less than five minutes.

My eye cautiously looked up the stairs, counting each one like a hurdler before a race.

"This is going to suck." I said to myself. Then I looked down at Virgil and added. "Sorry buddy, this might hurt when you wake up." With that, I grabbed Virgil to begin my difficult climb to the top of the staircase. I had only climbed a few stairs when my arms began to ache, I could feel my muscles tightening under my skin. My legs felt like gelatin beneath my weight, each step making them tremble more and more. After what seemed like an eternity, we reached the first landing. I collapsed to the floor as soon as I knew Virgil's body wasn't going to slide back down the stairs. Every joint and muscle inside of my body screamed out in pain as I laid back, looking at the ceiling.

There was a long moment of silence.

Get up James!

I pushed myself off the floor and grudgingly got back to my feet. I took in a deep breath as I bent over to pull Virgil; once I had a hold of him there was an overwhelming feeling that I couldn't let go until we reached the top of the stairs, or until we came tumbling back down them. My hands tightened around Virgil's shirt to maintain my grip on him while my left foot made the first step up the stairs. The rest was a blur, the next thing I knew I was on the second landing, with a door at my back and more steps on my right. I went through the door; dragging Virgil's limp body through with me. Once in the room my eyes glanced at the maze of cubicles before me, making me instantly feel like a mouse, hunting for cheese. I continued through the room until I found a cubicle away from any windows that would be good to rest in.

I laid Virgil's body on top of a desk so that he was resting completely flat. As soon as Virgil was in position, my body fell backwards into an old blue swivel chair. I sat there for a moment as my body fired signals at my brain, letting it know I was in pain. The ache was unlike anything I'd ever felt before; I felt like I'd been run over by a car and then thrown off a cliff. I looked down at Virgil, speculating on the extent of his injuries. "Come on Virgil, wake up." I said to the empty room.

Then a sound answered me.

A howl from outside echoed down the empty streets of Eugene until it made its way to my ears. Suddenly my heart leapt back to life as my mind processed what the noise meant. "They're hunting me." I said in a whisper.

I let my body loaf in the chair, waiting for something to happen; nothing ever did.

An hour passed, and as it did I felt the strength to stand return to me. I got up out of the chair, a bit shaky at first but a second later, I was stable. I walked to Virgil and turned his body over so that his stomach was facing the desk. Then I lifted his shirt in search of the place where he'd hit the fire hydrant. It was easy to spot, my fingers moved down his spine until they got to the wound, a deep indent right above the small of his back. The bruise that had manifested was overflowing with twisted color, blacks, purples, and reds, making Virgil's back look like some sort of sickening work of art. Once I was satisfied, I put his shirt back down, covering his torso and then returned him to his resting state.

I sat back down in my chair.

What if he doesn't wake up?

The pessimist in my head began to shout out ideas.

He will wake up, he has to—but what if he doesn't?

I tried to shake the thoughts from my head, but no matter how hard I tried, the fact remained that if Virgil was gone and was not going to wake up I would have to move on without him. Leaving him was something I didn't want to do; not because being on my own frightened me beyond belief but because Virgil had tried to help me, and I had made him a promise to help him. "I'll give you five hours Virgil, if you don't give me something by then, I have to leave." I said to Virgil's comatose like body.

The hours passed one by one. Every so often, I would hear another howl from outside which would put me on my toes for a few minutes. This continued for three hours as I watched Virgil sit lifeless in front of me. That was, until hour number four.

My eyes glanced down at my watch; I had been waiting for Virgil for a little over four hours when a croaking sound came from Virgil's throat. I instantly threw myself from the chair towards Virgil. "Come on buddy." I said as I began to tap on his face. "Come on, come on." I pleaded. Virgil let out a small nasally noise as my hand continued to pat his cheek. Then his eyes sprung open almost startling me as they did; Virgil was awake. His eyes darted around the room a few times and then he looked up at me.

"James, where—where—," his voice was hoarse. "Where are we and why can't I feel my legs?" He finally got out. I stared at him silently not wanting to answer either of the questions. Virgil's eyes looked at me with a look that seemed to say, *out with it*.

"You were hit by one of those—those wolves." I told him. "You hit a fire hydrant and I think it broke your back." I didn't know how he'd take the news, I didn't know how to prepare for his reaction, but nothing could have prepared me for what actually happened.

Virgil smiled at me and then began to laugh.

"Are you serious?" He asked almost jokingly. "Great, well I'll be on my feet in a few then."

I didn't understand, my eyes searched him for the root of his humorous outburst, I found nothing. He looked up at me; he must have seen my furrowed brow and understood immediately that I was confused because he then said. "James in The Shade, your body can heal just about anything, that's why you don't feel tired any longer." He was right; I had noticed the pain slowly fade to a dull burning then to nothing. I felt like I could run a marathon, like all my energy was back and I was ready for round two. "The DMT in your body can repair in seconds, damage that would leave normal people out of commission for weeks. So don't worry about me—," He said as he pushed his body up into a sitting position. "—short of losing a limb we can recover. So where are we exactly?"

My hand sifted its way through my messy hair as I tried to come up with a way to tell Virgil that I'd disobeyed his rule about entering the city. I swallowed a lump in my throat then spoke. "We're in—to get away from the wolf I ran, I might have run us into—," I paused not wanting to finish my sentence.

"Into where?" Virgil prodded.

"Into the city." I said and then moved back expecting an outburst of rage. Virgil didn't move, he didn't even respond he just absorbed what I'd said, From the look on his face I assumed he was trying to figure a way out of the city. "I'm sorry—," I began to say but Virgil's hand stopped me mid-sentence.

"It's alright James; we just have to get out of here quickly." He told me.

"Right—the wolves were just so massive. How do you stop something like that?"

Virgil opened and closed his hands to flex the muscles. "You don't. Only fight the wolves or the specters when you've got no options left. The only advantage we have over the wolves is that they're slower when they stand upright." He told me as he began to work his hands down his legs in an attempt to revive them.

"What about the specters?" I asked curiously.

The dead quiet in the office made my voice seem ten times louder than what it had been. I could hear a breeze rolling down the line of cubicles towards us. Unfortunately that wasn't the only thing that it brought. The sound was faint at first but as the wind breezed past us the sound became distinct and recognizable, the sound of a wolf howling. Quickly my body shot up to look over the cube that Virgil and I were in, I peeked over the top of the partition and scanned the room. "It sounded far off James, relax." Virgil told me.

I turned around and lowered myself back into my seat, listening to Virgil.

"Did you want me to answer your question?" The question was rhetorical because immediately he continued. "Remember when I told you that the body can't live without the mind but the mind can survive without the body? Well if a body dies and a mind remains, whatever corruption that that mind holds within it will slowly change it into a specter. However, if that mind has something to anchor it to the real world, then it becomes a ghost. They can't see you when you're in the shadows, as you figured out. They store their energy for fast bursts of speed; you can wear them out if you stay defensive." His advice echoed in my ears and I committed it to memory. Then Virgil tried to stand, grunting as he pushed himself off the desk. As soon as Virgil's leg hit the floor, he gripped it in pain, letting out an agonizing groan as he did.

"What's wrong?" I asked.

"The damn bone in my leg must not have set right." There was a long pause as Virgil thought about what to do. "You're going to have to break my leg again and help reset the bone."

My eyes widened at what Virgil told me. "Are—are you sure?" I stammered. He nodded his head at me with a grimace that told me that he was having second thoughts. He put both his hands on the desk and braced himself for the pain that he knew was coming. "You're absolutely sure about this?" I asked looking at the broken leg.

"Just do it, right here." He said pointing to the place he wanted me to break. "Give me your belt." I undid my belt and handed it to him. He put the thick leather between his teeth to be sure he didn't bite his tongue. I gave one good dry swallow and then drew my leg back. The kick was fast, but the sound of bones shattering under the force was sickening. Virgil let out a whelp of pain but the belt between his teeth muffled any noise.

He spit out the belt and then sank to the floor.

"Okay, now help me hold it in place." He said as he held the mangled leg.

"Like this?" I asked, putting my hands around his leg.

He nodded in pain. Virgil's discomfort was almost palpable; he made no effort to hide the pain. As we sat there in the abandoned office building an itch crept its way into my head, it was something that I had wanted to ask Virgil as soon as he had explained what had happened to his family, I would have asked him sooner if the wolves hadn't attacked. I looked at the ground for a moment then looked over at Virgil. His eyes were fixated on his leg, completely focused on nothing at all. "Hey." I said to get his attention. His head didn't turn to look at me but his eyes moved so I knew that he was listening. "What was she like, your daughter I mean?" I asked, hoping that talking about his family would take his mind off the pain.

There was silence for a long moment.

Is this the wrong time to bring that up? Maybe I shouldn't have tried to pry.

I quickly tried to correct myself. "I didn't mean to—," Virgil's hand stopped me.

"It's fine." He told me. He thought for a long moment then spoke. "Sarah was beautiful. I can still remember how her hair fell down over her shoulders. She had her mother's eyes, the most magnificent green I'd ever seen." He began to smile at the thought.

"How old was she?" I asked.

Virgil paused for a moment. His face sunk in and his eyes looked glossy. "She was seven. Only seven years old when she was killed—," Virgil turned away from me for a moment and his hand wiped something from his face. When he turned back, I noticed his eyes were significantly redder.

I said nothing.

"—the most distinct thing I can remember is her laugh. She always laughed." He smiled again. "Burke took my daughter and my wife away from me. I'm not even sure if he ever had my wife, but he used her to get to me and I've been here ever since." He told me as his eyes focused back on his legs. "Why do you bring this up now?"

I stood up in the cubical and looked around at the office.

"I wanted to know about them, about you." I said.

He smiled at the thought as he bent his knees up to his chest and then lowered his legs back down to the floor. I looked back down at Virgil. "You know, Angela and I talked about getting married after college." I said. Virgil peered up towards me. "She's always been beautiful to me, no matter what. Like this one time she was sick, I mean really sick—," I chuckled. "—she just looked like someone had taken all the color out of her face, she had all kinds of fluids coming out of her and when I saw her, I still thought she was beautiful. That's when I knew I loved her." I told him. "I knew that if I could still want to be around her when she was sick like that, then I could handle anything."

"So what happened?" Virgil asked.

What happened?

Virgil's question was the same one that I'd asked myself every day since the moment we broke up. "I'm not sure—," I hesitated. "—it was as if she ended things but didn't really *want* to end them. It always felt like there was something she wasn't telling me."

"Maybe she didn't want to leave you. Maybe she felt that she *had* to." Virgil said then went back to moving his legs. The thought had never crossed my mind before. What if she didn't want to leave me, what if something had forced her to. It was something I'd never even considered until that point.

"Why would she do that?" I asked Virgil.

He pursed his lips. "Not sure. But when we get you out of here, make sure you ask her." He said with a finger in my chest. I nodded in agreement. "My leg feels set now."

He reached his hand out and I grabbed it, pulling him back to his feet.

"Are you sure you're alright to walk?" I asked him as he tried to keep his balance.

"Yeah I'm sure." He told me as he steadied himself. "Let's get the hell out of this city."

XVIII

The drum of my heart rang in my ears. Virgil's hand covered my mouth as I stared intently at the large black animal prowling around in front of us. The wolf had tracked us to an old shipping warehouse. Virgil and I sat quietly inside the dark blue shipping container while the beast tried to sniff us out. The large door of the container sat slightly ajar, letting light from the warehouse slowly trickle in on us. I watched wide eyed as the wolf sniffed the outside of the container. Its hot breath blowing through the crack in the door. After a few minutes, the wolf shambled out of my field of vision. The sound of lumbered walking faded in the distance and as it did, my heartbeat began to slow. Virgil's hand uncovered my mouth; I looked over at him, knowing he was displeased.

Our eyes met.

"Don't you ever do anything that reckless again!" Virgil yelled at me in a whisper.

"I'm sorry but we've been running for three days now, I'm beginning to think we can't make it out of this city." I told him equally as frustrated. Virgil let a heavy sigh pass over his lips as he shook his head at me. Virgil then pushed the container open, poked his head outside to scout around. After a few seconds he pulled his head back inside, focused on me.

"I know you're tired, we're almost out of this okay?" He said trying to console me.

I rubbed my eyes with the tips of my fingers as Virgil spoke, wanting to believe what he was telling me. I nodded in agreement with him and asked. "Are they gone?"

"They're gone for now."

"Then let's go—," I said, starting to walk out of the container. However, before I could leave, Virgil put his arm out to stop me, his hand placed firmly on my chest.

"We'll go when I know that you're alright." Virgil said in an almost concerned tone of voice. It was a side of Virgil that I'd seldom seen. The only times that he'd opened up and let his true emotions come out were when he talked about his family. Virgil's words stopped me dead in my tracks; I contemplated for a moment what he'd meant when he said 'alright'. I was mentally exhausted, but so was he; staying one-step ahead of demonic wolves was hard work. The only thing I could deduce that he was talking about was what had happened right before we escaped into the shipping container.

"I'm fine." I told him.

Virgil's eyes scanned me for a moment.

"Then what happened back there?" His voice was worried.

I pinched the bridge of my nose as he asked the question. "I don't know. I came around the corner to quickly and, I made a mistake—," I offered my explanation, letting my voice trail off as I said it.

"Mistakes get people killed James; we've come too far for a lapse in judgment to undo us." His voice was firm, but not scolding. "You're making it incredibly difficult to keep you alive." Virgil's tone had changed to a more jocular one.

I rolled my eyes at him, as a silence filled the air around us.

"Speak for yourself old man, I had to carry you on my back all the way here." I joked.

"That's right, you are the reason we're in the city." He jabbed back.

I let out a slight chuckle. It almost startled me as it made its way out of my mouth. Virgil too was smiling, something I saw him do only on very rare occasions. We sat in the dark shipping container for a few more moments, allowing me the opportunity to drink in our sudden burst of happiness.

"Let's go." Virgil said as he pushed the heavy blue door of the container open. I followed him out into the warehouse. The expansive building was huge, almost the size of an aircraft hangar. Metal shipping containers lined the walls, while some sort of crane hung from the ceiling above us. As we headed towards the middle of the room, I noticed the three large doors immediately to my right. They were larger than the employee door we had used to enter so I surmised they were used for deliveries but I couldn't say for sure.

Virgil raised his hand in the air, signaling me to follow him. I did as he instructed, following close enough behind him so that I'd be able to keep up, but not so close he'd get hung up on me if he needed to make a quick retreat. Virgil and I crept along the wall directly across from the container we'd started in until we came to a solid white door with the words: Manager's Office, painted in faded yellow letters. Virgil opened the door cautiously, making sure not to make any more noise than he had to. Several seconds later, the door was open, revealing the abandoned managers office. The office sat in total disarray, with paper covering the white tile floor. We moved through the office, towards the door on the opposite end of the room. As we moved, we tried not to disturb anything in the room.

We continued out the other side of the office, which put us in another empty warehouse. I looked to my right and saw a set of metal garage doors. Above them was a sign that read: Out-Going Deliveries. The thing that caught my eye however was the door that sat slightly askew, allowing what little light there was on the street to filter into the musty warehouse.

"Let's get outside." Virgil spoke softly as he moved closer to the hangar doors. When we arrived at the entrance, Virgil turned to me. "Keep an eye out, I'm going to get my bearings."

I did as he requested and turned around to make sure nothing got the jump on us. I watched the empty room, it sat cold and lifeless as my eyes peered into it. "What do you see?" I asked, curious about where we were. Virgil didn't respond right away, he was working on something in his head the way he always did.

After a minute of waiting, Virgil answered. "I see a large commercial center across a four lane road. Fast food places and stores, an outdoor mall. Further from that is an apartment building, we should head for that next." He said looking back at me.

"As long as it gets us out of here." I said.

"It will." Virgil said as he glared back outside. "We better go now, while the sun isn't out."

Quickly, Virgil and I crossed the desolate four-lane road. The blacktop was cracked and splitting in places, allowing grass and other weeds to grow up through it. Once we arrived at the edge of the road I looked back at the warehouse one last time, then made my way up a grassy hill towards the shopping center. Once I crested the hill, I saw that we still had a lot of ground to cover before we made it to the apartments. Before us stood a commercial plaza, in the real world the plaza would have been drenched with the stench of fast food and alive with shoppers. However, in The Shade the stores sat idol, unused and unmanned. The sight was a bit saddening as if I had expected someone to be there. We walked across the large expansive parking lot, which was teaming with rusted out cars and destroyed asphalt.

We were half way across the lot when we heard the howl.

It pierced the silent veil of The Shade so clearly, there was no mistaking what it was. Virgil turned to me and gently said. "They haven't found us, keep going." My heart jumped into full swing, the sound of the wolves only helped to amplify my concern. We made it to the end of the parking lot to a clothing store; all we had to do was pass through the store and on the other side, the apartment buildings would be waiting.

Virgil walked into the store through the shattered front window. I followed behind him, allowing the broken glass to crunch underneath my feet. The store was small enough that once inside I could clearly see the exit. We continued to move through the store until we came to the emergency exit. The red exit sign illuminated the dark back corner of the store, my eyes focused on it for just a moment then I looked down at Virgil whose hand was already on the doors crash bar.

Virgil then pushed the door open.

Almost immediately an alarm sounded, the noise was a piercing screech as it echoed through the hollowed shell of the store. "You've got to be kidding me!" Virgil yelled over the alarm. "Get to the apartment!"

Quickly we ran across the open field towards the apartment block. Virgil and I both knew the wolves were coming for us; there wasn't any doubt about that. As the red brick of the apartment building came into full view it seemed like we'd finally caught a break. That was when the wall of the store we'd left exploded outward. I looked back, and saw two wolves dive through the concrete block; It took only a second and they started running towards us.

We made it to the front door of the apartment building. Virgil got there first, throwing the door open as soon as he hit it. We ran inside the dust-filled lobby of the apartment building. It wasn't large, in fact, once we'd entered the front doors it was a straight shot back to the stairs. A set of elevators lined both sides of the lobby, but we ignored them. Virgil sprinted up the stairs towards the first landing when the all glass door of the apartment lobby flew off its hinges towards us. I made it to the landing just as the door slammed against the stairs.

Virgil and I shot up another set of stairs when we heard the patter of paws against the cold linoleum floor. The wolves were coming for us. We reached the third floor landing, the sound of the wolves drawing nearer; we had two options, go up the next flight of stairs towards the fourth floor or take the rusted red door in front of us. Without much thought, Virgil threw the red door open, which lead us into the third floor hallway. We rushed down the hallway, past the rows of doors on both sides of us. We had gotten half way down the hall when the door behind us swung open, two massive black wolves entered behind us. They barreled down the hall at us as we ran helplessly towards the window at the end of the hall.

"We're going to jump." Virgil yelled in a panicked voice.

"Are you insane?!" I yelled back, but Virgil didn't answer. By the time the question had left my lips, Virgil had already slammed his body against the window, shattering it instantly.

I was going too fast to stop.

My body passed through the window frame, leaping outwards towards the gas station next to the apartments. I landed on the gravel roof of the gas station, my body rolled and I ended up close to Virgil. "Get up." Virgil's voice called as he yanked me back to my feet. There was no time to thank him because even though Virgil had picked me up with lightning speed, the first wolf had already made its jump across from the apartment. Before I could move out of the way, the wolf's body rammed into me. My back hit the ground and the wolf took its position over me. It snarled letting me see the razor like teeth that protruded from its mangled mouth.

Suddenly, Virgil's leg shot out and kicked the wolf. In an instinctual movement, the wolf reared its body upwards allowing Virgil to deliver a well-placed kick to its chest; the kick was so powerful the wolf stumbled backward, off the gravel-covered roof and down to the hard concrete below. "Thanks." I said in a sigh of relief.

"No problem." Virgil replied as he pulled me to my feet for the second time.

As my legs found their way underneath me, a howl broke the still air. I turned and saw the second wolf that had been chasing us, it stood stoic at the threshold of the apartment building window almost contemplating whether to jump over to the gas station. It stared at us, and instead of jumping over and meeting the same fate as its companion, the wolf let out a nasty snarl, then turned around and ran back down the hall. "Come on." Virgil said. "It's going to try and find another way around; we're not out of the woods yet."

Virgil and I ran across the roof, finding the ladder to the street below.

"I'll go first." He told me as he made his way half way down the ladder then let himself fall the rest of the way. "Come on." He commanded. I grabbed the ladder and quickly shuffled down to the street. My head swiveled back and forth trying to locate the wolves that were chasing us. The street seemed empty, but there was no time to think. A few seconds after my feet hit the ground Virgil took off running in a seemingly random direction, I trusted it was a way out of the city.

My eyes darted around as warm sensation filled my body. I didn't think my heartbeat could have gotten any faster but as soon as my mind realized what the source of the warmth was it tripled in speed. I looked up towards the sky. "We've got to move." Virgil screamed, already running in a seemingly random direction. I followed his instructions without hesitation and began to sprint after him. My feet slammed against the ground as I ran, kicking up dust and creating a cloud of smoke behind me.

As soon as I caught up to Virgil who was only a few paces ahead of me the sound of feet behind us became apparent. Not just the sound of the wolves', I counted fourteen in total that were hot on our heels. I looked backwards as we ran to see the oncoming death that trailed us; the sight of it was almost too much for me. Two wolves, fangs out and ready to rip through flesh; accompanied by three specters. "Virgil we've got a problem." I called to him.

He glanced back wide eyed and said. "Just keep moving."

We moved across a two-lane road and into a field, the horizon before us was free of buildings, we had made it out of the city. Then something happened, something that made me believe that the universe didn't totally have our number. The clouds in the sky began to swirl and twist in different shapes, creating a performance of grey and white above us. The clouds slowly moved in front of the sun, and a second later, all sunlight ceased.

Virgil and I both saw the change in the sky. "Virgil do you have any ideas." Virgil looked into the sky then back at the creatures bearing down on us. He seemed to be contemplating something, like he wasn't entirely sure of the thoughts in his own head. Virgil looked back over at me as the mass of fangs and death moved in closer behind us. "So?" I questioned urgently.

"I've got an idea—but you're not going to like it." He said in a huff as we continued to run.

"Anything's better than this." I replied.

Virgil hesitated for a moment. "Eh—I wouldn't say that."

"Just tell me what it is!" I pressed.

The creatures were only a few feet behind us.

"We fight them." He told me.

It took me a second to realize what he was suggesting.

"You were right." I replied.

"About what?"

"I don't like that idea."

"Look there's only a few of them, between the both of us this shouldn't be difficult." He tried to reassure me. "I've shown you how to do a few things, just remember. You're faster than they are; use that to your advantage." He told me. The creatures were almost on top of us. My heart beat quickly in my chest as they drew closer. One of the wolves let out a snarl that sent ripples through me and as if the noise was a starter pistol. Virgil stopped running, pivoted on his left foot, and spun himself around.

"We can do this." He told me just before he shot off towards the mob of creatures.

I had no choice. I stopped myself and spun around, following Virgil towards the darkness that followed us, towards death.

XIX

My heart was running in overdrive. It pounded in my chest as Virgil and I ran towards the creatures. We were seconds away from a clash of fists and claws. I prepared myself for what was coming. *"You're faster than they are."* Virgil's words echoed in my head. *"Get behind them."* My fist clenched as we approached the creatures.

Only a few feet away from them, the wolves used their powerful legs to propel themselves towards us, their jaws snapping at the satisfying thought of a quick meal. Seconds before the clash, the wolves' hind legs coiled backwards, launching them forward at the two of us. The sound that followed was a thunderous boom of power.

One of the wolves' leapt for me, the other towards Virgil. As it reached the apex of its jump, I tried to duck under it, but the duck turned into more of a roll and before I knew what had happened the wolf was behind me and I was seconds away from being ripped to shreds. Quickly I got up and saw a specter in front of me. It let out a feral scream that overtook all my senses. I forced myself to run towards the creature, dipping my shoulder low I rammed the monster sending it flat on its back.

Out of the corner of my eye, I could see Virgil. He was using his leg like a sledgehammer, knocking back one of the wolves, sending it flying like a ragdoll through the air. As soon as the wolf landed, a specter crept up from behind him, Virgil seemed unaware, but before the specter could attack, Virgil's fist shot out like a rocket. I watched as Virgil's hand went clear through the creature's midsection. The specter let out a terrible moan then burst into a cloud of dense black smoke. It was a small victory, but there was no time to celebrate, the wolf from before had returned and wanted to settle things with Virgil.

The specter that I had rammed lay at my feet. So taking Virgil's lead, my foot rose up and with one defiant stomp, I brought it down on top of the specter's head. Just as the specter had done with Virgil, the creature changed into a puff of dense black smoke and then was gone. Then, through the black cloud that surrounded me, a wolf leaped out at me. I tried to duck under the attack, but it wasn't enough. The animal's sharp claws shredded my shirt as it passed over me, but left my body intact. The blow took me by surprise and for a second I was stunned.

That was close.

The wolf landed behind me and stood up; immediately I readied myself. My fist shot up and nailed the wolf in the chest as it came towards me. The wolf snarled as another blow landed, then another. That's when it dropped to all fours, trying to get a lower angle on me. However, Virgil had taught me how to deal with wolves. Almost immediately, my leg swung around and smashed into the side of the wolf's face. It fell to the ground and I backed up a few feet from it, unsure if it was dead. The wolf twitched and then sprang back to life. Its eyes twisted towards me, black, filled with rage. Then it shot towards me, faster than I'd ever seen anything move before.

A moment later, the huge beast had me pinned to the ground.

My hands clumsily gripped its jaws as it tried to sink its teeth into my neck. I tried to push the wolf's oozing jaws away from me but the animal was overpowering. Then I felt something inside me change.

Something in me clicked on, as if someone flipped a light switch. Time seemed to slow down. My brain worked overtime and for a moment, everything became clear to me. My mind saw all the possible moves I could make and all of the countermoves to those ones and so on. It was as if my mind was playing a game of chess with itself and in that instant it knew every possible outcome of my current situation.

Then a warm sensation filled my entire body, different from what I felt the first day in the field. It felt as if someone heated my blood and now it was coursing from my heart to my extremities faster than it ever had before. I watched as my hands moved the wolf's mouth away from my neck and with one swift throw, tossed the animal aside. Quickly I found my feet and in an instant, I was ready for the next attack. My eyes stared at my hands in amazement of what I'd done.

What's happening?

The wolf slowly recovered and came at me once again. Its teeth chomped at the air, ready to sink them into my flesh. My body swiftly moved to the left the beast, letting it pass by me. With its back turned to me, my fist slammed against the wolf's back. I could hear its bones crack under the power of the attack. The wolf let out a painful screech, so loud in fact; I had to cover my ears. The wolf wasted no time. Before I knew what was going on it leapt at me once again. This time I didn't have time to move out of the way. Its shoulder hit me in the chest, making my bones rattle inside my body. I flew through the air and then crashed into the ground.

I rolled a few feet and then stopped. I blinked the dirt out of my eyes as the wolf came to finish me off. Everyone always tells you when you have a near death experience your life flashes before your eyes; that was not the case for me. Instead of my entire life, my mind only seemed to flash to the good parts, to the moments that truly defined me as a person. The first thought in my head was that of my family, knowing if the wolf killed me they would never see me again and I'd never be able to tell them how much they really mattered to me. After my family, Angela was the next thing in my head. I imagined her face, radiant against the light of the afternoon sun, her hair shimmering against the light of the moon, all of the things we had never done, all of the things we wanted to do together. All of those things would never come to pass if I died.

So I chose not to die.

My heart pumped faster and faster as my face turned towards the monster. I felt the warmth in my body grow like an inferno out of control. My breathing became heavy as the heat escaped my body.

Then something happened to me.

My eyes started to get dark, like going down a tunnel without any light at the end. Like a black hole that swallows up all the light around it, my eyes saw nothing but the darkness in front of them. My vision slowly got dimmer until finally there was nothing.

Then my body stood up, but I had not commanded it to do so. Then it darted towards the wolf, which was the opposite of what I would have done. It was as if I was no longer in control of myself, as if someone else had taken the driver's seat, as if I was lost in my fury. However, as scary as it was, the sensation was liberating, freeing me from worry and above all, I enjoyed it.

I ran at the wolf as it lumbered towards me, but just before impact, I dodged the beast to the left like some kind of matador. As the wolf ran passed me, I threw a kick to the side of the wolf's head. The blow landed solid against the animal's face, the subsequent cracking could only be described as revolting. The wolf's body crashed to the ground and then disappeared into a cloud of black smoke, just like the specters had. My fists tightened, waiting for the beast to come back to life somehow. I did not, so I moved on.

My eyes shifted to Virgil, who was still having trouble with his wolf. It had him pinned to the ground and its massive jaws snapped at Virgil who was struggling to save himself. Without thinking, without hesitation, I began to run towards them. I'd been twenty feet away from where Virgil and the wolf were, allowing me enough time to build up the speed I needed to tackle the animal. A split second later, my arms wrapped around the wolf's body and the momentum of the tackle sent us hurdling towards the ground.

We crashed against the ground and separated, only to be back on my feet a few moments later. My fist clenched shut as it rocketed towards the wolf's jaw. When the blow landed, my fist crushed the bones within the wolf's jaw. An ear-shattering crack reverberated off the hollow ground as the injured wolf fell to the dirt. My lungs drew in heavy gulps of air as I watched the wolf struggle for life. The wolf thrashed, trying to pick itself up off the ground, failing to stand back upright.

Then my mind flashed to a dark place.

Only a few moments ago, a wolf a lot like this one had been trying to rip my throat out and had it succeeded, it wouldn't have given me another thought. Why should I show them any mercy?

My body moved over top of the beaten wolf, with fists clenched tight my entire arm cranked backwards and then launched. The fist made contact with the animal so hard it let out one last whimper and then it fell silent.

But that did nothing to stay my hand.

Another fist came down on the animal, then another and another. My fists slammed against the wolf until my knuckles began to bleed. "James." I heard from behind me, but I did not stop. My fist continued to work their destruction over the wolf. "James." The voice said again, but still my fists pummeled the giant wolf's broken skull.

I had no control over myself. I tried to stop my fists from moving, to be done with the act of violence, and move on. However, I did not move. I just continued to beat the shattered remains of a broken beast. "James that's enough!" Virgil's voice called out to me. Virgil's hand met my shoulder and tore me off the wolf. The wolf transformed into a puff of black smoke and evaporated into the air. My body sprang up and moved towards Virgil.

STOP!

I shouted at myself. My body moved closer towards Virgil as he backed away from me slowly. "James, you need to calm down." He told me. "You need to stop, it's over. You won." He said as he continued to back up.

STOP MOVING!

My mind screamed for my body to listen. Then, much like before, a switch went off. I blinked my eyes and suddenly the world felt normal again. My body was suddenly at my command once more. I wobbled and fell to the ground; my body hit the soft dirt and in an instant, Virgil was helping me off the ground. "Are you alright?" He asked as he pulled me back to my feet. "Can you stand?"

I didn't answer, instead I tried to stand upright by myself.

My legs shook once more and I almost fell. Virgil's hand caught me quickly to keep me up. "Whoa—easy there. Can you walk?"

"I think so." I told him. "Why do my legs feel like noodles?"

Virgil chuckled. "Your muscles are just not used to the overexertion; you'll be fine in a little while." He told me. Virgil braced me as we walked towards a group of houses. "We need to get inside—," Virgil looked into the sky. "—I'm not sure how long this cloud cover will last us."

We came to a house on the corner of two streets. The house was a small one story with what used to be red paint that had all but flaked away. The door was accented by a green trim that seemed to make the door pop out. Maybe that was why Virgil chose the house, whatever the reason was, we walked to the front door, opened it up and we walked inside.

The house was quiet and still. Virgil carried me to the living room—which was fully furnished—and sat me down slowly on the couch. My head leaned back and it hit the wall.

Ouch.

Virgil turned his back to me and put his hand over his mouth as if he were thinking.

"Virgil?" I asked quietly. "Is something wrong?" Virgil turned and looked at me. His eyes were inquisitive as if he were seeing me for the first time. Virgil scratched his face and then said. "Do you know what happened back there?"

I looked at him, eyes blinking as every second went by. "I'm not sure—," I paused trying to collect my words but none came to the front of my mind. Virgil looked me over and then walked back over towards me. He sat down beside me and met my gaze.

"Tell me what you felt, what happened." He instructed.

I tried to remember, tried to recall every single detail of the experience. "I—I'm not sure. I was doing what you taught me, but it wasn't working. The wolf had me pinned and then I—,"

I paused for a moment, lost in thought.

"And then you did what James?" Virgil asked to snap me out of my stupor.

I shook my head and then resumed. "—then I, thought about my family and Angela. I thought about losing them, about all the things we would never experience. Then something happened, it was like something within me just took over."

"Your eyes were black, did you know that?" He asked.

I nodded my head. "Yes, or—or at least I think so. My vision got dark, like all the light around me was being overtaken by darkness. When the thing took me over it was as if I was watching someone else control my body. I didn't realize my eyes had turned black." I looked up at him. Virgil had moved towards the edge of the seat cushion and after I stopped speaking, he stood up.

"I've never seen anything like what you did today." He told me. "You see James; your power is controlled by your emotion." Virgil walked towards me and knelt down to my eye level. "Anger comes from here—," Virgil's finger pointed towards my heart. "—but so does compassion. If you use your compassion and humanity, you'll be stronger than anyone, that is why Burke's afraid of you. The number one rule you have to remember James is that no matter what, you never let yourself be overcome by emotion."

My eyes tilted towards the floor. "And my eyes?" I asked.

"It's got something to do with your anger. You were angry you would never get to see your family or Angela again, and that anger took over. You can't let that happen." He said. "I'm sure with my help I can teach you to control yourself and you'll be able to overcome it."

I wasn't sure if Virgil believed what he was telling me. The fact that I'd let myself get to the point that I actually lost control of my actions frightened me on a level I'd never known. The fear of letting my emotions take hold of me again and losing control sent a chill down my spine. My eyes slowly moved around the room trying to get a handle on the thought of something else controlling me.

Am I in control now? If I wasn't, could I even tell?

My head shook the thought from my head and I looked over at Virgil. "I'm going to show you how to control yourself. Don't worry James."

"What happens if I can't control it?" My voice slowly let the words roll out of my mouth.

Virgil sighed and then said. "I'm going to help you." Then he looked towards the ground, a hint of worry in his eye. I couldn't tell if he was scared or apprehensive, but whatever it was, Virgil looked legitimately concerned.

"Why don't you sound confident when you say that?" I asked him.

Virgil froze like a statue for a long moment and then looked straight at me. It was as if his eyes were trying to impress upon me something of dire importance. "James, those who lose themselves in emotion open themselves up to being taken by power." My brow furrowed, not exactly sure what Virgil was talking about, he must have noticed my confusion because he continued. "Those things out there—," his hand gestured to the outside. "—the wolves. Those animals were once men like you. The story goes, they were driven mad by the power The Shade granted them, and it slowly transformed their outside into the ravenous beasts that they were on the inside—,"

Virgil's story shocked me.

Is that true?

Slowly the question circulated through my head as Virgil's words continued to fill my ears. "—but becoming a beast inside isn't the worst thing that can happen. Sometimes, every so often a person so foul comes along that even The Shade can't twist. They let the power overtake them until there is nothing left of the person they once were."

"You're talking about Burke aren't you?" I asked.

Virgil nodded his head in the affirmative. "Yes."

I didn't even know where to begin with the new information.

"Am I just like Burke? Am I just a time bomb waiting for the day that I'll lose myself and everyone I care about, all because the power overwhelms me?" I questioned as the thought bounced around in my head.

"James. I'm not going to let that happen. I'm not going to let you do anything that's not your choice, do you understand me?" He said with an amount of concern in his eyes I'd never seen before.

"yes—," my voice said quietly as I shook my head.

"Good." Virgil said as he got back to his feet and walked towards the hallway. "I'm going to check the rest of the house. You rest up. We've got a lot to do." He told me as he disappeared into the hall.

My head leaned back against the wall once more and my eyes focused on the ceiling. I breathed out a heavy sigh as my eyes shut. I knew that Virgil had said he wouldn't let me succumb to anything that wasn't my choice but his words didn't make me feel any better. The only thing my mind could focus on as I slowly drifted off to sleep was—,

Maybe I'm more like Burke than I thought, and if that's the case, what hope do I have of beating him?

XX

My heartbeat picked up speed as I sprinted through the forest. My feet hit the ground with violent force, each step making my location clear as I ran. My eyes glanced behind me to try to figure out where *it* had gone. I caught a glimpse of nothing and as far as I could tell, there wasn't anything chasing me through the forest. Then with a sudden sigh of relief, my legs allowed me to stop in a large clearing. My eyes paced back and forth, as they tried to discern where *it* had gone. My lungs grabbed for air, taking in deep breaths one after the other, my heartbeat never slowed. There was a rustle from the woods behind me. Quickly my hands snapped up to defend myself.

But it was too late.

Before I could move, *it* had grabbed me. Slowly my body was sucked down, down into the darkness that surrounded the creature. My chest ran cold, my heartbeat went faint, and as the darkness reached my throat, I could feel the cold air being pulled from my lungs.

Then I let out one last gasp before the darkness consumed me.

My eyes shot open as I awoke in a cold sweat. Slowly I tried to wipe the beads of sweat from my forehead but my hand was too clammy, so it didn't help. It had been a month since the day in the field with the wolves. Since that time, Virgil had showed me how to defend myself more effectively. He stressed control over my emotions and every time I began to lose myself, we stopped our training to meditate, letting me rest for the remainder of the day. I wasn't sure, but it almost felt as if Virgil was frightened of my loss of control. I figured that was why I'd been having the same nightmare for over a month. It always started the same way, with me in a forest, alone. Then one of the specters began to chase me, but it didn't matter how fast I ran, because I'm always caught, always dragged into the darkness, always killed. It seemed to coincide with my fear of losing control. Like one day, my loss of control would catch up to me, find me, and ultimately, destroy me.

Virgil had done his best—given the short amount of time we had together—to show me how to control my emotion. Instead of focusing on things that made me angry, Virgil had taught me a meditation technique that focused on me remaining calm and serene. Everyday was a new lesson with Virgil, and everyday it felt like I could run just a little bit faster from that darkness that chased me through the forest.

My mouth felt dry as my lungs tried to breathe in, the room was cold, and because I was alone, I let out a long sigh and let my head fall back to the pillow. My eyes closed slowly while my brain tried to work out the bugs that had definitely affected it.

My hands met my forehead once more and I ran my fingers through my short hair. The sensation felt good, it had been such a long time since I had actually felt something and even the simple sensations had become more meaningful. The Shade was cold and dead, sometimes I thought about how easy it would be to lose who I was as a person.

If I hadn't lost it already.

I sat up on the couch and pondered what The Shade could do to a person who was willing to do anything to survive. I knew that it had warped Virgil and Burke; it's easy to see the effects of The Shade on a person trapped there for so long. I knew the only way to be absolutely certain of The Shades affects on me would only come in retrospect. I thought about the idea for a minute then let it fade from my mind. I wasn't sure what separated me from the creatures of The Shade, but if they had once been human my only thought was they must have lost something essential inside themselves. I glanced around the dark living room and noticed Virgil's absence. He had been nice enough to let me sleep, even though he had expressed on numerous occasions that sleep was useless in The Shade. However, like most things the more someone says not to do something the more you'll be inclined to do just that. This, in and of itself would have been fine, if my mind didn't conjure up dysfunctional dreams every time I closed my eyes.

Nevertheless, my body felt rested and I was grateful for that. Each day Virgil's training had become more intense, forcing more out of me. I felt a time crunch, as if Virgil knew the fast approaching fight with Burke was coming and he knew that I wasn't ready. Every day that passed felt like an eternity and every day I grew more and more concerned about Angela and my family. My concern being, that if Burke knew what we were up to, he could use them as an advantage against me.

Why not? I'd do it if I was in his shoes.

Virgil had assured me on numerous occasions that Angela was fine. Shaun, being Angela's cousin put her in the best position possible to be protected against Burke. My feet laid flat across the arm of the small couch. As the days passed, my memory had begun to unscramble itself. Every time I recovered memories however, it felt like someone trying to kabob my head with a white-hot poker.

After I got over the pain, my memories from before my crash began to fall into place. I could remember the woods, and hearing something that made me hurry back to my truck. I also remembered talking to Angela on the phone.

But there were still gaps.

A loud slam came from the front door, followed by the stomp of shoes on the hardwood floor as they made their way into the living room. Virgil entered the room, walked to his chair and sat down. He never looked up to acknowledge my awakened state; instead, he decided to stare at the floor as if he and it were having some sort of contest.

I wasn't sure, but I knew the floor would win if he looked long enough.

After a short while, Virgil finally looked up at me, his face wore a blank expression. One of horror mixed with desperation.

Things are worse than I thought.

Virgil had sat in his dusty armchair for a few minutes without a move.

What is he thinking?

My mind wanted to break the silence of the room, given a few more minutes and maybe I would have. "James." He said.

Seems like I wasn't the only one thinking that.

"Yes?" I answered.

"Tomorrow is the day." He said simply.

"Wait, you mean *the day*?" I asked, trying to clarify what made tomorrow, 'the day'.

"Yeah, Shaun's going to send members of the family to the hospital tomorrow to wake you up, which means we need to talk." He told me. My mind went into an all out blitz and for the first time in a long time, I felt excited to receive news from Virgil. My heart began to pound inside of my chest at the thought of finally going home. It was finally time to put everything that Virgil had taught me to work and I couldn't believe it.

"Has it really been five months?" I asked.

"No, we've had to accelerate our plan, which is why we need to talk." He told me.

"Something's changed in the plan?" I asked.

"No, not exactly. The family will still be taking you off your medication tomorrow." He explained. "After you wake up, Shaun's people should have stashed a weapon tucked in between your hospital mattress. Make sure no one sees you, locate Burke, and finish him off. You'll have to be quick about it, if Burke notices that you're gone, our shot is blown. All you need is one shot; when his guards down, you kill him." He told me.

"So why have we been training so hard here if I'm kill him out there?" I motioned upwards as if the real world had some sort of direction.

"Everything I've shown you has strengthened your mind." He told me. "You'll be sharper, faster, even in the real world. You'll also feel the effects of the residual DMT inside you, the effect will be limited, but they will allow you to do some of the things we can do here."

I breathed a sigh of relief.

It was reassuring that Virgil had trained me to defend myself at least a little against Burke. Virgil rose from his chair and walked towards me, stopping about half way across the room. He looked at me with an inquisitive look as if he wanted to tell me something important. My eyes focused hard on him for a moment to see if he'd say what was obviously on his mind; he remained silent. "Alright." My voice was quiet as I tried to convince myself he had all of his bases covered.

Virgil bent down and looked at me. "James, you can do this." His words sounded genuinely reassuring. "I've never seen anyone progress as quickly as you. If anyone can do this, it's you."

Even with Virgil's confidence in me I still felt as if I was going to be a lone fish in a narrow barrel. My head hit the back of the couch once more and my eyes focused on the wall. A few minutes passed and I let my eyes drift back over to Virgil. His hand was clinched in a fist and slowly rubbing his knuckles against his palm. His eyes were looking elsewhere so he hadn't noticed me. His hand fidgeted almost out of nervous habit.

That was the last thing I remember.

The next thing that my eyes saw was the hardwood floor. My nostrils blew up dust from the dirty floor as the pain in my head began to magnify. Virgil was over top of me in an instant. "James, are you alright?" The sound of his voice was muffled in my ears as he rolled me over onto my back. The pain in my head forced my hands over my face. My brain felt like someone had stuck a thousand needles in it at once and sent an electric charge through me. "James. Hey can you hear me?" Virgil said as he snapped his fingers at me. My head slowly stopped throbbing and everything around me returned to focus. "Are you alright?" Virgil said, as he stood wide-eyed over me.

I breathed heavily, each breath coming to me easier than the one before it. "I remember." I said over the sound of my heavy breath. "I remember everything." It was clear that at some point my body must have rolled off the couch and landed on the floor, which must have triggered the memories of what happened before my accident. Virgil looked at me as my eyes fluttered back into focus. My body sat back upright and slowly I got back up and to my feet.

"Are you okay?" Virgil asked.

Physically I was fine, but mentally it was as if someone had crammed another set of all new memories inside my head. Everything had fallen into place; every second of my lost memory had come back to me. "What happened?" I asked rubbing my head.

"You were sitting on the couch and you just rolled off. Then I flipped you over to make sure you were alright." He told me.

"The fall—," my hand rubbed the back of my head as I sat back down on the couch. "—it must have jogged my memory. I remember everything from before my crash." I told Virgil.

Virgil moved back to his chair and sat down. "My truck flipped." I told him. "But before that, there was something in the cab with me, something different. Like a shadow that wasn't quite there. Like something you couldn't see unless you were looking out of the corner of your eye. It was there but only to let you know you weren't alone." My voice shook as the pieces in my mind fell into place. Virgil just looked at me, his eyes wide as I explained the details of my newly recovered memories.

He stared for so long I thought he wasn't looking at me at all, but instead just staring off into space. His eyes worked over me with the same concerned look that he'd given me before. Again, he seemed to want to tell me something but then shrugged it off and said. "Sounds like a ghost." He said abruptly.

"A ghost—," the words trickled out from my mouth. "—why would a ghost want anything to do with me?"

"I'm not sure, but it doesn't concern me and it shouldn't concern you." He tried to brush the topic under the proverbial rug. A heavy sigh left my lips.

There's more to this. I know it.

Something inside of me, maybe something on the subconscious level knew this memory was important. "What if the ghost is working with Burke? What if it helped him put me here and it's going to help him again when I get out?" I told him. The argument was solid, something even Virgil couldn't dismiss without a proper explanation.

"Don't jump to conclusions. The two things could be completely unrelated." He told me.

To which I replied. "And they could be absolutely related."

Virgil let out a long huff of air then said. "Burke wouldn't use a ghost to get you here—,"

"—but what if—," I tried to interrupt.

Virgil held up his hand at me. "—He's powerful enough to get you here on his own he wouldn't need to employ another super natural being." Virgil's logic made me angry. Not because I was mad at him, but more because it was hard to argue with. "James, it's not like he'd taken notice of you before your accident. He wasn't stalking you." He finally said.

My head told me that what he was saying was logical, but my heart reminded me of the emotion I'd felt in my truck. As much as I wanted to dismiss what I was feeling for Virgil's logical explanation, I couldn't. "I'd gone to the woods before going to Angela's. I heard—and felt something; I think that's where the ghost came from."

Virgil rolled his eyes at me. "James, just drop this." My brow furrowed at his sudden remark. "Why are you getting so defensive?" I asked.

"I'm not getting defensive—I just want you to focus on what's important." His voice was even when he spoke. He showed no sign of hesitation and because he didn't I decided not to push the subject any longer. My mind told my instincts to stop worrying about the ghost and do as Virgil had asked.

Focus.

"Alright." I told him. He was satisfied I had conceded the argument and given up on the whole thing. He left the room and as he did, my head laid back down against the armrest of the dusty couch. I knew the plan, I knew what I had to do, and the only thing left to do was wait.

A few hours went by. I didn't sleep. Not that I wasn't tired, but I had too much to think about to sleep. I watched from the living room couch as Virgil paced from the front door, through the hallway which led to the living room and then into the kitchen. He'd done it over a dozen times which was just long enough for me to stop him and say something about it.

"Can I ask you something?" I asked as he passed from

the hallway into the living room. He looked over at me and nodded at me to ask. "What will happen to you, once Burke's dead?"

Had I been walking, Virgil's gaze would have stopped me dead in my tracks. From the look he gave me, it was clear that he hadd never thought of the scenario before. He'd never thought of a world outside of The Shade. That's when I finally realized why he'd pushed me so hard. He didn't want me to have the same life he'd had.

For that, I thanked him.

"Nothing, after he's dead I'll have what I want." He told me.

"I'm not asking if you'd have everything you want. I'm asking if you are going to be alright."

"Oh." He said somewhat startled by the question. "I guess I will be. We'll wake up and then we can meet in person."

"How long has it been since you've been back?" I asked.

"Too long." His voice trailed off.

I let his voice fade into background noise and then decided to switch the subject. "How much longer do I have—you know, before I wake up?" I asked. Virgil stopped the aimless pacing that he'd been dedicated to for the past hour and came into the living room.

"The family is going to stop your drip tonight. Given the amount of time it will take for it to work its way out of your system it should only be a few hours from now."

"How is it going to happen?" I asked.

"Well you can just fall asleep and when you wake up, you'll be back in the hospital." He explained. Virgil glanced at the front door. My eyes caught this action and I squinted at him trying to figure out what he was doing. "Have you been outside today?" Virgil asked as he noticed my curiosity.

"I've been here all day—," I motioned to the couch. "—Why?"

Virgil hesitated for a moment and then a small smile began to spread across his face. "Come with me." My head cocked to the side as I tried to understand what he could want to show me. He walked back out of the living room, down the hall towards the front door. From the end of the hallway, I heard. "Are you coming?"

I sat up on the couch and got to my feet. I strolled down the hallway to meet up with Virgil who stood by the door. He turned the knob and slowly opened the door to something truly unbelievable. Instead of the usual bright light that would have blinded me as the door opened. My eyes were met by a faint blue calm. I stepped out onto the porch and looked at the sky.

The sky was dark. Not the kind of darkness that occurred when the sun was obscured by clouds, it was a brand new kind of darkness. The sky was filled with tiny little lights each one twinkling bright in the blackness. The darkness that overtook the sky seemed to stretch out forever and then Virgil directed my attention to the dark glowing ball in the sky. "It's an eclipse." He told me.

"An eclipse?" I stammered.

"I've only seen it happen a few times before." He told me.

"So it's special, when was the last one?" I asked.

Virgil didn't speak immediately. Then turned to me and then said. "The last one happened the day before I found you. Seems like a proper farewell." I stared into the blackness that seemed to engulf the sky. My eyes traced every star and constellation, it reminded me of home, and it reminded me of her. One memory in particular stood out from all others.

My eyes looked back towards Virgil. "Virgil, do you think I could fall asleep out here?"

"If that's what you want, I can make sure nothing happens to you if you'd like." He offered. I looked at Virgil, his eyes met mine, I knew he'd have done anything I'd asked. It was a last request and even Virgil wouldn't have denied it.

"Go ahead, I'll be over here." He said pointing to the porch.

I nodded to him and he sat down on the cold cement of the porch. Slowly I walked into the front yard. Once I found a suitable position my body laid down in the grass. Sprawled out on the grass in front of the house, I let my fingertips move over every blade. I looked at the shining lights in the sky for a good thirty minutes until I began to feel faint. My eyes blinked as they began to feel heavy, I shut them, and waited. A white light engulfed me and on the other side of oblivion, there was my life, my family and one last score to settle.

XXI

My eyes opened to see the bright red of the autumn evening sky, like flames that shot from one end of the heavens to the other, seeming to stretch on into eternity. It was early February, seven before the accident.

I sat up on the blanket that was neatly laid out, waiting patiently. I had waited a long time for that moment, and I knew nothing was going to screw it up. I'd laid the blanket down in our usual spot and told Angela to meet me when the sun started to set, not because I was some sort of romantic but because I truly had no idea when the sun actually set. Our spot was one of the few places that provided us a decent view. The crackle of leaves betrayed her and I knew that she was near.

"Hello?" I said. She stumbled through the brush and finally appeared to me.

"James." She muttered with a half smile on her face. Her smile was breathtaking; I had never seen anything quite like it before in my life. The way her eyes looked against the sunset was something of absolute beauty and brilliance, something that rivaled the sun itself. My smile met hers and she ran for me, with her out stretched arms she tackled me.

"Well hello ma'am." I said in the cheesiest southern draw I could muster. She lay on top of me for a few extra seconds then kissed my forehead.

"Well sir, why did you make me hike all the way out here?" she asked.

"I'm not sure. Just thought we could have a romantic evening in the woods."

She smiled and rolled off me, now with our backs to the earth we stared at each other. She grinned at me and I brushed her hair back over her ear. I leaned in and kissed her lips, and felt a warm sensation like a shock through my entire body. My face pulled away from hers and I looked into her eyes. I would have done anything to stay in that moment forever with her. She smiled at me with a large grin, which made my heart race. There was nothing that made me feel more alive than being with her; the sunset and the wilderness were just an added bonus.

"What are you smiling about?" I said playfully.

"Guess what I did yesterday?" She said to me.

"I don't know. What did you do?" I said giving her a peck on the lips.

"I set up a college visit a few months from now—," she said excited. "—with Dartmouth."

I had been recognized by Dartmouth at the start of my Junior year. They had recommended that I apply after my junior year for their early acceptance program, which usually meant they were interested enough in a person that they would get in. Angela and I had thought we'd have to be separated because she was going to apply to Oregon State. Sufficed to say, I was happy to hear she had a chance to go to the same college as me. The thought of being away from her for an extensive amount of time seemed unbearable, this was because it wasn't until a few months ago that I realized I loved Angela. I knew I wanted to go to school, get a job, and one day marry her.

I leaned down and kissed her forehead. "That's great, so you might not be able to run away from me after all." I smiled.

THE SHADE

"You know I'm not the one running away." She said as she squeezed me.

I smiled at her and she smiled back. If I didn't need food or water I could have stayed there with her forever. My lips met hers and we kissed, this time my lips lingered around hers a few extra moments just so I could be close to her. "You're beautiful." I told her.

"Oh stop it." She blushed. Her face turned redder than they had been from the cold. Her rose colored cheeks shown against her skin and only intensified the glow that she emitted. I never was able to find the right words to describe how I felt when I was around Angela. Somewhere between immeasurable happiness and pure bliss was about right. She was always there for me, during the hard times she comforted me, and during the good times, she was there to hold my hand and smile along with me.

"I'm glad we can stay together." I said as she pulled herself in closer.

"Of course we'd stay together James." She kissed my nose. "You're the greatest guy I've met." I smiled and I knew from the way Angela looked at me that I had blushed, but I didn't care. She was mine and I hers, that's the way it was always going to stay.

"So you never told me." She said.

"Never told you what?"

"You never told me why I had to hike all the way out here." She explained.

"Well—," I stammered. "—the reason was—," I pursed my lips as I tried to think of the right words.

"Just spit it out." She said with a smile.

I fumbled in my coat for a few seconds until I found the parcel. It was a long box. Once my fingers touched it, I grabbed it and yanked it from my jacket. I pulled it out and when Angela saw the box, she covered her nose and mouth with both hands.

"James," She said with a very soft voice. "What's that?"

"Well I know you like older things, and I saw this and thought you might like it." I said. I removed the lid of the box, inside was an old necklace. The necklace was made of silver, a bit tarnished but that only added to its authenticity. There was a pendent on the end, a bright blue stone set in an oval of silver. The stone seemed to catch the light at every angle and make it dance around the forest. I removed it from the box.

"Do you like it?" I asked.

"James," She said. "Of course, I love it." She smiled at me as she came in to give me a hug. Her arms wrapped around me and made me feel like the luckiest man alive. I had the love of a beautiful girl, and better yet, she loved me back. That was all I needed.

"May I?" I asked with a motion to put the necklace on. She turned herself around and pulled her hair up out of the way from the back of her neck. I draped the necklace over her and fastened the two ends together. Then I kissed the nape of her neck and turned her around.

"Are you sure that it's alright?" I asked.

"Of course I'm sure, it's perfect." She said as she threw her arms around my neck and kissed me. She tackled me so hard that I toppled to the ground again. She lay on top of me and kissed me again and again. She rolled off me and we sat side-by-side my hand in hers.

"So what's the stone made of?" She asked as she prodded at it with her finger.

"I'm honestly not sure, the woman from the store said it was some kind of special stone." I told her.

"Special how?" She said in a very playful voice.

"Well my dear." I said. "She said it was once used to trap the good spirits in it and protect you from the bad ones."

"That's really nice; I always need protecting from bad spirits." She said in a jocular fashion.

"I also got it for the color." I laughed.

"I assumed." She smiled at me. She continued to look at the stone that seemed to shine, even in the dimly lit evening air. The stone sparkled as if it were alive.

Maybe there are good spirits inside the stone after all.

I hoped it would always keep us together, that it would be something that always reminded her of me and me of her. Something that connected us, no matter the distance between us; making sure, we were always in each other's lives. We sat beside each other the rest of the evening, my hand in hers; occasionally stopping to watch the setting sun and exchange a kiss. It's how I'd always wanted to feel with someone. The warm light from the sun kept the forest illuminated much longer than I'd thought. The shadows of the trees danced as we watched the sun recede behind the hills and then vanish altogether.

The early twilight was chilly, so we had decided to go back to the park entrance. We walked slowly through the woods towards our vehicles. I had my flashlight to help us over broken limbs and fallen trees. Angela hummed with excitement, I wasn't exactly sure why. Did she want to tell her friends she had a romantic time in the woods with me, or about the necklace she had received? Whatever the reason she was electric, and it made me smile.

"Why are you so smiley boy?" She asked as she danced through the forest.

"I'm just watching you." I said.

"And that makes you smile?"

"Yes, always does." I responded.

She smiled at me and continued to walk. It took us about a half hour to find our way out of the forest, by the time we reached the vehicles the moon had replaced the sun as our light. I walked Angela around to her car door. I pulled it open but she leaned against it causing it to close. I put my arms around her and kissed her lips softly.

"Thank you for coming here tonight." I told her.

"You don't have to thank me silly." She said as she smiled. Then she rose up on her toes and kissed my forehead. She pulled back and giggled for a second. Her hair fell in front of her face. My hand brushed it aside so I could see her better.

Her eyes were pale in the glow of the moon light, her cheeks and nose cold from the autumn air had changed to a red color.

"Are you cold?" I asked.

She nodded her head.

Of course she's cold, it's like forty degrees out here.

I took off the old cotton jacket I normally wore and placed it on her shoulders.

"This should keep you warm." I said with a smile.

"Aw James, you didn't have to do that." She said in a sort of protest, but seemed to take more joy that she was warm now and she let her protests die. "What about you?"

"I'll be fine." I told her. It was actually cold that night, I had to hide how cold I really was until I could get in my truck and turn on the heater. "Well I suppose this is goodnight." I flashed a big smile at her.

"I suppose it is." She smiled back. I moved in towards her lips and she met mine. It was a long kiss; I didn't want to part with her lips. We finally moved back from each other and she laughed. She threw her arms around my neck and kissed me again.

"I could get used to this." I said.

"We'll I'm glad you haven't already."

"Even if I did, I'd never tire of it."

I opened her car door. "Ma'am your carriage." I said as I motioned for her to get inside. Angela played along; she curtsied then got into her car. I shut the door when she was in. She rolled down her window and looked at me.

"What?" I asked.

"Nothing, just checking you out."

"Well take a good look; I'm not some piece of meat." I taunted. Then I leaned down and kissed her one last time. When we separated, I hovered to look at her eyes then shot her a grin. I stood back upright and hit the top of the car twice to signal it was time to go. She waved as she drove off into the distance until her tail lights faded into the fog.

I went to my truck and climbed in. My body shook because

of the cold, so I turned the heater on full blast and thought of only one thing, Angela. I started the engine and backed out of the woods. It was already eleven o'clock, I was sure my parents wondered where I was but I didn't care. For that one night everything was right in the world, there were no distractions, no consequences for actions, just Angela and me. I prayed that one day my life could be as simple as that day, I drove all the way home and collapsed on my bed and closed my eyes. A warm light overtook me and then a shape came into focus behind my eyes.

It wasn't a part of my original memory of that night, it was something new, something added. It looked like a detailed shadow, an outline from my memory. Then I realized I'd seen the shadow before. It was the shadow from my truck and all at once, I knew exactly what the shadow was.

PART III:
RESOLUTE

"He is a man of courage who does not run away,
but remains at his post and fights against the enemy."

-Socrates

XXII

A blinding light replaced the darkness that had overcome me. The electrical impulses in my brain suddenly kicked into overdrive, telling my muscles it was time to get up, time to move. A surge of energy pulsed through my body and as I surge with new life, the pain from the accident made itself known to me. There was a sharp ache in my left leg and a brief numbness in my left arm. Suddenly without warning, my body was under my control.

"The shadow!" My voice scratched out. As my eyes darted around the room, my heartbeat hammered away like a steady drum in my chest. I rolled over on my right side and stared at my hands.

Virgil was right. I still have all my fingers.

With that out of the way, I pulled up the side of my mattress looking for the firearm that was supposed to be stashed in my room. The mattress was heavy, and my muscles felt weak as they lifted it. My hand had pulled back the bedding, but my eyes were met with only the mattress underneath.

Where's the gun? Why isn't it here?!

I instantly began to panic, almost lapsing into a state of

shock. It seemed like it had been forever since I'd used my real body, coming with all the defects that had not ailed me in The Shade. I could feel every crick, every bruise, and aching joint. It was as if I was hyper-aware of every single problem in my newly awakened body. The Shade had given me reprieve from the aches' of everyday life, but in the real world, those aches felt like even more like a burden. My eyes quickly searched for the missing firearm, until suddenly, I heard a voice. "James?"

The voice came from the left. Through all of the excitement, I hadn't noticed the person sitting next to me. My body rolled to my left to investigate the sound.

It was Angela.

My eyes must not have been fully adjusted to the light because the soft glow of the fluorescents seemed to create a halo that surrounded her face. The outline around her face was so beautiful I momentarily forget how to communicate. My eyes stared at her and my heart began to take huge leaps in my chest.

What is she doing here, and where is the gun?

My heart continued to pound against my chest as I tried to think of a way to get Angela out of the room. I needed time to search for the gun, but one look at her told me that she wouldn't be swayed to leave. I figured Shaun's people could have placed the gun in a number of different spots below the bed and it could take some time for me to find it, time I didn't have. Instead, my mind snapped to the next best thing, a plan B if you will.

I'll get Dad's gun, come back here and finish this.

The plan wasn't much, but it was all I had, and as I stared up into Angela's eyes I knew I would have convince her to help me escape the hospital. My heartbeat began to lower as I let out a slow breath, trying to center myself. Angela looked as if she were in shock and she began to tear up without the look of sudden excitement leaving her face. "James, are you okay?" She asked as she broke out into a full-blown sob. My voice cracked as I tried to say something, but nothing but a raspy moan exited my throat. "James, sit still and drink this."

She handed me a cup of water and then hovered over me for a long moment. I coughed as I choked down the water. Her face looked like a combination of happiness and worried which only made me concerned about what had happened while I was asleep.

"Ang—Angela." I cough out the rest of whatever had blocked my throat. My eyes focused on her and suddenly my mouth formed into a smile. My arms lifted up towards her and she needed no instruction about what to do next. Her arms wrapped around my body and mine around hers. I could feel the faint flutter of her heartbeat against my chest. Angela looked up at me, her face filled with tears.

This is what I waited months for.

"James how do you feel, I can get the doctor for you." She said.

My eyes snapped open wide and I suddenly remembered what I was doing. "No, please. I'm alright." I answered weakly. I touched my arms to remove any drips or IV's, but to my surprise, there were none. I looked over to the EKG machine that sat by my bed, it wasn't connected to me. My eyes traced the wires back to their source until I finally came to a small black box that had been tucked under my bed, no gun in sight.

Shaun's people must have rigged this up so when I woke up the hospital staff wouldn't be alerted.

In fact, other than the misplaced pistol, Shaun's people had removed all my drips and IV's, even my feeding tube, before I had awoken. The pure fact that Shaun could orchestrate something of that magnitude both scared and comforted me. "I'm going to get someone to check you out really quick okay?" She said as I held the black box. Her intention was good but as she walked towards the door, I knew I had to stop her. Slowly my body tried to shuffle off the bed, my legs swung around and I placed them on the ground. My legs tried to stand up on their own but they shook violently. As I let go of the bed, my legs wobbled and then my body collapsed towards the floor.

Angela caught me before I hit the ground. I knew my bedridden body had lost some muscle mass but until I actually tried to use my body again, I didn't know how severe it was.

"James I'm happy you're awake but I need to get you the doctor." She told me with a smile on her face and a teary look in her eyes.

"Please don't get the doctor." I tried to calm myself as I spoke. My voice almost came out as a whisper, I hadn't meant it to, but it was hard to control. "I'm sorry I jumped out of bed, can you help me back up?" I knew the next words out of my mouth were going to make or break the whole plan. "Do you trust me?" I asked. Her eyes began to size me up. I knew the look; it was the same look that a normal person gives to someone who's obviously insane. "Do you trust me?" I repeated.

After a moment, she finally said. "Yes. What's going on?" It was easy to see she was worried about me and I couldn't blame her. The tears that had come down her face had now dried which made her cheek look as if it was shining.

"I'll explain everything. Did you drive yourself here?" I questioned.

"James do you know where you are?" She asked. That was a set of questions I'd wanted to avoid. I didn't have time to waste trying to explain every detail of what was really going on. "You know you were in a coma right?" She questioned again.

A heavy sigh left my lips and then said. "I'm in the hospital. I've been in a coma for the past few months and I'm thinking very clearly. I know all of these things but what I really need right now is to get out of here. No doctors, no nurses, just me and you." Angela looked stunned at my sudden clarity. She stood with a dumbfounded look on her face that told me she was going to take some convincing. "Please I'll explain everything when we leave we just have to go." I reassured her.

"But James we—,"

"I know it sounds crazy Angie but please."

"Fine we can go, but you have to explain everything." She demanded.

THE SHADE

Quickly, before she could change her mind, I said. "Deal." At that point, I'd have agreed to just about anything to get out of the room. She helped me walk with her arms wrapped around my body.

Her eyes suddenly looked up at mine. "It's good to see you again." She said with a smile.

"It's good to be seen."

We walked out into the hallway, it was eerily empty, but you could still tell the hospital was alive with color. It was such a contrast from the hospital in The Shade. Even the colorless white walls seemed to be beautiful compared to the rusted world I had left. We started to move quickly down the hallway, towards the back exit of the hospital. I assumed either it was past normal visiting hours or it had been lunchtime because of the emptiness in the hallways. Then, through a nearby window I noticed the sun coming in, which told me it was the latter.

We shambled quickly down the hallway. I had no extra clothes to change into, so I was still in my hospital gown.

Thanks for that Shaun.

We tried our best not to provoke any unnecessary attention as we left. The hospital wasn't very large, so it didn't take long to get to the staircase that lead down to the first floor lobby. We went down the stairs and once we reached the bottom, I opened the door slightly, poking my head out to see if the coast was clear, of course it wasn't. "Angie, there's only one doctor standing in the lobby, if you can distract him I can slip out the front." I told her.

"And what am I supposed to do?" She said as if suddenly she had realized it was mistake to be helping me sneak out of the hospital.

"I don't know, just make sure that he doesn't see me leaving, the rest is really up to you." I told her. She glared a familiar glare at me for a brief moment then turned to walk out of the door. Her walk morphed into a gleeful bounce as she approached the doctor. The conversation was clear as day. "Excuse me." Angela said as she tapped the doctor on the shoulder. "Which way is it to the west wing of the building?" She asked even though she knew full well where the west wing was, because that was where we had just been. It had made me smile a tiny bit when she asked the question. Angela was by no means stupid, so the thought of her needing help with a task so simple was humorous.

"Here I'll show you on a map." The doctor said as he motioned towards one of the maps on the wall. I poked my head out once more to see if her ploy had worked. Angela noticed me and gave me a wink to let me know I was clear to leave. Slowly I crept out of the stairwell and through the lobby. There weren't many people in the waiting room, only an old man reading the local newspaper and a young man absorbed with whatever he was scribbling to notice much else. I passed through the sliding glass doors and out of the hospital.

The light outside was almost unbearable, I had not used my real eyes for so long they took longer than normal to adjust. Each breeze that passed welcomed back smells that I'd long forgot about while I was in The Shade. It was like being born again, seeing the world through fresh eyes, I knew that life was something fragile and sometimes stripped from us, so we had to make the most of it.

"James!" Angela called from behind me as she ran to catch up to me.

"Where's your car?"

"Don't ever make me do that again." She said. "And just so you know I'm not going to forget about our deal." She wrapped her arms around me and gave me a hug that could have crushed someone. She buried her face deep into my chest and spoke softly. "Don't you ever scare me like that again, you aren't going to go anywhere without me." I wanted to hold her; there was nothing else at that moment I wanted more. I wanted to tell her everything was all right; however, before I could do anything my mind shot a sharp pain into my frontal lobe.

I had already broken one of Virgil's rules about seeing people. It couldn't be helped, so he'd have to understand, but there were still things that needed to be done. With those things invading my mind, I reached for Angela's shoulders slowly peeled her away from me and with a slight smile and in a calm voice, I asked. "Where are you parked?" Angela took out her keys and as she did, she began to walk. We jetted across the parking lot to the small silver Honda that had minor scrapes on the side from when she ran into my neighbor's mailbox.

I thought I'd never see this little car again.

"Get in." She told me; I did as she commanded. "Where to?" She asked as she pulled out of the parking space.

"Home—," I trailed off as I got in my own thoughts, home is where the gun is, get the gun, and kill Burke. Get the gun, kill Burke. Get the gun, kill Burke. I repeated the words again and again like a mantra.

We traveled for about five minutes in complete silence until Angela spoke up. "Are you going to explain what's going on? Why did I just help you break out of a hospital?" She asked. I looked over at her and smiled, her brow was half furrowed which told me that she was worried.

"I didn't want them to call my parents." I told her, which was halfway true anyway. The one thing that Virgil had taught me that really stuck was the ability to bend the truth.

"Why not? They're going to be relieved when they find out you're awake." She rebutted. The statement would have been true under any other circumstances, but me being awake put their lives in danger.

"It's not for them it's for me. Angie I'm not safe and there's so much I have to do."

"Like?" She questioned.

"I'm not sure if telling you is the best idea." I mumbled.

"James I'm here to help you, but you need to tell me what's going on." Her voice was quiet.

Where do I begin?

I knew I couldn't lead off with—oh while I was in a coma I was on another plain of existence and by the way monsters and ghosts exist as well. In addition to that—Dr. Burke wants to harvest my brain. Even I would think I was crazy. "Have you ever had an out of body experience?" I asked her.

Her eyes closed as I asked the question. "Like have I ever seen my body from outside of my body?—No, I haven't." Angela said with a sigh as she suddenly realized I had gone totally insane.

"This is going to sound crazy—," my hands covered my face.

Here goes nothing.

"—while I was in the coma I wasn't fully there, my body was here—," I thought for a moment how to phrase what I wanted to say without sounding as if I'd completely lost it. "—in the hospital I mean. But my mind wasn't."

"Are you telling me you went to heaven? Saw bright lights and a tunnel?"

"I wasn't in heaven. I'm just talking about another plain of existence." She looked at me with eyes that showed half worry and half sadness. I could tell she was having a hard time believing what I'd said, who wouldn't. "I can't explain it Ang." I started.

Angela put her finger up to hush me.

I remained quiet.

"Let me try and process this." She peered out the front of the car. She had wanted answers but she had never expected the ones I had given her. I thought about what to say to her and after five long antagonizing minutes, I finally decided to say something.

"Angela, I'm sorry." I said. "I know it sounds insane but everything I'm telling you is true. You just have to trust me." She turned to look at me and her eyes looked as if she wanted to believe me. "I've never given you a reason not to trust me and there was a time when we told each other everything." I pleaded with her. "I don't know how to say what I want to say to you so I'm just asking for your trust."

She looked back out to the road then after a long pause she said. "I believe you."

"What was that?" I asked half surprised with my head cocked.

"I said I believe you James, you heard me." She said with a smile beginning to grow on her face. I smiled back at her, it had been a long time since I had smiled at her, and it felt good.

"Thank you." I said quietly.

"What was that?"

"You heard what I said." I told her with a smirk. "Thank you." I said more clearly.

"You're welcome."

"Thank you." I said, so softly it was almost inaudible.

We drove out of the city, passed the apartments and businesses Virgil and I had fought our way through. Eventually the cityscape dwindled and changed into open fields and houses with big yards. Slowly we closed in on my parent's house. Every inch we moved closer only served to make my body feel tenser. My hands began to sweat and could feel myself get warmer and warmer. I caught eyes with Angela and she noticed I looked worried.

"Are you alright?" She asked.

"Yes I'm alright. I'm just a little worried about going home."

"Do you want to call your parents?"

"No." I said. "This is something I've got to do."

We approached the house. Its odd shape and features stood out more than ever before. Angela got out of the car first but I sat in the passenger's seat frozen; my eyes locked on the unopened garage door. I'm not sure why my body couldn't move, but it felt as if I had been glued to my seat. The door to the car opened. My head shook, breaking my trance. Angela looked down at me; her eyes asked if I was coming. I got out of the car with her and we made our way to the front door. My hands groped for my pockets and that's when I found there weren't any. My eyes glanced down and remembered I was still wearing the hospital gown.

"You still have the key?" I asked Angela. Angela found the key on her key ring and unlocked the front door. We walked into the house. A sudden wave of emotion washed over me that was almost overwhelming.

"You're sure you're fine?" Angela asked.

"I'm fine. I'll be alright."

"Why are we here?" She asked.

"I'll be right back, please just wait here." I smiled. Angela didn't reciprocate the smile but instead gave me a look that said she was not pleased with what was going on.

"What's going on?" She asked. "Why did I come here if you don't need me?"

"Ang, I just need to grab some things then we can leave okay?" I smiled again and again she didn't smile back, she just looked a little bit less annoyed.

I turned away from Angela and headed towards my father's room. I was sure his back up handgun would be there. I opened the door to the room and went inside. The metal box that housed the handgun was normally under the bed. I knelt down and looked. The metal case was right where it was supposed to be. My hands pulled it towards myself and then sat it upright. The combination hadn't changed; it was my birthday an easy set of numbers for me to remember. The two metal locks snapped open and with them, the side of the case popped opened.

The gun sat before me.

Slowly my hand reached inside and picked it up. It was light, small, but effective. I made sure the safety was on and then wrapped it in my hospital gown. After that, I returned the case back to its place underneath the bed. Then I left the room and walked through the kitchen. I stopped in the dining room.

My room

I moved down the hallway towards my room. Once there I opened the door, it creaked just as it always had. Nothing had moved since the day of the accident. I walked to the closet and decided to put some clothes on. Walking around in the hospital's gown would draw far too much attention to me.

I changed into a pair of blue jeans and a red long sleeve

shirt. After I was changed, my eyes noticed the odd shaped blue box on my desk. My fingers picked it up and put it into my pocket, then tucked my father's gun into my waistband and pulled my shirt down over it. My hand moved up and met my face. It could feel the stubble of my many months without a shave.

I made my way to the bathroom and shaved my face. After I was finished, I touched my smooth skin, making sure I had gotten all of the stubble. My eyes slowly fluttered up to the mirror and I stared at the man reflected back at me. "Are you ready?" I asked myself.

"No." I answered my own question. "There's still something to take care of."

"The shadow from my truck," I said softly. "It was the little girl, the girl in the woods." My hand flipped the lights off in the bathroom as I walked back to Angela.

XXIII

Angela was looking out the window at the front of the house. My feet moved slowly as I made my way towards her and as I did, I began to admire her beauty with each step that I took. Placing both of my hands on her shoulders, I leaned in to talk to her. "Are you alright?" I whispered in her ear.

She turned to face me. "Are you? James this is crazy, why are we here?"

I didn't know what to say.

"If I explain you'll think I'm crazy." I tried my best to comfort her.

"If you don't tell me I'll think you're crazy anyway." She retorted.

"Angie I know it's hard to believe but I've done and seen some amazing things. I can't even explain in words but they're too fantastic to believe, I barely believe them." I tried my best to be vague. She looked at me for a long time inquisitively then looked back outside. "See you don't even want to believe me." I told her with a sullen tinge to my voice. I moved closer to the door and placed my hand on the cold knob.

"What's next James?" She asked me as she looked back to me.

THE SHADE

"I need to go back to the hospital—," I began to say, but then let my words trail off. "—I need to go to the nature preserve, our regular spot."

"Wait what?" She exclaimed. "Which one is it?"

"The preserve, I've got to check on something before I go back to the hospital." I turned the knob and pulled the door open. We stepped outside and I felt the brisk air on my face. The sensation felt new as the air passed over my cheeks and blew through my hair. The air was cold and almost too thin; and when I tried to breathe in, the air never seemed to satisfy my needs.

One more thing to do.

Angela followed me outside, as we both approached the car I realized only one of us was aware of what was about to happen. "May I drive?" I asked.

"Are you sure you can— I mean, in your condition?" She questioned.

I stretched my arms out and worked out the kinks in my joints. "I'll be fine." I told her as I reached my hand out for the keys. She gave me a look of worry and then handed me the keys. I winked at her as she handed me the keys and we started towards the car again. Angela immediately got into the car and buckled herself in. I however, opened my door and couldn't help but stare at my parent's house. I let out a sigh and got an overwhelming sense like that was the last time I was going to see the place.

I got into the car and turned the key in the ignition, the engine of the Honda came back to life, and we headed towards the preserve, unsure of what I'd find there. The memories of my accident had begun to sharpen, the shadow I'd seen in my cab wasn't a shadow at all, it was a little girl. I still couldn't make out her face, but I was absolutely sure that whatever it was it had latched onto me when I visited the forest before going to Angela's. Suddenly I wasn't focused on driving, I was focused on all the reasons Virgil had told me to stay away from the woods. That's when a feeling began to scratch at my head;

now I had never been a pessimist so I'd never considered the plan that Virgil had hatched would fail, but at that moment, the thought of failure slowly crept up into my head and began to gnaw at me.

What if Burke sees me from a mile off and takes me out before I even have a chance. Who are the police going to believe? A doctor or a recently escaped coma patient?

Suddenly a sharp realization washed over and filled my body.

"This isn't going to work." I said in a whisper. So quietly in fact, that Angela either didn't hear or didn't care enough to look up at me.

Maybe the preserve is nothing; maybe it was my brains way of giving me a chance to run.

I contemplated that thought for a moment until a voice beckoned me back to reality.

"James?" I shook myself from my trance and looked at Angela.

"Yeah what's up?" I asked.

"We're stopped." She informed me.

I looked up from her and to my surprise, we had already made it to the preserve. I looked at the brilliant green leaves of trees. The budding new life of the preserve made me feel instantly at one with the forest. "The girl from my truck." I murmured.

Angela looked at me with a strange look. "What girl?"

I'd never believed in predetermination or fate, but something inside of me screamed that the forest was important, that I was supposed to be there. In that moment, I felt that universe seemed to need me there for one reason or another and my whole body felt compelled to get out of the car, walk into the forest, and never return to Eugene. I moved to get out of the car. "What are we doing here, exactly—," Angela asked as I left the car. "James?"

"I need to do something." I told her as she joined me outside. My hand wrapped around hers. It had been an instinctual action and not a premeditated one, but it made me feel good that she didn't pull away from me. Her soft touch was still as warm and comforting as I remembered it being. If I was blushing I didn't care, I knew I didn't have time to dwell on it. We began to walk into the woods; the sun was out but couldn't pierce through the treetops so it felt colder than normal. The slow crunch of twigs under our feet made a distinct sound in the emptiness of the forest. We walked deeper into the forest to a point I'd never been to before.

"Are you sure we should be going this far?" Angela asked. I looked over to her and as I did out of the corner of my eye, I noticed a white blur. It was something fast, something that was neither in this world, nor in the next. "The girl." I said out loud by accident.

"What girl James?"

"You didn't see that?" I said as my hand tightened around hers. She squeezed my hand tighter as we made our way deeper into the forest to follow the white blur.

We trekked through the forest for thirty minutes, every five minutes or so I caught another brief glimpse of the blur. Angela saw nothing every time I claimed to see it; she must have thought I was truly going insane. We had hiked deeper in the forest when we noticed a light coming from a break in the trees up ahead.

Was there a clearing up ahead?

I tugged for Angela to follow me once again.

"James what are you doing?" She asked as we began to walk towards the clearing.

"I just need to see what's up here and then we'll go back." I told her as we neared the edge of the forest.

"Look, I haven't seen anything this whole time; what if your eyes are just playing tricks on you?" We stepped out into the clearing. "We should just go back to the car, there's no one here there's nothing but—," Angela's words slowly died out as we entered the clearing.

It was wide and in the center, there were the scorched

remains of an old house. The home had long since turned to ash, only the foundation remained, but it was clear it had once been a wooden home of some kind. To the left of the house was a large tree with a broken swing under it, and there in front of the house stood a small girl dressed in white.

"James who is that?" Angela leaned to me and whispered.

"I'm not sure exactly." I told her as I walked towards the girl.

"What are you doing?" She yelled in a sort of whisper.

"I think she led me here for something."

"That's insane, you know that right?" She rebutted. I inched my way closer to the girl and as I got closer, it was easy to tell the girl wasn't solid like she had looked from a distance. She was slightly transparent in places, as if she were stretched too thin, almost as if she was mixed between life and death. She was a ghost, that much I was certain. My body stood frozen as I waited for her to speak, waiting for her to tell me why she had brought me to that place.

Finally, I decided to speak up. "Did you lead me here?" I asked.

She nodded up and down to signify that she had.

"You're a ghost right?"

Again, she nodded yes.

"A ghost? James what's going on?" Angela said as she finally made it to me. I looked at the girl and as my eyes focused on her face I noticed something peculiar. As I tightened my gaze, the realization of what I was seeing was almost too much for me.

The little girl looked exactly like Virgil.

"You're Virgil's daughter." I said to the ghost. Then she did something I had not expected. As if I'd said something odd, she stared at me with a strange and confused look. After a moment she began to walk around the house, but using the word walk would be wrong, the action looked more like she was floating. She moved her legs as if she was walking but she seemed to float over the ground. "Am I wrong? You're related to Virgil—I mean Michael?" I corrected myself as I chased her around the house.

From a distance, I hadn't noticed the small grave that sat nestled beneath the mighty tree. The girl that I assumed was Sarah sat situated between the tree and the small granite tombstone that marked a patch of bright grass. "Is this your grave?"

She nodded yes.

"I don't get it James, who is this?" Angela asked, obviously trying to understand what she was witnessing.

"She's a friend." I told her and then moved in closer to the grave. My hand reached out and brushed the dirt and grime that covered the face of the tombstone.

Then my eyes squinted as I read the slightly faded words:
Sarah Burke 1950-1957
Daughter of Michael and Lora Burke
Loved Always

I reread the words once, twice and even a third time to make sure I had comprehended them correctly. Virgil had told me his name was Michael; it would be too much of a coincidence to assume the name on the tombstone was someone else's. "Michael—Virgil—," I said quietly as my voice trailed off. My hand scooped up a hand full of dirt and crushed it in my palm. "—why didn't you tell me the truth, Burke's your brother."

Angela approached me from behind. "Burke. That's your doctor right?"

"No—," my voice trailed off. "—his name's Edwin." As soon as his name hit my lips, Sarah's eyes flared with a white-hot intensity.

Angela withdrew at the sight of Sarah's unwieldy temper. "She doesn't seem to like that name very much." She said as she backed away from the ghost.

"Edwin Burke is your uncle." I said to Sarah calmly.

She nodded furiously.

My mind began to spin. Unanswered questions whirled

around inside me like a hurricane as wicked thoughts began to enter my head.

Why didn't he tell me about this, why would he keep it a secret?

Virgil and I had grown close in the time we had spent together in The Shade. He had been a mentor and a teacher, but above that, he was a friend. He had saved my life on more than one occasion just as I had done for him. We had trusted each other, looked out for one another, I knew he had secrets but I never imagined that it was anything like what he had kept hidden from me. Then a sour thought entered my mind, one I didn't want to think about, but my mind forced me.

Can I still trust him?

Sarah's eyes remained glued to me as I racked my head with all the new information. Suddenly I realized something; I looked at Sarah and asked. "Did you make me crash my car so I could help your father?" Sarah's eyes met mine. She looked saddened as she nodded once more. It felt like the world's largest puzzle piece had fallen into place. Everything about Virgil and Edwin, both made sense and completely confused me at the same time. Burke had killed Virgil's daughter, his own niece. Then he imprisoned his brother in The Shade.

What kind of cruel animal would do this to his own family?

My eyes turned from Sarah's pale transparent face and stared at the headstone. My thoughts ran out of control. It felt as if my mind was trying to fit everything together but for some reason it couldn't make it fit. I slammed my fist down against the ground.

I felt anger beginning to well inside me. Heat from my anger swelled in my chest.

How could he do this to me? I was only trying to help him and he never told me the truth.

"*You can't trust anyone but yourself.*" A voice in the back of my head told me. Frustration mixed in with the anger, ready to burst forth from within me. My breathing became shallower as the heat inside my body seemed to set me on fire.

He didn't want me to come here, he didn't want me seeing the truth. He just wanted me to do his dirty work for him.

Then a sensation washed over me, a sensation I'd never felt in the real world. My eyes started to go dark, slowly cutting off all light.

Then, Angela's hand was on my shoulder. My eyes snapped back to normal and the heat inside my body subsided. "We need to get back to the hospital." My voice still carried a tinge of anger. My eyes looked down at my dirt-filled hands.

I'm still in control.

Angela had squelched the growing rage inside me. She had been the tether that bound me to reality. Once I was certain I was in control of my body, I turned to face Angela. As I turned, I noticed the tears rolling down the gentle curve of her cheeks.

"What's wrong?" I asked.

"What you said before about being somewhere else while you were in your coma, you were right, I didn't believe you." She sobbed.

"It's okay." I tried to comfort her. "If I hadn't seen it for myself I wouldn't have believed it either."

"It's not just that. While you were in your coma I felt so bad—because we weren't together anymore—," she paused to gasp for air and wipe the tears that flooded from her eyes. "—I felt like you thought it was your fault we broke up." She finished.

After she spoke, Virgil's words filled my head. He once told me that Angela might not felt like she had any other choice than to break up with me. "Then what happened?" I asked trying to get clarity.

"James I love you—," she paused. "—but after graduation I didn't want you to be tied to me, tied to Eugene. I didn't want you to forgo going to Dartmouth just to stay here because I am going to be here." She explained. "I thought pushing you away would let you have the freedom to do everything you wanted in life. I just didn't want you to give up a future because of me." She said as she wiped more tears away. I moved closer to her and placed my hand on her shoulders to console here.

"Everything I wanted in life?" I asked rhetorically. "*You. You're everything I want in life.*" My hands slid down from her shoulders to her waist. "We can make a life here, I don't need Dartmouth, I need you. Did you ever think to ask me about any of this?" My hands pulled her in closer not expecting her to answer the question and we kissed. Our lips met for a few seconds then I looked down at her.

"I love you." She said while I smiled and grabbed her hand.

"We need to get back to the car."

We walked the long journey back through the forest. I held Angela's hand the entire way. This time not with a sense of urgency, like before, but with more tenderness and caring.

We arrived at Angela's car, we got in and buckled up, I twisted the key, and the engine fired up. My mind told me to run, to cut all ties to Eugene, and leave with Angela. I had something to live for again. However, the more my heart tried to force myself to run, the more my head knew there was only one real choice. I had known from the beginning my situation could only end one way. I drove faster than normal to get to the hospital before visiting hours were over. Something in my gut told me that timing was going to be critical.

We arrived at the hospital and I pulled into the large west parking lot that we'd left from. I pulled into a parking space and stopped the car then turned to look at Angela. "No matter what you hear or see, please stay in the car okay?" I asked her.

"But James I—," my finger met her mouth to silence her.

"Just promise me."

"I'll be right here." She agreed as she kissed my forehead.

"If I don't come back in ten minutes get out of here." I

paused. "And don't believe anything they say about me okay?" I added.

She nodded to me. I pulled the handgun out from where I had tucked it in my pants. Angela's eyes lit up at the sight of the gun. I didn't say anything else to her, my hand pulled the slide back to chamber the first round, turned the safety back on and then put it back into my waistband. I turned to get out of the car before she could speak, and then started to walk towards the sliding glass doors. My feet hit the pavement, systematically in sync with my heartbeat. The gun felt heavy as its cold metal touched my skin. I continued to walk and as I did, I tried to remember what little my father had taught me about shooting. The sliding glass door of the hospital opened as I stepped on the black mat in front of it, releasing a cold blast of air as I walked into the hospital.

The waiting room was as empty as it had been when Angela and I left earlier that day. A young nurse stood at the lobby desk, I started to walk towards her. I got half way across the room before she noticed me and said. "Can I help you sir?"

Her voice was sweet, tender as if by helping me she could solve all the world's problems. I was somewhat sorry my voice wouldn't be. "Yeah I'm looking for a Dr. Burke." I told her. She looked down on her desk and started thumbing through a folder upon folders. She examined each one and then finally chose one in particular. Her index finger ran the length of the page and stopped. I assumed she found what she was looking for because she placed the folder back down.

"Yes Dr. Burke is making his rounds on the second floor, he's currently in room 214." She said in an even happier tone of voice than before.

"Thanks, I appreciate it." I said with a smile. She smiled back at me unaware of what was about to ensue. I nodded to her and made my way to the stairs. I climbed my way to the second floor, once there, my eyes glanced down the hall to make sure there wasn't anyone around. A sign on the wall told me that rooms 200-220 were to the left, so I made my way down the hall. After the short walk down the hall, I reached room 214 and could hear someone inside talking. I stepped into the room and noticed that it was my room. I hadn't realized it when Angela took me out earlier, but I knew it was definitely the same room I'd left. My hand trembled as I pulled out the handgun, pointing it at the man standing with his back turned to me.

"Turn around. Now!" I commanded.

"Well hello James." The man said as he turned to face me. He turned slowly to look at me and the eyes that met me were ones I knew. His pale yellow eyes were the exact same as Virgil's. His hair was darker, slicked back and out of his face. Burke's cheekbones sat high on his face and unlike Virgil, his features were more pointed. In his hand a small pistol glimmered in the florescent light of the room, it was aimed directly at me. "I believe you left this behind when you made your audacious escape." He commented in a condescending tone of voice.

Burke had found the gun that was meant for me. The plan was spiraling downwards quickly, and as we pointed the firearms at one another, I hesitated to do what I knew needed to be done. "You—you look just like him." I managed to stammer out.

"He didn't tell you? Well I don't blame him." He said with a smile. "I suppose you're here to kill me, with—," he leaned over to me in an attempt to see my weapon. "—a gun—," then he let out a heavy sigh. "Glad you could find another one, I've just barrowed yours." He said as he pointed at his pistol.

"It doesn't matter what Virgil told me, I'm here to stop you." I said.

"Do you wonder why he didn't tell you about me?" He moved closer to me, from the range he was at it wouldn't matter if I was a good shot or not. "You see, what Virgil fails to understand is, there are bigger things at work here than you or him, or even me."

"Well aren't you humble." I said and adjusted my aim at his heart.

I hesitated.

"Please James if you were going to shoot me, you would have by now." He told me.

I lowered the gun to see what he had to say.

"Speak." My voice frustrated.

"You're my brother's most trusted friend, which in the overall scheme of things doesn't say much. But in all your training, all your time together are you telling me that he never mentioned that *I* was his brother?" He continued to say.

"I'm sure he has a reason—,"

"—He did have a reason James. He set you up." Burke interrupted me.

My heart's pace quickened.

Is it true?

"So what if he did. What does that matter?" I questioned.

"Not much, seeing as you're going back to The Shade. That's where you're the most useful to me." He smiled. "You'll never see this world again. Your life is will serve something far greater than yourself." He smiled as he finished.

"And if I don't go back willingly?" I asked as I raised the pistol once more.

"Oh James," He chuckled. "I never intended for you to go back quietly." He said with a smirk. He raised his left hand and clenched his fist. The last thing before the room went dark was the sound of the two shots I was able squeeze off before I hit the floor.

XXIV

My eyes slowly adjusted and focused in the absence of light. They began to focus on the ceiling above me, it was the same ceiling I had seen before I fell, but with only one difference. The paint was peeling and as I turned my head sideways, I noticed the walls were just as damaged. "Damn it!" I yelled. I knew that I was back in The Shade, I'd missed my shot to kill Burke, and now everything seemed lost. "Damn it! Damn it! Damn it!" I cursed at the walls, the hospital, and even The Shade itself. Everything I'd worked for was lost in one moment. One moment of hesitation and my last chance to get back to the life I once knew had vanished.

In that moment, I had failed.

I sat up. The room was empty, the old gurneys were overturned, the walls, floor, and ceiling in total disrepair. My hands moved over my face, covering it as I took in a deep breath. As I dropped my hands to my side I used them to push myself up off the floor; slowly returned to my feet. "Shit!" I yelled, kicking some loose tiles across the room. They slammed against the wall and shattered.

I have to find Virgil. I have to ask him what's going on!

THE SHADE 239

The fear deep in my chest mixed with the anger and frustration, making a volatile cocktail inside me. I found the door and made my way down the abandoned hallway towards the entrance.

I have to find Virgil.

Even the thought of his name sent a sense of anger vibrating through my bones. I made my way out of the hospital without incident. Making my way out of the city would be easy because the hospital sat on its edge, but the sun wasn't out, so I'd decided to look for Virgil in the only spot I knew. I headed towards the house that we had squatted in just before I left The Shade. After living in the same house for a month, I'd memorized every route to get back there. This was just to ensure I'd have an escape plan if something ever went wrong while I was out.

I made my way out of the city with the clouds still shielding the sun. As the sprawling buildings gave way to simpler farmland, I found myself in a large open field. My feet dragged themselves across the field as my eyes tried to focus on the small shapes in the distance. The field was a large expanse of nothingness. More than likely, it was some sort of farm in the real world but in the dead empty void of The Shade, it was just a field, barren of the crops that should have been growing there.

Then I noticed something.

Something moved along the desolate landscape. It wasn't a house on the distance, the speck on the horizon was moving. It seemed to be coming straight for me. My fist's tightened preparing for a fight as my feet trudged toward the speck.

It took only a few minutes for the speck to become the silhouette of a person; the outline had become well defined by that point. My eyes focused tighter on the speck trying to figure out who it was. A few more feet and I would be able to make out who it was, but it didn't take a few more feet. Without warning, the figure raised its hand in the air and began to wave. My head cocked to the side at the action. "James!" The figure shouted.

It was Virgil.

My heart began to fly with anticipation. My fists still balled and ready, with only one thought on my mind.

Why?

He approached me slowly with what appeared to be a half-hearted look of worry. We stood in the middle of the field and he said. "James, what happened—," he tried to ask but before he was finished with the words I raised my hand to him.

"What happened?" I chuckled and then began to circle around him. His eyes stayed on mine as I did. "What happened?—what happened was your brother saw me coming." I told him, my tone vicious. His eyes widened at the term brother. "And that's not all." I told him. "He told me *you* set me up. So let me ask you a question. What the hell is going on?" The words flew from my lips poised to strike.

Virgil just stared at me.

"Well? Speak up, did you think I could kill him, or did you set me up?" I started to approach him as he just looked at me. "I said—," my voice sharply rose. "DID YOU, SET ME UP?!" My finger poked at his chest.

Virgil cleared his throat and he said. "I'm sorry. I can explain everything."

However, I didn't want an explanation, I wanted to be angry, to be furious. My mind tried to figure out why Virgil would betray me, why he would lead me down a path that had a giant pit at the end of it. I wanted everything in the moment to lash out against him, but instead my mouth uttered just one word. "Speak."

Virgil took a long second before speaking. "Okay. Yes. Burke is my brother. I'm sorry I didn't tell you James, but it was for your safety—," I rolled my eyes. "—it truly was. The less you knew the easier it was to get you to help me."

"So you used me."

"No—Yes—, It's more complicated than that. I was going to tell you—,"

"Oh you were *going* to tell me. *Going* to." I interrupted him.

He put his hands up to try to calm me down, so I pushed them away from me in defiance. "James, please. We need to go to the refuge. We need to talk to Shaun. We cannot be out here."

My lips pursed not wanting to relent. Then an exacerbated, "alright." huffed out of me.

"Okay. We've got to go before—," he started to say.

Suddenly a blue light erupted from the nothingness of the field. The light was blinding and seemed to stretch on forever. A figure stepped out from it and then as quickly as the light had filled the field, it disappeared back into the void. My eyes slowly adjusted to the regular light once again. Once they were in focus, I could finally see who the figure was.

"Burke." I seethed.

He stepped into full view as the words came pouring over my lips. As if a silent alarm went off, Virgil's body tensed up and he readied himself. "Brother, I didn't come here to fight, so let's skip the dramatics shall we?" He said as he walked closer towards Virgil and me.

"Then what the hell are you doing here?" Virgil's voice rang out. Burke looked at me with his hollow eyes and smiled a brief smile, as if I'd told a joke only he and I were privy to.

"I came for him." He pointed at me.

"You can't take him." Virgil said in my defense.

"I'm not going anywhere with you." I stated in confirmation of what Virgil had said.

He looked at me puzzled and then as if a switch in his head flicked on, he snorted and shook his head. "You've not told him I take it?" He asked Virgil. I looked at Virgil then back to Burke. "Oh this is just too good." Burke clapped his hands. "Well go on, get to it."

Virgil looked over at me. His face looked like he was searching for the right words to use. However, I knew deep down no words, no matter how feathered, would be able to soften what he was going to say. "James I—," his voice stammered as he tried to find the next few words. "—I'm working—I was forced to work—," then Burke who had been standing with his arms crossed filled in the rest of the sentence.

"Virgil's been working for me." He said with a smile. My eyes snapped to Burke. "What my dear brother is trying to tell you is that he's been working for me." My head spun. Anger built inside my body. The slow warmth began to work its way over me. "Go on Virgil, tell him."

My eyes peered back at Virgil, his face a mess. "He knows where my wife is, he told me if I didn't help him then he'd kill her, along with her family, anyone she was attached to. So for a time, I collaborated with him to save her." He told me.

My face felt warm, like standing next to a bonfire for too long.

"What do you mean by work?" I said through my teeth.

Virgil hesitated for a moment before he said to me. "Burke needs the chemical inside of our heads. Like I told you before, most people only have a limited supply of DMT and eventually dry up. Once they do, I was in charge of getting rid of them." He told me then focused on the ground.

Then the sudden realization of what the words 'get rid of them' meant. "You killed them?!" I yelled at him. By the look Virgil gave me, it was clear my face had twisted into something terrifying.

"I didn't want to. I was just trying to save my wife."

"And that gives you the excuse to kill innocent people."

"I didn't have a choice—,"

"You always have a choice!" I yelled. My breath became heavy. Frustration swelled in my chest and my mind raced out of control, each thought making me more and more livid. After a moment, Virgil spoke back up.

"James I stopped doing his dirty work a long time ago, I was never going to bring you to him, it was never going to be you James, it was never—," he was cut off.

Burke pinched his fingers together and like magic, Virgil's lips were sealed shut.

"That's enough out of you." Then he turned to me. "Now where was I? Oh yes, my dear brother here was going to sell you more lies." He said as he glared at Virgil. The look was one of immeasurable hatred, the same look I'd seen so often in Virgil's eyes when he talked about Burke. "It's true. When I trap someone here, Virgil was in charge of making sure they stay here for as long as I needed them." He explained.

My eyes went wild as they looked at Virgil.

"So why not me, huh?" I asked Virgil.

Burke opened his fingers and allowed Virgil to speak once more. Virgil's mouth spewed the words he'd wanted to say like a machinegun spewing bullets. "I only helped him because if I didn't he'd kill my wife. I'm his slave James." He tried to explain. My mind tried to work through the maze of what had been fabricated and what was the truth. I felt like I was being stretched out in every direction, then something snapped, and I realized, there was no way to twist the situation and make it better.

"Angela. Angela reminded me so much of her." He added.

"Shut your mouth." I told him. "You don't get to talk about her."

"James I haven't helped him in years, I wasn't going to take you—,"

"You what? You thought you could use me for your own purposes." I cut him off. "I don't care that you've not helped him for years, if that's even true. The fact remains you helped him to begin with."

Burke stepped forward and spoke.

"You see now James. He's unreliable, weak and devious. He's someone who's not to be trusted." My eyes snapped to Burke then back to Virgil. My head was on fire with all the new information. As Burke stood only twenty feet away and Virgil a few feet to my right, my mind flooded with everything they had revealed to me. Then something snapped. Something long dormant inside of my head flicked on and stirred to life. I twisted my head to Virgil.

"What about Christina?" Referring to the girl we'd found in the closet.

"Would you have taken her? Would you have sacrificed her? Had she outlive her usefulness?" Virgil stared at the ground. "Answer me!" His eyes rose back up and met mine.

"Yes." His voice filled with shame. "It was people like her that I took to him."

That's when I snapped.

It was like a freight train derailing in my mind. All of my thoughts seemed to make it to one point then collapse into nothing. My breathing quickened, my body felt the warm surge of adrenaline rush through my veins. I felt as if my body had been lit on fire, but the burning gave me a feeling of power.

I looked at Virgil as my vision began to darken.

"James please you have to stop this, I know you're angry but you can't let this overtake you." He shouted. His voice only fueled what drove me, I could feel the power swell within my body waiting to be released. The burning gave way to a hypersensitivity to my surroundings; everything seemed to be moving in slow motion. I could hear farther than my eyes could see, I could smell the grass all around me and I could feel, feel the presence of the two people with me. "James, please I'm begging you." Virgil shouted, but it was a dull sound in my ears. I waited for the moment, the moment when everything would go dark and my rage would take over.

I didn't fight the anger, I embraced it.

Then my vision went dark, and something else took over.

"Please James snap out of it—," Virgil began to say, but before he could finish his sentence my foot slammed into his chest. I could feel the bones shatter under the force of the blow, each one splintered down and fractured. He hurdled through the air. When he hit the ground his body rolled a good six feet, finally stopping motionless on the dirt.

"Very good James, now finish him off and join me. If you do I promise I won't touch a hair on your precious Angela's head."

Angela?

Her face shot through my head. The sound of her name

only fueled me more. She was the one I was fighting for, she was the reason I needed to kill Burke. I laughed a terrible laugh that wasn't mine, like two voices stacked on top of each other, mine and a much deeper one overlaying it. "NO. I'm going to kill you." I said. Then, without control of my actions, I darted forward as quickly as I could; my fist became a ball of rage and power, rocketing at Burke. I came within three feet of him when he held out his hand.

Suddenly I stopped.

Try as I might I couldn't move closer to him. I screamed a barrage of incoherent nonsense at him. "Join me or die like him." He pointed at Virgil.

"NO!" I yelled at him and struggled to break free of his grasp once more.

"Very well." He said.

He clenched his fist, as he did all of the bones in my body instantly felt like mush. My legs could no longer hold me and I collapsed. The soft grass caught me and with a light thud, I laid on the ground. I coughed up blood into the bright green grass, staining it a muddy red color. I couldn't move, my chest felt as if it had collapsed. Blood was streaming from my mouth and as I looked up, I only had enough time to see Burke step back into the real world before I blacked out.

XXV

The light was enveloping, it drew me in on all sides and seemed to reach inside of me. It filled me and made me warm, I wanted to stay in the light forever.

Am I dead?

I blinked my eyes back into focus. Someone had been shining a light into my eyes.

No not dead, I'm not that lucky.

My eyes slowly followed the light back and forth, without consciously making them move they flickered to the light wherever it went. "Alright, I think he's finally coming to." A familiar voice said. The sound echoed and rang in my ears. I forced my hand to reach up towards my face and wipe my eyes clear of their fog. With my eyes unhindered, they were able to get a good look at the ceiling. The stonework was familiar with high arches and pillars on all sides; the thing that stood out the most however was the mural of trees that was painted on the ceiling.

"The refuge?" I said. My voice raw as my vocal cords tried to make the correct sounds. My throat felt like it was on fire, my eyes couldn't seem to focus on any one object for any set period. My face turned to my right, focusing on the face of the person sitting across from me.

It was Virgil.

He sat across the room looking at me. The look in his eyes seemed as if they were trying to scream something at me, but I didn't pay it any attention. Then my eyes sharpened and I began to notice the amount of people that were in the refuge. Each person was carrying something, chests, chairs, beds. It seemed like they were gathering anything they could. "James, how are you feeling?" The same familiar voice asked. I looked around until my eyes finally made out where the voice was coming from.

Shaun's face hovered above mine.

He gave me a quick smile and then called someone to help him sit me up. That was when I realized my body felt heavy. Like someone had laid a thousand pounds of extra weight on it.

I tried to sit up.

"Easy there, you broke most of your ribs and had a collapsed lung, take it slow." He advised. Shaun and Kate propped me up. My eyes looked down at my chest.

I was covered in bandages.

My entire torso was patched up, almost making me look like a mummy from an old horror film. My fingers drifted down and touched the dark red spots that painted the bandages. "I wouldn't touch that." Kate said to me.

"How did I get here?" I asked.

There was a long awkward pause and then Shaun spoke. "Virgil carried you the entire way here; you were both pretty close to the end when you got here. But thanks to Kate most of the ribs you broke have already healed, but some may still be a bit off. You're healing quickly because of the DMT that's still in your system; you'll be alright in a few hours." Shaun explained. I glanced up at Virgil. He had remained silent for the duration of our conversation. My eyes moved from him quickly back to Shaun.

"What's going on here? Why are you moving everything?" Shaun took a good look around his refuge, seemingly heartbroken and said. "We're leaving here. Because our plan failed, Burke knows where we are, and since he knows we interfered he'll be gunning for us. It's time for us to go into hiding." He said with a type of sadness I'd never seen before.

"We have to have a backup plan right?" I said franticly.

"There is no backup plan, we run and hide, fight when we have to. We've lost too many people already." He said quietly. My eyes lowered then met with Virgil's.

Suddenly I remembered everything that had happened.

His betrayal, the lies, the fact that Virgil was not only Burke's brother, but also that he had also been working with him for the past sixty years. There was nothing I wanted more, than to fly off my cot at him. To yell at him with everything I had inside of me, to demand to know if everything that he'd ever told me had been one elaborate lie after another. Then I thought about telling Shaun, if the family knew what Virgil had really been up to, they could deliver some swift justice. "Shaun I need to talk to you about something—," my eyes glanced at Virgil. "—in private." I finished. Virgil's eyes widened, he knew what I wanted to say, and finally he broke his vow of silence.

"Shaun we do have a backup plan." Virgil declared.

Shaun looked stunned by Virgil's sudden outburst and turned to him.

"What's that?" He asked.

To Shaun he said. "We can still get James out of the hospital."

What is he trying to do?

"No." Shaun said firmly. "After he tried to kill Burke the hospital had him moved to a more secure wing. He's been moved to a padded room just in case he wakes up and tries to attack someone again. Even if I could muster the manpower, if we go for James, Burke will kill your body the first chance he gets." He told Virgil.

That option is off the table then.

My thoughts seemed to echo between their conversations.

"Shaun you know we need him out of here, whatever the cost. You do whatever you have to do to save him." Virgil looked at me with his pale eyes. "He's worth more than my life." No longer were his eyes screaming at me. They were soft, seeming to say: I'm sorry.

My eyes turned away from his, not wanting to acknowledge the apology. I looked at Shaun, his face painted a very different picture. He seemed like he was conflicted about something, and then it hit me. I'd known Shaun for a very long time, even if I hadn't known about his secret life in The Shade, I knew one thing about him that would never change. Once he committed to something, he was almost zealous in his pursuit of it. In that moment I knew he would do anything—short from sacrificing his own—he could to save the refuge, it was his home, his family, things anyone would regard as worth saving. At that moment, I knew Shaun would make just about any sacrifice to save his family and the refuge.

Thoughts of Virgil's betrayal filled my head at once. My mind tried to parallel the actions of Shaun and those of Virgil. Virgil had done what he thought was necessary to keep those he loved alive. Shaun was willing to do the same for The Family, and to a certain extent, I would have gone just as far, or further to do the same.

Could I blame either of them? How far would I go if Angela or one of my family members were in danger?

My eyes looked back at Virgil, his mouth twitched with something to say but nothing came out. His face spoke the apology that his words could not. It seemed to say sorry for everything, everything he'd done to me, to all the others before me, and to himself. As much as I wanted to be furious at Virgil, the only emotion that I felt was pity. My lungs let out a slow sigh as my head nodded, letting him know I wasn't going to say anything to Shaun. He seemed to understand the signal and with a sigh of relief, he let his head fall against the wall.

"Virgil, you're sure about this, knowing what it means?" Shaun asked him.

"I'm absolutely sure." He responded.

Shaun hesitated for a moment and then said to me. "Alright then, whatever you needed to tell me will have to wait. I've got to find some volunteers. We'll infiltrate the hospital, with force if it's necessary, and get James out." Then he walked toward a group of people carrying various items. I heard his voice grow fainter as he moved away from us, giving orders, planning his next move to free me from my padded prison.

Then my eyes lowered and settled upon Virgil.

"Virgil—," I began.

He held his finger to his mouth, which told me to be quiet.

"You don't have to say anything James. I know exactly what I'm doing."

My mind clawed to try to make sense of what he was doing. "What if—what if they get you out first? Then come for me." I offered my suggestion.

"That won't work, as soon as I'm out Burke will kill you and we'll be done. Besides, I've spent the past sixty years here, I'd be useless in the real world, but you—you still have a future. At least one of us is getting out and I'll be damned if that's not going to be you." His voice was calm, almost like the early morning hours as you peer over a placid lake.

"Why are you doing this? You don't owe me anything—," I tried to tell him.

"James I owe you everything, I owe you my humanity." He told me.

Then a million questions sparked to life. I knew then that to understand Virgil I'd have to understand why he'd done the things he had done. "Why," I asked. "What happened to you?"

He pondered the question for a few moments and then spoke.

"James, I've been in the hospital for sixty years. The only thing that kept me going all that time was the thought of seeing my wife again and finally being able to lay my daughter to rest. I'm not stupid. The reality is that even if I get out of here I don't have much life left to live." He confessed. "It was clear to me from the moment I saw you that I'd much rather give up my remaining years to make sure you can live out yours. Burke has destroyed too many lives and I promised myself yours wouldn't be one of them."

"You helped Burke take all of those people, why am I so special?" I asked him. However, in the back of my head, I knew there was nothing that Virgil could ever say that would give me what I truly wanted from him. Because what I desired most was for him to say something that could rebuild my shattered perceptions of him. However, those words didn't exist.

Instead, he said. "The thing is James. I saw a lot of myself in you. From the first time you mentioned Angela and the way you felt about her, I only thought of me and my wife. I can't ever justify the things I've done, but maybe this will make up for some of it."

I nodded to him as Shaun showed back up at our cots.

"Are we ready to get started?" He asked us both.

"In a minute, we need to go over some of the finer points." Virgil said.

"Well hurry up." Shaun pushed as he hovered over us.

"James, when you wake up, Shaun will help you. There's a good chance that by breaking you out Burke will dispose of my body before I can get back." I noticed he used the word dispose as if his body was a piece of garbage. "Shaun can help coordinate an attack." I thought about what he said, his words felt as if he was inscribing his own epitaph.

"Do you really think I can do this? Do you think I can kill Burke?" I asked, questioning my own abilities. Virgil had told me from the first day we met that I was special. He'd told me if anyone could destroy Burke it was me.

Virgil nodded his head and said. "Yes, I believe you can."

"How can you be sure?"

"Because the two of you are a lot alike." My eyes widened at the thought.

Virgil continued. "James I lost my brother to the power of The Shade, his power grew until it consumed him. His anger ruled over him and one day it took over." Every lesson Virgil had ever taught me about controlling my emotion flashed through my head and suddenly everything made sense. "I didn't want to lose you like I lost him." He told me.

"He's stronger than me." I shook my head at the ground. Then Virgil began to do something peculiar, he began to laugh. "What's so funny?" I asked.

"James it's not about who's stronger and who knows more. This fight comes down to heart. You have a good heart, your morality hasn't been compromised by this place. Those things make you dangerous to Burke." He said. "Remember the bleed over effect; you'll still have some power when you get back. Heightened senses, speed, and strength, make use of them. Keep in mind that if you use the power to often, the residual will dry up."

"I understand." My voice rang out.

He smirked at me, knowing that if I got a shot at Burke he knew I'd take it.

Shaun stepped forward for the first time in our conversation and interjected. "My people will back you up if they can, that way you won't have to face Burke alone. He knows you're coming for him, and he thinks we've played all our cards, show him he's wrong." He told me.

I nodded to Shaun and then looked at Virgil once more.

"There's still a chance he won't get the opportunity to—," I struggled to say the two remaining words. "—kill you."

"You're right." He said with a half-hearted smile. I knew he didn't believe his own words, but I had to hold on to some kind of hope that we would both come through this together. Shaun got up tired of the conversation and grabbed what two IV bags filled with some sort of clear liquid. "Can you both lay back on the cots for me?"

I lay back down on the cot; my eyes met the stone ceiling of the church. The bricks were old and I could tell that they had been laid by hand because of the minor imperfections that adorned them. "This is going to sting a bit." Shaun told me as he forced the needle into my arm. The pinprick was quick but Shaun was right, it did sting. As the clear liquid entered my body, it did more than sting it burned through me. The sensation ran down my arm, and with every pump of my heart it sent the liquid further and further into my system. I turned and looked at Virgil on the cot next to me, our eyes met.

I didn't want to think it would be the last time I'd see him, but it was the only thing on my mind. There was still so much I wanted to say to him. To thank him for being my mentor, for keeping me alive for months, for making sure that when the moment I had to face Burke alone came, I'd be able to face it. Above all, I wanted to tell him how much I understood him and what he did for his family. "When you fight him, don't lose control. You have everything you need. Don't waste this." Virgil said to me in a calm and even tone.

"I won't." I told him.

I would have said more but I had to choke back the lump that started to grow in my throat. Virgil turned his head back up and looked at the ceiling, from the corner of my eye I could see the smile on his face.

I'm getting what most people never get, a third chance.

Until that moment, I never in my life believed that extraordinary things could happen, at least not to me. I'd never considered myself a believer of any sort, but on that day I had something to believe in. Because for the first time in my life I'd seen that good was stronger than evil in men's hearts. That no matter what happened in the coming hours; I'd never sacrifice my humanity for anything. I knew what I was fighting for, not revenge, not myself, not for power. I was fighting for my friends, my family, and everyone who had come before me.

Then all of a sudden I found it hard to think about anything.

The liquid must have been working because my eyes began to move in and out of focus. Shaun stood over me checking my ribs, I would have twitched with pain, but I couldn't feel anything. I closed my eyes and waited for the familiar sleep that would take me to another world.

A world far away from this one, one with Angela, my parents, and maybe, just maybe, Virgil would be there as well.

XXVI

An intense wave of pain shot through my body, beginning at my lower abdomen and growing outwards through me. I was on my back, that much I could tell as the pain coursed through every nerve ending that my body had. Each beat of my heart made the stinging sensation scream out at me. My eyes snapped open as I tried to move my arms. I had little success and found that my arms and legs had been strapped to the table that I lay on.

That's when the panic set in.

My arms and legs began to struggle against their bonds. Quickly my eyes looked around as they tried to give me some sort of grip on where I was. The room was half lit; it was clean, almost too clean, like it didn't belong to a human, it clearly not a hospital. My heartbeat grew more rapid as I realized the futility of my struggling. It occurred to me this wasn't a problem I could force my way out of, not only that, but with every twist and turn of my torso a fresh bite of pain shot through me. I heard the door open behind me; someone entered the room outside of my field of view. I writhed in futility as I desperately tried to break free as the person's footsteps came closer and closer to me.

Shaun's head poked out from behind me.

"James, please stop struggling you're going to pop your stitches." He told me.

Stitches? How badly had I been hurt?

"Shaun please let me out of here." I commanded him.

"No can do, we have to keep you in here for just a bit longer until we know the full extent of the damage." He told me.

I tried to remain calm as I spoke. "Okay, Shaun you're starting to worry me, what's happened to me?" The sentence was quick and ran together as I began to panic.

"James you need to stop panicking. I'm going to explain everything to you." He said trying to reassure me. "We had some—*issues* getting you out of the hospital." He told me.

"Define issues?" I said to him in a stern voice.

"Well there was more resistance than we had planned for. It was a bit harder than we expected." He began to explain but his voice trailed off towards the end. My body felt weak, as if someone had drained me of my blood. My skin looked white, almost too white to be normal. I swallowed down the hard lump that had been growing in my throat and I focused my eyes up at the bright fluorescent bulbs that hung from the ceiling.

"Is Virgil here too?" I asked, my voice husky from the dryness in my throat.

Shaun looked at me then looked up towards the door as someone else walked into the room. "How is he doing?" A female voice said. I immediately identified the voice belonged to Kate; she had a particular velvety smooth sound to her voice that was unmistakable. Kate walked over to Shaun and me. She must have noticed something was wrong, because when they caught eyes, her demeanor changed dramatically. My heart began to thump heavily in my chest as Shaun turned back to me. Once his eyes met mine I knew what news was about to come, his eyes told the entire story.

"James, I'm sorry." He said in a low whisper.

"What happened to him—you got him out right?" They

both just stared. "Right?" I pleaded with them. Kate put her hand on my shoulder in an attempt to comfort me; it didn't. "Say something please, tell me what happened!" I screamed at them as I shrugged Kate's hand off me.

"Like I said James, they knew we were coming for you. Once we had you, they knew we would try to go for him." Shaun's hand covered his face as he shook his head. "It was a massacre. Burke knew exactly where to hit us, we lost six before we got the word that he'd already killed Virgil." He said. "I'm sorry." He added after the fact.

And just like that Virgil was gone.

He was gone and this time he was not coming back. Tears began to build behind my eyes. I couldn't reach my face because of the straps holding me down. The tear rolled down the side of my face, landing on the table next to my head it made an almost unperceivable sound in my ears.

Why am I crying?

The thought of crying hadn't crossed my mind before, not until then. It wasn't until I felt as if the world couldn't get any more unfair. People always say that life isn't fair, but at that moment, it was being outright cruel. Virgil was a good person at heart; he had only wanted to help the one's he loved, moreover he had helped me. My mind flashed to the memories of Virgil, to the promise that I'd made to him, to all the good that had been left undone. In stories, the good guy was always supposed to win, but in the real world all we can hope for is to not die before we finish what we have to.

Shaun looked down at me. "You need to stop." He said.

I didn't answer him.

He rolled his eyes at my act of defiance and then said. "You're safe now James, we've brought you to our refuge in the real world. We've been setting it up for a while now, using old sewer tunnels to get around. A lot of the old maintenance tunnels around Eugene are abandoned." He said as he let Kate look me over.

"Great, I'm safe, Virgil's dead, what more could I want?" I said sarcastically.

Kate looked down at me with teary eyes, I wasn't clear about her and Virgil's relationship but she looked just as torn up about it as I was. I peered up at her and asked. "So why am I on a gurney and why do I have stitches exactly?" I questioned.

Kate looked over at Shaun who was pacing around the room. She smiled then looked back down at me. "You were shot." She finally said. I couldn't see myself but if I had I'm sure that I looked white as a sheet.

Shot. Why was I shot?

The pain became present as I started to dwell on it. Like fire that shot up from my side, I could feel where the wound was now. "How was I shot?!" I yelled at the two of them. The anger in me, coupled with the pain from my wounds made me even more belligerent.

Shaun stopped pacing and walked over to the gurney. Putting both hands shoulder width apart, he leaned over my face and said. "There was a security detail at the hospital we hadn't accounted for, after we got you out one of them took a shot and it hit you, barely though, more like a graze." He said stumbling over his words.

"Great Shaun. What's the point of being able to see the future if you can't see something like security guards?" I questioned him angrily.

Kate looked over at Shaun and asked. "Are you going to tell him the rest?"

Shaun's forefinger and thumb pinched the bridge of his nose then to Kate he said. "I was getting to that Kate." Then he rolled his eyes as if Kate had revealed something to me I wasn't supposed to hear. "You may have also died while Kate was operating on you." He mentioned as my eyes widened in fear.

I was ready to go off on them, had I not been tied down I might have hit Shaun. "What do you mean died? A graze is not something you die from and it's certainly not something you forget to mention to someone Shaun!" I screamed at him.

Shaun let out a long sigh.

"See this is why I didn't want to tell him, he's so dramatic all the time." His words weren't intended for anyone in particular but more aimed at the universe in general.

"Its fine, he deserves to know." Kate said.

Shaun pushed himself up from the table then said. "There were complications when we tried to fish the bullet out of your stomach. You died but we resuscitated you, no big deal."

Even though Shaun was trying to play down the fact I'd been shot, the thought of actually dying twisted my stomach into knots. Trying to think about not existing gave me a headache, I had been close to death before, but suddenly I felt different. I had actually died and came back, for a moment I ceased to be, in this or any world. For one moment, I *wasn't*. I found it too hard to think about so I decided to dwell on it later when there weren't so many more pressing things at hand—like making sure Shaun knew how pissed I was. "What do you mean it's not a big deal? You weren't the one who was shot." I said through my teeth.

Kate held me down as I struggled against my bonds saying. "Calm down James it's going to be alright. If you calm down we can let you go." A few seconds later I let myself become passive externally, as a fire raged internally. When Kate was satisfied I wasn't going to struggle any longer, she began to undo my restraints. She released my right arm first followed by my right leg; as soon as she freed my hand however, I began to work on the restraints until all of my appendages were free. My hands rubbed my wrists because of how tight the straps had been. I sat up and noticed the small patch where the bullet had entered me.

"Don't touch it too much. You should be alright we just don't want to risk infection." Kate instructed. I looked at the bandage and then ignoring her warning my fingers touched the soft cotton.

My body flinched.

Kate was right I should have left it alone. My head tried to get a grip on the situation.

I scratched my head as I looked around the room. "So where are we exactly?" I asked.

"We're underneath Eugene." Shaun said.

My eyes adjusted to the whiteness in the room, then looked at Shaun. "How did you do all this?" I asked, questioning how many resources Shaun really had.

Shaun smirked and then said. "It has taken a few years but I think we've gotten this place running smoothly, and just in time, now that we can't use our refuge in The Shade."

I stared at him for a moment as the nagging thoughts of Virgil reentered my mind. Virgil had trusted me, not only while we were in The Shade, but he also gave his life to ensure we would finish Burke, so I might be able to live a normal life. I felt tears rolling down my face once more. Shaun saw this and put both of his hands on my shoulders. "You can't give up hope now James, we don't have that luxury." He told me.

I stared up at him.

I could only stare, as what he was trying to say to me blurred into a sea of white noise and hums. Lost in my own thoughts about what was going to happen next, a muffled voice that seemed to be directed at me came piercing its way through my fog. "JAMES!" Shaun shouted his hands tight around my shoulders.

"What?" I asked as I snapped out of my trance.

"Virgil's gone, we can mourn him later. We've got bigger problems James, he has Angela." Shaun said. The thought of Angela made my eyes widen, my neck snapped up to attention and my spine tingled.

"Who has her?" I asked knowing exactly what 'he' Shaun had meant.

"It's what I've been trying to tell you. Burke has her. We got a phone call from him after the botched rescue." He explained.

My heart jumped into overdrive as my fists tightened. I knew Burke's game, he was going to use Angela to draw me out in the open and then kill me or put me back into The Shade. However, I didn't care, I didn't care what happened to me, as long as I got Angela back. "Where?" I asked, my voice almost frighteningly calm.

Shaun saw my calm and told me. "He's at the old mental hospital, the abandoned one near the edge of the city." I shrugged Shaun's hands off my shoulders and jumped off the table I'd been sitting on. The pain from the bullet wound was minor, I could still walk, which meant I could still fight. Kate saw my sudden burst of energy. "Please, sit back down." Kate pleaded.

"I'm not sitting down, where are my clothes?" I asked.

Shaun looked at me with a broken look on his face as he realized what I was trying to do. "No, you've lost a lot of blood." Shaun said. "We've lost too many people today, let's play this smart, and not rush off to play hero." Shaun looked as if every life lost that day was his fault, he must have blamed himself for all that went wrong. It seemed like if I were added to the body count, it would just be one more failure for him.

"No one's playing hero, I'm going to get Angela." I told him. "Now where are my clothes?"

Kate looked at me with a furrowed brow, it was obvious she didn't like that I hadn't listened to Shaun. However the fact remained, I wasn't one of Shaun's soldiers so I didn't care if she was displeased with my decisions. Shaun moved closer to me saying. "You're going to have to take a step back and settle down." His voice intimidating.

"I'm not going to back down here Shaun. I owe you my life but I am not yours to control, you can either help me out or get out of my way. Either way, I'm leaving this room." I told him, my eyes glared straight through him.

There was a long silence.

"Kate get him his clothes." Shaun said as he stepped back from me.

Kate reluctantly handed me my bag. Once the bag was in my hands I scrambled through it, my red shirt, a pair of jeans, even the box I'd taken from my desk was inside. I took out the box and handed it to Shaun.

"Keep this safe for me please." I said as he took it from me.
"Alright." He acknowledged.

I changed into my clothes and put on my shoes.

"I'm ready to go." I told Shaun. He walked over to the door and opened it, the door howled as it came open.

"Take the hallway all the way to the end and there will be a ladder on your left take it up, you'll be on 5th street." He instructed.

Slowly my feet shuffled me to the doorway but before I left the room, my body turned and looked at Kate. "Thank you, for everything." I told her. She gave me a smile and I grinned back. Then I twisted, looking at Shaun. "Take care of yourself." I told him and then offered my hand to him. He took it and shook my hand.

"You too, remember James he knows you're coming. He's not going to leave you alive this time. Be careful." He said. "Oh and make sure that no one see's you." He added.

"Alright." I told him and then stepped out of the doorway into a long hallway. The large metal door slammed behind me and locked shut. I walked slowly down the sewer hallway, each step the sound of water under my feet became louder and louder. A few minutes passed and I reached the ladder to the street and began to climb. When I reached the top, my hands moved the old manhole cover; I slid it off the fittings and then looked out, making sure there weren't any people around. Once I felt safe, I climbed out of the sewer and onto the street.

The street was empty.

I felt an overwhelming feeling of being cold and alone as I moved down the street towards the mental hospital. Angela was the only thought on my mind. Enough people had died for me, I wasn't going to let Burke claim another victim.

I was going to kill him, once and for all.

XXVII

The street was vacant and lifeless. The two blocks that separated me from the abandoned mental hospital felt more like a million of miles. As I thought about the distance, an overwhelming the feeling despair set in. I closed my eyes, trying to calm myself but the wound from where I had been shot made me feel like I was on fire. Instantly my body began to sweat, which dripped down and entered the wound. My face cringed in pain as I started to walk towards the alleyway on my right.

Remembering what Shaun had told me, I knew that I needed to be as careful as possible.

I can't stop now.

My feet pounded the asphalt as I made my way into the alley.

The alley will be much easier to navigate unseen.

The alley was damp and dirty, with layers of sedentary grime that had developed over years of neglect. Loose newspapers and other trash swirled in the wind as it blew strong down the narrow passage. The papers cascaded down through the small alley and gently floated to the ground. The cool breeze on my face was refreshing. It calmed me and cooled my body. The sweat from my brow trickled down and landed on the ground before me. I welcomed in all the sensations, even the small ones, because I wasn't sure how much longer I'd be able to enjoy them.

I stood in the breeze of the early morning with my eyes closed as I listened to the sounds around the city. Cars drove their commutes to work, people hurrying along the sidewalks to get to wherever they needed to go. The trees that swayed back and forth, then a peculiar sound that I'd not heard before rang in my ears, for an instant it sounded like my name. It sounded as if someone, perhaps the wind itself, was calling out to me, "James!" The wind whispered then faded into the white noise.

My eyes opened quickly and took a long deep breath. I was ready to move on further towards the hospital. My body moved slowly as the pain from the gunshot ripped through me with every step, the agony was outweighed however, by my sense of urgency to help Angela. I trudged down the alley, as my beehive like mind buzzed with thoughts. Thoughts like the fates of Virgil, Angela and I, all of which seemed so uncertain.

Virgil stuck out in my mind the most.

He had been through so much; he had face so many years of trial and tribulation. Virgil had done things some people would question, but as I stumbled my way towards the mental hospital, I forgave him for those things. However, I came to the realization that ultimately, he was my friend and nothing was going to shatter that memory of him. Whatever Virgil was to anyone else, he was a good person to me and I didn't want to remember him any other way than as the man who saved my life.

I moved out of the alley and back out onto a street behind some shops, the street, seemingly used for deliveries to adjacent shops was just as empty as the alley had been. A large breeze came from the west and funneled down the street towards me. The force of the concentrated wind almost knocked me off my feet. I staggered backwards but regained my balance. The wind brought with it a bitter feeling and once again, my body remained still to listen to the wind.

Then the peculiar sound crept into my head again.

"James!" It seemed to be speaking directly to me.

"This has to be my subconscious playing tricks on me." I said to myself. "Great! Now I'm talking to myself." If there was anything that could make me seem crazier, it was creeping around abandoned alleys talking to myself. I'm sure Angela already thought I was insane, with all my talk about out of body experiences and ghosts.

She saw the ghost, she had seen Virgil's daughter. She must have known that I wasn't completely insane, either that or she felt as if she was going crazy too.

Whether Angela thought I was crazy or not, the only thing on my mind was that I needed to get to her and make sure she was safe. That no matter what happened to me, that the lunatic Burke didn't lay a finger on her. I moved from the street to the next alley and walked to its end, the mouth of the alley led out onto another road, which was being repaired for the local fair in a couple months.

Luckily, that meant the usual traffic would be detoured, so I didn't have to worry about being spotted. My eyes darted around to make sure the street was clear. It was, so quickly I made my way across the road and into the next alleyway. Graffiti decorated the brick walls of the alleyway with names of artists scribbled underneath the artwork.

I was only one block away from the abandoned hospital. In its heyday the hospital had been one of the city's first, and after it was deemed unfit for the more civilized members of society, it was changed into a mental institution. After it was decommissioned almost twenty year ago, kids began to break into it at night and have parties inside. Most of us maintained that ghosts haunt it, but no one had actually seen anything. Although with my newfound knowledge about the afterlife, I would bet there were a few spirits still lingering there.

I made it to the middle of the alley, when the wind suddenly stopped. This wasn't a slow taper off, but like if someone had flipped a switch.

Then the sound came again.

"James!" This time it was louder than before. The voice stopped me. My head darted around looking for its source, hearing like it was right next to me. I glanced back and forth trying to locate the origin but came up with nothing. "James!" The voice shouted into my ear.

I turned quickly behind me.

I was alone in the alley.

My fingers tightened into a fist as I prepared myself for an attack.

Is Burke behind this?

He could be trying to distract me before I can get to him.

"James!" The voice wailed through the alley.

"No!" I shouted "I'm not going to let you get inside my head Burke!" My voice reverberated off the hollow red brick of the alley. My eyes shut as tight as I could manage and when I opened them, the voice was gone. "I'm not going to let you inside my head Burke!" I repeated just in case the voice was still following me. Then, as if the wind were responding, a moan wailed down the alleyway. It seemed to be coming through a filter, muffled and distorted. I spun around to look again, finding that I was still the only one in the alley. "Where are you?" I said trying to reason with the voice.

"James!"

My hands met my head in frustration trying to keep the sound out.

Then a face appeared. Next to me, trying to come through the solid brick wall was a face. It stretched and contorted the brick so that it looked more like rubber stretched over someone's face. The face said nothing more, retreated into the wall, and was gone.

I got up close to the brick wall and touched the area where the rubber face had appeared. The wall was perfectly solid.

THE SHADE

Then the face pushed through the wall again, this time with more violent force. I could see its jaws snapping as it pushed through the once again rubberized brick. My feet stumbled backwards, away from the wall. The face ripped and tore at the air, looking like it was trying to break free of some sort of restraint.

Then it happened, the wall began to glow, like daylight emerging from a crack in a window. The face began to emerge from the wall, followed by an arm. My eyes looked up at the figure and immediately I knew what it was. The blackened, burnt skin of a specter was unmistakable. Its face looked tortured, as its hollowed out eyes sat like endless voids in the back of its skull. The specter's arms came through the wall, helping to push the rest of the vile creature into the real world.

"Oh my God." I said as my eyes opened wide. Virgil had told me that the specters could cross between worlds, but he never mentioned anything about them appearing in the real world. The specter must have been disoriented because for a few moments I thought it couldn't see me. As the seconds ticked by, my heart was pounding away in my chest. I tried to think of what to do, but with limited power in the real world, the only plan that I could come up with was to run. I slowly moved backwards, trying to get as much distance between me and the specter shadow before it noticed what I was doing.

It didn't take long for it to figure it out.

The specter let out a terrifying moan that scratched at my ears. My hands went to cover my ears but before they could, the creature turned in my direction and began to charge at me. With as much speed as I could muster, I turned to run. I ran as quickly as I could out of the alleyway. I made it to the mouth of the alley, looking both directions as I crossed the street and then continued down another alley. The last one before the hospital. My head turned to check on the specter that chased me; its blackened mass ran through the street towards the alley I had just entered. My head twisted forward just in time for me to run into a chain link fence that divided the alley in half.

I scrambled to get over the fence before the specter could catch up with me, believing if I made it to the hospital that I could slip away from the creature. It took me only a few seconds to scale the fence and drop down to the other side. I turned around to see the specter push its way through the fence like a bulldozer. My eyes widened as it continued coming for me. My feet carried me to the end of the alleyway, from there I could see the hospital just across the street.

The hospital's crumbling walls and broken windows made it look like a building from The Shade. A tall chain link fence stood around the building trying to keep any adventurous teenagers out of the old abandoned halls. Quickly I made my way across the street towards the fence that stood around the hospital. I knew immediately I'd be unable to climb it because of the barbed wire strung across the length of it. My fingers gripped between the links as my mind tried to figure out what to do.

Then a scream came from behind me.

I turned seeing the specter, it knew I had nowhere left to run. My fists clenched together prepared for an attack. Then it darted towards me, faster than anything I'd ever seen in my entire life. The specter zipped over to me like lightning and once it was within range, its charred fist punched my chest. The immediate feeling that rattled my bones was nothing compared to the pain of being thrown through the metal fence. The action happened so quickly my mind didn't have time to register the pain. I shook my head back into focus while my pursuer inched closer towards me.

On my back, I began to inch in the direction of the large metal doors of the hospital. My breath was labored, no matter how much oxygen I took in, my lungs never seemed satisfied. My body backed up until I hit the steps leading up to the doors of the hospital. I stumbled as my hands pushed me back upright, my legs wobbled under my weight. My eyes squinted and saw the specter moving closer and closer.

Then with one quick movement, the creature was in front

of me. It kicked me in the chest making my back slam against the metal doors, causing them to fly open as I stumbled inside. I lost my balance and hit the floor of the hospital lobby, scattering loose tile as my body rolled to a stop. My eyes crossed in and out of focus as I got up on my hands and knees. A metallic taste entered my mouth and I spit a mouthful of blood onto the dusty floor. My legs quivered as my body struggled to stand upright; I braced myself on a nearby desk and then looked out through the doors I'd crashed through.

My body felt like it was going to give out. Every second that ticked by, I could feel a little more of my life slipping away from me. Every step the specter took towards me was one more second counted down before it inevitably ended my life.

Is this it? Is this how I die?

Thoughts of my family and friends flooded my head. Everyone I'd known and cared about flashed before my eyes, but when my mind got to the image of Angela it stopped, and hers was the only face I could see. Her face hung there for a moment and then a scream shattered the memory as the specter beckoned me back to the present with its grotesque wail. Then I tightened my fists until my knuckles turned white.

No! Not like this!

The creatures darted towards me again while my veins pulsing with adrenaline. But it was too fast for me to defend against, the specter smashed against me, sending me hurtling through the air and through the wall behind were I stood. My back hit drywall snapping through the studs and everything else inside. When I hit the ground, I landed on my back. I rolled to a stop looking up at the ceiling, thinking only one thing.

This fight is nowhere near over.

XXVIII

An intense wave of pain shot its way up my spine. Slowly I opened my eyes, as my bloody fist clinched a hand full of tile fragments and crushed them into powder.

That didn't go as expected.

My hands shook as they slowly lifted my body back to an upright position.

Once on my feet, I scanned the empty room quietly. My legs quivered as they tried to keep me from doubling back over. Then I felt a presence in the room with me. It wasn't something tangible that I could see, but I knew that something was there. My breath remained slow and steady. My hand rubbed the back of my head as I tried to get my bearings. Then it happened, coming out from the wall in front of me, the specter emerged.

My fists balled tightly, readying myself for an attack. The creature leapt at me, its arms opened wide, ready to take me to the ground. I instinctively ducked, causing my assailant to vault over me. I rolled forward and then sprang back to my feet.

The specter landed softly, only a few feet behind me.

I spun around to face the creature and before it had time to attack; my fist was already rocketing towards its face. When the two forces made contact, a thunderous boom erupted in the room. The specter recovered quickly, and before I knew what was happening it had latched its arms around my waist and we were tumbling towards the ground. We slammed against the floor, rolling a few feet. When we stopped, my legs heaved upwards with all their strength, breaking the specter's grip on me, hurling it across the room.

The creature hit the floor as I quickly found my way upright and ran for the door. I headed down the long hospital hallway. I felt the side of my body begin to burn as the pain the specter had inflicted became apparent. Halfway down the hallway, I found a room and ducked into it to avoid the specter. My hand met my mouth to stop myself from breathing too heavily. My heart pounded so loudly in my chest I thought that it would give me away.

From down the hallway, I could hear the specter moving closer towards me. Closer and closer the footsteps of the creature passed by the room. It breathed heavily as it searched the hallway for me.

My muscles tightened.

I could feel the creature as it passed by the room.

One, two, three.

I counted in my head and then took off down towards the opposite end of the hallway. I ran back down the hallway, the sound of heavy footsteps running towards me echoed down the hall. The noise from the creature behind me grew closer, and closer. Each step that I took down the hallway the creature gained another few feet on me, I knew that within a few seconds it would be on top of me again.

So in a split-second decision, I stopped to make a stand.

My foot pivoted and my whole body turned to face the specter. I balled my hands into fists and readied them to defend myself. The creature lunged off the ground, leaping through the air towards me. My eyes watched the creature fly like a missile towards me. It grabbed me and we fell towards the floor together, slamming each other against the hard tile. My head felt woozy from the blow; while I was recovering, the specter positioned itself on top of me. Its arms reared up and its fist plunged down towards my face. The first blow landed. It felt like being hit by a car. A quick second later, another fist slammed into my jaw; then another in my eye, then another.

With all the strength I could muster, my hand shot up, catching the specter's punch. I summoned all muscles to tighten and crush the creature's hand. My body called every muscle in my body to throw the specter off me. With one quick jolt from my arm, I shoved the creature away from me. It stumbled backwards towards the wall, and then it disappeared into smoke.

My breath was heavy, as my lungs finally allowed me to breathe. My arms pushed me to my knees and from my knees; I rose to my feet. My body felt dizzy, like when you stand up too fast and all the blood rushes to your head.

I knew that the specter was still near, my eyes glanced around, looking for the creature. Then my whole body stiffened as the presence of the creature filled the hallway. I searched the dusty corridor with my eyes, taking note of everything. I looked downward to find my hand trembling in fear. In fact, my entire body shook with anticipation of what was coming next.

The specter leapt out from the wall towards me. My body ducked, causing the creature to miss me. The specter was headed for the floor but before it made contact, it disappeared once again. My eyes began to scan again, waiting for the next attack. Then from my left, the creature burst from the wall. This time my body was prepared. As the creature flew by me, I grabbed hold of it. While holding the specter, I gave it one solid toss, managing to send it crashing into the closest wall. The wall caved in where the creature struck it, creating a thick cloud of white dust before me. Frantically my eyes searched the dust for any signs of movement.

I continued to search as the dust began to settle.

My eyes turned up nothing. Then from behind me, something slammed into my back, which sent me stumbling forward towards a wall. I hit the wall, cracking the sheetrock in places.

I turned my body around to face the specter. Its hands grabbed my shirt and threw me to the ground. I hit the floor in a seated position, that was, until the creature kicked me in the face. The blow snapped my body completely backwards, causing my head to smack the tile.

"Is that all you've got." My voice choked out through layers of blood and saliva.

The specter looked at me as if it were annoyed. As if any emotion could be distinguished from a face so evil. I watched as the specter stood above me, then in one swift motion its leg went back, and then came forward towards my gut. My hands moved to intercept the foot but they did nothing to soften the blow. The kick sent me sliding across the floor towards the wall, only stopping when my back made contact with the wall.

I opened my eyes. The world around me was out of focus and a dark figure approached me. Time itself seemed to slow as the specter walked, each stride taking longer than the last. I fluttered my eyes to regain focus but by then the creature stood over me. Slowly my eyes looked up at the creature. Blood dripped from my face, and my body ached, but I knew there would be no mercy, no repose. Then I watched the creature raise its leg in the air, and then propelled its leg down towards me.

Two point five seconds until his foot slams me into the ground and I'm nothing but a stain on the tile.

Two point five seconds was enough time for my mind to think of everyone that I was about to leave behind. My family, my friends—Angela. Then my mind moved from those I'd leave behind to the things that I'd never get to do. All the things that I would miss out on, all of the things that I regretted not doing, everything, all at once passed in front of my eyes.

Then as the shadows foot was nearing my face, a voice called out of the darkness.

"That's enough!" The voice called.

The specter stopped its foot short from hitting my face. I could see the charred flaky skin as the specter removed its foot from my face and placed it back on the ground. My head twisted to see who had saved me from my fate. My eyes took a second to adjust but as soon as they did, I saw the face of my savior.

"Burke." I said through my bloodied teeth.

He held out his arms in a showy gesture and said. "One and the same."

I pushed myself up with my arms, under pressure to get myself upright, I felt as if it was made of liquid. My feet trembled as I stared at Burke walking closer and closer to me. I looked to my left where the specter stood, passive, and obedient to Burke's will.

"Do you like my pet?" He asked strange twisted sense of happiness in his voice.

"Your pet?" I questioned.

Burke looked at me as if he were confused. Then his furrowed brow changed to a grim smile that seemed to say he knew something I didn't. "Do you not recognize him?" He asked me allowing me to look at the specter.

There was a long moment of silence as I stared.

Then Burke stepped forward and said. "This is my dear brother, everything that's left of your precious Virgil." His mouth spit Virgil's name out as if it were some sort of bile. My eyes widened as I looked at the specter, I could find no trace of Virgil in its inhuman form.

"What did you do to him?!" I screamed.

"Me?" He said gesturing to the specter. "I did nothing to him, He did this to himself. Despite what you may think James your miraculous Virgil wasn't without his sins." My fists tightened as he mentioned Virgil's name. All I wanted in that moment was to run at him with everything I had. However, that isn't what I did. I remained calm, just as Virgil had taught me.

"They were the things that you made him do." I told him.

"I didn't make him do anything, like you said James, you always have a choice." He told me, throwing my own words back in my face. Burke looked at me with disgust as I defended the brother he despised so much. "He's stolen, lied, and murdered. This is what his mind became after I killed his body; usually it takes years for this kind of degeneration to happen."

My eyes shifted to the specter who was as still as a stone. "The only reason Virgil did any of that was to protect his family. You're the monster here Burke, not him." My voice became louder as I spoke. The sound of my voice echoed off the empty walls of the hospital.

Burke began to laugh. "I'm the monster, eh?" He rubbed his chin. "Okay then, try and reason with him James." He gave me a bleak smirk and then to the creature and said. "Kill."

Instantly the specter's hand was around my neck.

The creature lifted me up until my feet were off the floor. It slammed my back against a nearby wall holding me there. The hollow sockets of the specter glared towards me, I struggled as my hands tried to free myself from its death grip. "Virgil—," I coughed out. "—I know you're still in there somewhere, you can fight this, I know you can." My legs kicked as they tried to brace my body against something. Burke stood by and from the corner of my eye, I could see him, arms crossed watching the life being choked out of me.

"You see James, you can't reason with monsters." He told me.

I turned away from him and looked back at the specter. "Virgil, I know it's you—," the monster tightened its grip on me. "—I know you don't want to do this, just try and fight it!" I yelled. The air in my lungs was getting stale, unable to grasp another breath. I knew the next time that I spoke could be my last. That's when I remembered something Virgil told me about the nature of the specters. "Virgil—Virgil I forgive you." My voice croaked out.

The creature's grip loosened a tiny bit, allowing me to get a breath of air.

"I forgive you Virgil." I continued. "Not just me but everyone you wronged, all the people that your brother made you deceive, all the people that had to die in your pursuit for justice." The specter's grip loosened even more. "We forgive you, and if you need a reason to hold on to your humanity, hold onto it for me, because I need you now more than ever." I pleaded.

Then something unexpected happened.

The specter dropped me back to my feet. I hit the floor and almost lost my balance, rubbing my neck where the creature had held me hostage. The specter stared down at me, its head twisted as if it were trying to think. "What are you doing?!" Burke called. "Kill him now!" The specter didn't respond, it looked at me and for a moment I thought I could see Virgil's face. Suddenly, with violent force the specter began to shake. It twisted and contorted as a guttural rumble began to emanate from within it.

I watched as the skin of the specter began to crack, and through those cracks shown the brightest light I'd ever seen. The light blinded me for a moment and as it began to erupt from the specter, I covered my face. The room around us shook with violent intensity and then a second later the creature was gone, and in its place stood Virgil. He looked the same way he had when we were in The Shade. He stared at me for a long moment and then smiled. "Thank you." He said.

If my heart could have, it would have ripped its way out of my chest. I couldn't believe the vision standing before me. "You're—you're welcome Virgil." I stammered out then he turned to Burke, fists readied to fight.

"Well I have to say I didn't see that coming." Burke smirked then darted through the dust-covered hallway and slammed his fist into Virgil's face. Virgil's body flew backwards into the wall next to me.

"Virgil!" I called out as I quickly ran to see if he was okay. When I got to him, his face was a mess of blood, his nose broken and out of place. "Hey, Virgil are you alright?" My voice was frantic as I checked him for other injuries.

"James." He said faintly as blood flowed down his lips and onto the ground.

"What?" I asked.

He pointed behind me and my eyes followed his finger, tracing it back to where Burke was standing. Burke cracked his neck then grinned at me. My heart raged. I got up to my feet and offered a hand to Virgil, helping him back to his feet. My hand balled into a fist and as it did I could feel a faint surge of energy flow through me, it wasn't as strong as the ones I'd felt in The Shade but I hoped it would be enough to keep me alive.

My anger boiled over and I couldn't help myself. Without a second thought, I threw myself straight at Burke. My fist flew through the air towards Burke, but he caught it with his hand. His fingers wrapped around my fist and clamped down, and I felt the bones in my hand fracture. Our eyes met for a moment, he smirked at me then tossed me backwards. I flew back a few feet then stumbled to the ground. Virgil ran at him as I hit the ground, but with no avail. Burke hit him in the ribs and he flew back, meeting me on the floor.

"Boys, boys, boys why all the hostility?" Burke finally said. My eyes watched him as I reached down to pick myself up off the ground. My hand throbbed, clearly broken from what Burke had done. I paid it no attention as my feet slowly found their way under me.

"You've got Angela." I said to him. "I'm here to kill you."

He snickered at me.

"I don't have Angela, Mr. Langley. You see that's the value of misinformation. I set a trap for you and like a fool, you walked right into it." I glanced down at Virgil. He was out cold.

That last hit must have done some serious damage.

With Virgil incapacitated I'd have to continue alone. I had prepared for that moment, the moment when I would have to face off against Burke. "I don't care about your misinformation; I'm here to end you." My voice sounded like a low growl as it came out over my teeth.

Burke put his hands up in the air as if he was surrendering to me. "James, you've got so much potential, please don't throw it all away." He said in a tone that was almost pleading. "Didn't my brother mention why you're so important to me?"

I searched my mind for the reason Virgil had given me.

"He said it was because I'm different, that you need what's in my head." I sneered.

Burke shook his head at me. "You're not just different James, you're someone very special." Burke began to move in closer towards me, his arms were down, not in an offensive posture. "You can't possibly imagine the painstaking effort it has taken to get you to this point, right here." He explained. "I don't want to fight you James. I've already won, because even if you kill me, here and now, this won't end when I do."

I looked at Burke confused. My mind tried to process everything he'd said to me, Virgil had warned me not to let Burke distract me, to seize my opportunity to kill him when I could. I hesitated then swallowed back a hard lump in my throat. "So why go through all the effort just to kill me?" I asked.

Burke let out a snicker as he walked even closer towards me and said. "James I never intended on killing you, you're far too important. You've just got your priorities mixed up."

My face formed into a scowl.

Burke noticed. "What? I know you're more like me than you care to admit." Walking closer he continued. "I know about your anger. How you lose control. It's really quite impressive." He was a few inches from me. "I know about your thirst for power and how you're consumed by it. You see James. You and me, we're just different from other people."

His words cut me like a knife in the chest. However, it didn't faze me, it didn't stop my aggression, it fueled it. "I'm nothing like you." My voice laced with a thick tone of hatred.

Burke pointed at me with his finger and smiled. "Well that's where you're wrong. We're not ordinary. Ordinary people cannot walk through walls or crush stone into powder. No, you'll never be like those people again. So you see James, I'm the closest thing you've got to family." He told me. "That's why I don't want to kill you. I'm just the tip of a much wider spear pointed at the throat of the human race, at the ordinary people."

It took me a second to realize what Burke had said, and then something snapped inside my head. "I get it now." I told him. "You're not in charge here, you're just following orders." A smile crept across my face as I realized the truth. "So why am I even talking to you then?"

In an instant, the few inches that had separated me from Burke cease to be as he grabbed my shirt. He twisted the fabric and picked me up off the ground. I laughed in his face and the rage he'd been hiding spilled over, changing into open unbridled anger. "You insignificant worm. I swear if I didn't have orders not to harm you I would enjoy pulling the flesh from your bones." He said with a calm voice then launched me backwards. I reached out, trying to use my hands to brace myself but as they made contact with the floor, they did little to stop me. My back hit the floor with a thud, making me slide a few inches across the dusty tile.

I lay on the tile and held my hand.

"Your life belongs to The Speakers, so it's not mine to take." He said with a stern tone. "Fight it all you want Mr. Langley, they already have control over your life and soon enough, there won't be anything you can do about it." Burke said with a smug smile.

I tried to get up but couldn't lift myself off the ground. Then I tried again, using my forearm and elbow to lift myself in liue of using my hands. I managed to get my feet under me having my legs lift the majority of my weight to push me upright. "I'm no one's puppet Burke."

"He said as he could hardly stand." Burke mocked me.

"Like it or not your pathetic human race will be coming to an end."

"I don't believe you."

"Believe me or not it doesn't matter. Nevertheless know this, human kind will fall, and you will be the architect of its destruction." Burke said. The statement sent my head into a tailspin, unsure of what he was telling me.

It can't be true.

"What do these "Speakers" want?" I asked.

He paused. I assume for dramatic effect then said. "They want you. You're the key James. The Speakers have been around since the beginning; they always have been and always will be. The Speaker's feed off energy, and what creates more energy than a human being?" He posed the question. "They've manipulated human history for their own means. The Speakers influenced every single choice that has ever been made, and those choices led to this moment right now. Centuries of manipulation to get you here, right now James. They're the little voice in your head that tells you to go right instead of left. They control everything, so make no mistake, you are their puppet." He told me.

"So what, you think I'll help you?" I asked him.

"You don't get it, do you? You do not have a choice. There have been hundreds of generations of persuasion that went into getting *you* to this moment." He informed me as his finger pointed at me once more. I couldn't move, I was frozen in that moment. Frozen by the thought of a group of beings so powerful they could orchestrate what Burke had told me. For the first time since I'd awoken, my brain allowed me to feel frightened as wave of panic washed over me.

A few seconds of silence passed until I finally found the courage to speak. "So what you're saying is I don't have free will." My voice shaky as I spoke.

Burke caught it immediately.

"No what I'm saying is, it doesn't matter what you choose to do the result will always be the same." Burke said through

THE SHADE

the hall. "James I offered you a chance to join me and you threw it back in my face. Instead you cast yourself in with this lot." He pointed at Virgil who had begun to stir awake.

I looked down at him and asked. "You okay?"

"I've been better but I'm alright."

I reached down and pulled him up. His icy hand hit me like a shock and yanked him to his feet. His sudden awaking revived my fighting spirit. "You see Burke." I started to say as I moved closer toward him. "I'd rather cast my lot in with Virgil and the rest of the human race than join you or your Speakers."

I felt powerful in that moment, understanding something Virgil had once told me. *"If you use your compassion and humanity, you'll be stronger than anyone, which is why Burke's afraid of you."* Virgil's words echoed in my head.

Burke began to laugh.

Then in an instant, he appeared next to Virgil and with both fists sent him into a wall. Burke had hit Virgil so hard that the wall actually caved inward as Virgil's body slammed against it. Then Burke glanced at me, less than a second away he threw a wild punch.

The fist came so quickly I didn't even see it.

The blow landed just below my neck, the force sent me at least ten feet down the hallway. My body tumbled until I finally ended up on my back. Looking up at the decrepit ceiling tiles and hanging electrical wires as pain shot all through my body. Clumsily my hands checked my chest. Nothing felt broken, but the pain was strong, I got back to my feet but my lungs felt compressed, not allowing me to take a complete breath. I wheezed as I finally stood upright.

When my eyes were finally able to see straight they locked on Burke who was standing down the hall holding Virgil by the throat. Burke snapped a grin at me. "I may not be able to kill you." He pointed at me. "But there's nothing that says I have to leave him alive." He smiled and looked at Virgil.

"James, RUN!" Virgil shouted.

I darted quickly down the hall towards them; I was only ten feet away.

Five feet.

Then they vanished, straight into The Shade.

I ran to where they had been standing but I found nothing but air.

My mind went frantic. I didn't know what to do. If they were in The Shade, Virgil wouldn't last long without me. My eyes scanned the dust-ridden hall for anything that could help me. As my eyes examined the empty hallway, an unnatural light shot out beside me. "James!" Virgil's head and shoulders became visible through the light, and then a hand from nowhere pulled him back.

I caught a glimpse of Virgil's face as he called out to me. His appearance haunted me, it was clear that Burke was making fast work of Virgil without me to help him.

I couldn't save him, just like I couldn't save him before.

My heart beat fast in my chest. I squeezed my fists until my knuckles were white.

Everyone I try to protect I let down. Virgil would never get the justice he deserved for his daughter's death. I'd never be free of Burke if Virgil couldn't help me kill him. Angela would most likely be punished for what Virgil and I did today, along with my parents, my friends and all of the others that would come after me. I'd failed them.

My eyes welled with tears but none fell from my face.

Unexpectedly a surge of energy washed over me like a wave. I could feel the power permeate through me, crashing, pulsing. Virgil had told me that the bleed over effect from The Shade was minimal, but the power the circulated through my body felt as if I could do anything.

Maybe I can use it to my advantage.

I let the waves waft over me until I was filled with energy. My breath slowed and my eyes darkened. The moment my eyes shut, I could feel everything around me. From the dust on the walls and floor, to the old tiles that had become worn and cracked. The termites that ate away at the foundation of the building, even the stale air in the room all came alive. I could feel that, as I flexed, so did the walls around me, my energy seemed to be pushing them outward.

I gathered as much energy as I could muster and started to run.

I ran quickly, faster than I'd ever run before. I saw my goal. I needed to break the bond of the real world. I needed to pass through. The end of the hallway was sixty feet away.

Forty feet. Closer and closer.

Thirty feet, my legs moved faster and faster.

Twenty, I made no effort to stop.

Fifteen feet.

My eyes slammed shut and then the light enveloped me. I turned around to find Burke standing above Virgil's body, without any indecision I ran straight at Burke who had his back turned to me. When I reached him, my hand grabbed the back of his head and all of my fingers dug into his skull. My body leapt forward into the air and landed flat on my chest, bringing Burke's face crashing down into the old tile.

The sound that echoed through the hallway was one of bones being crushed.

I got up off the floor, breathing heavily as I looked down at Burke, kicked him onto his back, and said. "Get up!" I said through my teeth. "I'm just getting started."

XXIX

I looked down at Burke and kicked him in the gut again. I looked at my work, seeing a small pool of red liquid forming around his lips. Then I realized.

Virgil!

My eyes glanced around and saw Virgil as he tried to reclaim his footing. I went to help him back to his feet. My arm wrapped around his neck and grabbed his shoulder, helping him until he stood completely upright by himself. "You alright?" I asked.

"I can't believe you made it." He smiled at me. "How did you do it?"

That's when I fully realized where I was. Virgil's question sent my head through a loop. While my anger for Burke began to subside, my mind began to ponder how I had made it back into The Shade. My memory felt like it was unorganized, I could remember running quickly, then the bright light, but it wasn't intentional, it just happened. "I'm not completely sure." I said as my voice trailed off as I began to think about it again.

"Well I'm not sure how you did it but I'm glad you got here when you did."

Burke stirred and quickly pushed himself up off the floor, his eyes looking at us. There were no bruises, scrapes or blood on him. He had been completely healed. Burke rose to his feet and chuckled. "Well, well, well." He said as he dusted himself off. "Sorry to break up the reunion boys but you see, I've got work to do."

I readied myself for an attack. "I told you, I'm not finished with you yet."

"Be careful James. He's a lot stronger here." Virgil advised.

"Don't worry, so am I." My palms were wet with anticipation, I clenched my fists and darted at burke, I ran to the wall on my left. My feet ran along its face until I was within five feet of Burke. My legs launched me off the wall and I flew at him, my fist aimed straight for his jaw. However, I had misjudged the distance, and instead of a punch, my leap turned into more of a tackle. When my shoulder met his lower torso, I instinctually wrapped my arms around him and used my momentum to fly both of us towards the nearest wall. My eyes clenched shut as they braced for the impact.

However, there wasn't an impact.

There wasn't anything. I had expected to hit the wall with all the force I could muster but instead I didn't feel the pain until we hit both hit the ground. We slammed hard against the ground breaking the rest of the tile that weren't already broken. We rolled away from each other when I noticed we were in a completely different room.

We both must have phased through the wall.

I sat upright and a sharp pain came from my left shoulder, my hand immediately rose to check it. Then I looked up to find Burke standing over me, his fist driving down on me. His knuckles dug deep into my cheek and I could hear the reverberation of the blow through the rest of my skull. The force knocked me backwards, pushing my face back down to the ground. I tried to regain my orientation and I looked back up to see Burke's fist as it came back down again. The force of the second blow was just has hard as the first. My face tried to look up again and another fist slammed into me.

The blow didn't hurt as much as the previous ones did, partially because my face had become numb to the pain, and because my head couldn't have been working right after so many blows.

I can't take this kind of punishment for very long.

I closed my eyes expecting another blow to hit.

Focus. Breath and focus.

My eyes quickly snapped open.

The fist that had been rocketing towards my face seemed different, like it had been slowed somehow. I had time to think, time to break Burke's stranglehold on me. I threw my hands up quickly in an effort to deflect the blow.

Right before Burke's fist reached me however, Virgil phased through the wall. He flew at Burke and tackled him to the ground. I could hear the violence when they landed, rolling, and struggling to subdue one another. My hand touched my broken face and could feel how damaged it was. I was bruised and beaten but somehow I found the strength to stand. Before my eyes had time to observe what was going on, Virgil's limp body flew past me and hit the ground. He rolled and sprang back up next to me. We watched as a broken faced Burke moved closer to us. "You're finished." Virgil said in disgust.

"We'll see about that." Burke said spitting out an enormous amount of blood. Burke then hunkered down and dashed his way towards me. The blow to my ribs was immediate as Burke's whole body crushed itself against me. Interlocked we flew backwards towards the wall behind me, I felt helpless to stop myself. I shut my eyes, bracing for impact. At that moment, something happened, before we came crashing through the wall I felt as if my body hit a barrier. Like an invisible glass wall that separated The Shade from the real world. My body slammed against the invisible wall, breaking it. In a matter of seconds I was back in the real world, with just enough time to realize it before my back slammed through the old drywall behind me. The studs in the wall snapped and the old sheetrock gave out, collapsing a hole in the wall. My face hit the floor as my body rolled across the room I'd been thrown into.

Burke stood over me with a smile that shot terror straight into my veins.

Then a ruffling came from Burke's left and his smile morphed. As Burke turned to look at what had caused the noise Virgil's body flew out of The Shade, slamming Burke's body through the wall adjacent to the one I'd come through. Virgil stood over me and helped me back up.

"Is Burke gone—,"

The words had almost left my mouth when Burke rounded the corner to our right. As Virgil saw Burke, he suddenly disappeared into a puff of smoke. Burke looked at me in the middle of the hall, all alone. "James you have to know there's no way to win this, just accept defeat." He told me.

"I can't do that. I've got too much at stake, too much to lose."

"Even if you kill me here James, there are more people out there like me." He said. "Are you going to kill us all?"

"I'm tired of talking philosophy with you. The only people I care about are my family and you will not take them from me" My fists were ready as the pain from our fight began to envelope me.

"No, maybe not me, but losing them is inevitable. That's the way of the world James. Your friends will not last the coming storm, no matter how hard you try, you can't protect them. You never could. Everything has been predetermined for you." He told me with a matter of fact kind of tone. Now I wouldn't say I'm a violent person but the things that were spewed from Burkes lips filled me with a rage I could not measure. I wanted to tear him limb from limb and smile while I did so. The adrenaline burned deep in my veins and I knew what I needed to do.

Keep him talking. Let him get you angry.
"I'm not going to be anyone's puppet."

"You'll do exactly as The Speakers want, this is your destiny." He said.

"I make my own choices. Get your Speakers down here, Virgil and I will show them that they can't make our decisions for us."

"Them." He said. "No you misunderstand; The Speakers are a, mutli-mind being. While there is only one body it contains seven different entities." His logic confused me. It was hard to conceive of a concept like the one he'd proposed. I stood there, debating what he had told me when he finally added. "They are gods, they have no time for you or my brother petty ideals about family and honor."

My fist tightened. "Why did you kill your own brother?"

Burke scoffed at the question as if it were somehow irrelevant. He thought for a moment then said. "Michael was never worthy of calling himself my brother." The disgust and anger flowed from his mouth; each word he spoke seemed to make me angrier. "He was always too soft, too weak. Never could do what needed done. He sickened me, every aspect of his life made me hate him that much more."

"You didn't answer the question." I said through my teeth, my blood boiling.

Good. It's working.

"He was always the golden child. Even after all my accomplishments. *He* was the one that everyone adored. He never deserved the praise. The two of us are special, like you. We came to The Shade when we were kids. To us, this was our escape. You see, our father was a drunk and a cruel bastard of a man."

"Am I supposed to feel sorry for you?" I sneered.

He ignored the question and continued. "We were kings of this place, powerful beyond measure. Then The Speakers found us, offered us both more, more than we could have ever imagined. I of course accepted, Michael however, said no. He was a disgrace, unworthy of their power, and if he couldn't help me directly I knew I could harvest him for his power."

I watched from my periphery as Virgil materialized behind Burke. He was unaware of Virgil's presence as far as I could tell. I continued to distract Burke from the approaching Virgil. "So you killed his daughter and let him wither away in a hospital?!" I screamed.

"Tragic that I couldn't use Michael for anything else, but letting him sleep away his life was still beneficial." Then a smile spread across his face, it was cold and eerie. "My niece Sarah however—," he paused. "—I enjoyed that. I couldn't allow Michael to have everything he wanted while he shut his own brother out. He had everything, a wife, a child. I knew I had to cut all his ties to the world. So, I came in the night, quickly, as not to be discovered. I went too little Sarah's room, crept to her bed and wrapped my hands tight around her neck." He didn't look ashamed for what he'd done. He continued to smile, a smile I wanted to beat right off his face. "She didn't struggle, she accepted her fate. When I finally watched her eyes roll back, I knew it was over. I can still picture her eyes looking up at me, questioning me. Asking me why I was doing this to her, why I was cutting her life short."

Virgil winked at me, which I assumed was the signal.

"You must be proud of yourself you prick." I seethed.

Then from behind Burke, Virgil's arms shot around him. "What the—," Burke said in surprise. With Virgil's hands interlocked around Burke's body there was nowhere for him to go. Burke struggled to break free, but with every movement, Virgil's grip just became that much tighter.

"You see Burke it's good to have friends."

"I'm going to destroy you." He struggled against Virgil's strength.

"Don't worry this will be over quick." I said as my fist readied itself for an attack. I ran towards Burke who was still in Virgil's grip. Seconds away from impact, my fist took off towards Burke's face, but right before the moment of impact, something happened. Burke ducked out of Virgil's grip and my fist slammed into my ally's jaw. His hands immediately reached for his face, letting Burke free.

Burke kicked my chest and I flew a few feet from where we had been. With Virgil defenseless Burke smiled a malicious grin. Virgil's eyes widened at the smile. Burke placed both of his hands on Virgil's chest. Then from out of Burke's hands, a blinding light shot out in all directions. I tried to cover my eyes but the light was too quick, temporarily blinding me.

Everything went white.

By the time my eyes adjusted, Virgil was across the room his face black and blue with blood flowing from his nose and ears. The ring in my ears muffled all noises. I focused my eyes on a large tan object and just as they focused, I realized the object was Burke's fist. Time slowed down, and as Burke's fist came towards me, I ducked and avoided it to my astonishment, maybe to Burke's as well. My ears still rang. I was fighting deaf and half blind. Burke swung at my face. I jumped backwards to dodge it.

A right hook aimed for my ribs followed. I crouched and avoided it.

Burke threw a front kick towards my chest. My arms crisscrossed and I caught his leg before it made contact. I knew there was a grin on my face but I couldn't help it. I was better half blind and deaf than when I was completely functional. Burke came at me again with everything he had, left hook, right jab, front kick, side kick; every attack he threw at me was met with a dodge or a block.

He threw a right jab. My hand caught his and deflected the blow, which opened his chest for an attack. I made my move, a right hook into the ribs, some of them cracking under the pressure. Then a left jab to the sternum, then a right jab. I made sure to hit him hard enough that he'd not have time to recover and respond. Both my hands met his chest just as Burke had done to Virgil. My hands began to glow and then a spark shot from my hands into Burke's chest. Burke flew backwards ten feet then rolled across the ground another five.

I looked at my hands in astonishment.

What did I do?

"It's an electromagnetic burst." Virgil said as he steadied himself. He walked up towards me, placing his hand on my shoulder to stabilize himself. "Hurt's like hell." Then he turned and his back hit the wall beside me and his body slid down. "Causes slight paralysis." There were more questions I wanted to ask Virgil but time was short and Burke was already stirring from the blast. I left Virgil sitting on the floor, unable to stand on his own and approached Burke. He laughed his normal maniacal laugh as his hands pushed himself off the floor. With one swift kick, I rolled him over so that he was facing me.

"You're finished." I said.

Burke coughed as he tried to speak. "I'm—just getting—started." He choked out.

"You're done and you know it."

"I'd never fight you unless I had an ace up my sleeve." He told me with a grin.

I knew immediately. He was referring to Angela.

"Where is she?" My voice grew louder as my fist readied back for one final blow. Burke stared at me with a smile. His teeth bloodied from the blast. "If you're not going to tell me, than you're going to die." Without hesitation, my fist rocketed forward towards Burke.

"Angela will die!" Burke yelled just before the blow landed. I struggled to stop my fist and the counter momentum I applied knocked me off balance.

"What did you say?" I questioned.

"If you kill me, she dies too." He said as he smiled with his bloody teeth.

"You're lying, you never had her, that was misinformation you said that yourself."

"Ah, but that's the value of misinformation, hard to distinguish truth from lies."

My eyes tightened. "Where is she?" I demanded.

"She's safe, for now."

I grabbed his shirt and pulled his face towards mine. "Tell me now!"

From behind me, Virgil yelled. "He doesn't have her James, finish him!"

"Listen to your good friend Virgil. He's always been *so* honest with you." Burke's words slithered like a snake through his teeth. "I'm sure he's telling the truth now."

"Your mind games aren't going to work." I pulled him closer. "Now tell me."

"I'll never tell." He taunted.

"This is a waste of time James let's just kill him." Virgil shouted still unable to walk. My head spun as I tried to figure out what to do.

Did Burke have Angela or is he lying about this too? Did Virgil know anything about it? How could he be sure Angela would be safe after we killed Burke? Was he so driven by revenge he'd endanger Angela's life?

I tightened my grip around his neck. "Tell me now or I'll kill you."

"You'll kill me if I tell you."

"James, just do it." Virgil yelled. "We aren't going to get any more opportunities like this."

"Think about Angela, James." Burke said. "Scared and alone."

"Tell me!" I shouted.

"Let me go."

"Kill him James!" Virgil screamed.

Then I brought him so close to my face I could see each wrinkle in his face and forehead. Burke smiled a malicious smile and laughed. "What's so funny?"

"You boys never learn do you?" He said as he put his hands on my chest. My eyes widened, knowing what was coming next. A flash of light came from Burke's hands, brilliant light emanating from his hands burst forth into my chest. The radiant beauty of the light was only outdone by the amount of pain that it inflicted. The shock reverberated through my body and tossed me aside like a ragdoll. My arms and legs were numb. My body struggled to get back up, but it was completely paralyzed.

Virgil moaned on the floor. "You should have killed him when you had the chance."

"I couldn't risk it." I slurred as I regained some use of my tongue. "I couldn't risk him hurting her." Virgil stared at me. I heard a dozen footsteps running down the hallway, followed by muffled voices. My eyes turned upwards and saw Burke as he ran down the hall and around the corner. I lost sight of him; we'd missed our chance to kill him.

"I'm sorry Virgil, he's gone." I said as I tried to roll onto my stomach.

"Damn it!" Virgil said as he hit the ground with his fist.

"I'm sorry." I said again, this time I felt faint.

"COWARD!" Virgil yelled to the walls of the hospital.

"I'm sorry" My voice had grown even softer.

Then my head fell back and I blacked out.

XXX

It wasn't a kind hand that woke me. It wasn't someone who had been slowly trying to get me out of bed. It felt more like someone who was trying to shake the sleep out of my body. When my eyes flickered back to life, disorientation and confusion set in. I glanced around until I saw the face of my shaker.

It was Shaun.

He and Virgil both stood over me as they shook me back to life.

"He's up now." Virgil said with some finality in his voice.

"I know he's up, these last few shakes are for letting Burke escape." Shaun said as he continued to make my body convulse.

"Look it wasn't his fault, I was there too." Virgil defended me.

I stared at Shaun, almost too tired to speak.

"What are you looking at?" He said.

My throat was dry and sore. I coughed to clear an invisible obstruction. "What's going—," I coughed out more. "—what's going on?" I asked. My eyes glanced around the familiar room. It was the same room that Shaun and Kate had taken me to when they'd broken me out of the hospital. The room was a tint of white to bright to describe and the light hanging above me beat down on me like the sun. "I thought this was too risky to send people with me?" The question was more for my benefit. I knew if Shaun had sent his people with me in the first place, we could have ended Burke then and there.

"It was." He said with a stern voice. "But that didn't stop you, did it?"

"I guess not." I said raising my hand to scratch my head. My muscles felt like they'd been bruised and beaten over and over again. Everything felt sore, it was as if someone had taken a meat tenderizer and used it on my entire body. Virgil offered me a hand up.

I took it and pulled myself upright.

I felt ridged. My joints squeaked and cracked like a man four times my age.

The electromagnetic shock that Burke had used must have made my muscles seize up, just like when someone's in a car accident.

"How do you feel?" Virgil asked after I finally straightened myself out.

"Like a million bucks." I told him with a smile. "Why am I so stiff?"

"You were hit with an electrical shock—," Kate said as she appeared beside me. "Your bones and muscles seized up—"

I was right.

"—and now you should be experiencing an increased level of soreness." She finished.

"How are you Kate?" I asked as she moved closer towards me.

"Fine. Better than you I assume." She started to say as she pulled my shirt over my head and began to listen to my heartbeat. Virgil and Shaun looked on, watching my examination. It was a bit uncomfortable when Kate put her ear to my chest, listening to my heart and lungs. Virgil and Shaun watched me as if I were some sort of sideshow oddity. A few seconds later Virgil and Shaun walked over to where Kate was examining me.

"You're safe here James." Shaun said.

"I figured." I let out a deep breath.

Kate said. "Breathe in"

I took another breath in. "Did you and your people find Burke?" I asked

Shaun looked at the floor then to Kate; I knew the look. "No, we only found you two in the hospital. Virgil was trying to wake you." He told me with a slight grimace on his face.

"Take a deep breath please." Kate instructed.

"So he got away?!" I exclaimed while I tried to take another breath.

"Yes. Due to your carelessness Burke was able to slip through our fingers." Shaun said.

"Our fingers? Our fingers—," I looked hard at Shaun. "—by our fingers do you mean Virgil's and mine? Because as I recall you didn't want to help us." Shaun and Virgil both looked at me stunned.

"Yes I mean—," Shaun began.

"—No, you don't get to say you had anything to do with this, at least *I* did something." I said pointing to myself.

Kate put her ear on another part of my body. "Another breath." She instructed.

"James, cut it out." Virgil said. "We don't need to blame each other for what we did or didn't do. James, you were reckless and though I agree with you, I also think Shaun was right not risking everyone here on an attack." There was a momentary pause then Shaun added. "Besides, Burke was bluffing about having Angela and she was the only leverage he had over you." He stated.

I looked blankly at him as my mind tried to comprehend what he had said.

Angela's alright?

A wave of relief spread over my body and I let out a long sigh.

"—hey I need you to keep holding your breath." Kate said.

"Sorry." I said, taking a quick breath inward. I was elated to know Angela was safe. Even if we hadn't killed Burke I'm sure if anyone could find him it would be Shaun. "So how did we get here?" I asked taking a breath.

Shaun said to me. "We moved you at night so no one would see. You've been asleep for the better part of a week." The processes that occur when in The Shade aren't an exact science but Virgil had taught me the basics. I knew that while in The Shade we experienced accelerated healing, the bleed over effect should have granted me that power in the real world. I knew it shouldn't have taken a week for me to get back on my feet. As the thought passed through my head I said. "Why am I still sore? Shouldn't my residual DMT have healed me by now?"

Virgil walked forward. "Normally yes, but I think when you shocked Burke you drained what little supply you had left." He explained.

Shaun then said. "So for now we're just letting your body do its thing. Although we are glad you're awake, there are tons of people waiting to meet you."

"Breathe in for me." Kate told me again as she checked my back.

I took a deep breath and held it until she told me to exhale. I looked at Shaun puzzled with his statement, after a couple of moments passed I finally had to ask. "Who needs to see me?"

Virgil scoffed at the question.

"Everyone—," he told me. "—everyone here wants to meet you James."

I looked at Virgil's smiling face with the same puzzled look I'd given to Shaun. "Why would they want to see me?"

"You lived." Kate said looking at me as she moved my left leg back and forth, seeing if it still worked. "No one ever has."

Virgil walked up to me and put his hand on my shoulder.

"James, you're a hero. These people see you as the one who stopped Burke."

"But I didn't stop him. He got away." I stated. "He's still out there."

Shaun looked over at me. "We have it on good authority he's left town."

My mind slowly began to process what Shaun was saying. Burke was scared.

"What happens next?" I asked.

Kate looked up at me. "For you—," Kate said as she threw me back my shirt. "— get some sleep and don't get into anymore fights." She smiled, it was a promise that I could keep. I slipped the shirt over my head and said. "We have to find Burke. I mean we can't just let him go."

Then Shaun said in a serious tone of voice. "We don't have any other options James. We have to pick up the pieces here before we can even think about going on some wild goose chase."

There was hesitation in the air until Virgil added. "We'll be lucky if we see or hear anything from Burke again. He's not stupid, he'll bide his time until he knows he can kill us." My heart sank. The thought of Burke being able to do what he did in Eugene to another city left me speechless; it was never our intent but more of an unfortunate side effect. I'd missed my chance to kill Burke more than once, I knew that I needed to make things right. I knew there was something that we could do to keep pressure on him. "We have to do something." I said.

Virgil put his hand up to stop me. "No." He said. "Not now, you're awake and alive, two victories worth celebrating, no matter how small."

I smiled at him.

Virgil was right.

Throughout all the hardship we endured over the many months we'd been together, it was finally time to allow ourselves to relax. "Alright." I said with a smile. Then Virgil helped me off the bed. I found my feet in working order, even if the muscles in my legs were sore. The four of us made our way to the large metal door of the medical room. Shaun gripped the metal wheel that opened the door and began to twist it counter clockwise, releasing the lock.

"Get ready." Shaun said then he opened the door. As the large door swung open, the eyes of at least a hundred other people greeted me. The people in the hallway looked overjoyed to see me, staring in the same way people marvel at nation monuments. Instantly I felt nervous, then with Virgil's help we began our way out of the room. As soon as my foot came over the threshold, applause broke out in the damp hallway. The echoing sound of people cheering and clapping made me feel like a sports star.

As we walked, people came up to shake my hand and thank me for what I'd done. It took a few minutes but once we were clear of the crowd I noticed they were following us. The twisted hallways of the service tunnels were lined with lights making it look brighter and homier than one would have expected. We traveled down the twisting and turning hallways until we arrived at a large room. When we made our way into the room, another crowd of people was already waiting to greet us. They wanted to shake my hand, talk to me, and hear about what had happened. I felt as if in that moment, Shaun and his family had accepted me. Not only me, but Virgil also, who had been considered an outcast. People greeted me, telling me how amazed they were with me, letting me know what a huge burden I'd lifted and some just simply wanted to thank me. I didn't need their thanks. I did it for Virgil, first and foremost and as much as I wanted to think I'd done it for myself, even that wasn't necessarily true. It was for Angela, my family and now since the people from the refuge felt like a new family, I decided I'd done it for them as well.

Quickly the introductions turned into festivities.

As the nights activities progressed, I found myself sitting at the bar. Kate had come by and offered me a drink of some concoction she'd devised. I declined, telling her I wasn't interested. She smiled a brilliant smile at me then walked away. Virgil appeared behind me and put his hand on my shoulder. "Seems like someone's got a thing for ole' James here." He said with a laugh.

"What are you talking about? I've got Angela back now." I chuckled. "Besides isn't she like a hundred or something?"

"She's closer to a thousand actually." He laughed a hardy laugh.

For as long as I had known him, I'd never seen Virgil laugh the way he did that night. He seemed free, no longer burdened by any preoccupation or worry. "How are you feeling?" He asked.

"Pretty tired actually." I told him. "I was thinking of going to find somewhere to lie down."

Virgil nodded to me. "Well I'll show you where to go."

We made our way out of the large room, saying goodbye to a few people on the way out. The main hallway we entered seemed as if it was devoid of all sound. I slowly followed Virgil as he led me to a place to sleep, it was the first real chance I had gotten to be alone with him since he'd died. "What was it like?" I asked him.

His head turned around and looked at me with curious expression. "What was what like?"

"Dying?" I questioned quietly.

Virgil let out a quiet puff of air and then said. "Darkness—," the word floated out of his mouth. "Like swimming in a sea made of nothing but darkness. It was terrifying. But then I saw a light, like the warm rays of the sun, and then there you were." He told me.

I digested what he said then added. "I'm sorry again about Burke."

Virgil stared at his feet for a long while then finally looked back up at me. He smiled a half smile and shook his head. "It's alright James, we did our best. I don't blame you for anything."

"But you died because of me." I told him.

"No—," he said. "—I died because of Burke. I died because of my own choices. I'm okay with this new life, if that's what this is. I'll get used to it, just like everything else." He smiled.

A thought scratched at my brain, it was a question I'd wanted to ask Virgil since he'd emerged out from the specter. "So you're a ghost now, right?" I asked.

Virgil chuckled a bit then said. "Yes, I'm a ghost."

"Alright—," I paused, looking for the right words. "—why do you still look young?"

Again, Virgil laughed at my question. "I'm not sure why I'm still in this youthful body, it must have something to do with the image my mind had when I died, next question." He smiled.

I couldn't think of anything else to ask him so I simply said. "That's all the questions I have." We began to walk again, and then I remembered. "I saw your daughter." I told him and Virgil stopped walking.

He turned to look at me and said. "How did she seem?" He asked with a slight tinge of sadness in his voice.

"Peaceful." I said with a smile.

Virgil flashed a smile back to me and then we continued to make our way down the curving hallways and tight corners of the refuge. We eventually arrived at a large room lined with cots; I could see from the outside that the room was a sleep quarters used for just about everyone that lived in the refuge. We stopped in the hallway and with his arm outstretched, he said. "Here you go." There was a pause and then he added. "So you're back in your real body and I'm a ghost, we're no longer what we once were—," voice trailed off. "—so what does that make us?"

I thought about what Virgil said, and in that moment I knew exactly what to say.

My hand outstretched towards him. "You can call us friends." I smiled.

He smiled back and took my hand in his and we shook. Then my hand felt hot, like abnormally hot. I looked at Virgil and he shrugged. With my hand still in his hand, I tried to release my grip but couldn't, Virgil attempted to pull away from me but it only pulled me closer to him. We tried to pull from one another at the same time but with no success. Then a light shot from my hand. Then another light came, and then another, until both of our hands had been immersed in a glow of brilliant light.

Then the glow stopped.

The glue that had held us together lost its cohesiveness and we were free of each other. I looked down at my palm and rubbed it. There weren't any marks but my hand was hot, like the top of a stove kind of hot. Virgil and I stared at each other, I'm sure we were thinking the exact same thing.

Virgil leaned in towards me. "What the hell was that James?"

I shrugged. "How should I know, should we tell someone?"

"No I'm sure it's nothing." Virgil wrote it off.

"I'm not sure if that constitutes nothing." Then a sudden wave of exhaustion hit me and I rubbed my eyes. "I'm going to sleep this off; I'm going to talk to Shaun about it in the morning."

"Alright then." Virgil said as he smiled then disappeared before me.

I walked over to a cot and lay down. The cot was old and rusted, most likely one stolen from the hospital, which seemed reasonable for how uncomfortable the hard green canvas was. I looked up towards the ceiling and the unfamiliar brick looked back down at me. My only want was to sleep in my own bed, to be back with my family. As much as I complained about my parents throughout my high school years, I never dreamed I'd miss them as much as I did.

I wondered what they would say when I got home, what their reaction would be. I wondered how my mother would act, if she would break down at my return or not. I knew my father would give me a hug but nothing too affectionate; he had always been that way. I longed to see Angela again, to explain everything to her.

My body ached from all of the bruises, but due to the excitement of the party, I'd forgotten about them. My fingers touched my chest and winced as a slow achy pain immediately shot from the point. The bruises were mostly black and blue with some purple and the outer edges were yellow. My fingers traced the edges of the largest one on my arm, running from my shoulder almost all the way down to my elbow. My face cringed whenever my finger fumbled over and hit the actual bruise itself. After a few moments of this I could no longer stave off the forces that were trying to close my eyes.

My eyelids closed while my ears listened to the sound of the celebration going on downstairs. I smiled when I thought of the people that I'd helped. All of the people that no longer had to live in fear of a man bent on destruction. I was happy for them, happy I could help so many, happy I could help my friends, but above all happy to be home.

XXXI

I awoke six hours later. Immediately I realized the room looked very different in the daylight. The empty cots that lined the room were filled with sleeping celebrators. My body sat up and moved to get off the hard green cot. My feet touched the cold hard floor and I found my shoes and put them on. I stood up and wandered quietly through the room, trying not to wake anyone.

My eyes glanced down at my watch.

5:45

It's too early to be awake. Surly no one else will be awake for a few more hours. I thought with a yawn. To kill time I began to wander around the halls of the sewer maintenance tunnels, that was, until my stomach started to grumble. I put my hand over my stomach and decided I'd look for the kitchen. I searched my mind for the correct way to get back to the bar from the night before, knowing that there would still be food there. I walked slowly down the hallway until I found the correct doorway.

I stopped just before the door, there were voices coming from inside. I couldn't make out what they were talking about but Virgil's voice was definitely one that I'd heard. Quickly I composed myself as best I could, ran my fingers through my hair, greasy from the few days without wash, and then strutted in. The room that had once contained hundreds of partygoers had been converted into a war room. Maps of all kinds laid about the table with Shaun furiously typing on a computer. I had been correct about Virgil's voice. He was standing in the middle of the room right next to Shaun. They kept pointing at the laptop then back to the maps then back to the laptop. I rubbed my face a bit until I reached the table where they stood looking down at the maps. "Good morning James." Virgil said.

"Is it?" I asked him with a yawn. "It's too early to be up."

Shaun gave Virgil a look but Virgil didn't notice.

"What are you two up to?" I asked.

Shaun seemed reluctant to say anything to me. He spoke after a few seconds. "We're compiling data on where Burke might be. Virgil thinks that we might be able to catch him if we move fast enough." He said. "We think he's headed south."

My eyes widened. "That's great news."

"Hardly, we don't know where he's going, just the direction". Shaun said with a snide tone.

"But we know something, that's better than nothing." I tried to say.

Shaun said nothing, instead he just typed with even more ferocity on his keyboard. Virgil shook his head and came over to me. He placed his hand on my shoulder and moved with me out of the room. "What's up with him?" I asked.

"Shaun's a bit—upset." Virgil started to say.

"At what?"

"He saw the way Kate was talking to you last night."

"And?"

"He doesn't like her flirting with other guys." He said.

"We weren't flirting." I said with a chuckle. "She just offered me a drink." Although I wasn't sure if that was entirely true. Maybe we had been flirting, maybe her smiles meant something more, and maybe Kate just wanted Shaun to notice her. I wasn't sure but my intention was never to flirt with her.

"Alright James." Virgil said with his hands up. "You don't have to explain anything to me."

"Thanks."

After my run in with Shaun, Virgil gave me a proper tour of the tunnels. He taught me how to navigate the subterranean lair with relative ease. We sat down in the mess hall and ate oatmeal. I'd never been particularly fond of the stuff, but because it was the only food they had on hand I ate four bowls. Virgil told me how he had mapped out the entire tunnel system last night. He informed me that ghosts don't sleep, so with his free time he thought he'd use it for something productive. After I finished my meal, I pushed the four empty bowls to the side and looked at Virgil. "Can I help you James?" He said noticing me looking.

"Just wanted to know how we're going to get Burke back."

"I've decided to head south and look for him." He said.

"You can't go alone." I told him almost in a panic. Then I thought about it and the truth was, he could go alone. Virgil wasn't tied down to anyone or anything anymore, he could move freely around wherever and whenever he pleased. Virgil looked at me with a long hard stare then got up. "Come on James we need to get going." He said, almost with a tiny bit of reluctance.

We walked back from the mess hall. That's when I noticed more and more people had started to clamber out of bed. They seemed like zombies in an old horror film, slowly shambling around trying to go get something to eat. I watched as a group of people passed by Virgil and me who were walking in the direction of the mess hall. "James." He called me out of my stupor.

"Yeah, what?" I answered.

"Have you heard a thing I've said?"

I remained silent, trying to recall what Virgil had said while I was clearly not paying any attention. "I'll take the silence as a no then?" He said

"Sorry, I've got other things on my mind right now."

"Do these other things have a name?" He asked

"Possibly." I said with a smile. The first thing I wanted to do was to see Angela. She'd been on my mind ever since the accident, and since I was back in the real world she was the first person I wanted to see. Most of my bruises had healed, there were some that could be hidden under my clothes, still in the process of healing, but overall I was presentable. What I really wanted was to let my friends and family know I was okay.

"I'm sure." He chuckled at me. "Come on we're going to be late." Then he took off, walking quickly down the hall toward the war room.

"Late for what?" I said as I trailed behind him.

"We're having a meeting, to plan our next move on Burke." He told me. By the time we arrived at the door there were at least twenty other people trying to get into the room. After pushing our way through the crowd, we finally made it inside. My eyes scanned the crowd counting almost fifty people already seated. Virgil and I sat down near the back, I assumed it was because Virgil still didn't feel comfortable sitting with the actual family.

"Why are there so many people here?" I asked

"They have meetings like this to determine the group's course of action." He told me. "Shaun may be a tough leader but he's no dictator." Then Virgil pointed to the front of the room. I followed his finger until my eyes finally settled on the place where Shaun and he had been standing earlier that morning. Shaun appeared from a door and walked over to the table. Everyone watched and waited, waiting for their leader to say something.

The room went quiet, everyone calmed down, and all attention was on Shaun. To say you could hear a pin drop would have been an understatement. Shaun took center stage and his audience awaited him. He cleared his throat. The cough sent a sharp echo through the silent room. "I'm sure you all know why we're here." He said. "We've had some *developments* in the past few weeks that are forcing us to change our game plan. But as always, you are my family and I'll never do anything without your agreement." I looked around, everyone was nodding in agreement. I hadn't been fully aware of the family dynamic the group possessed until then. That's when I truly felt like an outsider looking in. "Due to some recent information we are being faced with a new threat." Shaun said as he looked at Virgil and I. "Virgil would you please come up here?"

Virgil patted my leg and looked at me. "I'm up." He said as he made his way towards the front of the room. He walked to the table with the maps and stood beside Shaun. Virgil looked around, he seemed unsure of what he had to say. "For those of you who don't know me, my name is Virgil." A heckler shouted something from the back that was inaudible. Virgil cracked a fake smile and then continued. "Also for those of you who don't know I'm Edwin Burke's brother." He said. There was a round of gasps that flowed across the room like a wave. Everyone grumbled, the crowd was quickly slipping out of Virgil's control. Shaun raised his hands and calmed the room just as quickly as it had erupted. It was clear Shaun had full control of his people.

"Thank you." Virgil said to Shaun then returned to the audience. "Despite what you think of me, I'm here to give you a warning. Burke, the man we thought was our only immediate threat has now confirmed he is just a messenger. This whole time we've been dealing with nothing more than a henchman." The crowd erupted in quiet whispers and groans. "Please do not be discouraged. While his masters' whereabouts are still unknown, we do know this. Burke is headed south, we're not sure where exactly but we know he's moving fast." I looked around the room. Everyone focused on Virgil. Virgil then showed a graph of Burke's movements up until that moment.

We were closer than I'd thought to catching him.

"We can track his moves but we are lacking manpower." Virgil looked around the room. "Unfortunately Burke's masters want to bring about an Armageddon of sorts. They realize we know their plan and now have hastened their movements. We've had reports of more and more creatures from The Shade making their way into the real world. We cannot allow them to infect this world and destroy its inhabitance. So that's why I say, we need an army." Virgil backed away from the table, no one clapped, no one cheered, everyone just looked, afraid.

Shaun stepped up and looked out among his people.

"I know we've tried to stay out of affairs that did not concern us. Burke has been our enemy for a long time, but now we have someone else to fight. These Speakers are going to unleash a devastating attack on the humans. If those things from The Shade are released, there will be millions of lives lost. We knew there was a storm coming and if we do nothing to stop it then we're no better than the monsters who commit the atrocities."

Shaun paused for dramatic effect.

"We must fight. We must defend the human race. I know a lot of you distanced yourselves from your families and friends a long time ago but hear me. If we do not band together, everything we know will be destroyed. This is a request, stand and fight with me, or retreat, I won't force you, but each and every one of you will have to make that decision for yourselves. Anyone who wants to leave, do so now."

Shaun paused.

No one got up, no one even moved, they just stared straight ahead.

"Good." Shaun smiled.

Shaun passed the floor back to Virgil.

"I'll be leading a two man team to track Burke. The rest

of you will be split into four man teams to mop up anything that may come through and gather any information we can. Anything you hear about Burke, Speakers or monsters you report back here. Shaun will lead the operations and manage forces. We will use frequent dead drop locations to deliver your orders." Virgil said.

Shaun then stepped forward and said. "Pack your stuff ladies and gentlemen. You're dismissed." Everyone got out of their seats and made their way towards the door. Everyone was abuzz about all of the new information, speculating what it all meant. However, it was clear that even with all that Burke had told us, we still knew very little about The Speakers. We knew they were old, like beginning of creation old. They needed energy from a living source to survive, and above all, they wanted to wipe us out.

Which was exactly what we wanted to prevent.

Most everyone had moved out of the room, Shaun and Virgil were looking at a map and when the room emptied, Virgil looked up at me. He pointed at me and motioned for me to join them. I walked up to the center of the room and joined them. "Nice speech." I jabbed. "Never took you for a diplomat." Virgil didn't respond, he just gave a slight sigh, looking at the ground.

"What's wrong?" I said. "Someone die?"

Virgil, still looking at the ground said. "You're going with me James." Then he let out a sigh. "You're the other part of my two man team."

Shock hit me and then I said. "Well, I'll do what I can, but now that I'm back in my body I'll need to be able to see my family." Virgil and Shaun looked at each other. Shaun just shook his head. I stared at them both wanting one of them to tell me what was going on.

"James you can't go back to your family—," Shaun said.

Virgil shot him a glare.

"—what?! I'm tired of dancing around this with him."

"What?" I said. "What are you talking about?"

"It's not our choice." Virgil said. "Before Burke took off—," he hesitated. "—he claimed when you made your initial escape from the hospital that you contracted a new form of rabies. He went public with, telling everyone that the symptoms occurred so quickly that you died before they could diagnose you. He did it after you confronted him, before he skipped town." Virgil's voice began to trail off.

"What does that mean?" I asked.

Virgil was reluctant to speak. "Well," he stumbled over his words. "Because Burke was the medical examiner he had authority to cremate your body without authorization from your parents—it's standard procedure when dealing with infectious diseases."

There was a long pause as I slowly took in everything Virgil told me. Shaun quickly filled the void of silence. "—so you see we can't have you showing up when everyone thinks you're dead."

My head went frantic. My mind tried to cling on to anything it could. "I have to tell Angela I'm not dead." I told them. "Just let me tell her."

Virgil wouldn't look at me.

Shaun crossed his arms and turned back towards the table.

"James." Virgil said. "This is the only way they're going to be safe. If Burke thinks he can use the people you love to get to you, then he will—,"

"—just look at what happened with Angela." Shaun interjected.

"I don't need your help." Virgil told him harshly. Then he looked back at me and said. "I'm sorry James. You know if there was anything we could do we would, Burke will use the people you love against you. You don't want them to be in danger do you?" His words hit me like a ton of bricks.

My entire body felt heavy. I sank down to my knees.

I felt compressed. Like someone was pushing on every side of me, squeezing me like someone trying to get the last bit of toothpaste out an empty tube. Pressure in my head made it feel like it was going to crack open. I had waited a long time to see the people I cared about, but that too was being stripped away from me.

Tears filled my eyes and ran down my cheeks.

The thought of leaving everyone filled my head, the thought of never being able to say goodbye. The thought of my parents never knowing what truly happened to their son.

Oh God my parents! Why is this happening to me?

I'd done everything correctly. I'd fought my hardest and even made Burke flee Oregon, but it wasn't good enough, I hadn't truly won anything. It was only the illusion of success that I had.

I sobbed, still on my knees while Virgil and Shaun looked on.

I didn't care that they could see me, nothing mattered anymore, everything I'd known had been taken away from me. In that moment I knew, Burke was right. There was no way for me to have beaten him, because even in victory I still lost. My eyes itched from the well of tears coming from them. Then a spark flashed in my head and then fizzled out.

The flash was a thought, a realization of sorts. Virgil was right. He was right about everything. The only way for my family to truly be safe was for Burke to be destroyed.

That's when I decided.

That was the moment when my mind became fully committed to the idea.

I've got to destroy Burke. That's the only way I can go home.

My hand reached up and wiped the tears from my face.

I looked up at Virgil who had been standing next to me with his hand on my shoulder. I could see in his eyes that he was truly sorry, he knew the pain of loss, and I knew he never wanted me to feel that same pain. My hands met the floor as I tried to compose myself. Then, once I felt like everything was in place, my legs slowly began to lift me back up.

I stood back up and glared at Shaun.

He looked back at me with an unapologetic stare.

"Don't blame me for this. This isn't my fault." Shaun told me, but I didn't blame him, I knew in my heart what was happening wasn't his fault. I knew what they were saying to me was rational. It would protect the ones I loved; it was the only way to make sure they were safe.

"When's the funeral?" I asked.

"Which funeral?" Shaun said with a sort of surprise. "Yours?"

I nodded. Shaun began to say something that sounded like he was going to forbid me from going but before he could Virgil spoke up quickly. "It's tomorrow, at noon."

"I suppose you want to go." Shaun said with frustration in his voice.

"Yes. If I have a last request then that's it." I looked at Virgil and he nodded, I didn't look for Shaun's approval, he didn't control me. Instead, I stretched my hand out towards Virgil. "Then after that, I'll go with you." I said.

He took my hand in his and we shook.

Then when we tried to pull away, we were stuck again.

"Not again." I said.

We tried to pull apart but the power keeping our hands bound seemed even stronger the second time. Virgil yanked hard away from me but only managed to pull me towards him.

I stopped myself before I ran into him.

"What is this?" Virgil questioned. Then a light came from my hand, then from Virgil's, then all at once, my hand lit up so bright I couldn't look at it directly. There was a loud boom in my ears then we released. The force was so strong I stumbled backwards then hit the ground. My eyes danced as I tried to regain focus. Virgil and I picked ourselves off the floor.

Shaun stood in the middle of the room looking back and forth at the two of us.

"What was that?" He asked.

"It's alright, everything's normal." Virgil said.

"Yeah it's happened to us before." I added.

"This has happened before?" Shaun's voice began to rise.

"This happened before and you didn't tell me?" Virgil and I exchanged a glance but said nothing. We had no idea where the light came from; all it seemed to do was want Virgil and me to stay together. "I take it you two have no idea what this is?" He looked at us. "No? I've seen this before. You see James, your Virgil's anchor to this world; you two share a link beyond all others, so much so that even at a subatomic level your atoms are trying to bond together. They want you two to join together to make—," his voice trailed off.

"To make what?" Virgil and I said in unison.

"—uh, well. I'm not sure." Shaun said. "But what an excellent way to start a partnership." Virgil and I flashed each other a look that didn't quite share the same enthusiasm as Shaun had for our situation.

We're bound together now, the universe must be screaming at us.

Then a heavy feeling entered my body. "If you don't mind I'm going to go." I said as I stepped back away from the table and began to walk out of the room.

"James." Virgil said as I looked back at him. "We'll leave after the funeral tomorrow alright?" I knew that it had to be alright, so I nodded okay. It's not like I had a choice in the matter. I was just doing what I was told. As I left, a feeling of emptiness swelled in my chest. Slowly my legs clumsily carried me back to the area with all the cots.

I'm never going to see my parents again.

My face was wet. The soft roll of tears had already begun to fall before I entered the sleeping quarters. I wanted nothing more than to be alone. However, in the busy refuge, that was next to impossible. I was sorry I had to let my parents think I was dead. Sorry that Angela was going to have to go on without me. Sorry that I'd failed to get home. My legs wobbled as they moved me closer towards the cots. Once I found mine, I lay down and stared at the ceiling. I could feel the tears run down my face. If anyone saw me, they didn't say anything.

Why would they? Why would anyone care about a boy who'd lost everything?

XXXII

The next day came too soon.

My backpack was loaded with everything I needed, everything that was going to keep me alive while we headed south after Burke. I looked at my watch, which told me it was ten o'clock. Virgil had informed me that the funeral would be taking place at noon. I knew I couldn't be seen by anyone, so I wore a hooded sweatshirt and some sunglasses to obscure my face.

Before I left, I wanted to talk to Virgil so we were both on the same page about when we were heading out of Eugene. My feet carefully carried me towards Virgil's cot. He was sitting on his cot looking at some maps. He seemed to be calculating where good spots to check for Burke would be. He already had a graph of Burke's early movements but as we stayed put, Burke moved further and further away and we let his trail get colder and colder. Virgil watched me as I approached then stood up.

"Are you all packed?" He asked.

"Yeah, I've got everything."

"Knife, phone, five days of rations, the alternate ID's Kate made for you?" Virgil questioned skeptically.

"I've got everything I'll need." I said as my eyes stared at the ground.

"I know that's not true James." He told me as he put his hand on my shoulder. "I promise when we finish Burke you can come back here and live a normal life."

I scoffed at the idea.

Me, a normal life, those things just weren't in the cards now.

"All the more reason to find him quickly." I said with a half-faked smile. Virgil gave me a half smile as well then sat back down on his cot. "I'm going to get going to the funeral."

Then Virgil said. "Alright I'll meet you there. We won't be heading out until tonight."

I gave him an odd look "But Shaun said to leave as soon as we can." I said. "I figured he meant after the funeral."

"He did, but I thought leaving later would give me the time I needed to tie up loose ends." He winked.

"Thank you." I said with a smile.

I knew what Virgil was doing. He was giving me the extra time that he never got. Although I couldn't directly speak to anyone I could still make peace with leaving Eugene. I could be okay with leaving for a short while, and then once we completed our mission, I could try normal life. Virgil was plotting our route as I walked away from him. It was then I realized that I couldn't have found a better friend, no one else would have done the things that Virgil had done for me. I walked back through the halls towards the mess hall.

I had to pass by the war room. I tried to sneak passed the door unseen. However, Kate's eyes were much faster than my body so as I walked by she called me in. "Come in here love." I strolled into the room acting as if I hadn't just tried to slip past them. I gave Kate a smile and hers sparkled back at me. Shaun cleared his throat and my head turned quickly over to him.

"I was just headed to the mess hall to eat before the funeral." I told them.

"Then you and Virgil will be on your way right?" He asked.

"That's the plan." I lied. "I just finished packing." Then I faked a smile.

"Glad to hear it. I have some very specific orders for you two." He said. "I've informed Virgil that if you find Burke, capture would be preferred to death." My jaw sank. He wanted me to capture Burke after everything he had done. There was no way Virgil would follow that order, there was no way his hatred for Burke would be offset by some loyalty to Shaun.

"What!" I exclaimed. "If we have a shot we're going to take it."

"I'd have to advise against that. If we kill Burke then we lose any connection we have with The Speakers. We don't need to destroy our most valuable intelligence asset if we can help it." Shaun said back to me.

"So this is all a game for you?" I asked. "This isn't about politics, this is a war, and we need to defeat our enemy!"

"You're right." Shaun raised his voice. "This is a war, which makes me your commander. You do not destroy valuable intelligence if you can help it, regardless of feelings."

"I'm done with this." I said as I turned to walk away.

I was seething with rage as I walked towards the door, the nerve of him to ask for something like that. I spun back around and faced Kate and Shaun. "Virgil and I work alone—," I pointed my finger at Shaun then back to myself. "—we help each other out, but him and I don't work for you got that?" I said infuriated. "We'll keep you posted, *sir*." I said with such thick sarcasm I could almost taste it on my lips.

Then I stormed out of the room and down to the mess hall. I was still boiling with anger as I made my way through my second bowl of oatmeal. The bland taste did nothing to calm me and only seemed to exacerbate my rage. After I ate, my only goal was to get out of the refuge. I made my way out of the mess hall, down a set of corridors until I finally came to the door we were using to get in and out of the sewers. The man who identified himself as Charles shook my hand and told me what a great honor it was to meet me. I shook so many hands at the party the other night I wasn't sure if we had already been introduced.

"The pleasure is mine." I told him.

We shook hands, he turned the large wheel, and then the door cracked open. The light that escaped was blinding. The door fully opened and I was enveloped in the soft warm glow of the Eugene sun. Then I stepped outside, for the first time in days.

The air was cooler then I remembered.

What month is it?

I put my hood up and my sunglasses on and made my way out of the door. I walked ten steps when I heard the sound of the metal door slam shut behind me. The wind lapped my face and I stood in the breeze. The anger I'd felt earlier had completely subsided. It had been replaced by a sense of serenity I had not felt in a long time. With one deep inhale, the cool air filled my lungs, and with that breath, I began to walk towards the cemetery.

I arrived at the cemetery shortly before the funeral started. It would have been strange for my family if a man in a hoodie stood to watch their son's funeral, so I chose to stand beneath an old tree that grew only about fifty yards from where the crowd had formed.

I watched as my family and friends gathered around my casket, unaware that what the hospital had given them were not my real ashes. There wasn't a body in the casket. Burke had deprived my parents of even seeing their son one last time before putting him in the ground. It wasn't like someone could distinguish human ash from other human ash, in a way Burke solved all his problems with me by just burning my body. He deprived me of my family, I'd made peace with that, but to deprive my family of a proper burial was cruel. I watched as my mother wept openly in front of all my family and then three yellow buses appeared and stopped on the road beside my grave.

My grave.

That was something I'd never thought I'd have to say. The buses were filled with kids from school. It seemed like they were all there to support my family. I could make out my old friends Rich, Gabe, even Zach.

Then I saw Angela emerge from the bus.

She was so beautiful; she wore a black dress, her hair blowing in the breeze. Even though she looked amazing, it was obvious that she had been crying. She walked over to my mother and father and gave them both a hug. How I longed to be in her arms again, to hold her in that way, I yearned for it so much it burned the inside of my chest. Then Angela took her seat beside my mother, holding her hand for comfort.

In that moment, I wanted to make myself known. I wanted to walk out from the tree and announce myself to everyone. I wanted to do that.

However, that's not what I did.

I held my breath and grabbed the tree tight. My heart pushed me forward but my mind gripped the tree, preventing me from moving. I thanked my mind for having more restraint than my heart did.

My family doesn't deserve to believe I'm gone.

They needed to know the truth. However, every time I tried to justify a reason for telling them that I was still alive my mind snapped back to Burke. I could never put any of my friends or family in danger. Shaun and Virgil were right. I had no other choice; I would have to play dead to protect the ones I cared for. I could never bear to lose Angela, not to Burke, not to anyone.

I couldn't put her in harm's way just because I loved her.

Virgil appeared to my left and walked to me slowly.

"Has it started yet?" He asked solemnly.

"It just did." I told him, pointing to the priest that just arrived.

The priest began to speak a verse from the Bible; I wasn't a person of faith but I liked the message: *Gone but not forgotten.*

"We don't have to watch this." Virgil said.

"No, I'd like to." I said, trying to hold back my tears.

"I heard about your argument with Shaun." Virgil said. "I just wanted to let you know that I agree with you."

I smiled at him. "I'm glad to have a friend like you."

"What? One that tried to kill you?" He chuckled.

"I'm serious." I smiled. "You're the reason I'm still here."

Virgil let out a long chuckle then said. "Well I wouldn't want my atoms to try and fuse me to anyone else." Then there was a long moment of silence between Virgil and me. I watched the priest as he started to call up others to speak about me. It was almost unbearable to watch. I knew there were tears on my face, but I wasn't aware of how much I was crying before my hand wiped my face.

My parents went to the podium first, my father holding up my mother as she wept over the microphone. They spoke about how beautiful I was as a child, about how playful I was, and how I was a friend to everyone. I couldn't remember a time when my parents thought of me this way, but I suppose losing a son makes you long for days gone by. After my parents were finished, my hand picked away the last tears and turned back to Virgil.

"I know you wanted us to leave later tonight because you want to give me time to tie up loose ends." I said.

"I didn't say that." Virgil winked at me. "I just needed extra time to pack."

"Well I'm glad you did." I told him. Angela was up next, she had tears in her eyes before she reached the stand. I turned away from the funeral, knowing if I heard what she had say I'd have lost it. "I think I'm done here." I told Virgil. He nodded and we started to walk away. Angela's words muffled in the background until they slowly died out into a dull ring and finally into nothing.

My afternoon was spent alone. Mostly meandering around town, watching the children play in the cool breeze. I walked past my favorite shops, all of the places my friends and I used to hangout, I even made my way all the way out to my parent's house. I stayed a good distance away. I didn't want to interrupt any of the grieving.

It was nice to see the house one more time before we left Eugene, it was also an hour and half walk from the cemetery so it helped to pass the time. Virgil had gone back to make sure everything was ready. I didn't really like the idea of taking orders from Shaun, but I supposed we could have had a worse leader.

I made it back into the city a little bit before eight, the sun was already hanging low in the sky and as it drooped further and further down it seemed to be putting a close on my day.

I walked to a park bench that Angela and I had always visited; I sat down and watched the sun finally set among the cascading hills and treetops. My eyes looked up, and watched the stars one by one twinkle into life. It was the same sky I'd looked at every night we were away. As I looked, I wondered if Angela was looking up and watching them as well. It was the closest I could come to being beside her, it wasn't the real thing, but I'd have to settle for it. Then an idea flashed into my head, like a bright burning light, it burned all of the oxygen in my brain. My hands fumbled as they tried to get a scrap of paper and pen out of my bag. When I'd finally managed to grab one I took the pen and scribbled on the paper furiously.

When I was finished I tucked the paper into my pocket and put the pen back into my bag, then made my way towards Angela's house.

It was late but I had to see it.

When I arrived at her house the lights were turned off, but her car was in the driveway so I knew she was home.

She must be sleeping.

I moved to the backside of the house. Her room was on the second floor. I found her window and used the tree near the house to climb over to it. My hand unzipped my bag and pulled out the odd shaped box that I'd been carrying and my note.

My hands shook as they opened the box up.

My eyes looked down at the necklace that had once been hers. I set it on her windowsill and placed the note on top of it. I peered into her room, she was sleeping. I banged on her window to get her to wake up, just as I had done many times when I snuck over in the middle of the night. My hand hit the window one more time for good measure then I jumped to the ground.

I hit the ground and rolled, stood upright and brushed myself off.

I looked up at Angela's window as her light came on.

Slowly I moved to the side of her house so as not to be seen. The window slid open with a familiar creek. I could see her, looking around, wanting to know who had knocked on her window. Then she found the box on her sill and gasped. She ran away from her window, leaving it open. I could hear her yelling for her parents. It was done, and because it was, I decided to meet back up with Virgil. Didn't want anyone getting suspicious of me, standing outside a house in the middle of the night.

Sometime later that night I went back to meet Virgil at the entrance to the refuge. A half hour went by until Virgil finally appeared. "Ready to go?" He asked.

I shrugged. "Where are we headed?"

"We have a report that Burke was seen in Nevada, we'll start there."

"I've never liked the heat." I said to him.

"Come on, Shaun gave us a truck." He said as he dangled the keys. "We've got miles to go and places to be." We piled our stuff into the old pickup truck that Shaun had given us. Virgil took the first shift driving. I sat in the passenger seat and gazed out of the window. The night sky was brilliant with the light of a billion different stars as we headed further away from the city.

As we left the city limits, we passed a sign that read: You are now leaving Eugene, Oregon. My eyes read the sign as raindrops began to pelt the truck. I looked ahead of us, seeing a storm cloud growing ominously on the horizon.

It's the first time I've been away from home by myself. But I suppose I'm not by myself, I've got Virgil. I'm not totally alone.

The thought brought a smile to my face as we drove further away from the city.

Eventually Eugene sat like a bright speck on the horizon as the cascading rain swept sheets across the road in front of us.

I'll make it back to Eugene. I will see Angela again, maybe not tomorrow or next week, but someday. I will return to the ones that I love, to Angela and my family.

It was a promise I made to myself. I knew that I would make it back to Eugene someday, but as we headed towards the storm on the horizon, I knew it wouldn't be easy.

Angela opened the note with hesitation. Her fingers fumbled on it until it had been fully unfolded. The box with the necklace that James had given her almost a year ago sat on her bed. She looked down at the note:

> *I will return to you. I will come home.*
> *Don't believe what they say.*
> *I love you.*
> *James.*

Angela held the note to her chest and wept.
"I love you too." She said. "Come back to me soon."

SPECIAL THANKS

Writing this book has been a long and sometimes difficult journey for me, so naturally there are people that I need to thank. No matter what amount of help I received form someone they all deserve a medal for putting up with me.

First, I want to thank my wife to whom I dedicate this book. She nurtured my writing, even when it cut into time we could have spent together. She was the encouraging light that allowed me to complete the book you've just read.

I would like to thank my parents who have always told me that I could do anything, for always pushing me to finish my projects and for helping to finance this book.

I'd also like to thank everyone who edited the various versions of this book. Thank you for making me take such hard looks at things that I had been reluctant to change before. Thank you for taking time to help a friend and know that I appreciated every comment you made about the book. So thank you to: Chris, Gary and Katy.

Thanks to Lisa J Wilson of Pixel Pixie Design. I don't know if this book would have felt as complete if the cover art was done by someone else. Thank you for making my vision for the cover a reality.

Thank you to Emily M Tippetts of EM Tippetts book design for formatting this book.

Thanks to everyone else who I forgot to thank in the above section. Thank you to everyone who bought the book and who supported me through my journey.

This paperback interior was designed and formatted by

E.M. Tippetts
Book Designs

www.emtippettsbookdesigns.blogspot.com

Artisan interiors for discerning authors and publishers.